STILL
OF
NIGHT

JONATHAN MABERRY
AND RACHAEL LAVIN

JOURNALSTONE
YOUR LINK TO ARTIST TALENT

"Fat Girl with a Knife" © Jonathan Maberry Productions, LLC, was originally published in
Slasher Girls and Monster Boys, edited by April Genevieve Tucholke; Dial Books, August 18, 2015.

JournalStone books may be ordered through booksellers or by contacting:
JournalStone
www.journalstone.com

ISBN: 978-1-947654-34-1 (sc)
ISBN: 978-1-947654-35-8 (ebook)

JournalStone rev. date: November 9, 2018

Library of Congress Control Number: 2018952027

Printed in the United States of America

Cover Art & Design: Robert Grom
Interior Layout & Back Cover Design: Jess Landry

Edited by Vincenzo Bilof
Proofread by Sean Leonard

STILL OF NIGHT

From Jonathan:
This is for Brian Keene—great writer, cultural influencer, world-class curmudgeon, good dad, true friend.
And, as always, for Sara Jo.

From Rachael:
For Matt, who inspires me to bring the worlds inside my head to life.

ACKNOWLEDGEMENTS

Special and heartfelt thanks to Dana Fredsti for editing and generally putting out all kinds of fires. (You rock in so many ways!) And thanks to David Fitzgerald for utility infield work. Nice!

CONTENTS

AUTHOR'S FOREWARD
JONATHAN MABERRY

There are some things you need to know. The first of which is that I love my life-impaired fellow citizens. We have some history. A lot of history, actually.

My first exposure to "zombies," as we've come to know them in the current pop culture world, goes back to October 1968, when I snuck into the movies to see the world premiere of *Night of the Living Dead*. A truly landmark horror film. Prior to that, zombies were a kind of somnambulistic slave in old black-and-white movies about Haiti. They didn't eat human flesh and they weren't really dead. Just dead-ish.

Then George A. Romero gave us that movie. And, before anyone throws down this book in semantic frustration, yes, I know that Romero did not make a zombie film. Yes, I *know* that the word "zombie" was inaccurately applied to one of his later films. Yes, I know that George fought tooth and nail to remove that word (and completely failed in that attempt). And, yes, I know his movie was about living dead ghouls. All of that is on the table.

But...these monsters are what we *now* call zombies. Everyone calls them that. Even George gave up and began calling them that in his later years. So, yes, this is a zombie book. There are zombies in it. None of those zombies are from Haiti. Just so we know where we stand.

Now, here's the nicely complicated part of this.

In 2011, St. Martin's Griffin published my novel, *Dead of Night*, which was my attempt to tell the story of the rise of the living dead with as much plausible science as possible. I wrote it for a couple of reasons. First, because I was always a little frustrated that zombie stories seemed to start with things in motion. Even *Night of the Living Dead* starts hours after the outbreak. These stories skip over the cause, or gloss over it. Romero certainly did. His movie had characters alluding to the possibility that it was radiation from a returning space probe as the root of the plague. This bothered me, even as a kid, because there wasn't enough science behind it. I was a science nerd and that explanation made no sense. So, I wanted to tell a story that gave the science. Not just a passing reference to a "disease," but the science *of* the disease. I worked with a number of top experts in epidemiology, infectious diseases and parasitology to come up with as reasonable an explanation as natural science, bioweapons research, and genetics could manage. What disturbed me was how close I was able to get to something that could be concocted in a biological warfare lab. Luckily no one has been insane enough to authorize, let alone fund this; and Mother Nature, even at her crankiest, couldn't create it.

The other reason I wanted to write the book was to honor George Romero. He was always one of my favorite people. I loved his movies, and (as a young man) read countless interviews with him and he seemed like a truly decent guy. Later, after I was working in the horror field and doing the convention circuit, I got to meet and become friends with him. And, yeah, nice guy for sure. Whip-smart, funny, inventive and humble.

So, I dedicated *Dead of Night* to him. I later found out that he really enjoyed the book. A lot. In late 2015 I reached out to George to see if he'd give me his blessing to edit an anthology of stories set, approximately, in the forty-eight hours surrounding his landmark movie. We spoke on the phone at length and he said he'd agree under three conditions. The first was that he wanted to co-edit it with me. Not a problem. Second, he wanted to write a story for the anthology. Again, all good with me. And third, because he loved *Dead of Night* and its sequel, *Fall of Night*, so much, he asked that I write a story that specifically connected the events of those books with the events in *Night of the Living Dead*. He told me that as far as he was concerned, my books were the official "backstory" of his movies.

Yeah. I'm a grown-ass man, but that put tears in my eyes.

And so I did that. The short story "Lone Gunman" picks up a few minutes after the events of *Fall of Night*, and does indeed take the main character, Sam Imura, into that ill-fated house from Romero's first film. The anthology George Romero and I did together was *Nights of the Living Dead*, and was published by St. Martin's Griffin in 2017. It was the last project George completed before he passed, and I was actually at a book signing five days after the book's debut when we got the call that he had died. I grieved then and grieve now, but I also celebrate with a full heart at how much he brought to the world of horror entertainment. Try to find *anyone* who doesn't know what a zombie is. You can't. It's a global cultural phenomenon.

Think about it. Without Romero's old B&W movie, and the new spin on flesh-eating monsters he created, there would be no *World War Z*, no *The Walking Dead* or *Warm Bodies*, no Michael Jackson's *Thriller*, no Stephen King's *Pet Sematary*. No *Santa Clarita Diet*, *iZombie*, *Z Nation*, *Marvel Zombies*, *Train to Busan*, *Return of the Living Dead*, *Resident Evil*, *28 Days Later*, *Dead Set*, *Zombie Survival Guide*, *Shaun of the Dead*, *Pride & Prejudice & Zombies*, *Call of Duty: Black Ops* (zombie mode), *Star Wars: Death Troopers*, *Dead Space*, *Zombieland*, *The Evil Dead*, *House of the Dead*, *Left 4 Dead*, and even no *Game of*

Thrones, because the Night Walkers are fucking zombies.

Now, we jump forward to my post-zombie-apocalypse series of novels collectively known as the *Rot & Ruin* series. Those novels are set fourteen years after the events of *Dead/Fall*. They're young adult novels about what it's like to grow up years after the apocalypse. There are four novels in the original series: *Rot & Ruin, Dust & Decay, Flesh & Bone* and *Fire & Ash*; as well as a graphic novel, *Rot & Ruin: Warrior Smart*, set between books 2 and 3; and a collection of short stories, *Bits & Pieces*.

In one of the stories in *Bits* I introduce a character known as Rachael Elle. She is a cosplayer (someone who dresses up in costumes, often those of super heroes, anime characters, movie/TV characters, etc.) who is at a convention when the end comes. Because she emulates the heroic qualities of the characters she plays, Rachael is able to both survive the attack and lead a group of other survivors to safety.

More tricky math. Rachael Elle is the cosplay name of an actual person, Rachael Lavin, who was—once upon a time—a student in my Experimental Writing for Teens program. She was also an active cosplayer and her group would do charity appearances at places like children's hospitals. I found that so admirable that I used her as a basis for the warrior woman character in *Bits & Pieces*. Later still, when I decided I wanted to continue the story from *Dead/Fall*, I asked Rachael if she would like to collaborate on it. She would write the Rachael Elle/Warrior Woman storyline and I'd write two converging subplots featuring Dez Fox, the protagonist of my first two novels; and Joe Ledger, the hero of my ongoing series of weird science thrillers, of which *Patient Zero* is the first.

And, to complicate the math even more, Sam Imura was the sniper for Joe Ledger's special ops team.

Yeah. It's convoluted. The short version of that is this: The Joe Ledger thrillers take place more or less right now. *Dead of Night* and *Fall of Night* take place roughly fifteen years after whenever the last Ledger novel will be. *Dark of Night* takes place several months after that, and *Rot & Ruin* takes place fourteen years later. A new spinoff series, *Broken Lands* (debuting in December 2018), will take place a year after *Rot & Ruin*.

There is a complete reading list in the back of this book.

So, that brings us to *Still of Night*.

This story takes place a few weeks after the events of *Dark of Night*. The book is made up of three short stories and one novella. There is a solo Rachael Elle/Warrior Woman story written entirely by Rachael Lavin. There is a brand-new Joe Ledger story. And there is one reprint called "Fat Girl with a Knife", also by me, which ties into the events of the novella. Then there is the novella, which is another full collaboration between Ms. Lavin and me.

You don't need to have read any of the previous novels or short stories in order to read this, but it's kind of fun to take the whole trip. It goes through some weird territory and over a lot of bumps. A few deadfalls, too.

So, buckle up and enjoy the ride!

PART ONE

HOT TIME IN THE OLD TOWN TONIGHT

JONATHAN MABERRY

DURING THE OUTBREAK

–1–

NOW

E ver been in a helicopter crash?

There is no way to brace. There is no way to deal with any part of it. Your only hope is to get right with Jesus as fast as you can and hope that he isn't playing golf with Buddha, with his phone switched off.

In the split second the pilot yells that he has a dead stick and that you're all going down hard, you become acutely aware that a helicopter is a small metal box. It's filled with sharp edges and a lot of incidental shit that's suddenly going with you into an industrial dryer. The world spins and you can feel the subjective floor beneath you drop away. Gravity whispers bad promises in your ear. Adrenaline speed-bags your heart. You hear grown men and women—all of them tough and hardened—begin to scream. Through the windows you see the world whip around like a tilt-a-whirl.

You know the ground is waiting for you and it loves to kill things. Consider all of the billions of dead whose bones rest in the ground. It's a hungry thing and it is never satisfied.

All of this is bad. All of this is absolutely fucking terrifying.

But any bad thing can get worse. Much, much worse.

Like when the guy strapped into the seat next to you on that falling helicopter is trying to bite you. Not out of fear, but because he has a hunger so deep that nothing, not even death, is going to stop it.

That's how we fell.

It's why we fell.

– 2 –

SIX HOURS AGO

It started in another aircraft. A plane. One of those big-ass air force C-5m Super Galaxy transport jobs bringing my team back from a base in Japan to LAX. We were alone in the plane, having dropped off the rest of the human luggage in Hawaii. Just me, Top and Bunny, sitting in shocked silence as we watched the news unfolding on our laptop screens.

We'd been radio silent for nearly a week because Echo Team had crossed the North Korean border to find a factory where they were developing a new kind of DSRV that could transport high-yield nukes right into American harbors. Intel from Japanese, South Korean, and American spies agreed that these deep-water vehicles were invisible to our best sonar. My boss, Mr. Church, took ownership of the case away from the U.S. JSOC people and put my Rogue Team International into play. I took Top and Bunny with me because I needed brains and muscles for a situation where lack of numbers would work better than a crowd scene. Because we operate outside of American law—we don't even return the president's emails most of the time—if we make a mess, then it's all on us. The U.N. Security Council knew about us, but only off the record. No one else knows we exist, which is kind of the idea. Covert ops, you dig?

We found the base and discovered that the North Korean DSRV program was only days away from launching. That is some scary shit right there. Ten mini-subs armed with single-use missile launchers, each capable of carrying one fifty-megaton nuke. We hacked their network and identified all ten targets. New York, Los Angeles, Port of New Savannah, Port of Seattle, Port of Virginia, Port of Houston, the naval base in San Diego, as well as the Jebel Ali port in Dubai, Busan in South Korea, and Tokyo Harbor. And there were twenty-eight more of the machines in various stages of construction.

When we left, there was a smoking crater where the factory had been and a tapeworm in their computer system that did irreparable damage to their research databases. We made sure we were in the air, hitching a ride with the air force, before we switched our radios back on. And that's when we all got kicked in the nuts. The world we just saved was already dying, and we were too late to do much of anything about it.

− 3 −

The devil slipped the leash in a small nobody-gives-a-fuck town in western Pennsylvania.

The devil's name was *Lucifer 113*. One of those old Cold War bioweapons people created to kill everyone if their side lost. A doomsday weapon.

People, as I've said way too many times, are assholes. Not all of them, but enough of them. Especially the kind of entitled asshole who thinks the world is his bitch and—because he's a jealous, childish and petty asshole—he'd rather burn it down than let anyone share. Maybe I'm mixing a metaphor. Don't know, don't care.

Military intel divisions—especially SpecOps teams—are always calm, cool and collected. There could be missiles inbound and they'd sound like they're giving color commentary on a golf match. That wasn't what we were hearing on the military channels. What we heard were screams. And weeping. And prayers. The story came out broken and jagged and it left us bleeding.

Dr. Herman Volker had been a young and brilliant bioweapons developer in the last few years of the Soviet Union. Some CIA spooks cultivated him as an asset, turned him and eventually brought him to the U.S. to help us develop a response to the weapons he'd helped create. That weapon, *Lucifer*, was based on parasites rather than something as fragile as a virus. These parasites were the ones you sometimes saw in internet news stories called "zombie wasps" or "zombie ants." Volker and his team found a way to use them to create a real motherfucker of a bioweapon that rewired the human brain so that higher reasoning was gone and a lot of what they considered less important body functions were allowed to go idle. At the same time the parasites drove the hosts to spread their larvae through bites, and the weapon supported this by amping up aggression.

Yeah, process that for a moment.

In the decades since the Cold War ended, maniacs like Volker were semi-retired. A lot of them were given jobs in R and D projects tied to DARPA or in corporations doing government contract work. There was always supervision so they didn't do anything hinky. Which is like saying condoms are one hundred percent effective.

So, Volker said he wanted to stay active and asked for a job as a doctor in a super-max prison. Sew up some tough guys after yard brawls and maybe do some quiet research on the side with "test subjects" who wouldn't complain a whole lot. Wasn't supposed to be working on anything within a million miles of *Lucifer*. What his handler failed to grasp was that Volker had history apart from his work with the Soviet bioweapons lab. Family members of his had been torn apart by a serial killer, and that left him scarred. Or, maybe "warped" is a better word. His hatred of those kinds of predators was the fuel that fired his engines, but also consumed his humanity.

When a particularly vicious serial murderer came up for lethal injection, Volker decided to get a little of his own brand of revenge. He replaced the usual chemical cocktail with a brand-new version of the one he'd helped develop—*Lucifer 113*. His plan? He wanted the killer to go into the ground and then reanimate inside his coffin. Awake, aware, connected to all five senses, but totally unable to control his body. He would lie there, feeling himself rot, kept alive by the parasites that fed on him with infinite slowness.

Problem was that an aunt nobody knew about filed papers to claim his body after the execution and had it transported to her home town for burial on family land.

In the mortuary of that little town, the killer woke up. He woke up hungry, too.

That's how it started. A big-ass super-cell storm hitting the area was how containment failed. People fleeing the area in cars, trains, on foot and on planes was how it spread.

Now it was everywhere.

We sat on the plane and watched the end of the world. Three big, tough, ruthless, capable special operators. Helpless as fucking babies.

– 4 –

And then the phone rang.

– 5 –

"Captain Ledger," said a male voice. "This is Scott Pruitt, National Security Advisor—"

"I know who you are," I interrupted. "Tell me you're calling to tell me this shit isn't as bad as it looks."

There was a beat. "It's worse than it looks," said Pruitt.

"Tell me."

"*Lucifer 113* has a one-hundred percent infection rate," he said. "It has a one-hundred percent mortality rate."

The three of us were clustered around my satellite phone, the speaker on. Command Sergeant Major Bradley "Top" Sims and First Sergeant Harvey "Bunny" Rabbit had walked through the Valley of the Shadow with me more times than I could count. No matter how bad things ever got there was always a light shining somewhere, however small and fragile.

Bunny, who was a hulking kid from Orange County, mouthed the words "*one hundred percent.*" His face had gone pale beneath his volleyball tan. Top, the oldest of the three of us, looked stricken.

"What's the response protocol?" I demanded.

Another beat. Longer this time. Then Pruitt said, "We have one chance, Captain. One, and it's slim. But that's why I'm calling you. The White House, Camp David, and the other secure locations here on the east coast are compromised. Half of the Joint Chiefs are dead, and so is most of Congress. The president flew from D.C. this morning to San Diego, where he met with senior military staff and was scheduled to go to the Blue Estate."

The Blue Estate was a codename for a government safe house near El Cajon in Southern California. It was a massive bunker built half a mile below a *faux* warehouse on a remote corner of the National Guard base.

"But he never made it," I said, knowing where this was heading.

"No," said Pruitt, "his detail was attacked, sustaining heavy losses. The crucial materials for our only viable response were in a briefcase carried by one of the president's aides. That aide was killed in the convoy attack and his body—and the briefcase—cannot be recovered. A backup briefcase is aboard Air Force One, which is at Gillespie Field in El Cajon, twenty miles from the president's current location. He is barricaded in a suite of rooms at the Marriott Marquis Marina in San Diego, next to the convention center."

"What about local law?"

"San Diego has fallen," said Pruitt bleakly. "The city is a war zone. Infrastructure failure has collapsed and there is rioting in the streets. We are unclear as to whether that rioting is predominantly panic and looting, or if the citizens are fighting the infected."

"Okay, how about National Guard? They're in El Cajon, too, a couple of miles from Gillespie Field."

"A detail has been sent to protect Air Force One, but the majority of their forces have already been mobilized. There are over three million people in the San Diego metropolitan area. If even one percent of them are infected, that means there could be as many as three hundred thousand violent vectors in play."

Top closed his eyes and Bunny looked around like he wanted to run. The big, empty airplane offered no avenues for escape from the truth.

"What do you need from us?" I asked.

"Find the president," said Pruitt, "and get him to El Cajon before our window of opportunity closes."

"How much time do we have?"

"Almost none at all," he said. "I've taken the liberty of rerouting your plane."

As he said it I could feel the big bird tilt and the engine whine rise to a roar.

− 6 −

On the approach to California I went aft where I could be alone and placed a call to my wife, Junie. She answered on the first ring, as if she'd been waiting for my call.

"Joe!" she cried. "Where are you? Are you okay?"

"I'm fine, baby," I said, closing my eyes and leaning my head against the wall. "How are you? How's Ethan?"

"We're good, Joe," said Junie. "We're in Baltimore with Sean, Aly, and the kids."

Sean was my younger brother. He was a detective in Baltimore, a good husband and father of two great kids. There was talk about him being on the shortlist for commissioner and I hoped like hell he'd have the chance. But I could hear the TV on in the background and the news reporters were yelling.

"Listen to me," I said quietly, "you need to get out of town. Get out to my uncle's old farm in Robinwood. Load up with everything you can carry—water, canned food, medical supplies."

"Joe, is what they're saying true? Has this plague really spread out of control?"

I don't lie to Junie. If there are things I can't tell her because of mission restrictions, then I tell her that. That was yesterday's rulebook. I told her everything. She isn't the kind of person who falls apart. She's been through the badlands herself. Junie is tough in the way that real women are tough, which is pretty fucking tough.

"It's going to be crazy out there," I said. "People will panic, so—"

"Sean has plenty of guns," she said. "I'll make sure we bring them, too."

Sean's wife, Aly, was a good shot, and so was Lefty, their son, who'd just started college on a full-ride baseball scholarship.

We talked details for a few minutes. Junie was so practical that it actually calmed *me* down, and I'd called to reassure her. I heard the *bing-bong* signal telling us that we were beginning our descent.

"Call me as soon as you get to the farm," I said.

"I will."

"Call me if anything happens along the way."

"Joe…I will. We'll be fine."

I didn't say anything for too long.

"Joe…*will* we be fine? I mean, this is going to pass, right? We're doing something about this, aren't we?" By "we" she meant me, and people like me. Special forces, agents of the infrastructure, the methods and protocols and everything that went into motion when there was a major crisis.

"I'm going to give it a hell of a try," I promised. It was not the reassurance she wanted to hear or I needed to give. But it was all I could offer, and Junie knew it.

"I love you," she said.

"I love you, too."

"Come home to me," said Junie, which is what she always said when I was going off to war.

"I will," I said.

I meant it. I really did.

The plane tilted toward the mainland.

-7-

San Diego looked normal from the air.

Distance is a liar.

Perspective, on the other hand, is a brutally honest motherfucker. As the Galaxy began our descent we could see the fires. Closer still we could see whole sections of Old Town and the Gaslamp District thronged with people. On any other day you'd have thought it was a party. Fourth of July. A Day of the Dead joke occurred to me, but I kicked its ass back into the shadows of my mind.

"Gear up," said Top.

We did.

Top is the oldest active shooter in anyone's special ops group. He should have retired a long time ago. He is a muscular fifty-something with scars all over his dark brown skin and intelligent eyes filled with equal measures of compassion, intelligence, and tightly controlled anger. If you get between him and something he cares about, you are going to regret that you were the fastest swimming sperm.

He and Bunny went through the motions of selecting weapons and equipment with a familiarity that can only exist because of mutual trust, certain knowledge, and years of experience on the battlefields of this troubled little blue planet. They selected magazines and grenades and other gear, and buddy-checked the Kevlar limb pads and body armor.

Bunny's stuff was never off the rack. He's six-and-a-half feet tall and two guys wide. Perfect for the volleyball he once played to Olympic standards, and well-suited to the rigors of combat and hardship. Blond hair, blue eyes, and a goofy smile that went exactly one millimeter deep. Behind the surfer boy look was a good-natured killer. He was truly one of the good guys, but in combat he was something else entirely. His strength was a thing out of legend and he somehow managed to keep his idealism intact despite the things we'd all seen.

I was younger than Top and older than Bunny. A little over six feet, a little over two hundred, a little off the mark when it comes to my psychological profile. My shrink says that I manage my damage in useful ways. Fair enough.

We sat down for the landing but were up again while the bird rolled toward the most distant point in the San Diego airport.

"Looks clear," said Bunny as he peered out of the window. "Bunch of people over by the terminal, but no one over here."

"Where's our ride?" asked Top, looking out of another window. "It's a little better than five klicks to the hotel. If there's trouble in town that could be a long walk."

As if in answer, a big black Nissan Armada came tearing across the tarmac toward us. It was a brute of a civilian SUV, which was fine. We were big guys and we were bringing a lot of toys to this playground. We gathered our equipment bags and deplaned. I ordered the flight crew to refuel as long as it was safe, but otherwise button up and hold tight.

The driver spun into a skidding, shrieking stop that kicked up a cloud of friction smoke. The driver's door popped open to reveal a woman dressed in the black of a San Diego city police uniform. She was short and solid, with a Mexican face and hair that was falling out of a tight bun.

"Captain Ledger?" she yelled, pitching it almost as a plea.

"I'm Ledger," I said, walking toward her.

"I'm Torres, SDPD. Get in. *Now.*"

Top was studying her, but Bunny had a flat hand up to shade

his eyes as he stared at the people over by the terminal building. He said, "Oh…shit."

And ran for the SUV.

Top and I turned, and that's when we saw it. Those people were coming toward us. They were ordinary people. Some in regular clothes, some in various airport uniforms. A few soldiers and TSA agents among them. The one uniting theme about them was the color.

Red.

It was splashed on all of them. Hands and arms. Clothes. Mouths.

Maybe seventy of them.

Top threw his gear bag into the SUV and climbed into the backseat next to Bunny. I saw him draw his sidearm as he did so. I lingered for a moment. I wasn't rooted to the ground by shock or anything like that. I'm not known for hesitating.

No, my heart was breaking.

These were people. So many people. And they were infected. Which meant they were dead.

Pruitt had told us. One hundred percent infection rate, one hundred percent mortality rate. The parasites in Volker's bio-weapon killed them, and the parasites woke them up again as aggressive vectors. They were dead.

And they were coming for us.

− 8 −

"Drive," I growled as I slammed the front passenger door.

Sergeant Torres drove. She drove like hell was chasing us.

It was immediately obvious that the Armada was not a government-issue car. No radio or tactical computer, no lights or sirens. There was a bloody handprint on the left side of the windshield and shell casings on the floor.

She spun the wheel and kicked the pedal down as the first of the infected reached us. As the SUV turned, I saw a panorama of faces. White faces, a lot of shades of brown. Their mouths snapped at the air as if trying to chew their way toward us; their hands reached and fingers slashed in our direction. Their lips curled back from bloody teeth but their eyes—damn, that was the worst part. There was nothing in the eyes. No flicker of hate, no anger, no anything. They weren't even the black eyes of a shark. The eyes of all of these people were empty. Vacant.

Dead.

If the eyes are the windows to the soul, then these windows looked into vacant rooms of empty homes. No one and nothing lived there.

Behind me I heard Top murmur, "God Almighty."

Bunny said nothing at all.

Torres crushed the pedal against the floor and the Armada shot past the crowd. I heard the slithery, raspy sound of fingernails on the door and then we were beyond the crowd. We looked as they turned and began to follow. It was not exactly a pack response, but something colder and odder. The parasites within each of them reacted with identical single-mindedness and reflexive efficiency. The prey moved and so each of them moved.

"Welcome to San Diego," said Torres, trying for a glib joke and failing.

There were other people on the airport grounds. We saw bizarre tableaus as we raced past.

A pair of baggage handlers were beating an infected pilot with vicious swings of heavy suitcases. The pilot's bones were shattered, with white ends stabbing outward through skin and uniform, but even with all that he kept trying to get back up, kept trying to grab them.

A mechanic knelt on the ground, worrying at a co-worker's throat like a dog tearing up a squirrel. He did not even glance at us as we passed.

A little Middle Eastern boy walked blindly across the tarmac, most of his lower face gone. His empty eyes turned toward us and he reached out with small hands.

A fat woman with most of her blouse torn away walked in a sloppy circle, hands clamped to her stomach to try and hold her intestines in place. Her strength failed and her guts spilled out and I heard Bunny gag.

"What the fuck, boss?" he begged, but I had no answers.

Instead, I turned to Torres. "What can you tell us?"

She cut me a brief look. "The president is in his suite," she said quickly. "He has some Secret Service left, and there are some officers on the scene, but it's all falling apart. We have the lobby barricaded, but it's a big hotel and it's right next to the convention center. There's a couple of dozen ways in. When I left, the place was already under siege."

"Can you get us in?" I asked.

She took too long to answer that. "I'm not even sure I can get you all that close. People are going crazy in the streets."

Top leaned forward. "Did anyone tell you what this is? Do you know what's happening?"

"I heard a lot of crazy rumors. Some kind of terrorist attack. A bioweapon or some shit. Or an accident at some government lab. Everyone has a story."

"What do you think is happening?"

She looked at him in the rearview mirror. "I think someone left the back door of Hell unlocked."

We said nothing.

"I shot a guy in the chest. Three rounds, center mass," said Torres. "He went down because one of my bullets must have hit his spine. But even on the ground, even with a hole drilled through his fucking heart, he kept trying to bite me."

"Jesus fuck," said Bunny.

"I put another round in his head," said Torres, but there was a hitch in her voice. "I shot him while he lay there on the ground." She wiped at a tear and then looked at the wetness on her fingertips. Then she smeared it on the arc of the steering wheel. "I don't know what's going on. All I know is that death is broken."

She reached Airport Terminal Road, which was choked with cars, some of them stopped in the middle of the road. People—

alive and undead—were fighting between the cars.

"Hold onto your dicks," she said. She crossed herself and wrenched the wheel over to send the Armada punching through a line of neatly-trimmed hedges. The big vehicle had four-wheel drive but it wasn't built for this, and seatbelts or not, we were whipped and slammed around as the wheels crunched over curbs, shrubs, and fallen bodies. Then we burst out on North Harbor Road, which was also congested but not as badly. The engine roared as she accelerated while zigzagging around cars and people.

A man stepped out into our path and there was a godaw-ful thump. He went flying, crashing into the windshield hard enough to punch a spider web of cracks into the safety glass. I had a microsecond to see the man's face. I saw the pain and panic in his eyes. Maybe Torres saw it, too. Maybe knowing that she'd crippled or killed an uninfected person would ruin her. Maybe she was already gone by then. Don't know. The car muscled on and she never took her foot off the gas. The wind blowing past us pushed beads of dark red through the labyrinth of cracks.

"They didn't tell us it was this bad," said Bunny.

Torres laughed. A single snort that was a shuffle step away from hysteria. "I walked my dog this morning," she said after a few seconds. "I had coffee with my boyfriend at Starbucks before my shift." She shook her head. "When all of...*this*... started, it seemed to just explode, you know?" She cut us looks, hoping we'd understand. Needing it, as if to say that this was bigger than her, that it wasn't her fault.

"Yeah," I said, which was lame, but what else could I say?

We roared on. She steered the car like she'd spent her entire life training for this ride. My heartbeat was like a machine gun and my blood pressure could blow bolts out of plate steel, but I kept it off my face and out of my voice.

"It's a plague," I said. "A bioweapon."

I told her the story. I told her the truth. Because why? Be-cause fuck it. The world was falling off its hinges and this cop was in hell. In actual hell. And because she deserved to know the truth. I did not give a cold, wet shit about national security or need-to-know. That was as dead as the bodies in the street.

I knew that Torres appreciated the truth. I knew it hurt her, too. The truth is like that.

"Turn on the news," suggested Top. I did, and most of the channels were filled with pre-programmed music. Not the time for an Eagles retrospective or classic hip hop. I found the local news and the reporter was weeping so brokenly that I couldn't make out a single word. On another station, there was a field report from some guy back in Pennsylvania that was being broadcast nationally. His opener would have been a joke two hours ago. It wasn't now.

He said, "This is Billy Trout reporting live from the apocalypse..."

The story he told was about him and a cop named Dez Fox and several busloads of school kids trying to make it from Western Pennsylvania to Asheville, North Carolina. The roads were mostly blocked and the dead were everywhere. I heard gunshots and screams, and then the feed died. There was dead air for maybe ten seconds and then a reporter came on and tried to apologize for losing the feed.

Apologize. Jesus Christ.

He said that the station was switching to the Emergency Broadcast Network, but there was only dead air after that. I turned it off.

"It'll come back on," said Bunny, but Top just looked away out the window.

We could see the hotel and the sprawling convention center beyond it. There was a huge inflated rubber monster truck floating above the center, and signs everywhere for a monster truck convention. Dozens of the trucks were parked along the far side of the drive, and a few were sitting at haphazard angles in the street. One was burning.

Even over the roar of the SUV's engine I could hear a cacophony of sounds that I've only ever heard in the streets of countries in the midst of a civil war. Sirens wailed like demons; gunshots *pokked* and banged; screams rose to the skies. There were explosions, too, and the crunching of cars into each other and into meat and bone. Columns of smoke rose from between buildings on both sides of the bay. The sky was filled with helicopters—news and military.

I was born and raised in Baltimore, but a while back I ran Echo Team out of a pier in Pacific Beach. So, for several years *this* was my town. I knew the streets, knew a lot of the people, knew the vibe of the place.

What I saw around me belonged to some alien world. Not my town. Not any town that could *be* mine.

We drove.

I saw the Marriott rear up in the distance.

Behind me I heard Top say, "She-e-e-eet." Dragging it out.

The hotel was burning.

– 9 –

"What floor's POTUS on?" I demanded, looking through a pair of binoculars Bunny handed me.

"Top floor," she said, "executive suite." There was real dread in her voice.

Half the windows on the top floor had been blown out, and a lot of the rest were pock-marked with black dots. Bullet holes. Gray smoke twisted its way out of three windows on the north tower.

"Tell me that's not him," said Bunny.

But Torres shook her head. "He's in the south tower."

The south looked intact.

"Get us close," I told Torres, but she was already swinging us around onto a ramp that led to the valet parking entrance. The big glass doors were streaked with blood and two local cops were trying to hold it against a pack of screaming people. Some of those people had visible bites; others looked whole but terrified.

They were all desperate to get in because a dozen of the infected were closing in on them.

Torres gripped the wheel. "Call it," she said.

"Pick a side and own it," I told her.

She actually smiled.

Then she revved the engine, spun the wheel and then stamped hard on the brakes so that the big SUV slewed around. The back end crunched into the infected and sent them flying. But I could hear a huge metallic *crack* and the vehicle tilted down on a broken ball joint, the jagged metal screeching along the asphalt. Bunny and Top were out before it stopped moving, their guns up, fingers slipping inside the trigger guards. I was right there with them.

There was no discussion of rules of engagement. We'd faced infected like these before. Not the same plague, but the same bioweapon design philosophy. There was no reasoning, no Geneva Convention, no mutual agreement of honorable warfare between us and the hungry dead. Their humanity had been stolen, stripped away from them, leaving them as mindless aggressors. They were no more human than a swarm of wasps, and far deadlier. *Lucifer 113* was a serum transfer pathogen. Any bite would be a death sentence. Blood in our noses, eyes, mouths, or in an open wound would be as deadly as a bullet to our hearts. We knew all that.

And yet…

These were people. They weren't dressed in battle dress uniforms. They weren't extremists acting on a skewed ideology. These were housewives and homeless people, kids and business execs, tourists and conventioneers, vendors and bystanders. None of them had a gun or a rocket launcher.

It was going to break our hearts to pull those triggers. We all knew it. This was going to scar us forever.

We fired anyway.

Top tucked the stock of an M4 CQBR into his shoulder and fired, shifted, fired, shifted. Double-taps to the chest. His eyes were cold, and they didn't blink, and he never missed. But then he jerked erect as every person he shot recovered from the impacts and kept coming forward.

"Head shots!" screamed Torres. "That's the only thing that takes them down."

"Fuck me," murmured Top. He raised the barrel and put the next round through the forehead of a pretty woman in a torn yellow dress. She puddled down as if a light switch had been thrown. "Fuck me all to hell."

Bunny has an AA-12 drum-fed shotgun. He calls it Honey Boom-Boom. Bunny has some long-standing issues. He opened up and the heavy gauge buckshot did terrible work at such close quarters. There wasn't time for the pellets to spread, so they instead hit in clusters that disintegrated snarling faces and blew everything into clouds of red, pink and gray.

I had my old M9 Beretta in a two-hand grip and backed toward the doors, firing as the infected rushed me. They fell one by one.

But then I shot one in the head and he did not fall. He kept coming. It froze the moment for us all because it seemed to change the math. I shot him again as he leaped at me. The second bullet took him below the right eye and blew out a chunk of the back of his skull.

The motherfucker did not die. He tackled me around the legs and I fell.

I twisted as I landed, putting a lot of torque into it so that he landed first. He snapped his head forward and locked his teeth on a corner of my Kevlar chest protector. Before I could swing my gun between us, Torres put the barrel of her Glock against his temple and fired. The blast knocked his head sideways and the tension vanished from him all at once.

She helped me up and while Top and Bunny kept up the barrage we stared down at the corpse.

"Three headshots," I said.

Torres was breathing hard. "Maybe...maybe it's not *just* the brain," she said. "Maybe it's a special part? Like the brain stem or something?" She shook her head. "I've been trying to make sense of it all the way here. I think it's like that."

The firing diminished and I turned to see the last of the dozen infected go down. Top and Bunny began swapping in fresh magazines as they backed toward us.

"Did either of you have trouble dropping these things with a head shot?" I asked.

Bunny shook his head, but Top nodded. "Yeah. Got to get it right. High and center. I clipped a couple and it didn't do shit. Punched into the brain, but maybe not the sweet spot."

"That's what Torres thinks," I said. "Brain stem or something else."

It was Bunny who came up with the answer. "Motor cortex. Got to be."

"Why's that, Farm Boy?" asked Top.

"That's where the control is," said Bunny. We all looked blankly at him. "Look, the motor cortex is the part that controls the voluntary functions and like that. If the parasites have hot-wired these poor bastards, then they have to be using *some* part of them. So, motor cortex." He tapped the front and top of his head. "Put a hot round through here and they'll go down. And the brain stem thing makes sense, too. Unless this is some voo-doo shit, running around, biting and all that shit needs nerve conduction. That's the cranial nerves going down through the brain stem."

"How the fuck you know this?" demanded Top. "You ain't cracked a damn book in years."

"TED talks, old man," he said. "I listen to 'em while I jog."

"Okay," I said, cutting in. "Brain stem and motor cortex. Christ. It's bad enough we need headshots, now we got to be accurate as fuck."

We turned to the people huddled behind stacked chairs and tables on the inside of the hotel doorway. A guy in a black suit and bloody white shirt came out to talk to us. He had a wire in his ear and a look of profound shock on his too-white face.

"Captain L-Ledger...?" he asked in a wavering voice. He held a gun in his hand, but the slide had locked back and he hadn't replaced it. His eyes had a jumpy quality that told me he was standing on a windy cliff and wasn't sure which way to step.

"Secret Service?" I asked, more to remind him of who he was rather than identify him.

"Yes, sir," he said with a bit more certainty.

"What's your name?"

"Murphy," he replied. "Julius Murphy."

"Okay, Murphy, where's POTUS? Is he safe and can you take us to him?"

He said the president was safe and told us to follow him inside.

I looked down the ramp to where more of the infected were shambling our way. It was a surreal sight. They did not move as slow as movie zombies, but they weren't fast, either. It was more a lack of coordination and maybe a disconnect from muscle memory. That and the injuries that had killed them. So many had chunks bitten out of their arms and legs, and that loss of muscle and tendon made them clumsy. They staggered and limped and sometimes crawled our way. You could outpace them with a brisk walk.

That wasn't the point, though.

Despite those terrible injuries, they moved forward with a relentless consistency that spoke to an inability to fatigue, or to tire, or to stop. Sure, you could outwalk them, but for how long? It was like trying to outrun a glacier. Eventually it would catch up.

They would catch up, and sooner or later you'd have to deal with the implacability of them. There was no way to ever outrun their utter reality.

The realization terrified me on a level I'd never felt before. When Echo Team had faced other infected monsters similar to these, it had been in contained settings. A warehouse and a meat packing plant in Baltimore, inside the Liberty Bell Center in Philly. Not out in the open. Not with it spread so far already.

I think that's when I realized that the world had changed. It was no longer creaking on broken hinges. It had fallen off.

Unless there was some radical way the president had to reverse this, I knew that I was looking at the future.

I was staring through a ragged hole in the now to an actual apocalypse.

To Armageddon.

I wanted to cry. I wanted to hide.

I wanted to die.

I did not do any of that. Instead I turned and shoved Murphy toward the hotel door. "Let's go," I roared. Top, Bunny, and Torres walked backward behind me, firing at the oncoming tide of death.

− 10 −

We helped the people reinforce the doorway as best we could, and we shared a few of the weapons we'd brought with us. Murphy led us through the hotel to the elevators. There were a lot of scared people in there, but so far none of them were infected.

However, I took Torres aside and asked her about the people at the barricade who had visible bites.

"You understand that they're going to get sick, right?" I said quietly.

She nodded, eyes big and filled with pain.

"Have you seen how fast this plays out?" I asked. "From bite to, um, *transition*?"

"Depends on how bad it is," said Torres, and Murphy, who overheard, nodded.

"From what I've seen, sir," said Murphy, "there seems to be some connection to consciousness. If they pass out then something happens and it accelerates, but someone with the same injury who stays awake seems to be able to fight it."

"Fight it or last longer?" asked Top.

Murphy shook his head. "I...don't know. This is all just happening now."

"Okay," I said, "but if anyone gets some reliable intel on this thing then we have to get it out to everyone. Bunny, call your theory in to Pruitt. Top, watch our backs."

All of the hotel's power was still on and the fires were in the other tower. Murphy said we could trust the elevators, so we crammed inside. When the doors opened on seventeen, Torres nearly blew the head off a terrified room waiter. The poor little guy staggered backward, let out a cry like a kicked seagull, whirled and fled.

After the door closed Top nudged me and touched his hand. I nodded. I'd seen the bloody bandage, too. Poor bastard.

We stopped at four other goddamn floors. Twice people tried to get on. They were scared, crazed, but we could not let them in. One of them held a baby in her arms. It was slack and smeared with red, and when the door closed Top leaned his forehead against the wall, eyes closed, and cursed God. Bunny stood with his hand on Top's shoulder but didn't say anything. Really, what the hell can you say to that?

The last time the doors opened on the wrong floor we saw a scene out of some kind of nightmare. Two completely nude women knelt on the floor eating the face off a third. I don't know what the story was. They all looked like they'd been beautiful. They were all too young for what happened to them.

We shot them before the doors closed. Call it a mercy. That's what we told ourselves. Didn't really help all that much.

Then the doors opened on the top floor and suddenly there were guns everywhere. Pointing out from the inside of the car; pointing at us from the hall. A mix of Secret Service agents and cops. All of them disheveled, splashed with blood that was more black than red, with eyes that were too wide and showed too much white around the irises.

"Okay, let's all calm the fuck down," I said. When nobody moved, I showed good faith by raising my pistol barrel to the ceiling, and told my guys to stand down. The door started to close and I put my foot against it. "We're U.S. Special Forces. Who's in charge here?"

A tall Asian woman pushed past the others, snapping at her people to lower their weapons, which they did grudgingly and with hands that visibly shook. She wore a black suit over a torn white blouse spattered with blood. She looked to be about forty but there were deep lines around her mouth that aged her. I suspected they'd been carved there over the last day or two.

Guns were lowered but nobody holstered anything. I stepped out of the elevator and faced the woman.

"Mary Chang," she said, "assistant special agent in charge."

"Where the AIC?" I asked.

Her eyes wanted to shift away from mine, but she was too well trained. "Dead," she said. "We lost seventeen of twenty-two agents on this detail. This thing it…it's worse than we thought."

"No shit. Where's POTUS?"

"I'm here," said a voice.

I turned to see the president standing in the doorway to a suite halfway down the hall. He was in shirtsleeves and there wasn't a drop of blood on him. His hair was even combed. He had one agent and four cops with him, all of them with guns drawn and barrels pointing to the floor in front of them. Only one was so scared that his gun barrel was pointing at the top of his own foot. The president looked me up and down as we walked toward each other. "Captain Ledger. I've heard a lot about you."

Over the years I've worked with a lot of commanders in chief. Some I respected, some I was indifferent to, and a few were worthless cocksuckers. This guy was pretty good, from what I'd heard from friends on the inside of the White House power circles. A moderate who tried to work with people on both sides of the aisle. Fifty-something, slim, black haired and gray eyes. But there was something too slick and polished about him. He looked like a movie version of a president rather than the real thing. He was one of those people that other people usually liked at once. Charisma and a good plastic surgeon. My immediate take on him was "manipulative self-absorbed asshole."

He didn't offer his hand and instead stood there, giving me the kind of measuring look that was supposed to make me think he was assessing everything about me and making reliable deductions. Good luck with that. I don't look like a psychopath, but my shrink tells me otherwise. I have a smile that crinkles the skin around my eyes, I have good teeth and a deep-water tan. I could just as easily have come from Central Casting. I know for sure he didn't know my backstory because it's been comprehensively erased from all databanks. A side-benefit of working for Rogue Team International. We are, for all intents and purposes, ghosts. We get the backgrounds we need for a mission. All the president could really know was when he asked for the right guy.

Thing is, I *am* that guy. And I wish to fuck I'd been in-country when *Lucifer* slipped the leash. Maybe I'd have figured something out. I usually do. I know that sounds arrogant as fuck, but it is what it is. There's a reason I get sent into places like this. Top and Bunny, too.

"Where do we stand?" I asked. Maybe I should have added "sir," but I wasn't in the mood.

"My motorcade was hit on the way here," said the president. "They swarmed us. We lost…nearly everyone. The press corps, my aides…gone. I need to get out of here. I need to get somewhere safe. Air Force One is at Gillespie Field in El Cajon."

"I thought we were supposed to take you to the Blue Estate on the National Guard base."

"Plans change. I need to get to my plane. They tell me you can get me there."

He said "I" and "me." Not "us."

I searched his eyes, looking for remorse, looking for some trace of compassion for the people who'd died to get him through the swarm and up to this room. Not seeing all that much of it.

"Had to be a hundred of those *things*," he said.

"They're people," I said, mostly to be a dick.

"They *were* people. They're not anymore," he said, which was fair enough, but I did not give him even so much as a grunt of agreement.

Murphy, who stood next to me, said, "We came here because it was a pre-selected rally point. But there were more of the, um, infected in the streets. The motorcade was swarmed. That's when we lost the AIC and a lot of the others. Had some marines in plainclothes, too, but the crowd…well…"

I nodded. "How many made it up here?"

"Counting Mary here," said the president, "and Murphy over there, I have five Secret Service left in my detail. And two of my aides."

"That's it?" I was appalled. The president motorcade is made up of twenty-five to thirty vehicles. Lots of security, as well as members of the press, and key aides. There's often a hazardous materials team riding point with local police behind them and more cops in follow cars at the tail end. It's a lot of people in a lot of vehicles. And the president's car is armored. Traffic is blocked ahead and on cross streets. "Sir, what about your family? Were they with you?"

The president shook his head. "I sent them to a secure location in Virginia." He paused, then added. "We haven't had a status report yet."

I listened for some real heart, some pain, some depth of feeling in his tone, but there was not enough of it there. It surprised me. The news reports always showed him with his pretty wife and three kids. They were always smiling, always clinging close to one another. Which meant what, when measured against his reaction now? Was he so good at playing the controlled politician that his hurt didn't show? Or was he one of those sociopathic types for whom everyone else—even family—were a little unreal, like window dressing?

Or was I being too hard on him? After all, he'd just seen a lot of friends die, along with the people sworn to protect him. If San Diego was any indication of what was really happening across America, then there could be hundreds of thousands of people dead. Maybe a million. Was the calm, indifferent façade just that—a front erected over his very human fears? Pretending detachment so that he stayed detached? The more human part of me wanted to give him the benefit of the doubt.

"Okay," I said, "we'll get you out."

The president took my elbow and guided me a few yards down the hall, away from his guards.

"Your orders are to get me out, Captain," he said quietly.

"That's what I—"

"*Me*," he repeated, leaning on the word. "If you have enough transport to get everyone else out, that's fine. But I need to know that you understand the key element of your mission here."

He still held onto my elbow.

"I want us to be clear here," he said stiffly, "I *need* to get to Air Force One. This plague is spreading exponentially. We have a window of opportunity, but it is closing very quickly. I had a certain resource with me when we were swarmed and it's lost. Backups for that resource are aboard my jet."

"What kind of resource?" I asked.

He shook his head. "That's above your pay grade, Captain."

"I—"

He cut me off. "If I can't get to my plane within six hours then all of our computer models tell us that we will lose."

"Lose what, exactly?"

He half-smiled in surprise. "I thought you knew," he said. "I thought they told you."

"Maybe *you* should tell me."

"Captain Ledger, if we can't initiate the response protocol within six hours, this entire country is going to be a graveyard. And if we fall, the whole world is going to follow."

And now I saw it in his eyes. Behind the control was a total, insane panic.

I removed his hand from my elbow and very quietly said, "Then let's get you to your plane."

– 11 –

"How we going to get to El Cajon, Cap'n?" asked Top. "Our ride's for shit and I don't think we can Uber it."

"Plan B," I said.

"Which is?"

I pointed out the window. Down there, surrounded by a full-blown battle between the living and the dead, were a dozen monster trucks.

Bunny gave a sour little laugh. "Seems somehow appropriate."

– 12 –

So, yeah. Monster trucks.

There was one I had my eye on. The chassis was from a Ford F350, but the mechanic had gone a little ape shit on it and created some kind of mutant psychedelic retro hippie thing. The words "Mystery Bus" were painted in swirling colors along its side.

Understand something, I'm not into truck porn. I'm not into these kinds of things. I'm very comfortable with the size of my own dick and don't need to make statements with machinery. That said, my Uncle Jack was into them when I was a kid. One summer Sean and I helped him trick one out. Stunt monster trucks usually run on methanol alcohol and corn-based fuel, but the ones on the street here were likely diesel. The axles are salvaged from school buses or decommissioned military trucks and have a planetary gear reduction at the hub to help turn the massive tires that probably came from a dump truck.

There were a lot of trucks down there to choose from, but the Mystery Bus could take more people than the rest. And it was set high up.

"What if it doesn't have the keys in it?" asked Murphy.

"I grew up in Baltimore," I said, and left it at that.

"Lot of those things down there," said the president. "Feel

free to run them over with that truck. Might as well have some fun."

Maybe it was meant as gallows humor, but it landed flat and nobody cracked even a little smile. The president gave a disgusted shake of his head. I saw him mouth the word "*pussies.*"

Top unzipped the equipment bag he'd brought from the SUV. It was full of guns, grenades, and ammunition. The president walked over and looked at them, and he gave an appreciative nod. He even chuckled.

"Isn't this the point where you SpecOps jocks make some hard-ass quip about kicking ass and taking names?" he asked.

Top straightened and gave him a warm, genial, almost fatherly smile. "I'm probably going to die out there, Mr. President, and I'm definitely going to get my ass in trouble for anything I say," he said quietly, "so I guess I better make it good. Fuck you. Fuck you all to hell and back. Fuck you to death. Fuck you and everyone you ever knew." His smile brightened. "How's that for a quip?"

The Secret Service agents all started to take a threatening step forward. Bunny was standing right behind Top, and I was behind him. They looked at us, at their president, and then into the middle of nowhere. POTUS stood there with a face that had gone as red as the blood on the streets.

"Get me to my goddamn plane," was all he said.

– 13 –

We went down in the elevators. Chang and Murphy, POTUS, my team, and Torres in one car; everyone else squeezed into the other. We'd brought spare body armor and had helped the president strap it on, and I gave him my ballistic helmet. Top didn't like that but kept it to himself. Bunny asked him if he knew how to use a gun, but the president shook his head.

When the elevator doors opened, we stepped into one of the inner rings of hell.

The barricaded door had failed. All the people who had been trying to keep the infected out were among the first to rush at us with dead eyes and bloody teeth. I heard someone in our car sob. Not sure who it was. Could have been me for all I know.

We stepped into madness.

Bunny led the way with his shotgun. It holds fifty rounds of twelve-gauge and it was a target-rich environment. Top and I flanked him while the others formed a defensive ring around the president. We waited as long as we could for the second car to arrive.

It never did.

It must have stopped on another floor, as ours had on the way up. There was too much noise and distance to hear if they were up there making a fight of it. I hoped they were alive, but I never found out. We never saw them again.

"Move, move, move," I yelled. I had one hand on Bunny's broad back and fired my Beretta dry with the other. Dropped the mag, reloaded, fired.

Head shots look easy in the movies. The good guys never miss on *The Walking Dead*. Even amateurs nail the bad guys in the sweet spot time and again, at long distances, while running. Which is total frigging bullshit. Ask any soldier who has been in a running fight about it. It's usually a matter of putting enough ordnance downrange, and the cumulative effect does the trick. In Iraq and Afghanistan it was estimated that American soldiers—who are among the most highly trained in the world—capped off two hundred and fifty thousand rounds for every enemy KIA. Yeah. How's that for some scary math?

Now, factor in that our sweet spot wasn't center mass but a couple of sections of the brain and brain stem that were roughly the size of a child's fist each. If I had a .22 with light loads in the bullets maybe it would have been easier. Those rounds usually lack the power to exit something as dense as a skull and instead bounce around inside, turning the brain into Swiss cheese. My Beretta was loaded with hollow-points, so I was blowing holes in whatever I hit, but hitting exactly those spots was a bitch.

It was scary.

It was closing in on impossible.

Bunny had the smartest weapon, and I wish to Christ I'd thought to bring a shotgun. If we survived it, that would be my go-to weapon.

If wishes were horses, beggars would ride.

There were seven of us with guns. Most of us had never worked together, and even though the other four all had training, it wasn't the same kind. We had to create a rhythm. We shouted "Out!" and "Reloading!" and hoped each other heard.

The fight in the lobby was a bloodbath. There were fifty or sixty of the infected. It didn't matter that some of them were kids. It didn't matter that they could not think and could not return fire. They rushed at us in a mob. Soldiers aren't trained to deal with a swarm of unarmed civilians attacking with teeth and hands, or to fight enemies who did not easily go down in any conventional way.

We lost Murphy before we ever got to the door. I felt a hand on my shoulder and the grip half-turned me. I spun to see him trying to grab onto me like I was his lifeline, but there were two of the infected clamped like lampreys onto him, biting an ear and a calf. He knew he was dying but he tried to cling to life by clinging to me, to the living.

Then he was gone and we had to let him go.

The president was screaming at the top of his lungs. Shrill. I wanted so badly to hit him. But he wasn't the only one screaming.

"Top," I bellowed, "plow the road."

He dipped into a pouch and came out with a fragmentation grenade. "*Frag out,*" he roared and hurled it underhand so that it arced over the monsters trying to squeeze through from outside.

We dropped into a momentary huddle, all of us crowding around POTUS.

The blast radius of the grenade cleared the door and showered us with bloody debris and jagged glass. I hooked an arm under the president's shoulder and jerked him to his feet.

Bunny cleared the last of the obstructions and then we were on the valet parking ramp.

"Oh…fuck…" breathed Torres.

The Mystery Bus was half a football field from where we stood. Fifty long goddamn yards. Between it and us were hundreds of the dead.

Hundreds.

I did not see a single living person out there. Not one.

"Grenades," I barked, and the three of us, Top, Bunny and me, began bombarding the throng.

We threw half a dozen grenades each. The blasts shook the world, deafened us, punched us over the hearts. Then we ran into the red-tinged smoke, skidding on blood, firing in all directions, killing anything that moved.

We slaughtered our way to the monster truck.

– 14 –

The keys were in the truck.

So was the driver. He had no arms, no face, no eyes, but he thrashed because he was belted in place. I put a shot through his temple and Torres popped the lock and pulled him down. I saw Bunny pick up the president and actually throw him in through the back door. There was a sharp cry of pain, but then Bunny shoved Chang up after him. I turned to yell at the two remaining Secret Service agents, but they were gone. I never saw them fall. They had simply been edited out of the world. Top crowded in behind the wheel. Doors slammed and hands began banging on the truck's metal skin. The blows were weird. Hard, but also soft. Limp hands striking without skill, powered by raw need.

"*Go, go, go,*" I yelled, but he was already turning the key. The powerful engine roared to life and I nearly wept with relief when the little arrow on the fuel indicator swept up to full.

"Hold onto your dicks," Top said and put the truck in gear.

The crowd, weakened and dismembered as it was, still wanted to keep us there. They had numbers and weight and they could not feel pain.

The truck was truly a monster. The over-built engine roared like a mad bull and the massive wheels turned. We braced ourselves for impact, but it wasn't like that. Not at first.

No, the truck *ground* its way down the street. The tires were sixty-six inches high and forty-three inches wide, with deep tread. The massive weight of the vehicle and those brutal tires crushed the fragile bodies into pulp. I made the mistake of looking into the rearview mirror and saw that we were leaving a lumpy red road behind us. Nothing I've ever seen was as awful.

When I looked at Top, his face was set in immoveable stone and he looked ten years too old.

I pulled up a map program on the small tactical computer strapped to my wrist. It was a little over eighteen miles along Route 94 to 125 and then California 52 east to Gillespie Airport. We had five hours left.

It took us more than four hours to kill our way there.

Four long, goddamn hours. Night caught up with us. It kicked the sun off the edge of the world and tried to smother us with blackness. The lights of San Diego vanished behind us, curtained by smoke even before twilight burned off. The highway was packed, but the fucking truck was designed to crunch its way over everything. We did a lot of that, and it felt like the Mystery Bus was shaking itself to pieces. We saw plenty of fights that I wish we could have helped with. People still alive and trying to stay that way.

The mission, though, the response protocol—that mattered more than anyone or anything, but damn if it didn't hurt to have to keep moving forward.

In the back, Bunny, Torres, Chang and the president clung to restraining straps and tried not to look at each other. Bunny reloaded all the weapons. We had two grenades left and five or six magazines for each gun.

We were still a mile away when we saw the base.

No, that's wrong.

From a mile out we could see the flames.

– 15 –

Top circled around to Kenney Street, on the north side of the field, near the biggest runway. We idled on the road outside the gate, watching the big Jet Air Systems factory burn. The light from it painted the sides of Air Force One in Halloween colors. Shadow goblins seemed to caper along the curved sides of the big Boeing 747.

There was a very stout wall and heavy gate, which was closed and locked.

"Ram the gate," said the president, but Top shook his head.

"Steel construction," said Top. "We'd wreck this truck and not put a dent in it."

There were a lot of infected wandering around the field, and signs of one hell of a battle. The National Guard had clearly been called in to protect the president's plane. Maybe a hundred of them. A dozen of them were on the roof of the burning building. They were the only ones I could see.

On our side of the fence were maybe three hundred infected. They clawed and scratched and even tried to bite the big truck, as if they were hoping to eat their way to us.

We all watched the plane through binoculars.

"Door's closed," said Chang. "Lights are on inside."

"Call them," ordered the president.

Chang made the call and when the pilot answered, POTUS snatched the phone from her hand. "Major Arlin, this is the president."

"Thank the lord, sir, I am so relieved to know that you're safe and—"

The president interrupted him. "What is the status of Air Force One?"

"All secure inside," said the pilot. "Systems are green for

take-off. We fueled up, Mr. President, but we were ordered to keep everything flight ready. We've burned through some of it."

"Do we have enough to reach Hawaii?"

"No, sir, and the fuel truck and crew have been compromised."

"The whole damn field has been compromised, Major, where the hell can we go?"

Major Arlin rattled off a list of secure destinations in California, Nevada, and New Mexico.

"Groom Lake," said POTUS quickly. "It's remote."

"Very well, sir. What is your ETA?"

I took the phone and explained where we were. "There's a gate between us and it looks too solid for us to crash. We're going to have to open it. That's going to let all these infected in."

"Who cares?" demanded the president.

I had to fight back the urge to slap him. Not because he was becoming hysterical or anything, but he *was* irritating the pure shit out of me.

I pointed. "See that big shiny jet? See those engines? Once they spin up for take-off, they're going to be sucking in a lot of air. You got a few hundred dead people wandering around and one or more of them are going to get sucked in and then you have *no* engines."

"Well, shoot them for Christ's sake. Come on, Ledger, you're supposed to be the number one gunslinger. Surely you're not going to let this stop you. Not with what's at stake. I *need* to get onto that plane and it's your job to make it happen right goddamn now."

"First things first, sir," I said tersely. "We need to open and then secure the gate after the truck's inside."

"Can't you use one of your grenades to open it?"

"No," said Top. "Not what they're designed for. We need to use a blaster plaster."

He explained. It was a technology developed for use by the Department of Military Sciences, which is the group I was in before Rogue Team International was formed. Proprietary technology. Looks like a sheet of bubble wrap, but much tougher.

The little blisters are filled with chemicals and the flat parts have wires in them. You peel back a clear film to expose a strong industrial adhesive, place the thing on any surface you want to destroy, and either pull a small wire that activates a ten-second timer or use a remote. The timer triggers tiny electrical charges that rupture the walls of the blisters. The instant the chemicals mix they detonate with about six hundred times the explosive force of detonation cord. A ten by ten sheet of blaster plaster would send a standard mailbox fifty feet into the air or blow the front end off a Ford F250.

The trick for a barrier like this is that we wanted to blow the lock without destroying the function of the gate.

"Half of one'll do her, boss," suggested Bunny, and he immediately began cutting one to fit. "But that's only half the problem. We got to close the gate and hold it long enough for the plane to take off. Once we blow the lock that means physically closing and holding the gate."

"Once the Mystery Bus is inside we can close the gate and back the truck up to hold it," Top suggested.

"That's good," said Bunny, "but someone's still going to have to place the charge, open the gate, and close it after the truck's inside."

"That's a suicide mission," said Chang, appalled.

"It's your goddamn duty," snarled the president.

"Mr. President," said Chang, her face draining of blood, "maybe there's another way."

"I got it," said Bunny and we all looked at him. "I'm the biggest, the strongest, and I have Honey Boom-Boom. We all know I have the best chance."

Top's hands tightened so hard on the steering wheel that the leather creaked. He wanted to tell him not to volunteer, to find some other way, but he knew—as we all knew—that Bunny was right.

"I'll do the gate," said Torres quickly.

Bunny shook his head. "Don't even try."

"She volunteered," said the president. "Let her do it. We are running out of time here. Do *something*, for Christ's sake."

"Okay," I said, "Torres, you place the charge. Bunny and I will provide cover. Top, you're at the wheel, and Chang, you stay at the door to this bus. We go out, get it done, and *everybody* gets back inside. Hooah?"

"Hooah," said Top and Bunny.

"Not sure what that means," said Torres with a brave smile, "but hooah."

Chang said it, too, and the president rolled his eyes.

– 16 –

Top began moving the Mystery Bus forward. We tried to tune out the sound of bones snapping under the tires.

I scouted around inside the bus and found two six-packs of beer, grinning as I handed one to Bunny.

"Seriously?" groused the president. "Beer? Now?"

I ignored him. Bunny and I quickly wrapped blaster plasters around as many beers as we could, sealing them with the adhesives. When Torres realized what we were doing, she said, "Coooool." Dragging it out.

"Got to throw them pretty far," cautioned Top.

"That's my job," I said. "I taught my nephew how to pitch a fastball that would make you cry."

I went to the back of the bus. "Chang, I need you to open the rear window when I tell you. Do it fast and then cover me. I'm going to try and get some of the infected to pull back."

She nodded. The windows were part of the old bus shell built on top of the truck. It had pinch-clips to lower the windows.

"Now," I said, and she dropped the window. We were too high for anyone walking to reach us, but some of the nimbler infected had climbed onto the structure.

"I'll clear it," she barked as she drew her weapon, aimed with two hands, and fired five spaced shots. Three head shots, two kills. It was enough. I hurled the plaster-wrapped beer through the open window and Top immediately stepped on the gas. Chang jerked the window up, but then I hooked an arm around her and pulled her down as the blaster plaster detonated.

I'd used a quarter of a sheet, but it was enough to shatter all of the windows in the back of the bus.

"Oh...fuck," I said. "Step on it, Top."

Chang rose up and began firing, but the lurch of the truck made her stumble and two shots went into the roof. She corrected and fired at a white face that filled the rear window. It burst apart and as it fell I yelled, "Frag out!" and threw another bomb.

The force flung bodies everywhere, but the noise was louder than what the truck was making and the fire drew the eyes of the infected. A third of the crowd turned toward the detonation point.

I threw another. And another. With each explosion more of them hurried toward the noise. I saw dozens of them on fire, stumbling into each other, spreading the blaze.

"Coming up on the gate," yelled Top. "Get ready."

"On deck," said Bunny.

I wheeled and hurried over to the side door, where Bunny and Torres crouched, ready to go. I slapped the big man on the shoulder.

"I saved a couple of cold ones for when you two get back," I said.

Bunny's grin was a familiar one, the kind I'd seen him wear on battlefields when the shit was raining down. He was in that zone now, past ordinary fear, operating on the highest level of combat awareness. Torres, on the other hand, looked terrified beyond speaking. Her face was slick with sweat and there was a fever brightness in her eyes.

"You're a cop," I told her. "Remember your training. Do your job and trust Bunny to watch your back. You've earned enough combat points to make you a full-fledged badass, Torres. You can do this."

"Thank you, s-sir," she said, tripping over the last word.

"Enough with the pep talks," yapped the president. "Tick-goddamn-tock."

I gave Torres' arm a squeeze, nodded to Bunny, and then opened the door.

The truck was still rolling. I drew my Beretta and shot four infected in the head. Dropped all four.

"*Go!*"

Bunny was out first, firing his shotgun before he even landed on the ground. He blasted six rounds and then reached up, took hold of Torres and pulled her down like she weighed nothing. He brought his gun up and fired. I crouched in the doorway and fired. Top rolled to within inches of the door, stopped, then opened his window and fired.

Chang was behind us, killing anything that tried to crawl in through the shattered windows. Thunder deafened us all. I took my last fragmentation grenade, leaned out the door and threw it in as high an arc as I could over the crowd. It dropped to about chin level before it exploded, killing at least a dozen of the monsters and drawing every single dead eye.

Torres stuck the blaster-plaster around the lock and then they began running toward the door. They were both shooting; Top and I gave them cover, but something went wrong almost at once. I don't know if Torres accidentally pulled the detonator cord or if maybe somehow it malfunctioned, but the plaster exploded too soon.

Torres and Bunny were plucked off the ground and flung like ragdolls. The blast blew out the windshield, but Top threw an arm across his face in time. When I looked, I saw the gate swing inward, but no sign of Torres or Bunny.

Through the ringing in my ears I heard Bunny bellow out her name and then everything was drowned in continuous gunfire from his shotgun. Three seconds later Torres came flying in through the door. She was alive, but badly hurt. Bleeding. Screaming. I dragged her inside and then gave Bunny cover fire as he scrambled up. His body armor glistened with red.

The gate stood ajar. Top stomped on the gas and the bus slammed into the barrier, knocking it all the way open. He rolled inside and before he stopped the bus, I was out, down on the ground, running to grab the gate. Bunny, dazed and bleeding, knelt in the doorway and offered cover fire. Even so, I had to slam the gate on a half dozen infected. Their sheer weight stopped me there, and more of the dead were coming. Then I heard the *beep-beep-beep* as Top backed the Mystery Bus toward me. I threw myself sideways just in time. The gate opened inward two feet and then it hit the bumper. Top kept backing up until the gate was closed.

I staggered to the doorway. "Get out!" I screeched.

Top and Chang helped the president down through the front passenger door. Bunny handed Torres down to me, and then he climbed down. Half his body armor was gone, torn away by the force of the blast, and there were burns on his chest, left shoulder and face. Half his hair had been melted away. Still, he fired the big shotgun one-handed, which would have put most people on their asses. With his other hand he supported Torres, who was barely able to walk. She was flash-burned, too, but her right hand was mangled. Two fingers were missing and the wound did not look like it had been caused by shrapnel. Bunny briefly met my eyes.

"It happened while she was setting the charge," he said loud enough for only me to hear. "She reached through to wrap it around one of the bars. There was one of those things inside."

Already I could see that beneath the soot and burns Torres was going pale. Her eyes danced with pain and fear. Bloody tears leaked from her eyes. She knew.

We ran.

The door to the plane was open and a flight officer and two Secret Service agents were there. The agents spotted us and ran down the stairs, MP5 machine guns in their hands. They raced over to meet Chang and the president. In a tight cluster, we fought our way to the plane.

As we ran, I saw that on the other side of the burning factory were two National Guard UH-60 Black Hawk helicopters. One was burning, one wasn't, and its propellers were turning slowly, engine on.

Maybe the soldiers on the roof could use it to get out. Not my immediate problem.

Ten feet from the stairs Torres fell. She took a last staggering step and then went down. I waved Chang and the other agents on. Top and Bunny stood guard while I knelt by the wounded cop.

Except she wasn't a cop anymore. Everything that had been Officer Torres was gone. Her eyes stared up at nothing and her last breath rattled out between slack lips.

"Cap'n…" said Top. "We have to leave her."

It hurt to do it, but that's what we did.

We ran up the stairs and into Air Force One. I found the president hunkered down at a small desk in his private office, and an aide was helping him open a small leather case and he was speaking on a tan-yellow satellite phone. He had Chang and the two other agents with him, all of them armed.

"Sir," I said urgently, "do you have the response protocol? Can you stop the plague?"

He looked up at me with a triumphant smile as he lowered the phone. "I just did."

"What is it? A counter-agent or…"

My words trailed off as I realized what that leather case was. My mouth went totally dry.

"I just spoke with the Secretary of Defense," he said in a weirdly calm voice. "I confirmed the gold codes, Captain."

The gold codes.

Good god.

The protocol is complex and yet frighteningly simple. The leather case contained a secure device that allowed him to input a set of codes. It nominally follows the two-man rule, but the Secretary of Defense can't really act without those codes from the president. Once they were given, once an agreed protocol was initiated, the machinery would move with terrifying swiftness and efficiency.

"Are you out of your *mind*?" I demanded, and the Secret Service agents moved to get up in my face. I ignored them. "What are your targets, for Christ's sake? We aren't at war with a foreign power."

"We *are* at war, Captain. The cities are falling. New York,

D.C., Philadelphia, Pittsburgh, Los Angeles..." His voice trailed off and he shook his head. "All of them are overrun. The only chance we have is to remove those centers of congestion and limit the spread of the infection to the suburbs and rural areas. People are already being told to evacuate."

"You *can't* do this."

"It's done," said the president. "We're going to take back this great nation. We will make it ours again."

I knew those words. They were trademarks from his campaign speeches. *Make it Ours Again* had been his platform.

"You're going to drop nukes on the major U.S. cities? What about fallout? What about living people trapped in the blast areas?"

"There is always collateral damage in war."

I don't know that I have ever heard that phrase used with less humanity or more coldness. The engine whine of the plane was increasing.

"You need to stop this while you can," I begged. "It's going to make it worse. You're killing us all."

I looked from him to Chang. Her eyes were bright with shock, but she had her Glock in her hand and she stood by the madman with the nuclear football. The other agents had their barrels half-raised and their eyes were hard as flint.

"Captain," said the president, "someone needs to move the stair car away from the door so we can take off."

"Make the call, you motherfucker," I growled, and now the barrels were pointing at my face. Top and Bunny had their guns up, too, but I knew it was too late. The codes had been given, the machinery was running.

"Get off my airplane," said the president. "That's an order."

"There are more of them coming," yelled the pilot. "We need to clear the runway."

"Cap'n," said Top, "this is done." When I still did not move, he took my arm. "We can take the Black Hawk."

He pulled me back and I let him.

At the doorway to the office I stopped, though, and pointed

a finger at the president. "God damn you to hell."

His smile was small and sad. "We're already in hell, Captain."

I turned and left. At the top of the stairs I jerked to a stop. Torres was crawling up toward us. Her eyes were completely empty and her lips curled back from white teeth. Bunny made a small, heartbroken sound and raised his gun.

"No," I said and ran down to the dead cop. She snapped at me, but my Kevlar pads were still in place. I pulled her up and drag-carried her into the plane and shoved her into one of the seats reserved for the press. The pilot frowned at me.

"She'll be fine," I said. "Spin this thing up. We'll move the stairs."

He gave me an uncertain nod and went into the cockpit and closed the door.

Then I whirled and ran, pulled the outer door shut and ran down to where Top and Bunny were positioning themselves at the base of the stair car.

We moved it away, then ran for the Black Hawk, killing whoever and whatever was in our way. We got in, got it started, got it in the air.

Top flew. He opened up with chain guns and cleared the runway, then banked away as Air Force One lifted into the air.

Neither Bunny nor Top asked me why I'd done what I'd done. They understood. Top nodded and Bunny put his hand on my shoulder. The fuel gauge said we had enough gas to go maybe a thousand miles. We'd have to refuel somewhere. Top had family in Georgia. Bunny's folks were on vacation in St. Thomas. My family was in Maryland, hopefully at my uncle's old farm in Robinwood, far away from the cities.

When the nukes dropped there would be EMPs, so maybe they would kill our electronics and drop us all down to the ground. Maybe we'd been the timetable. Maybe the generals would mutiny and refuse to follow orders.

Maybe.

Maybe.

Maybe.

We flew into the night, knowing that no matter where we went or what happened, this was the world now.

And it wasn't our world anymore.

– 17 –
NOW

You can't outfly an electromagnetic pulse.

We tried.

We saw the flash over San Diego and we poured it on.

By then Air Force One was well out of range, flying at thirty thousand feet, punching along at five hundred miles an hour. We opened the throttle to the never-exceed speed of two-hundred and twenty-two miles per hour, but we flew low over the landscape.

The EMP rode the shockwaves and chased us like a pack of dogs. It killed the bird. Killed the avionics, the motors. Everything. The rotors stopped turning with anything except wind friction.

And we fell.

Fell.

All the way down.

Maybe if we'd been luckier the crash would have killed the three of us. But, we haven't been lucky in a long time.

I stood there, watching the bird burn. Watching the sky burn. Feeling the blood run in lines down my face, my chest, my arms. Listening to the howling wind. Listening to the hungry moans.

Top and Bunny were hurt. We all were. Hurt. Not dead.

I slapped a fresh magazine into my Beretta and raised it as the first of the shambling figures broke through the wall of smoke.

Not dead yet. Not them. Not dead like they're supposed to be. And we were still alive, too. Death sang its mournful, tuneless songs in the moans of the things that came to us. Death sang, but we did not know the songs, did not know those lyrics. Not yet.

Not goddamn yet.

We raised our guns at the unstoppable wave of death.

"Well," I said, "fuck it."

Top and Bunny laughed. Actually laughed. So did I.

We fired.

PART TWO

FAT GIRL WITH A KNIFE

JONATHAN MABERRY

DURING THE OUTBREAK

–1–

D ahlia had a pretty name, but she knew she wasn't pretty. Kind of a thing with the girls in her family. None of the Allgood girls were making magazine covers.

Her oldest sister, Rose, was one of those college teacher types. Tall, thin, meatless, kind of gray-looking, with too much nose, no chin at all, and eyes that looked perpetually disappointed. She taught art history, so there was that. No one she taught would ever get a job in that field. There probably weren't jobs in that field. When was there ever a want-ad for art historian?

The sister between Rose and her was named Violet. She was the family rebel. Skinny because that's what drugs do; but not skinny in any way that made her look good. Best thing you could say about how she looked was that she looked dangerous. Skinny like a knife blade. Cold as one too. And her moods and actions tended to leave blood on the walls. Her track record with "choices" left her parents bleeding year after year. Violet was in Detroit now. Out of rehab again. No one expected it to stick.

Then there was the little one, Jasmine. She kept trying to get people to call her Jazz, but no one did. Jasmine was a red-haired bowling ball with crazy teeth. It would be cute except that Jasmine wasn't nice. She wasn't charming. She was a little monster and she liked being a little monster. People didn't let her be around their pets.

That left Dahlia.

Her.

Pretty name. She liked her name. She liked being herself. She liked who she was. She had a good mind. She had good thoughts. She understood the books she read and had insight into the music she downloaded. She didn't have many friends, but the ones she had knew they could trust her. And she wasn't mean-spirited, though there were people who could make a compelling counterargument. A lot of her problems, Dahlia knew, were the end results of the universe being a total bitch.

Dahlia always thought that she deserved the whole package. A great name. A nice face. At least a decent body. A name like Dahlia should be carried around on good legs or have some good boobs as conversation pieces. That would be fair. That would be nice.

Failing that, good skin would be cool.

Or great hair. You can get a lot of mileage out of great hair.

Anything would have been acceptable. Dahlia figured she didn't actually need much. The weight was bad enough; the complexion was insult to injury. But an eating disorder? Seriously? Why go there? Why make it *that* much harder to get through life? Just a little freaking courtesy from the powers that be. Let the gods of social interaction cut her *some* kind of break.

But...no.

Dahlia Allgood was, as so many kids had gone to great lengths to point out to her over the years, all bad. At least from the outside.

No amount of time in the gym—at school or the one her parents set up in the garage—seemed able to shake the extra weight from her body. She was fat. She wasn't big boned. She wasn't a "solidly built girl," as her aunt Flora often said. It wasn't baby fat, and she knew she probably wouldn't grow out of it. She'd have to be fifteen feet tall to smooth it all out. She wasn't. Though at five-eight, she was a good height for punching loud-mouth jerks of both sexes. She'd always been fat and kids have always been kids. Faces had been punched. Faces would be punched. That's how it was.

But, yeah, she was fat and she knew it.

She hated it. She cried oceans about it. She yelled at God about it.

But she accepted it.

Dahlia also knew that there was precedent in her family for this being a lifelong thing. She had three aunts who collectively looked like the defensive line of the Green Bay Packers. Aunt Ivy was the biggest. Six feet tall, three hundred pounds. Dahlia suspected Ivy had thrown some punches of her own in her day. Ivy wasn't one to take anything from anyone.

Mom was no Sally Stick Figure either. She was always on one of those celebrity diets. Last year it was the Celery and Carrot Diet, and all she did was fart and turn orange. Before that it was a Cottage Cheese Diet that packed on twenty extra pounds. Apparently the "eat all you want" part of the pitch wasn't exactly true. This year it was the Salmon Diet. Dahlia figured that it was only a matter of time before Mom grew gills and began swimming upstream to spawn.

Well, maybe that would have happened if the world hadn't ended.

− 2 −

It did. The world ended.

On a Friday.

Somehow it didn't surprise Dahlia Allgood that the world would end on a Friday. What better way to screw up the weekend?

− 3 −

Like most important things in the world, Dahlia wasn't paying that much attention to it. To the world. To current events.

She was planning revenge.

Again.

It wasn't an obsession with her, but she had some frequent flyer miles. If people didn't push her, she wouldn't even think about pushing back.

She was fat and unattractive. That wasn't up for debate, and she couldn't change a few thousand years of developing standards for beauty. On the other hand, neither of those facts made it okay for anyone to mess with her.

That's what people didn't seem to get.

Maybe someone sent a mass text that it was okay to say things about her weight. Or stick pictures of pork products on her locker. Or make *oink-oink* noises when she was puffing her way around the track in gym. If so, she didn't get that text and she did not approve of the message.

Screw that.

It's not that she was one of the mean girls. Dahlia suspected the mean girls were the ones who hated themselves the most. And Dahlia didn't even hate herself. She liked herself. She liked her mind. She liked her taste in music and books and boys and things that mattered. She didn't laugh when people tripped. She didn't take it as a personal win when someone else—someone thinner or prettier—hit an emotional wall. Dahlia knew she had her faults, but being a heartless or vindictive jerk wasn't part of that.

Revenge was a different thing. That wasn't being vindictive. It was—as she once read in an old novel—a thirst for justice. Dahlia wanted to be either a lawyer or a cop, so that whole justice thing was cool with her.

Justice—or, let's call it by the right name, revenge—had to be managed, though. You had to understand your own limits and be real with your own level of cool. Dahlia spent enough time in her head to know who she was. And wasn't.

So, when someone did something to her, she didn't try to swap cool insults, or posture with attitude, or any of that. Instead she got even.

When Marcy Van Der Meer—and, side note, Dahlia didn't think anyone in an urban high school should have a last name with three separate words—sent her those pictures last month? Yeah, she took action. The pictures had apparently been taken in the hall that time Dahlia dropped her books. The worst of them was taken from directly behind her as she bent over to pick them up. Can we say butt crack?

The picture went out to a whole lot of kids. To pretty much everyone who thought they mattered. Or everyone Marcy thought mattered. Everyone who would laugh.

Dahlia had spent half an hour crying in the bathroom. Big, noisy, blubbering sobs. Nose-runny sobs, the kind that blow snot bubbles. The kind that hurt your chest. The kind that she knew, with absolute clarity, were going to leave a mark on her forever. Even if she never saw Marcy again after school, even if Dahlia somehow became thin and gorgeous, she was never going to lose the memory of how it felt to cry like that. Knowing that *while* she cried made it all a lot worse.

Then she washed her face and brushed her mouse-colored hair and plotted her revenge.

Dahlia swiped Marcy's car keys during second period. She slipped them back into her bag before last bell. Marcy could never prove that it was Dahlia who smeared dog poop all over her leather seats and packed it like cement into the air-conditioning vents. Who could prove that the bundle of it she left duct-taped to the engine had been her doing? No one could be put under oath to say they saw Dahlia anywhere near the car. And besides, the keys were in Marcy's purse when she went to look for them, right?

Okay, sure, it was petty. And childish. And maybe criminal. All of that.

Did it feel good afterward?

Dahlia wasn't sure how she felt about it. She thought it was just, but she didn't spend a lot of time actually gloating. Except maybe a couple of days later when somebody wrote "Marcy Van Der Poop" on her locker with a Sharpie. That hadn't been Dahlia, and she had no idea who'd done it. That? Yeah, she spent a lot of happy hours chuckling over that. It didn't take away the memory of that time crying in the bathroom, but it made it easier to carry it around.

It was that kind of war.

Like when Chuck Bellamy talked his brain-deprived minion, Dault, into running up behind her and pulling down the top of her sundress. Or, tried to, anyway. Dahlia was a big girl, but she had small boobs. She could risk wearing a sundress on a hot day with no bra. Chuck and Dault saw that as a challenge. They thought she was an easy target.

They underestimated Dahlia.

Dahlia heard Dault's big feet slapping on the ground and turned just as he reached for the top hem of her dress.

Funny thing about those jujutsu lessons. She'd only taken them for one summer, but there was some useful stuff. And fingers are like breadsticks if you twist them the right way.

Dault had to go to the nurse and then the hospital for splints, and he dimed Chuck pretty thoroughly. Both of them got suspended. There was some talk about filing sexual harassment charges, but Dahlia said she'd pass if it was only this one time. She was making eye contact with Chuck when she said that. Although Chuck was a mouth-breathing Neanderthal, he understood the implications of being on a sexual predator watch list.

Dahlia never wore a sundress to school again. It was a defeat even though she'd won the round. The thought of how it would feel to be exposed like that…Everyone had a cell phone, every cell phone had a camera. One photo would kill her, and she knew it. So she took her small victory and let them win that war.

So, it was like that.

But over time, had anyone actually been paying attention and keeping score, they'd have realized that there were very few repeat offenders.

Sadly, a *lot* of kids seem to have "insult the fat girl" on their bucket list. It's right there, just above "insult the ugly girl." So they kept at it.

And she kept getting her revenge.

Today it was going to be Tucker Anderson's car. Dahlia had filched one of her dad's knives. Dad had a lot of knives. It probably wasn't because he was surrounded by so many large, fierce women, but Dahlia couldn't rule it out. Dad liked to hunt. Every once in a while he'd take off so he could kill something. Over the last five years he'd killed five deer, all of them females. Dahlia tried not to read anything into that.

She did wish her dad would have tried to be a little cooler about it. When they watched *The Walking Dead* together, Dahlia asked him if he ever considered using a crossbow, like that cute redneck, Daryl. Dad said no. He'd never even touched a crossbow. He said guns were easier. Ah well.

The knife she took was a Buck hunting knife with a bone handle and a four-inch blade. The kind of knife that would get her expelled and maybe arrested if anyone found it. She kept it hidden, and in a few minutes she planned to slip out to the parking lot and slash all four of Tucker's tires. Why? He'd Photoshopped her face onto a bunch of downloaded porn of really fat women having ugly kinds of sex. Bizarre stuff that Dahlia, who considered herself open-minded and worldly, couldn't quite grasp. And then he glued them to the outside of the first-floor girl's bathroom.

Tucker didn't get caught because guys like Tucker don't *get* caught. Word got around, though. Tucker was tight with Chuck, Dault, and Marcy. This was the latest battle in the war. Her enemies were persistent and effortlessly cruel. Dahlia was clever and careful.

Then, as we know, the world ended.

− 4 −

Here's how it happened as far as Dahlia was concerned.

She didn't watch the news that morning, hadn't read the papers—because who reads newspapers?—and hadn't cruised the top stories on Twitter. The first she knew about anything going wrong was when good old Marcy Van Der Poop came screaming into the girls' room.

Dahlia was in a stall and she tensed. Not because Marcy was screaming—girls scream all the time; they have the lungs for it, so why not?—but because it was an inconvenient time. Dahlia hated using the bathroom for anything more elaborate than taking a pee. Last night's Taco Thursday at the Allgood house was messing with that agenda in some pretty horrific ways. Dahlia had waited until the middle of a class period to slip out and visit the most remote girls' room in the entire school for just this purpose.

But in came Marcy, screaming her head off.

Dahlia jammed her hand against the stall door to make sure it would stay shut.

She waited for the scream to turn into a laugh. Or to break off and be part of some phone call. Or for it to be anything except what it was.

Marcy kept screaming, though.

Until she stopped.

Suddenly.

With a big in-gulp of air.

Dahlia leaned forward to listen. There was only a crack between the door and frame and she could see a sliver of Marcy as she leaned over the sink.

Was she throwing up?

Washing her face?

What the hell was she doing?

Then she saw Marcy's shoulders rise and fall. Very fast. The way someone will when . . .

That's when she heard the sobs.

Long. Deep. Badly broken sobs.

The kind of sobs Dahlia was way too familiar with.

Out there, on the other side of that sliver, Marcy Van Der Meer's knees buckled and she slid down to the floor. To the floor of the girls' bathroom. A public bathroom.

Marcy curled herself into a hitching, twitching, spasming ball.

She pulled herself all the way under the bank of dirty sinks.

Sobbing.

Crying like some broken thing.

Dahlia, despite everything, felt something in her own eyes. On her cheeks.

She tried to be shocked at the presence of tears.

Marcy was the hateful witch. If she wasn't messing with Dahlia directly, then she was getting her friends and minions to do it. She was the subject of a thousand of Dahlia's fantasies about vehicular manslaughter, about STDs that transformed her into a mottled crone, about being eaten by rats.

Marcy the hag.

Huddled on the filthy floor, her head buried down, arms wrapped around her body, knees drawn up. Her pretty red blouse streaked with dirt. Crying so deeply that it made almost no sound. Crying the way people do when the sobs hurt like punches.

Dahlia sat there. Frozen. Kind of stunned, really. Marcy?

Marcy was way too self-conscious to be like that.

Ever.

Unless…What could have happened to her to put Marcy here, on that floor, in that condition? Until now Dahlia wouldn't have bet Marcy had enough of a genuine human soul to be this hurt.

The bathroom was filled with the girl's pain.

Dahlia knew that what she had to do was nothing. She needed to sit there and finish her business and pretend that she wasn't here at all. She needed to keep that stall door locked. She needed to not even breathe very loud. That's what she needed to do.

Absolutely.

– 5 –

It's not what she did, though. Because, when it was all said and done, she was Dahlia Allgood.

And Dahlia Allgood wasn't a monster.

– 6 –

She finished in the toilet. Got dressed. Stood up. Leaned her forehead against the cold metal of the stall door for a long ten seconds. Reached back and flushed. Then she opened the door.

Turning that lock took more courage than anything she'd ever done. She wasn't at all sure why she did it. She pulled the door in, stepped out. Stood there. The sound of the flushing toilet was loud and she waited through the cycle until there was silence.

Marcy Van Der Meer lay in the same position. Her body trembled with those deep sobs. If she heard the flush, or cared about it, she gave no sign at all.

Dahlia went over to the left-hand bank of sinks, the ones

farther from Marcy. The ones closer to the door. She washed her hands, cutting looks in the mirror at the girl. Waiting for her to look up. To say something. To go back to being Marcy. It was so much easier to despise someone if they stayed shallow and hateful.

But…

"Hey," said Dahlia. Her throat was phlegmy and her voice broke on the word. She coughed to clear it, then tried again. "Hey. Um…hey, are you…y' know…okay?"

Marcy did not move, did not react. She didn't even seem to have heard.

"Marcy—?"

Nothing. Dahlia stood there, feeling the weight of indecision. The exit door was right there. Marcy hadn't looked up, she had no idea who was in the bathroom. She'd never know if Dahlia left. That was the easy decision. Just go. Step out of whatever drama Marcy was wrapped up in. Let the little snot sort it out for herself. Dahlia didn't have to do anything or say anything. This wasn't hers to handle. Marcy hadn't even asked for help.

Just go.

On the other hand…

Dahlia chewed her lip. Marcy looked bad. Soaked and dirty now, small and helpless.

She wanted to walk away. She wanted to sneer at her. Maybe give her a nice solid kick in her skinny little ass. She wanted to use this moment of alone time to lay into her and tell her what a total piece of crap she was.

That's what Dahlia truly wanted to do.

She stood there. The overhead lights threw her shadow across the floor. A big pear shape. Too small up top, too big everywhere else. Weird hair. Thick arms, thicker legs. A shadow of a girl who would never—ever—get looked at the way this weeping girl would. And it occurred to Dahlia that if the circumstances were reversed, Marcy would see it as an open door and a formal invite to unload her cruelty guns. No…she'd have reacted to this opportunity as if it was a moral imperative. There wouldn't be any internal debate over what to do. That path would be swept clear and lighted with torches.

Sure. That was true.

But part of what made Dahlia *not* one of *them*—the overgrown single-cell organisms pretending to be the cute kids at school—was the fact that she wasn't wired the same way. Not outside, God knows, but not inside either. Dahlia was Dahlia. Different species altogether.

She took a step. Away from the door.

"Marcy..." she said, softening her voice. "Are you okay? What happened?"

The girl stopped trembling.

Just like that. She froze.

Yeah, thought Dahlia, *you heard me that time.*

She wanted to roll her eyes at the coming drama, but there was no one around who mattered to see it.

Dahlia tried to imagine what the agenda would be. First Marcy would be vulnerable because of whatever brought her in here. Break-up with Mason, her studly boyfriend du jour. Something like that. There would be some pseudo in-the-moment girl talk about how rotten boys are, blah-blah-blah. As if they both knew, as if they both had the same kinds of problems. Dahlia would help her up and there would be shared tissues, or handfuls of toilet paper. Anything to wipe Marcy's nose and blot her eyes. That would transition onto her clothes, which were wet and stained. Somehow Dahlia—the rescuer—would have to make useful suggestions for how to clean the clothes, or maybe volunteer to go to Marcy's car or locker for a clean sweater. Then, as soon as Marcy felt solid ground under her feet again, she would clamp her popular girl cool in place and, by doing that, distance herself from Dahlia. After it was all over, Marcy would either play the role of the queen who occasionally gave a secret nod of marginal acceptance to the peasant who helped her. Or the whole thing would spin around and Marcy would be ten times more vicious just to prove to Dahlia that she had never—*ever*—been vulnerable. It was some version of that kind of script.

Marcy still, at this point, had not turned. Dahlia could still get the heck out of there.

But...she *had* reacted. She'd stopped sobbing. She was listening.

Ah, crap, thought Dahlia, knowing she was trapped inside the drama now. Moving forward was inevitable. It was like being on a conveyor belt heading to the checkout scanner.

"Marcy?" she said again. "Are you hurt? Can I...like...help in some way?"

An awkward line, awkwardly delivered.

Marcy did not move. Her body remained absolutely still. At first that was normal. People freeze when they realize someone else is there, or when they need to decide how to react. But that lasts a second or two.

This was lasting too long. It wasn't normal anymore. Getting less normal with each second that peeled itself off the clock and dropped onto that dirty bathroom floor.

Dahlia took another step closer. And another. That was when she began to notice that there were other things that weren't normal.

The dirt on Marcy's red blouse was wrong somehow.

The blouse wasn't just stained. It was torn. Ripped. Ragged in places.

And the red color was wrong. It was darker in some places. One shade of dark red where it had soaked up water from the floor. A different and much darker shade of red around the right shoulder and sleeve.

Much, much darker.

A thick, glistening dark red that looked like...

"Marcy—?"

Marcy Van Der Meer's body suddenly began to tremble again. To shudder. To convulse.

That's when Dahlia knew that something was a lot more wrong than boyfriend problems.

Marcy's arms and legs abruptly began thrashing and whipping around, striking the row of sinks, hammering on the floor, banging off the pipes. Marcy's head snapped from side to side and she uttered a long, low, juddery, inarticulate moan of mingled pain and—

And what?

Dahlia almost ran away.

Almost.

Instead she grabbed Marcy's shoulders and pulled her away from the sinks, dragged her to the middle of the floor. Marcy was a tiny thing, a hundred pounds. Dahlia was strong. Size gives you some advantages. Dahlia turned Marcy over onto her back, terrified that this was an epileptic seizure. She had nothing to put between the girl's teeth to keep her from biting her tongue. Instead she dug into the purse she wore slung over her shoulder. Found Dad's knife, removed the blade and shoved it back into the bag, took the heavy leather sheath and pried Marcy's clenched teeth apart. Marcy snapped and seemed to be trying to bite her, but it was the seizure. Dahlia forced the sheath between her teeth and those perfect pearly whites bit deep into the hand-tooled leather.

The seizure went on and on. It locked Marcy's muscles and at the same time made her thrash. It had to be pulling muscles, maybe tearing some. Marcy's skirt rode high on her thighs, exposing pink underwear. Embarrassed for them both, Dahlia tugged the skirt down, smoothed it. Then she gathered Marcy to her, wrapped her arms around Marcy's, pulled the soaked and convulsing enemy to her, and held her there. Protected. As safe as the moment allowed, waiting for the storm to pass.

All the while she looked at the dark stains on Marcy's shoulder. At the ragged red of her shirt. At the skin that was exposed by the torn material.

There was a cut there and she bent closer to look.

No. Not a cut.

A *bite*.

She looked down at Marcy. Her eyes had rolled up high and

white and there was no expression at all on her rigid face. Those teeth kept biting into the leather. What *was* this? Was it epilepsy at all? Or was it something else? There were no rattlesnakes or poisonous anythings around as far as Dahlia knew. What else could give a bite that might make someone sick? A rabid dog? She racked her brain for what she knew of rabies. Was that something that happened fast? She didn't think so. Maybe this was unrelated to the bite. An allergic reaction. Something.

The spasms stopped suddenly. Bang, just like that.

Marcy Van Der Meer went totally limp in Dahlia's arms, her arms and legs sprawled out. Like she suddenly passed out. Like she was...

"Marcy?" asked Dahlia.

She craned her neck to look at Marcy's face.

The eyes were still rolled back, the facial muscles slack now, mouth hanging open. The leather sheath slid out from between her teeth, dark with spit.

Except that it wasn't spit.

Not really.

The pale deerskin leather of the knife sheath was stained with something that glistened almost purple in the glare of the bathroom fluorescents.

"Marcy?" Dahlia repeated, shaking her a little. "Come on now, this isn't funny."

It wasn't. Nor was Marcy making a joke. Dahlia knew it.

It took a whole lot of courage for Dahlia to press her fingers into the side of Marcy's throat. Probably the toughest thing she'd ever had to do. They taught how to do it in health class. How to take a pulse.

She checked. She tried to listen with her fingers.

Nothing.

She moved her fingers, pressed deeper.

Nothing.

Then.

Something.

A pulse.

Maybe a pulse.

Something.

There it was again.

Not a pulse.

A twitch.

"Thank God," said Dahlia, and she realized with absolute clarity that she *was* relieved that Marcy wasn't dead. Dahlia fished around for the actual pulse. That would have been better, more reassuring.

Felt another twitch. Not in the throat this time. Marcy's right hand jumped. Right hand. Then, a moment later, her left leg kicked out.

"No," said Dahlia, fearing a fresh wave of convulsions.

The twitches kept up. Left hand. Left arm. Hip buck. Both feet. Random, though. Not intense. Not with the kind of raw power that had wracked Marcy a few minutes ago.

It was then that Dahlia realized that this whole time she could have been calling for help. *Should* have been calling. She shifted to lay Marcy on the floor, then dug into her purse to find her cell. It was there, right under the knife. Directly under it. The knife Dahlia forgot she'd put unsheathed into the bag.

"Ow!" she cried, and whipped her hand out, trailing drops of blood. Dahlia gaped at the two-inch slice along the side of her hand. Not deep, but bloody. And it hurt like hell. Blood welled from it and ran down her wrist, dropped to the floor, spattered on Marcy's already bloodstained blouse.

She opened the bag, removed the knife, set it on the floor next to her, found some tissues, found the phone, punched 911 and tucked the phone between cheek and shoulder, pressing the tissues to the cut.

The phone rang.

And rang. And, strangely, kept ringing. Dahlia frowned. Shouldn't the police answer 911 calls pretty quickly? Six rings? Seven? Eight?

"Come on!" she growled.

The phone kept ringing.

No one ever answered.

Dahlia finally lowered her phone, punched the button to end the call. Chewed her lip for a moment, trying to decide who to call next.

She called her mom.

The phone rang.

And rang. And went to voicemail.

She tried her aunt Ivy. Same thing. She tried her dad. His line rang twice and the call was answered.

Or—the call went through. But no one actually said anything. Not Dad, not anyone. After two rings Dahlia heard an open line and some noise. Sounds that she couldn't quite make sense of.

"Dad?" she asked, then repeated it with more urgency. "Dad? Dad?"

The sounds on the other end of the call were weird. Messy sounding. Like a dog burying its muzzle in a big bowl of Alpo.

But Dad never answered that call.

That's when Dahlia started to really get scared.

That was the point—after all those failed calls, after that bizarre, noisy, not-a-real-answer call—that she realized that something was wrong. A lot more wrong than Marcy Van Der Poop having a bad day.

She turned to look at Marcy.

Marcy, as it happened, had just turned to look at her.

Marcy's eyes were no longer rolled up in their sockets. She looked right at Dahlia. And then Marcy smiled.

Though, even in the moment, even shocked and scared, Dahlia knew that this wasn't a smile. The lips pulled back, there was a lot of teeth, but there was no happiness in that smile. There wasn't even the usual mean spite. There was nothing.

Just like in the eyes.

There…

…was…

…nothing.

That's when Dahlia really got scared.

That's when Marcy suddenly sat up, reached for her with hands that no longer twitched, and tried to bite Dahlia's face off.

−7−

Marcy let out a scream like a panther. High and shrill and ear-shattering.

She flung herself at Dahlia and suddenly the little princess was all fingernails and snapping teeth and surprising strength. The two girls fell back onto the wet floor. Dahlia screamed too. Really loud. A big, long wail of total surprise and horror.

Teeth snapped together with a porcelain *clack* an inch from her throat. Marcy bore her down and began climbing on top of her, moving weirdly, moving more like an animal than a girl. She was far stronger than Dahlia would have imagined, but it wasn't some kind of superpower. No, Marcy was simply going totally nuts on her, throwing everything she had into attacking. Being insane.

Being...

Dahlia had no word for it. All she could do or think about was not dying.

The teeth snapped again and Dahlia twisted away, but it was so close that for a moment she and the crazy girl were cheek to cheek.

"Stop it!" screamed Dahlia, shoving at Marcy with all her strength.

Marcy flipped up and over and thudded hard onto the concrete floor. She lay there, stunned for a moment.

Dahlia was stunned too. She'd never really used her full strength before either. Never had to. Not even in jujutsu or field hockey or any of the other things she'd tried as part of a failed fitness and weight loss program. She'd never tried to really push it to the limit before. Why would she?

But now.

Marcy had gone flying like she was made of crêpe paper.

Dahlia stared for a second. She said, "Hunh."

Marcy stared back. She hissed.

And flung herself at Dahlia as if falling hard on the ground didn't matter.

Dahlia punched her.

In the face.

In that prom-girl face.

Hard.

Really damn hard.

Dahlia wasn't sure what was going to happen. She didn't think it through. She was way too scared for anything as orderly as that. She just hauled off and hit.

Knuckles met expensive nose job.

Nose collapsed.

Marcy's head rocked back on her neck.

She went flying backward. Landed hard. Again.

Dahlia scrambled to her feet and in doing so kicked something that went skittering across the floor.

The knife.

She looked at it. Marcy, with her smashed nose and vacant eyes, looked at it.

With another mountain lion scream, Marcy scrambled onto hands and feet and launched herself at Dahlia. For a long half-second Dahlia contemplated grabbing that knife; it was right there. But this was Marcy. Crazy, sure, maybe on something, and certainly no kind of friend. Still Marcy, though. Dahlia had known her since second grade. Hated her since then, but that didn't make this a grab-a-knife-and-stab-her moment.

Did it?

Marcy slammed into her, but Dahlia was ready for it. She stepped into the rush and hip-checked the little blonde.

Marcy hit Dahlia. And Marcy rebounded. As if she'd hit a wall.

Any time before that moment, such a clash, such a demonstration of body weight and mass, would have crushed Dahlia.

It would have meant a whole night of crying in her room and eating ice cream and writing hate letters to herself in her diary.

That was a moment ago. That was maybe yesterday. This morning.

Now, though, things were different.

Marcy hit the edge of a sink and fell. But it didn't stop her. She got back to her feet as if pain didn't matter. She rushed forward again.

So, Dahlia punched her again.

This time she put her whole heart and soul into it. Along with her entire body.

The impact was huge.

Marcy's head stopped right at the end of that punch. Her body kept going, though, and it looked like someone had pulled a rug out from under her feet. They flew into the air and Marcy flipped backward and down.

Which is when a bad, bad moment got worse.

Marcy landed on the back of her head.

The sound was awful. A big, dropped-cantaloupe splat of a sound. The kind of sound that can never ever be something good.

Red splashed outward from the back of Marcy's head. Her body flopped onto the ground, arms and legs wide, clothes going the wrong way, eyes wide.

And Marcy Van Der Meer did not move again.

Not then. And, Dahlia knew with sudden and total horror, not ever again.

She stood there, wide-legged, panting like she'd run up three flights of stairs, eyes bugging out, mouth agape, fist still clenched. Right there on the floor, still close enough to bend down and touch, was a dead person. A *murdered* person.

Right there was her victim.

Her lips mouthed a few words. Maybe curses, maybe prayers. Maybe nonsense. Didn't matter. Nothing she could say was going to hit the reset button. Marcy was dead. Her brains were leaking out of her skull. Her blood was mixing with the dirty water on the bathroom floor.

Dahlia was frozen into the moment, as if she and Marcy were figures in a digital photo. In a strange way she could actually see this image. It was framed and hung on the wall of her mind.

This is when my life ended, she thought. Not just Marcy's. Hers too.

She was thinking that, and the words kept replaying in her head, when she heard the screams from outside.

– 8 –

For a wild, irrational moment Dahlia thought someone had seen her kill Marcy and that's what they were screaming about.

The moment passed.

The screams were too loud. And there were too many of them.

Plus, it wasn't just girl screams. There were guys screaming too.

Dahlia tore herself out of the framed image of that moment and stepped back into the real world. There were no windows in the girls' room, so she tottered over to the door, her feet unsteady beneath her. The ground seemed to tilt and rock.

At the door she paused, listened. Definitely screams.

In the hallway.

She took a breath and opened the door.

The bathroom was on the basement level. This part of the school was usually empty during class. Just the bathroom, the janitor's office, the boiler room, and the gym.

She only opened the door a crack, just enough to peer out.

Dault was out there, and she froze.

Dault was running, and he was screaming.

There were three other kids chasing him. Freshmen, Dahlia

thought, but she didn't know their names. They howled as they chased Dault. Howled like wildcats. Howled like Marcy had done.

Dault's screams were different. Normal human screams, but completely filled with panic. He ran past the bathroom door with the three freshmen right behind him. The group of them passed another group. Two kids—Joe Something and Tammy Something. Tenth graders. They were on their hands and knees on either side of one of Marcy's friends. Kim.

Kim lay sprawled like Marcy was sprawled. All wide-open and still.

While Joe and Tammy bent over her and . . .

Dahlia's mind absolutely refused to finish the thought.

What Joe and Tammy were doing was obvious. All that blood, the torn skin and clothes. But it was impossible. This wasn't TV. This wasn't a monster movie.

This was real life and it was right now and this could not be happening.

Tammy was burying her face in Kim's stomach and shook her head the way a dog will. When tearing at...

No, no, no, no...

"*No!*" Dahlia's thoughts bubbled out as words. "No!"

She kept saying it.

Quiet at first.

Then loud.

Then way too loud.

Joe and Tammy stopped doing what they were doing and they both looked across the hall at the girls' bathroom door. At *her*. They bared their bloody teeth and snarled. Their eyes were empty, but there was hate and hunger in those snarls.

Suddenly Joe and Tammy were not kneeling. They leaped to their feet and came howling across the hall toward the bathroom door. Dahlia screamed and threw her weight against it, slamming it shut. There were two solid thuds from outside and the hardwood shook with what had to have been a bone-breaking impact. No cries of pain, though.

Then the pounding of fists. Hammering, hammering. And those snarls.

Far down the hall, Dault was yelling for help, begging for someone to help him. No one seemed to.

Dahlia kept herself pressed against the door. There were no locks on the bathroom doors. There were no other exits. Behind her on the floor were three things. A dead girl who had been every bit as fierce as the two attacking the door. A cell phone that had seemed to try to tell her that something was wrong with the world.

And the knife.

Dad's knife.

Just lying there.

Almost within reach.

She looked at it as the door shuddered and shuddered. She thought about what was happening. People acting crazy. People—go on, she told herself, say it—*eating* people. Marcy had been bitten. Marcy had gone into some kind of shock and seemed to stop breathing. No. She *had* stopped breathing. Then Marcy had opened her eyes and gone all bitey.

As much as Dahlia knew this was insane and impossible, she knew there was a name for what was happening. Not a name that belonged to TV and movies and games anymore. A name that was right here. Close enough to bite her.

She looked down at Marcy as if the corpse could confirm it. And…maybe it did. Nothing Dahlia had done to the girl had worked. Not until she made her fall down and smash her skull. Not until Marcy's brain had been damaged.

All of those facts tumbled together like puzzle pieces that were trying to force themselves into a picture. A picture that had that name.

Began with a *z*.

"Aim for the head," whispered Dahlia, and her voice was thick with tears. "Oh God, oh God, oh God."

Tammy and Joe kept slamming into the door. The knife was still there. Very good blade. And Dahlia was very strong. She knew how to put her weight into a punch. Or a stab.

"...*God*..."

When she realized that she had to let go of the door to grab the knife, it changed something inside of her. She waited until the next bang on the door, waited for them to pull back to hit it again, then she let go and dove for the knife, scooped it up as the door slammed inward, spun, met their charge.

Tammy, smaller and faster, came first.

Dahlia kicked her in the stomach. Not a good kick, but solid. Tammy jerked to a stop and bent forward. Dahlia swung the knife as hard as she could and buried the point in the top of the girl's skull. In that spot where babies' skulls are soft. The blade went in with a wet crunch. Tammy dropped as quickly and suddenly as if Dahlia had thrown a switch. One minute zombie, next minute dead.

That left Joe.

A freshman boy. Average for his age. As tall as Dahlia.

Not quite in her weight class.

She tore the knife free, grabbed him by the shirt with her other hand, swung him around into the sinks, forced him down and...*stab*. She put some real mass into it.

Joe died.

Dahlia staggered back and let him slide to the floor.

Outside she heard Dault screaming as he ran in and out of rooms, through openings in the accordion walls, trying to shake the pack of pursuers.

Dahlia caught a glimpse of her own face in the row of mirrors. Fat girl with crazy hair and bloodstains on her clothes. Fat girl with wild eyes.

Fat girl with a knife.

Despite everything—despite the insanity of it, the horror of it, the knowledge that things were all going to slide down the toilet in her world—Dahlia Allgood smiled at herself.

Then she lumbered over to the door, tore it open, and yelled to Dault.

"Over here!"

He saw her and almost stopped. She was bloody, she had that knife. "W-what—?"

"Get in here," said Dahlia raising the blade. "I'll protect you."

Yeah.

She was smiling as she said that.

PART THREE

ORC NIGHT

RACHAEL LAVIN

SIX MONTHS AFTER FIRST NIGHT

-1-

"Left! Right! Strike! Strike! Watch your footing!" A young woman's voice carried across a grassy field as she paced between the long lines of fighters, dark green eyes watching her students run through training exercises. Dozens of people, from mid-teens to late forties, lined up in front of her in slightly askew rows, wooden training swords or large sticks gripped firmly in their hands, moving in unison through careful forms. "Don't stop. I don't care if you're tired. Remember, the orcs don't get tired. Ever."

Orcs. It was what she'd nicknamed the living dead. It was maybe a silly name, borrowed from *The Lord of the Rings.* The difference here was that these orcs were *real* monsters. And they were dead. All of the millions, or perhaps billions, of people who'd died when the plague swept across the world had risen to become monsters. To become orcs.

She was not exaggerating to the people she trained. The orcs never got tired, they never gave up, they were relentless and insatiably hungry for the flesh of the living. Half measures and half-assed training were not going to help anyone survive. Only real *warriors* would live long enough to maybe try and build something, to take back some land from the dead and claim it as theirs. And so Rachael Elle worked her people harder and harder every day.

The late spring day came with an unseasonably warm breeze, the sun rising in a clear sky. In a normal world this would be a beautiful day, the sort where you wanted to be outside, enjoying and relaxing.

But this was not that world. Rachael knew that better than anyone here. She had led a group of cosplayers and other survivors out of a hotel in New York, fighting floor by floor against thousands of the dead. It had taken weeks, during which Rachael had changed from a fangirl playing at being a super hero to an actual warrior. Maybe not a hero—at least not in her own eyes—but a practiced killer. She got her people—and by then they *were* her people—out of New York and down into rural Pennsylvania, then to Virginia. Fighting every step of the way. Refining her skills and becoming more of a warrior, and more of a killer, every day.

And it wasn't just the orcs she'd killed. While out on a scouting mission to find resources for her people, she'd come upon a bus full of terrified little kids. She'd pieced together that they were waiting for their protector; Dez, a raw and violent cop from Stebbins—the town where the outbreak began. Dez was in a running fight with a group of human monsters—all very much alive, but all the more evil for that. They called themselves the Nu Klux Klan, and they were rounding up women and children for the sickest kind of entertainment. Into this mix came a man, Captain Joe Ledger, who said he'd been a Special Ops soldier before the world fell apart. Ledger and his big combat dog, Baskerville, joined up with Rachael and Dez.

There was a terrible battle at a farmhouse, and when the smoke cleared the Nu Klux Klan had been butchered.

The Rachael who left that carnage was immensely far removed from the naïve and earnest cosplayer who had been at the comic convention in New York. She wondered how she would look to her family, but forced herself to turn away from that thought. That kind of loss was a much more destructive bite than anything the orcs could do.

Rachael propped the long stick she used for training across her shoulders, hooking her arms over it, standing back to watch. She looked like an average early twenty-something, having exchanged her superhero costume today for a worn geeky T-shirt with a Batgirl logo, loose fitting jeans and heavy-duty, knee-high leather boots. Her long auburn hair was pulled up into a loose bun, wavy tendrils escaping around her face and blowing in the breeze. The only thing that seemed out of place was the sharp elven sword and dagger strapped to her hips.

"Brian!" she called out. "Foot! Stop crossing over. That's how you trip yourself."

They had only been training for a few weeks, but she was pleased how quickly her team was developing their skills. Brett and Rachael took turns training them, putting their little combat experience from LARPing—live-action role playing—to some use. Their form wasn't perfect, but it kept them alive, and that was the best they could do.

It wouldn't help them against a trained, living opponent.

But their targets were slightly easier.

"Again!"

Listening over the sighing wind for any sounds of the dead, she watched her trainees run through the exercises over and over.

Practice meant perfect.

Practice meant fewer people died.

Over the last few months, their numbers had exponentially increased. What once had been a tiny traveling band of survivors that had barely escaped New York was now a full-fledged group. As their numbers increased, travel grew increasingly difficult, so the old hospital located on an earlier foray had proven useful as a refuge. After clearing it out and repairing the makeshift chain-link fences, they'd expanded the yards and added more outside areas—gardens and open areas for people to escape, even briefly, the confines of concrete walls. They set up traps in the surrounding woods, building fences next to it, upping their levels of security, and they drove the dead away.

It was almost like having a home.

But homes needed protecting, and the rumors and tales spread of the woman dressed as a superhero and armed with a sword, cutting through the undead. People traveled to join them, looking for safety, for a place to belong in their new, more dangerous world.

As their numbers grew, however, so did the threats. They would welcome anyone who wanted security and agreed do their part, but there were always enemies who would try to take their home, and orcs who stalked the landscape. Rachael couldn't protect them all herself, even with Brett at her side. He was a brute of a man who used to cosplay Thor without having to use padding. Brett was enormously powerful and moderately quick, but he did not share Rachael's combat intuition. Or her ruthlessness.

Then Alice, one of the women who had joined around the time of the battle at the farmhouse, expressed interest in learning how to fight so she could help, and that had given Rachael an idea. But she never expected the number of volunteers who stepped forward when she posed the idea to their group.

Wandering through the lines of training survivors, she tapped her stick lightly against legs and arms, adjusting stances and grips.

"Andy, foot farther forward," came a familiar voice. Rachael smiled at the sound. Brett came up to join her on the field. She was glad he hadn't left with their last patrol. The group was safer for having another competent fighter and...well, she was happier when he was around.

"Take a break," she called out, handing her stick to one of the fighters as they walked away, "we'll resume in twenty minutes. Make sure to stretch!"

She turned, walking with Brett a short distance away.

"How are they doing?" he asked. He brushed strands of long blond hair that had escaped from his ponytail out of his face and leaned back against a tree, folding muscular arms as he did so.

"They're getting better," she responded. "Some of them seem to be picking it up faster than others, but they all want to learn. They all want to protect the people they care about."

"They have a good teacher, a strong leader." Brett smiled at her, reaching out to tuck a strand of hair behind her ear before pulling her close and draping an arm around her shoulder. "You'll get them to where they need to be."

Leaning against his side comfortably, she rested her head against his chest. They watched together in silence as Andy and Brian began to spar, the sound of wood hitting wood echoing across the field. It was a lighthearted practice spar, neither of them trying very hard, but Rachael could see how much they'd improved over the last few weeks.

In the moment of calm, it seemed that everything could be right with the world. No orcs, no bloodthirsty gangs threatening their safety, no loss.

So when the small pack of orcs emerged from the tree line behind Brian and Andy as they fought, the words of warning stuck in her throat…lost on the wind that carried the unsettling death rattle of the undead.

Andy froze in terror as Brian turned, trying to get his sword up to defend himself. He tripped over his feet, landing hard as one of the orcs grabbed for him. His weapon flew out of his grasp, off to the side and out of reach.

Swallowing hard, Rachael ducked under Brett's arm and charged forward, her mouth open to warn the rest of the group. Before she could get the words out, however, another warrior already had her heavy wooden sword out, running full speed to strike quickly—Maria, a shy, quiet teen who'd joined their group recently. Before Rachael could react, the girl slammed her sword into the orc's head—once, twice, three times in quick succession.

It dropped to the ground, unmoving. Maria stood over it, making sure it didn't rise again, before reaching out a hand to help Brian back to his feet. Andy, in the meantime, snapped out of his shock and attacked the other orcs.

The rest of the group sprang into action without an order. Rachael watched proudly as they moved together as a unit to clear out the last standing dead. Some held back, but as the last of the orcs fell, the chatter and excitement of success filled the air.

Smiling, Brett joined Rachael, standing at her side. He mussed her hair lightly.

"Welcome to your army."

− 2 −

The morning sun glowed across the grounds as Rachael helped weed one of their gardens. She smiled, listening to the sound of children playing in the parking lot; drawing on the asphalt with chalk and playing with toys. This was the world she wanted, a taste of normality in the chaos.

Mark, another recent arrival to their community, jogged in between the beds of plants, stammering out-of-breath apologies for being late to his duties. Cute in a thin, intense way, with a shock of brown hair that hadn't seen scissors in months. Rachael smiled, handing him a small shovel. "Pull up some dirt," she said, gesturing to the rows of damp, dark ground.

The work was hard, but getting lost in thought made the hours pass. Rachael found herself tuning out most of the sounds around her as she dug her fingers through the dirt.

When the sound of children shrieking broke through her

reverie, she thought it was just a playground scuffle. Then the shrieks turned into screams of pure terror, pulling her out of her thoughts, jarring her back to attention. Rachael grabbed her sword instinctively, tossing the scabbard to one side as she bolted toward the commotion. The screams grew louder.

"The fence!" someone shouted. "There's a hole! The fence is broken!"

Dread filled Rachael's chest as she rounded the corner. Orcs filled half the lot, dozens of them, shambling with rotted hands outstretched and grasping at the panicked children fleeing in every direction.

No one but Rachael had a weapon. She snapped into action, charging the closest orcs, slicing and kicking and stabbing. She scooped up children on the run, handing them off to anyone she could as she charged toward the horde of walking death.

There was no way she could take on this many by herself; there were more than she'd ever battled alone. She battled ice-cold fear in the pit of her stomach as more and more orcs grasped at her, broken teeth snapping the air.

"Focus," she growled as she stumbled against a broken curb, almost losing her footing. Catching herself, she adjusted her grip on her sword, cutting through the orcs grabbing at her sleeve, knocking them away and moving on to the next without pause. Stopping meant death for her, for the children...for their home.

Charging through a pair of orcs, she swung her sword, dragging it across the backs of their necks as she spun, kicking out to knock them to the ground. There were too many; the orcs came in never-ending masses, and she couldn't take them on herself. She needed to focus on getting everyone to safety instead of trying to reduce the enemy's numbers.

Most of her people were back at the hospital, but Rachael could still hear screaming from across the lot, behind the orcs that changed direction to trail her. Throwing caution to the wind, she took a deep breath and charged, ducking and dodging and weaving, chasing the screams.

She was vaguely aware of someone yelling her name behind her, but she couldn't focus on that now. Swinging her sword arcing down into an orc's skull, she yanked hard, pulling it out of one orc's head to slice through another's neck, never stopping long enough to let any of them grab her.

She spotted a man with a boy and a girl backing away from the orcs. The man—Rachael couldn't remember his name—stood in front of the kids, doing his best to protect them.

"This way!" Rachael yelled, waving to them.

The boy bolted toward her, and she kicked an orc back with a solid foot to the chest, grabbing the small child and pulling him up onto her back.

"Hold on tight," she shouted as he wrapped his arms and legs around her. She gestured to the man to do the same with the little girl, but he was frozen in fear, the child's terrified screams drowning out Rachael's yells.

She made a split-second decision and charged the orc that stood between them, swinging her sword more slowly with the extra weight on her back, but still managing to land a solid blow that knocked the rotted form out of her way.

The girl ran to her as soon as the orc was down.

"Run!" Rachael yelled to the man to follow, to run, but it was too late. He screamed as orcs swarmed him, ripping and biting. Rachael grabbed the toddler, hoisting her up on her hip, fighting back the wave of nausea that threatened to overcome her.

Too weighed down to fight, and barely able to run, Rachael panicked as the orcs turned their attention away from the now dead man to her. Struggling to move with any agility or speed, she tried to dodge around an orc as it grabbed at her shirt, shredding the cloth but missing her skin.

Suddenly something smashed down on the orc's head, and Brett was there, spinning his steel hammer like it was a children's toy.

"Move, Rachael!" he yelled as the orc crumpled in front of him. He moved on to the next as she struggled to keep pace, her legs screaming from the extra weight, but she gritted her jaw and fought through the burning muscles, focusing on safety.

They made it to the door of the hospital a few paces ahead of the orcs, and Alice held the door open long enough for them to get in before slamming it shut, barricading it. Letting the crying children climb to the floor and run for their parents, Rachael collapsed against the door as her legs gave out, adrenaline crashing. A hand stretched out in front of her. She looked up at Brett, letting him help her up off the floor and into his strong embrace.

− 3 −

The grounds were overrun with orcs, lurching and moaning as they roamed looking for their prey. Rachael watched with anxiety from a second-floor window, leaning on the sill, forehead pressed against the cool glass. She tried to ignore that each one of the horrible, ruined creatures below her were once humans, each one with their own story. No time for that now. They needed to get to the fence. They needed to block any more of the orcs from getting in, and they needed to clear out the ones that had gotten in already.

"They're not ready," Rachael said, disheartened. "I can't ask them to fight that many, not yet." She paused. "I'm not ready to lead them. I let them all down, I trapped them here."

Brett stood behind her silently for a few minutes, before setting something down next to her hand.

"You're more ready to lead them than you think," he said as he walked away. She looked down at the Wonder Woman tiara he'd laid there, her fingers wrapping around the metal.

− 4 −

Rachael stood on a chair, pieces of metal Wonder Woman armor strapped over layers of clothing and leather, a mismatch of costumes and protective layers. Her eyes traveled across all of the men, women and children watching her silently, one by one, meeting their eyes. She could feel the fear in the air, but she could also feel their hope. Their faith. Their trust in her.

"You've faced every challenge to get this far," she told them. "No. You've *defeated* every challenge to get this far. You're not afraid. You're not weak. You are survivors. Yes, we're no army. We don't need to be. You are strong. Every single one of you. You are heroes."

She looked from face to face, her fingers clutching the tiara.

"I won't ask you to fight if you don't want to. I won't make anyone do anything they don't want to. But know that we fight to protect our home; to protect our family. This is our family. *You* are my family—and I will fight to defend you."

There was silence for a moment, then a rising murmur in the crowd as Alice stood.

"You fought for us before you knew us. I'll fight with you."

One by one, all of her students stood, followed by more and more people until every single person in the cafeteria was on their feet.

Pride rose in Rachael's chest as she looked around.

"We must move fast before more of the orcs come through. I know we can block the fence and clear out the orcs. Gather anything you have that can be a weapon."

As she stepped down from the chair, Maria and two other teenage girls, Eden and Kate, pushed through the crowd gathered around her.

"We...uh...we were on the track team," Maria started shyly, "and...um...we wanted to volunteer to run to the fence to try to block it."

"We're fast and strong and we can outrun anything that tries to get us," Eden piped up.

"We want to help," Kate added.

Rachael looked at the three teens with a smile. "If you promise me you'll be safe, I will gladly accept your help."

"It was Maria's idea, but all three of us were the fastest on our team and we all want to help!" Eden said.

Maria wouldn't meet her eyes, and Rachael smiled at her proudly. Holding up the crown, she gently placed it on Maria's dark hair. The teen looked up in surprise and confusion; then reached up to feel the crown on her head.

"I'll make you proud," Maria whispered.

"You already have," Rachael replied.

– 5 –

"Do you think you can do it?" Mark asked nervously. "Do you think you'll survive?" He watched Rachael's group gathering their weapons, his own hands empty.

"I think we can," Rachael said with more confidence than she felt. "You don't have to worry; we'll make sure we still have a home come morning. Plenty more plants for you to weed," she added with a small smile. He didn't return it. She put it down to nerves.

Turning away, she moved over to her waiting army. Walking up and down their ranks, she split them into five teams of equal size, making sure each squad had the right balance of muscle, fighting skills, and common sense.

"We need to clear out the orcs," she said, "and keep them away from the fence while Maria, Kate, and Eden secure it. They should be able to barricade it temporarily with some of the metal sheeting we have in the yard, but it will take some time. We need to buy them that time."

"It's dark, and we will use that to our advantage. We need to be as quiet as possible, take the orcs out a few at a time so we don't get swarmed. We're going with a buddy system, groups of four. Know where your team is at all times. We want to come out with the same number we go in with."

Brett headed up one team, while Rachael joined another. Alice, armed with a butcher's knife from the kitchen, stuck close to Rachael's side as they made their plans: all the teams would split up, defending and clearing the courtyard from different angles, hoping to spread the horde thin.

The runners—with Sophia, Maria's mom, as backup—would sneak to the fence and make the repairs as quietly as possible, hoping that darkness and silence would would give them enough time before more orcs came through. Once the fence was fixed, they would clear out the rest of the orcs a few at a time, and hopefully have them all cleared before morning.

Rachael gave each of the runners a hug before they left, wishing them luck.

"May the odds be ever in our favor!" Eden said with a smile, giving Rachael a salute before they moved off into the darkness.

The odds are never in our favor. The ominous thought struck her, but she hushed it, focusing on sending each team to their starting point, and readying the attack. The runners slipped into the darkness, silent shadows keeping to the fences and weaving undetected between the orcs. Rachael crossed her fingers for luck. Playing at being heroes was one thing, but actually being heroes—being *warriors*—was something else. The armor and weapons and occasional bits of speech cribbed from a fantasy novel or movie helped support the affectation, but once they were in combat they were going to be ordinary people faking it until they made it as heroes, or until they died. Rachael could not will them to be better fighters, she could not make them remember their training and drills. All she could do was pray, and she was not great at that.

She said a prayer anyway. In Elven, because…fuck it. Why not?

Then led her own team out to begin their assault.

Rachael had left the most dangerous approach for her own team: the barricaded front door. Moving with quiet caution, they unbarred the door and she stepped up to peer through the gap. There were more orcs than she had anticipated, and most of them had come close to the hospital, following the sounds and smells of living flesh. Turning to her team, she gave them a brave smile.

"On three. Ready?" They nodded, and without making a sound, she drew her sword and dagger before silently mouthing the countdown. On three, she kicked the doors wide open and led the charge.

Immediately out the door they were deep in battle, and Rachael moved with practiced skill as she sliced and stabbed through heads and necks, digging her dagger into the eye socket of an orc and driving her sword through the skull of another.

Bracing her foot against the second orc to pull the blade out, she turned to watch the rest of her team. They weren't as skilled or experienced, but all four of them moved with purpose, Alice slashing the head of one orc with her knife while Andy slammed a club into the skull of another, crushing it with an explosion of black decayed brain matter.

Rachael heard the yells of other teams as more and more orcs began to notice them. She returned to her attacks with renewed determination, focusing only on her strikes and the sound of her breathing. The orcs fell, but where one went down, two more took their place as more and more were drawn to the sound of combat.

Slice, cut, dodge, stab. Her sword and dagger were a blur as she struggled to make a dent in the sea of monsters. Each time there seemed to be a lull, more orcs poured into the courtyard. She didn't have the luxury of checking on her team to see if the screams were sounds of triumph or of one or more of her people dying.

Then she heard a blood-curdling scream of pain and terror come from the fence.

Rachael's stomach dropped, and she lunged past the orc she was fighting, sprinting forward. She didn't stop to fight, instead dodging under outstretched arms and clawing hands, ignoring the decaying faces. Right now she had one focus in mind—the girls at the fence.

The darkness near the barricade made it nearly impossible to see, and Rachael nearly tripped over a fallen orc sprawled on the ground. It snatched at her ankles, catching the leather boots with its sharp nails, unable to break the surface. She stomped on it a few times, driving shards of skull into its brain and silencing it forever.

The screaming had also stopped, though, and Rachael feared the worst.

Shapes moved by the fence, but Rachael couldn't tell if they were friend or foe, so she sheathed her sword, keeping only her dagger out, not wanting to attack an ally by mistake. Still, when a small form hurtled into her from the darkness, only the sound of all too human sobs stopped Rachael from lashing out with the dagger.

"Kate...?"

The figure nodded.

"Are you okay? Were you bit?"

Kate shook her head. "No, but..." She couldn't finish, her body wracked with sobs.

"Stay here," Rachael ordered, and crept forward, counting the bodies along the ground, struggling to see who or what was in front of her.

Cursing the darkness, she pulled a small flashlight from her belt pouch and, holding her breath, flicked it on.

Four figures at the fence turned away from their feast, rotted faces in permanent snarls created by flesh ripped away from bone. She swallowed bile as she recognized the orc's victims: Eden and Maria's mother. Their prone bodies were torn open, their ripped clothes soaked with blood.

Rachael lunged forward, thrusting the dagger into the eye of one of the feasting orcs, tore it free and plunged it through the skull of another. She kicked a third into the fence. Pulling up one of the metal stakes providing extra support to the fence, she drove it into the fourth one's head, before kicking the punctured skull off in time to finish off the remaining one with a power swing into its hideous face.

The fence behind her shook in a rattle of metal, and Rachael leapt to her feet, ready to fight more hordes of orcs. But instead, she was faced with Maria, the Wonder Woman crown askew on her head. The girl was clearly terrified and covered in blood, but in one unbitten piece. Rachael wanted to hug her, but Maria turned, sliding the last of the fence into place and wrapping the wires tightly.

"It's done," she said, voice both shaky and numb. Rachael recognized that tone; the same one she'd used when she realized her phone was dead and she could no longer contact her family. Not exactly defeat, but close. A weariness of the soul that ran deep.

"The fence was cut, Rachael," Maria added flatly. "I looked. It was cut, and big enough for the orcs to get through. I think someone did it on purpose…"

"Please, I want to go back," Kate sobbed. Rachael yanked her knife out of the orc's skull, holding it at the ready as she ran behind the two girls back toward the hospital building. Pushing them toward the door, Rachael returned to the fight, drawing her sword again and slashing with anger through the orcs that stumbled her way.

This was their home. It was supposed to be their safe place, and her anger drove each strike of the blade as she cut down orcs, littering the ground around her with their fallen bodies.

They were down to the last tattered remnants of the horde, at least as far as she could see. Only a handful of orcs still shambled and moaned at them, reaching out with bloody hands.

Alice yelled out to her left, and Rachael turned to see her friend sprawled on the ground, clutching her ankle. Rachael lunged at the orc trying to claw at Alice, slicing its hand off and sending the rotted appendage flying. She swung the sword at faces and arms and legs, sending other orcs stumbling backward against their fellow undead. Rachael kept after them, weaving a protective circle of steel around Alice with the gleaming arcs of her sword and dagger.

"*Keep it going!*" she bellowed to her forces, slicing with her sword to keep an orc back. It collapsed as a club smashed into its head. Andy nodded at Rachael before bounding back into the fight.

Rachael turned and watched as the last of the orcs fell and

their teams—their family—gathered back together. She looked around at the grim scene. Most of the squads were down to only one or two members. A quick count told her that at least fifteen of them had fallen.

Rachael felt numb, her heart sinking. They had trusted her, put their faith in her. Would they think she failed them?

As if the survivors read her mind, a number of fighters reached out to her, offering a hand of support or a squeeze of solidarity. They didn't need to say the words; she could hear them even in silence. They had made their choice. They fought for their home, and they would do it again. They fought for each other, and they fought for her.

A figure stepped toward her out of the gloom. Brett. And then he was there, cradling her face in his hands as he looked into her eyes. He kissed her deeply and she melted into the kiss, her terror and sadness momentarily gone as he hugged her to his chest.

Rachael wanted to stay there forever, but there was work to be done. Injuries to tend to, wounds to heal. She took a deep breath and pulled away to help Alice to her feet, slinging an arm over her shoulder and guiding her through the door into the darkened lobby of the hospital. Into the home they'd protected at such a great cost.

A gunshot rang out, the bullet echoed past Rachael as it struck the wall a foot from her shoulder, shattering the tile. She froze, still supporting Alice and unable to get to the sword at her side, eyes darting around for the source of the attack.

"Well, I guess I'll need to take care of you myself, since the dead couldn't handle it."

Rachael looked up and around, following the sound of the voice. She recognized it, but not its tone of confidence.

There. Up on the dimly lit lobby balcony overhead.

Mark leveled his weapon at Rachael, eyes pools of dark shadows as he stared her down.

"Mark, put the gun down. Please." She tried to keep her voice level. Seeing her distress, Brian moved in to support Alice. Rachael stepped forward, putting herself between the gunman and the rest of her people. Out of the corner of her eye, she saw some of her trainees moving along the wall, out of Mark's eyesight, stealthily creeping towards the side stairwell.

Keep him distracted, the voice in her mind whispered. *Keep him talking.*

"Why?" she asked. "Why are you trying to do this? You can have this as your home, you can be part of something bigger—"

"I don't want to be part of your home," Mark scoffed, shifting his grip on the gun. "You've made this a perfectly hospitable place, and we want it for our own."

"'We'?" she prompted, crossing her arms and raising an eyebrow, putting on a mask of confidence. Shadows shifted up above, prompting anxious cries from her friends as four men, armed with gleaming knives, appeared along the railing. Rachael swallowed hard.

"And there's more where they came from," Mark added with a smug smirk.

"There's more than enough room for all of—" she began, but Mark cut her off, pacing back and forth along the railing.

"No, there's not enough room for you," he snapped, gesturing with the gun. "This place is *ours* now. Ours. That's how it is now. You don't like it? Tough shit. We earned this spot. You couldn't keep it and that means you don't deserve to have it. Simple math." He paused for a moment and shook his head. "I was hoping you'd move out when the fences fell, but you didn't. Kind of hoped you'd all get bitten. That would have been easy. Well…for us, I mean. The rotters chow down on you and then we get rid of them. Easy peasy. But don't get me wrong, if I have to just shoot you myself, I will. You can count on that shit."

Keeping her eyes on Mark, Rachael clasped her hands behind her back, pointing off to the side away from the stairwell with one hand, hoping that one of her people would understand what she needed. The traitor went on with his tirade. Hopefully he wouldn't notice what was going on in the shadows behind him.

"So, what now?" she asked. "There's a lot of us here, Mark. Do you really want to have that many murders on your conscience?" *Please let him focus on me and not turn around*, she prayed to anyone or anything that would listen, her fingers wrapping around a small knife tucked in a sheath at the small of her back. Taking one, two, three steps forward, she continued to talk.

"Fuck," laughed Mark, "I'm not even sure murder is a crime anymore. Seriously...go ahead and call a cop. Oh, wait, you can't, because they all got eaten. That's how it is now. It's a big scary world, so I'm doing what I need to do to protect me and mine."

"Okay," said Rachael, keeping her voice calm, "I agree with you. The world is really scary out there. It's terrifying. But, come on...you have to at least take a chance for some peaceful way for us *all* to survive. I don't know who you are, I don't know your friends, or what any of you have done, but you can start over. Don't you want that? We're already at war with the world out there. Don't you want a chance for something better?"

A clatter of something sliding across the tiles on the second floor echoed like a gunshot. Mark flinched, and his gun went off. Rachael cried out as a bullet grazed her shoulder, hissing as white-hot agony seemed to ignite in her skin.

"That's just a taste, bitch," Mark yelled. "Unless you want more you'd—"

In one fast, fluid movement, Rachael whipped the knife from its sheath and flung it at Mark, then dove behind the lobby desk. He dropped his gun off the balcony and let loose a stream of curses. In the dim light of the unlit lobby she heard the echoes of the pistol clattering off the tiles.

He yelled a command to his partners, and Rachael's warriors sprang into action at the same moment, roaring out battle cries like a pack of marauding Vikings.

Pulling the long knives out of the sheaths at her hips, she crouched, moving as silently as possible. Then she launched forward, propelling herself off the wall and diving over the counter toward Mark's henchmen charging down the stairs. Swinging her knives in the half-light, she felt them sink into living flesh. Men screamed in shock and pain, and Rachael pulled her knives from their bodies, rolling through the dive to slide behind a pillar.

Parkour and sneak attacks and fighting undead were one thing, but going up against trained men with knives was still far outside Rachael's realm of expertise. This wasn't LARP or tabletop or cosplay; this wasn't make-believe. All of their lives were at stake, their home, everything they'd worked for.

Rage surged through her, and she used it to throw herself against the closest man, the momentum driving him to the floor and knocking his knife out of his hand. She slammed her knife hilt against his head three times, knocking him out. A second man grabbed at her, swinging his knife at her face in retaliation. Ducking out of the way, she sunk her blade into the soft flesh on the inside of his thigh, causing him to collapse in a howl of pain.

Rachael didn't want to kill them. She didn't like to kill; not people, not animals, not anything. She didn't even like killing the undead orcs, though that was a survival necessity.

It is, however, somewhat fuzzier on the subject of kneecaps, the *Firefly* quote popped into her fangirl brain. She scurried back to the shadows as more men streamed into the lobby. She was getting used to the near-darkness. Shapes were beginning to form, helping her make sense of what was going on around her. More fighting upstairs from the sound of it, shouting and screaming. No gunshots, but the grunting and thumping of bodies hitting the floor worried her.

"Please let them not be mine," she murmured to herself, creeping along the wall. Her whisper was louder than she intended, and two dark shapes in the center of the lobby turned, looking around for the source of the sound. At the same moment, a smaller, feminine shape appeared in the gloom by the front door. Maria.

The men turned, raising their knives, only a few yards away from the young teen. Rachael stood, using that moment to slide across the tile and slash at the backs of one man's ankles. He collapsed with a yell as Maria swung a wooden sword hard at the other man's head, cracking the weapon down the middle with a sickening sound of breaking bone.

After that, silence.

Brian clicked on their electric lantern, restoring some light to the lobby. Better. Rachael climbed to her feet. "Are you okay?" she asked. "Is everyone okay?"

"Th-they're fine," Maria replied, as the two came in for a hug. "I-I-I was worried, I wanted to make sure you were okay," she said, blinking back tears. She looked at the blood staining Rachael's arm with concern.

Rachael stroked the girl's hair comfortingly. "It's okay, I'm okay. But I need to check on everyone upstairs."

None of Mark's men were still standing; most of them appeared to be either dead or unconscious. Mark, however, was nowhere to be seen.

"Have you seen Mark?" she asked as her warriors secured the fallen men. They looked at her and shook their heads.

"He must have taken off during the fight," Alice suggested.

Rachael didn't feel so confident. She crept past the others, eyes darting around as she made her way cautiously down one hallway, then another in the dark. The hairs on the back of her neck stood up. She sensed the presence of another person, heard the quiet breathing of someone around a corner.

Instinctively bringing her daggers up in front of her head, she blocked the machete that would have gouged a chunk out of her face, immediately throwing herself back from the onslaught of swings that Mark threw at her. Her adrenaline rush was fading; the strain in her arms aching as she attempted to parry his blows.

With the last of her energy, she ducked a wild swing and darted past Mark, kicking out at his ribs as they passed. He lost his balance and she kicked again at his groin, letting out a yell that echoed through the darkened halls. Her kick missed, catching him instead in the hip. The hit sent him staggering back a few steps, but he caught himself, raised his machete overhead, and rushed her again.

"*No!*"

The scream was nearly as deafening as the gunshot that followed, and Mark staggered, arms still raised, before he collapsed to the ground, unmoving.

Maria stood behind him, her arm out, frozen, before dropping the gun with a clatter. She let out a sob and fell to the floor. Dropping her own weapon, Rachael gathered the girl into her arms.

"I...I wanted to...to be brave." Rachael could make out the words between Maria's broken sobs, and she hugged the girl against her, holding her tightly.

"You are brave," Rachael countered quietly. "Even the brave can be afraid or sad. But your mom and Eden would want you to keep going. They would be so proud of you. You are the real hero. You are the real Wonder Woman."

Maria didn't speak, but her sobs shook her body as she cried for her mom, and Eden, and for herself. For everything she'd lost, the life she'd had before. A life with cellphones and friends and crushes and school. For the lost innocence of a teen forced to grow up before her time.

This was their world now, Rachael realized. They all had to grow up too fast. But, she would do everything she could to change this world, to make it a place where children could be children. Where heroes could exist and bring hope.

– 6 –

"What next?" Brett asked quietly. They sat on the edge of the low roof of one of the hospital buildings, under the late summer full moon. Rachael leaned her head against his shoulder, her fingers entwined with his, watching her fighters, her warriors, her army, practicing in the moonlight. "We took back our home...so, seriously, Rachael, what's next?"

She was silent for a moment, considering, weighing her options.

"Next? We take back our world."

PART FOUR

STILL OF NIGHT

JONATHAN MABERRY & RACHAEL LAVIN

SIX MONTHS AFTER THE OUTBREAK

−1−

THE SOLDIER AND THE DOG

The dead rose. We fell. That's the short version of current events.

Well...not so current. We're still falling. It's a long damn way down to nowhere.

I've spent months going from one side of the country to the other. Me and my dog, Baskerville. There are no planes, no trains, no automobiles. At least none that work. Some geniuses in the military decided that nukes were the only proportional response to the armies of the dead. They dropped a lot of them.

Huge sections of North America are gone, buried under ash that glows in the dark. The radiation is probably going to kill more people than the zombies will. And the electromagnetic pulses fried all of the electronics. Which means any chance there was of driving somewhere safe is gone. The power is out, taking with it the controls for water, sewage, and every other damn useful thing.

Oh, yeah, and don't get me started on radioactive walking corpses. If I ever find anyone alive who was party to the decision to try nukes, I'm going to fucking kill them and when they wake up as zoms, I'm going to kill them again.

If I could fly or drive I might have gotten home in time. If the phones worked I could have called.

Instead it took weeks to go from California to Maryland. A lot of weeks, because I had to fight my way through some places, and circle way the hell out of my way to avoid others. When I got to my uncle's farm in Robinwood, Maryland, I found nothing but ashes and bones. I don't know if any of those bones belonged to my wife. The fact that I didn't find the charred bones of an infant gives me hope. A slender needle of hope that is buried all the way into the center of my broken heart. That's not poetry. It's a fucking tragedy.

I think I went a little crazy.

I mean, I guess I had to.

Days are gone. Maybe weeks. Time stopped having any meaning for me. There are days when all I have left are fragments. Shivering in a rainy ditch near the farm, covered in vomit and rainwater. Kneeling in the ashes, screaming, punching the ground, punching my own face. Wandering down roads I no longer recognized.

One day I woke up naked and covered in scratches, in a creek miles and miles away from anywhere. I had a dog leash clutched in one hand and when I could focus my eyes I read the name on the heavy steel tag: *Baskerville*. I knew that dog. He belonged to a neighbor and was one of the many descendants of my old combat dog, Ghost, and an Irish wolfhound named

Banshee. I think he was Ghost's grandson, out of a litter of seven. We'd gifted the dog to the teenage girl, Sandra, daughter of a neighbor, a lovely girl with Down syndrome.

I made my stumbling way to the farm where Sandra and her folks lived, but there was only heartbreak waiting for me. All the sweet gentleness that was Sandra was gone from the thing I had to fight in the living room of the old house. I buried her and five other members of her family, stole her uncle's clothes, and began drifting along the Maryland back roads. Finding no one alive.

Not. One. Person. There are some blank spots in my memory there, too. There is absolutely nothing in my brain to fill in those blanks. Even now, months later. My voice was gone, though. Raw. I spat blood onto my hands. Screaming can do that, if you do it long enough and put your heart into it.

The leash stayed with me, wrapped around my waist. Don't ask me why. I was wearing it when I became aware of who I was again. Days blurred by. I had the sense that I was being hunted, and gradually my old skills came back to me. Not on a conscious level at first, but instinctually. The lizard brain working toward its goal of survival while the monkey brain still went mad at times.

It was maybe a week before I even organized my brain enough to wonder how Top and Bunny were doing. After the cluster fuck that was our so-called "mission to rescue the president" and the subsequent helicopter crash, we split up. Bunny had a lot of family in Orange County; Top had people in Georgia. We each wanted to be there for the others, but we couldn't. We parted ways with an agreement to meet at an off-the-books base we all knew of in Nevada. It was fortified and had a hardened facility with a full laboratory, hospital, and room for hundreds of refugees. We'd each try to bring our families there. Parting was tough, though. It was a bitch, and we held each other and wept because none of us had much hope left. Not much at all. The thing driving us was fear. And need. But not hope.

Robinwood nearly destroyed me. Sandra's farm pushed me all the way to the edge and the only thing in the world that looked like it would offer a shred of comfort was the big fall into the welcoming black.

I wandered like a ghost, haunting a dead landscape, waiting until I dropped my body and drifted on as a spirit. Then, maybe, dissolve like mist and become nothing. If that meant there were no more memories, then I wanted it. Craved it. Needed it to be true.

Then something changed one day, and maybe changed me. Like a slap when you're on the edge of hysteria.

It was a dog barking.

Terrified, angry. A deep-chested sound. It reminded me of Ghost, though he was long dead. Old age. He'd run through hell with me all over the world. Wish to fuck I'd had him with me now. He could track anyone or anything. Ghost could have found my family. One way or another, he would have found them. Given me an answer. Not closure, though, because the mouths of some wounds stay open so they can scream at you day and night.

This dog wasn't Ghost. I knew that.

But it was *alive*. The first living thing other than squirrels and birds that I'd seen since I reached my uncle's farm.

And so I ran toward the sound of the barking. Blocks away. I was dressed in farmer's coveralls and a Pittsburgh Penguins T-shirt that was several sizes too small, and boat shoes that were too big. No weapons at all. My mind hadn't recovered enough for that to have been a thing. Barehanded. Stupid with shock. Running toward the sound of a frightened dog and endless hungry moans.

When I rounded a corner by the Antietam Tractor and Equipment store in Hagerstown, I nearly ran into a shambler. In life this person had been a cop of some kind—deputy or state trooper—but now there were only rags left of a tan uniform. He wore a gunbelt, though, but no gun. A rubber baton, the kind with the handle jutting out at a right angle, based on the old Okinawan *tonfa*, was looped through his belt. I skidded to a stop. Beyond him was a throng of dead ones all clustered around an overturned Ram Mega-cab four-wheel-drive pick-up. The dog stood on the top, on the passenger door, just out of reach of the grasping hands.

He was a brute. A monstrous mix of white shepherd and Irish wolfhound. One hundred and fifty pounds of muscle and fang.

I stood there and stared.

It was Baskerville.

He caught sight of me and for a moment we gaped at each other across a sea of the dead. His pale coat was crisscrossed with cuts and crusted with blood and dirt, but he looked strong. Terrified, too, because there was no way for him to get down from his perch without being torn to pieces. Against a pack of living people, he might actually have stood a chance because they bleed, they feel pain, and they would be individually ter-rified of the dog. The dead have none of those vulnerabilities. They are simply driven by an all-consuming need to feast on the flesh of the living. Human, animal, insect. Anything except plants. They don't tire and they don't fear anything at all. Given time, they would pull Baskerville down and eat him.

Like I said, I was unarmed and more than half out of my mind.

But something in me was awake now. I am not a normal person. I'm not nice and I'm not sane. Even before all this shit. At best I'm usefully batshit crazy, and I have done awful things more times than I could count. Not to the innocent. No. My kind of crazy edges a different way. If you're a bad guy? Differ-ent story.

I could feel something shift inside my skull and inside my chest. Here was an animal I knew. A dog. Alive. More than that, he was the grandson of the best dog I ever had. Ghost. A true hero dog.

All of this was processed in my brain in less than a microsec-ond. The dead cop was still turning toward me, just beginning his reach for my throat when I went from shock to action. I bashed his arms aside, spun him, grabbed his chin and the back of his hair and gave his head a vicious sideways twist. In the movies everyone seems able to do this, to break a neck. It's actually extremely hard because the neck muscles don't want to turn that far, and the bones don't want to break. You have to know how to do it, and you have to put real speed and muscle into it. Which I did.

I let go and snatched the baton from his belt loop as he puddled down.

Then I was moving.

I am over six feet tall and over two hundred pounds. Even with days of hysterical madness, dehydration and starvation, I was fit and fast and strong. They had no consciousness, no understanding of how to fight. They turned toward noise and movement; they howled out their hunger; they surged toward me.

A fool rushes into the center of a crowd. I fought the edges of it, moving, moving, moving. Turning and deflecting, knocking them into one another, never remaining still and so never getting caught. I used the club to smash arms and break knees. Even the living dead need their bones intact in order to stand, walk, grab, hold. I smashed skulls, aiming as often as I could for the base of the skull, working to damage the nerve conduction down the brain stem. They stumbled and fell. Some of them died.

It was brutal work. I don't know how many there were. Fifteen? Twenty?

I had so much rage in me. Grief is a terrible fuel because it burns hot and never seems to burn out. Frustration stokes that fire. Desperation pours gasoline on it. And yet beneath all that were skills honed over a lifetime in jujutsu, the police, the army and then Special Forces. I am a killer, and I proved it right there, witnessed only by a dog and the milky eyes of the undead.

I killed them all.

Every single one.

There was a strange time of stillness afterward. The dog stood on the overturned truck and stared at me. I stood and looked up at him. Maybe neither of us was all that sure we recognized the other. It was that kind of world. Birds sat in rows on telephone wires and the edges of roofs and watched us.

I cleared my throat and then spat dust and fear onto the ground.

"Baskerville," I said. Not a question. Saying his name. Letting him hear it and know it. Then he did something that absolutely broke my heart.

He wagged his tail.

That was six months ago. That was when he didn't die, and I no longer wanted to.

– 2 –

THE WARRIOR WOMAN

The night air was still, quiet. Too quiet. It made Rachael uneasy, raising the hair along her arms and the back of her neck. Too quiet meant nothing nearby trying to survive—no animals or birds or humans. Too quiet meant nothing living.

Too quiet meant dead.

Holding up one hand, she signaled the four young people behind her—two women and two men—to stop. Then she crouched down, moving quietly through the brush, pushing aside the thorny branches that plucked at her clothes, snagging on her leather armor. She didn't make a sound beyond a slight rustle of leaves and the creak of well-oiled leather as she unsheathed an elvish style dagger strapped to her belt, holding it at the ready.

For a moment all she heard was the rhythmic pounding of her own heartbeat. Then the sound of something shuffling along the ground with an uneven gait. First a crunching noise, then a *swoosh*. Maybe someone limping, dragging an injured limb behind. The smell of rotting flesh settled any doubt of whether it was human or orc.

Crunch, swoosh, crunch, swoosh. The sound carried across the night air as her eyes scouted for its source under the shards of moonlight filtering down through the treetops.

There. Up ahead to the right of the path. The bramble bushes trembled as a slumped figure emerged, ignoring the sharp thorns that tore at its skin and ragged clothing.

Gesturing to her friends to follow, she scanned for any more orcs before leaping to her feet and charging toward the lone figure. It turned toward the sound of her footsteps and moaned; an unearthly death rattle that echoed through the trees, sending a shiver down Rachael's spine despite the countless times she'd heard it.

She could see in dim light that this particular orc was in lousy shape—it looked like it had spent some time submerged in water. Mottled skin peeling away from its bloated face. Moss growing in an otherwise empty eye socket. Fingers swollen and splitting open at the tips.

It reached for her and she ducked easily under one decaying hand, spinning around the orc to position herself behind it, driving her dagger directly into the base of the skull with an awful crunch. It crumpled to the ground, the stench washing over Rachael and her group.

"Ugh! That one was ripe." Alice grimaced, dark hair falling around her face as she covered her mouth and nose with one arm.

The dagger made a squelching sound as she pulled it out of the orc's skull. Rachael wiped the viscous black blood on a handful of leaves and tucked it back into her scabbard. "At least it was only one," she said, trying to sound reassuring.

She felt less than reassured, however. It had been three days since they'd seen a living human other than the small scouting group that had splintered off from their original group of travelers, and three weeks since they'd seen anyone outside of that. No survivors, no towns hidden away from the dead. Nothing, except for orcs.

It felt like they were alone in the world.

The five took to the path again, moving quietly and cautiously through the trees, ready for attack, ready for any trap that might spring shut on them.

Rachael was still worried they weren't ready, but she knew that if they waited much longer they ran the risk of being unprepared for winter, so she'd set a date and pushed for preparations. Some of their group were afraid to leave the safety of the hospital, and others were unable to make the long trip, so the number that set out from their temporary home was lower than Rachael had wanted. But she would never force someone to make the journey. She knew it was a risk, even if she was optimistic of the endeavor.

Of her small team, the two fittest and most promising were Claudia and Jason. He was in his early thirties, with skin the color of milk chocolate and brown eyes flecked with bits of gold. Claudia, ten years younger, had lighter skin and green eyes. She looked like a fashion model, and he looked like an accountant, but they moved well and could fight.

After two weeks of slow and strenuous travel, they'd found a school with fences and walls intact, and very few orcs in the immediate vicinity. Everyone was exhausted, so Brett had suggested they take up camp for a few days, give people a chance to rest. Despite her own desire to keep moving, Rachael had agreed, dealing with her own restlessness by deciding to scout the surrounding area for supplies and survivors. Alice and three others had volunteered to go with her.

After two days of cautious exploration, they'd found only meager supplies and there were no signs of survivors anywhere. It was disconcerting, and Rachael decided to give them one more night of searching before heading back to their group and declaring this area an orc zone.

Sunrise breached the horizon as the five broke through the edge of the forest. They paused for a moment to appreciate the pure light reflecting off a stream that wound its way between scattered suburban-style homes and spacious farmland. At first glance it was if nothing bad had ever happened here. But, as they took a closer look, certain details became obvious: shattered windows, doors hanging on broken hinges, garbage scattered along the ground, and the slow movement of a half dozen or so orcs shambling through the streets, looking for prey.

"Let's go around," suggested Claudia.

Rachael nodded. There were not likely survivors here and the odds of supplies still remaining in the gutted buildings were too low to risk drawing out more orcs.

As they turned away from the dead town below, a sudden movement out of the corner of her eye caught Rachael's attention even as Alice called her name in a low, urgent voice. Rachael spun, dagger already in hand as something pushed its way through the bushes on either side of a deer path ahead in the tree line. The others took out their weapons swiftly and silently, ready for anything.

Well, almost anything.

None of them were prepared for the little boy that emerged. He looked seven or eight, tops. Hair combed and slicked nicely to the side, dressed in country club best, looking as if he had wandered away from a family luncheon in the World Before. His light green button-down shirt was well kept, no holes or patches other than a small rip in one sleeve that could have come from wandering in the woods. Even his shoes were in good shape.

For a brief moment Rachael thought she might be dreaming. His cheeks were rosy and clean and round, not gaunt like the children back at the hospital. This child didn't know hardship. Didn't have to fight for survival. This was not a child from the end of the world.

"Hold," Rachael said softly to her team, dropping her dagger to her side and quickly slipping it back into the sheath. She stepped forward with a non-threatening posture, hands out front and low, the way you'd approach a strange dog. The boy saw them and nearly bolted, but froze when Rachael spoke.

"Hey there."

He looked at her warily, eyes red and swollen from crying.

"I'm Rachael." She spoke in a calm and soothing voice. "What's *your* name?" She walked a few steps closer, keeping her eyes and ears open for a possible ambush. The boy blinked through his tears.

"T-T-Tommy," he stammered.

She smiled at him, trying to put him at ease, taking a few more steps forward until she was directly in front of him. Crouching down on one knee so she and the boy were face to face, Rachael put on her best friendly this-is-not-the-apocalypse smile. "Where's your family, Tommy?"

Sniffling, he glanced back at Alice and the other three before finally settling his gaze on Rachael. It suddenly occurred to her what a sight they must be—her in jeans, T-shirt, and Wonder Woman armor mixed and matched with Sif and Valkyrie and Asgardian armor pieces, and her fellow travelers wearing a mix of costumes, armor, and well-worn everyday clothes.

"Do you know the Apple Man?"

Not the answer she'd expected. Rachael glanced back over her shoulder at her friends. They looked at one another, confusion registering on their faces. Alice shrugged and Rachael turned back to the boy.

"I'm sorry, Tommy. My friends and I don't know him. But maybe we can help you find him. Who is the Apple Man?"

"The Apple Man is my friend," Tommy answered, "but he went out where the Bad Things are and hasn't come back. The Apple Man used to work for my daddy but then he left. I wanted to go find him, but no one would let me. They said it was bad out there, and that the B-B-Bad Things would get me, but I was worried about him so I climbed the wall and went looking for him. But then there were s-s-scary sounds and I ran and now I can't find my way home." His sniffling, which had started to subside, threatened to turn into tears again. Hoping to forestall it, Rachael quickly pulled a bandana out of the side pouch of her backpack, offering it to the boy. He stared at it, lower lip quivering.

Alice stepped forward, setting her sword down as she knelt next to Rachael. Taking the bandana, she gently wiped Tommy's face, mopping the tears away before pressing the cloth into his hand. "Where's home, Tommy?" she prompted. "We can help you get home to your family and look for the Apple Man on our way there. Would you like that?"

Tommy looked from Rachael's Wonder Woman armor, to Alice's Superman shirt, then up at their faces.

"Happytown," he replied, wiping his nose on the bandana and rubbing his eyes on his shirt sleeve. "They're in Happytown."

– 3 –

DAHLIA AND THE PACK

"If he's just some old guy," said Trash, the second oldest of their pack, "why are you afraid of him?"

Neeko, the pack's scout, looked up from the careful work he was doing wrapping bandages around the head of one of the other scouts. Neeko wore bandages, too. Both of them were covered with small bruises that were as intense as blueberries growing ripe on their skin.

Trash, who was one of the best fighters in the pack, recognized the bruises as the marks from single-knuckle punches. Full fists, edge-hands, Y-hands and palms left different kinds of marks. Trash had fought in semi-pro mixed martial arts for years before the outbreak. He'd taken and given enough injuries to be able to read them. Both Neeko and the other scout looked like they'd been worked over by club bouncers.

"You saying *he* did that?" he demanded.

Neeko tied the bandage, patted his friend's shoulder and

blew out his cheeks, nodding as he did so. "He kicked our asses and didn't work up much of a sweat doing it, man."

"One old guy?"

"Yeah."

"How old?"

"I don't know. Pretty old. Had white hair and a white beard and all."

"You're telling me you got your asses handed to you by Santa Claus?"

Neeko rose from the cinderblock he'd been using as a seat and came over to the card table where Trash was cleaning and loading pistols. He didn't sit.

"He didn't have elves, didn't say 'ho-fucking-ho,' and the only thing he gave us was a beating," he said. "Old fucker could have killed us, but he didn't."

"He chased you off?"

"He let us go."

"*Let* you go? Meaning, what? He couldn't beat you and chased you with his walker, so you ran off?"

"He could have killed us if he wanted," said Neeko. "We snuck up on him, and you know how quiet I am. He was sitting in a beach chair, hat down over his face. Looked like he was sleeping. And even if he was awake I was ghosting my way past him and keeping like a hundred feet between us. Bushes and some stacked boxes and all. He had this pimped out motor home. Really sweet, and in great condition. Reinforced, too. And there was one of those storage pod trailers hooked up in back. It was open, though, and he had his stuff all around his campsite. I think he was doing some kind of inventory on his shit."

Trash leaned his forearms on the table, interested now. "What kind of shit?"

"Boxes of food. Bottles of water. Medical stuff. All kinds of shit."

"How much?"

"More than we could use in, like, six months. A fuck lot more than we have," said Neeko. "That's why we followed him. Smelled cooking and there he is with a campfire and like six rabbits on a gas grill. Some potatoes and corn, too. God, the smells were driving me crazy."

"Yeah? So what did you do?"

Neeko's eyes slid away for a moment. "Two of us, and we had the edge. We both had our hatchets and all."

Trash gave him a skeptical look. "Why didn't you just kill the old fucker and take all that shit, man? What the actual fuck?"

"I, um," began Neeko, licking his lips. "I wanted to scare him. Maybe rough him up some and take *most* of his stuff. Take the mobile home, too. Wanted to roll up here behind the wheel of that sweet ride. Guess I wanted to see the look on everyone's faces."

Trash laughed. "But you came limping your ass in here like a pussy. Both of you."

"You weren't there, man. You didn't see what happened."

"So…stop dicking around. What *did* happen?"

Neeko cleared his throat. "We were coming up on him from behind, each of us with our choppers out, ready for anything, and then without moving his hat or moving a muscle, he said, 'You're doing this wrong.'"

"What?"

"That's what he said."

"Fucker told you you're doing it wrong?" Trash laughed a big donkey bray, his blond dreads dancing as his big shoulders shook. "What else he say?"

"He pointed to a stack of cans and bottles over by a tree and said we could take that and go. His gift. That's what he called it. He said to take it and go. But if we tried anything we wouldn't be allowed to take anything."

"*What…?*"

"Hand to god."

"What'd you do?"

Neeko looked down at his bandaged hands. "Andy rushed him," he said, referring to the other scout. "I guess I did, too, because Andy did."

"And...?"

"And I don't know. It was all so fast. The old guy was out of the chair and was hitting us and then he took our hatchets and...and..." He stopped and shook his head. "It was too fast, man. Before I knew what was going on we were in the woods, in a little creek. Both of us pretty banged up. The old guy was standing on the edge of the bank with our hatchets and I thought that was it, I thought we were dead as shit, but then he knelt down and chunked the blades into the mud and walked away."

"He just up and left? Didn't say shit?"

"Well..." said Neeko, "he said something weird. He said something about we got one pass because we're kids. Then he said that if we come back, we need to do it with manners. We need to ask nicely and shit. He said that we had to act like people and not animals or we're not worth saving. Something like that. I don't remember the actual words."

Trash stood up. At seventeen he was the third oldest, but easily the biggest, with massive shoulders and arms packed with ropey muscles. His skin had a permanent peeling sunburn that never seemed able to become a tan even after all these months running through the woods and farmlands to escape the biters. Like all the fighters in the pack, he wore jeans with a flexible weave, a camo tank top and a vest with lots of pockets, as well as a belt from which hung a holstered Glock and a big hunting knife. When the pack had raided a Wal-Mart, their leader, Dahlia, had decided that everyone needed a uniform. That rig for the fighters, full camo for the scouts, all black for the security, and jeans and T-shirts for everyone else. Dahlia liked order, and Trash was cool with that.

He towered over Neeko, who was fourteen, scrawny. "Listen, fuckface," he said, "you're going to tell all this shit to Dahlia and then you're going to take us all to this old asshole's camp. I'm going to personally shove your hatchet up his ass and break off the handle."

Neeko nodded quickly, forcing a smile, but Trash saw a look

in his eyes. Equal parts fear and doubt. That bothered Trash, but it also made him really fucking mad.

– 4 –

THE SOLDIER AND THE DOG

Baskerville and I hunted the woods and streets and fields of a dying world. He was bigger now, more muscular, because I'd spent some days making armor for him. Dogs couldn't become zombies, as far as I knew, but they could be killed. So I made him a suit of leather armor fitted out with studs and spikes and blades. He didn't have the full rig on all the time, but enough of it so that he added extra mass to support it. He even had a helmet.

At first I thought I was going to have to muzzle him so that he didn't bite any of the dead. If he did that then his mouth would be a danger for me to be anywhere near. But Baskerville had some kind of instinctual abhorrence to dead flesh. He wouldn't bite any of it, and I later found out that if we came upon someone who'd been bitten but wasn't presenting with symptoms, the dog knew it. He'd growl and stay at a distance. That saved my ass a lot of times.

We hadn't yet gone west to Nevada. I knew I'd get around to it, but I was stalling. We'd been back to my uncle's farm a dozen times, trying to pick up the scent of Junie or the baby. Or anything. But Baskerville only sat and howled. I did that sometimes, too.

There were travelers, refugees, wanderers out in the storm. We met a bunch of those. Most were deep inside a bubble of their own PTSD. Gone mad or gone feral, or just…gone. Some were cool, though. I met a guy named Billy Trout, a reporter from Stebbins, the little town where the plague started. He was stuck with a bunch of school buses that had been killed by the

EMPS. The buses were filled with kids, and Trout was taking care of them while waiting for his girlfriend, a local cop named Dez Fox, to find him. Her bus had gotten separated from a convoy before the power was blown out. The plan had been to take the kids to the post-apocalyptic version of the Promised Land, Asheville. Rumors were that people had made a successful stand there and were trying to build something. A community.

I helped Trout fortify his place and then moved on.

Then I ran into Dez Fox, who was in real trouble. She was something. A fiery redneck blonde badass who took no prisoners and cut no one any slack. I liked her in about the same way you can like a pit bull. We fell in together because she was protecting her bus of kids against a bunch of assholes who—and I'm not joking here—called themselves the NKK, the Nu Klux Klan. No, it doesn't make any sense no matter hard you stare at it.

They were exactly what you'd expect them to be, and there were a whole lot of the bastards. They were ranging through the woods and farms, gathering up women and children. Rape and every other kind of vile abuse you can imagine. Women and kids.

Naturally Dez and I took some umbrage at this and sternly disabused them of the notion that they had permission to act like total parasites. We had some help from a young woman, early twenties, who was dressed like some kind of Viking or Asgardian or something. A cosplayer who used to do the comic convention circuit and after the dead rose decided to embrace the characters she played. A little crazy, sure, but tough as fuck. The three of us, and my armored mutt, stood up to the whole NKK army.

We walked away. They did not.

The warrior woman, Rachael Elle, went east. Dez went off to find Trout, using a map I gave her. And I kept wandering. Kept looking for the family I knew I'd never find.

Days lost their meaning after a while. Most things did.

I found some pockets of the NKK and vented on them in very bad ways. Found some wanderers and helped them out of some scrapes and sent them on toward Asheville. Stayed alone, for the most part. Me and Baskerville.

One cold spring morning, though, I heard people. I heard screams and yells. And moans. It was a mélange of sounds I'd heard so often that even before I got there I could paint the picture—one or more of the living caught by a group of the dead. In a field or farmhouse, in a forest or on the banks of a stream. That kind of drama was probably playing out all over the country. Probably all of the world, in cities and in the woods, maybe even in the arctic and on remote islands. Wherever the disease was, and last I heard it was everywhere.

The screams were male. Two or three voices. And a lot of moans. Baskerville froze and stared. His armor prevented me from seeing the hairs rise along his spine, but his body language told me.

We broke into a run.

Even though we are a formidable team—big SpecOps guy with guns and a damn samurai sword and a hundred-fifty pounds of armored killer dog—we never acted like we could just blunder in and solve everything. Caution kept us alive, so we only ran as fast as safety allowed.

We stopped on the near side of a gully about a mile into some overgrown woods. All around us the birds had fallen silent. Never a good sign. The sounds of some kind of fight were coming from the other side of a thick stand of maple trees, with the gully in between. Baskerville wanted to run, his body quivered with that kind of excitement, but he wasn't running yet. Not because I'd given him the command to stay, but because his instincts were at war with his desire to fight. This was a combination I'd seen in him time and again. It meant that there were living and dead threats.

Before the run-in with the NKK goon squad, I'd go running in any time I thought a living person was fighting for his or her life. That's when I naively thought that the worst things out here were the zombies. The sad truth is that the living dead have no choice in what they do; they're driven by parasites and there is no human control left at all. No will, no choice, no animus. It's totally different with the living. When they bring hurt and harm, when they rape and steal and beat and torture, it's because they want to. People have always scared me more than any of the monsters I've ever fought.

I clicked my tongue for him and we moved forward more slowly, going down one slope, stepping across the narrow trickle of runoff from yesterday's rain, and then climbing the far side. An old oak climbed precariously to the edge with too many of its roots exposed by erosion. Worked for me, though, and I used the thickest ones as handholds. Baskerville ran slantwise up the slope and met me at the top, looking pleased with himself.

I scrambled over the edge and we went off around the copse of trees, but we didn't get far before the shape of things began to emerge. Bodies lay tangled in the tall grass and weeds. Some of them were pale and withered, gray-skinned and bearing the marks of the bites that had killed them the first time and the blunt-force trauma that had stilled them forever. Mixed in among them were bodies painted in blood, with throats torn out or such traumatic injuries that blood loss killed them. These bodies twitched and jerked as the parasites transferred into them from the bites sought to rewire the central nervous system. Soon all of them would rise and join the fight, changing sides from defenders to relentless attackers.

That's how we lost. Every one of us that died became one of them.

There were no gunshots. Ammunition was rare. In the old monster movies, the heroes never seemed to run out unless it was for dramatic effect. In the real world, you could burn through three or four full mags in a minute or two.

I heard grunts of desperation and whimpers of pain. I heard the moans. And I heard the heavy thud of something hitting flesh—crushing it, breaking bone. Hitting again.

Baskerville moved into line-of-eyesight with me and I gave

him two hand signals—a loose hand and then a cutting motion. The loose indicated that he was allowed to attack the zombies, and the cut was to remind him to use his body armor. We'd spent thousands of hours over the last six months on that. He was smart and experienced and he wanted to fight.

He ran, and I ran.

On the far side of the copse there were three living people and nine zombies. All three of the living were bleeding. All three had already been bitten.

They were dying; they were lost. I saw one of them, a medium-sized guy with brown skin and an Arab face. He saw me and hope flared for one terrible moment before it was replaced by a clear awareness that we weren't going to be able to save him.

Baskerville and I attacked anyway.

– 5 –

DAHLIA AND THE PACK

Dahlia liked being the queen. She deserved to be the queen. Not that she called herself that, or required any of the members of the Pack to call her that, but it's how she thought of herself. Queen of the Apocalypse.

Besides, probably everyone who was an *actual* queen was dead. Ditto for kings, princes and princesses, dukes, earls, and all of those royals. The same was likely true of presidents and prime ministers. Dead. If any of them were alive, they were keeping a low freaking profile about it. The news reporters said that the President of the United States was going to give a speech one night, but that never happened. Air Force One went down somewhere. Nevada, maybe, if the reporters were right; but you couldn't ask them, because they were dead, too. She'd actually watched MSNBC the night Rachel Maddow bit the throat out of that guy with the glasses and bowtie. The news went off the air after that, and nothing came back on. Not even the Emergency Broadcast thing, and that's what it was supposed to be for. Times like this.

Except, there really weren't times like this, were there? Never before, and definitely not now. Or ever.

The world was dead. Mostly.

Practically everyone she knew was dead. There were a couple of people in her Pack who'd been kids in her own school, but they weren't friends. Not family either.

All dead. All eaten down to the bone or walking around looking for warm meals. Not her family, though. She'd seen to that. Knife to the head. Mom, aunts, all of them. Knife, knife, knife. The actual mechanics of it had been easy. After the first time it was rinse and repeat.

But the mechanics were the smallest part. It was Mom. It was her family. Dahlia had screamed and screamed and screamed. And thrown up. And gone black inside. For days. Curled up on the floor of her living room, surrounded by dead things that she used to love.

It was her own hunger that brought her back. Not hunger for flesh, but a raw hunger for *anything*. She woke up, covered in sweat and dried blood, smeared with her own piss and shit, trembling and alone. For a while all she could do was lie there and watch the flies as they flew in endless patterns through the broken front window, crawled over the faces of her family, and flew out through the open front door. Like a machine. Like a video on some kind of loop.

Then Dahlia heard voices and when she got up, she saw that the kids she'd saved at school—the ones who followed her here—were sitting around the table in the kitchen. They'd eaten their way through most of the food in the cabinets. They were drunk off the bottles from the upper shelves. They hadn't gone away, but they hadn't helped her, either. They waited like idiots for her to snap out of it and tell them what to do.

Weak, trembling, faint with hunger and dehydration, Dahlia

had nevertheless beaten the shit out of all of them. Five of them. They didn't even try to fight back. They screamed and wept and cowered, but they didn't fight back. She kicked their asses and left them all bleeding on the floor. Then she staggered upstairs, found that the water—against all expectations—was still on. No heat, though. She took a cold shower, screaming into the stinging spray. The water washed away the filth and the blood and the acid stains of her own tears.

Later, dressed in clean clothes, she went downstairs to find the five of them sitting at the table. Wounds dressed, eyes crusted with dried tears, faces turned toward hers like kicked dogs hoping for a forgiving pat.

That's when Dahlia understood that she *had* to be a queen. Their queen. She had to keep them alive because left to themselves they were going to die. Three girls, two boys—both of who towered over her. None of whom had ever been nice to her in school. Maybe that's why they took their beatings. Maybe they knew it was their due.

Whatever.

That was then.

Now she had the Pack.

Sixty-seven in all. Most of them kids. A few lost adults. No one over twenty-four, though. A lot of them were tough as fuck. Trash was twice her size and could probably bench press her entire weight. But the one time he tried something, Dahlia had gotten a lucky shot in and damn near kicked his nuts off. The weird thing was that he seemed almost relieved. It meant that he didn't have to make any real decisions. Not for himself or the few people he'd been leading when he met her. He was happy to be her muscle, her enforcer. The knight to her queen.

Yeah, the world was *that* broken.

Sometimes Trash shared her tent and they filled the night air with growls and cries and screams and sighs. Most times she slept alone. There was a seventeen-year old black girl, though... and Dahlia spent a lot of time wondering how to open the right kind of conversation with her. Not as queen, but girl to girl.

Sex was one problem. Love was another. Most of the time, though, it was all about survival. Staying away from the biters, feeding her people, finding a good place, knowing when to fight, knowing when to run.

Dahlia kept it all running right. And she still carried the knife she'd used to escape the outbreak at her high school. The same knife she'd used to hush her family. It was sheathed on her thigh, the handle angled to where her hand fell. Ready. Always ready.

Each time she picked a camp for the Pack, she walked the area to look at how it could be defended, and how they could escape if a swarm of the dead came out of nowhere. There were sentries in the trees, trip wires and weapons stashed along escape routes. Her tent was always positioned against a wall, a wrecked car, or some other structure so that threats could only come at her along her line of sight. None of the Pack asked where she'd learned all that, which is good because didn't want to admit it was all from video games and those doomsday prepper shows on cable. Who knew those bearded fuckers would be right?

She sat on a folding chair next to an overturned equipment box, halfway through a game of solitaire when Trash brought Neeko to her to give a report on the failed scouting run. Neeko was young and skinny and scared of his own shadow. He was also scared of Trash, who liked to hit things. The dead, people—whatever.

"Go ahead, Neeks," said Dahlia, "tell me what happened."

Neeko licked his lips—a flicker of a tongue, fast as a lizard. He told her what he'd told Trash, though he stuttered, skipped words out of nervousness, and made a mess of it.

Dahlia listened with patience and without emotion. She was not the kind to fly off the handle. Never. Impulse control was key to survival. She didn't jump into any fight just because she could. She didn't run away just to be safe. For her, everything she did needed to have a reason. It had to be weighed for risks and rewards, but also for lessons. There was no Google anymore, no one she could call, no authorities to solve problems. She needed to be smart and practical, and to use those qualities to lead her people. To provide for them and keep them safe and even help them be happy. That was all part of the code she now lived by, and it informed the code that kept the Pack alive when everything else was dying.

"Get the shit out of your mouth and tell it right," growled Trash, taking a swat at Neeko, who cringed and shied away.

"Let him talk," she said, pulling a disgusted grunt from the enforcer. Then, to Neeko, she added, "I need to hear every last bit. We need to know every detail so we can figure out our play. You were telling me about how this old guy fought...?"

Neeko licked his lips again and shifted a few inches sideways, as if trying to be out of Trash's swatting distance.

"He was fast," he said. "Fast as you." He flinched, but when no one chastised him for that, he continued. "I don't know what kind of stuff he knows. Karate or something. I can't tell. Didn't kick us. But he wasn't exactly boxing."

"Were his hands open or closed?" asked Dahlia. She'd taken some martial arts, but since the End had read up on it. There were a lot of books around that no one seemed to need, and if she picked the right one there was good advice. She'd even found some police hand-to-hand combat manuals and had pored over every page.

"Kind of both," said Neeko after a moment's thought. "He used his fingertips and punched us with one knuckle, but not the big knuckle. He stuck his first finger out so the second knuckle was what he hit us with."

Dahlia nodded. "And you say he took your hatchets away? How?"

"I...I don't know. He just took them. Twisted them, like. My wrist still hurts."

Neeko went through all of it. The camper, the food supplies, the comments about how they could have had supplies if they asked nice. Neeko gave her a lot of details but he wasn't very sharp about people.

"Thanks, Neeks," she said. "Do me a favor, okay? Draw me a map of exactly where this guy's camper is parked. Make sure you include as much information as you can about trees, that stream, the position of his camper, anything else in the area. Do that right now."

"Sure," said Neeko quickly. "No problem." He turned to go and then paused, looking back at her. "He could have killed us, Dahlia. I mean easy. We were nothing to him."

Dahlia said nothing, and Neeko left.

She indicated the other folding chair with an uptick of her chin, and Trash sat.

"What's your read on this?" she asked.

The truth was that she could have predicted Trash's exact words. He was useful but predictable. His strengths were all about his abilities as a fighter, as a leader during kill raids, as an enforcer, and as a strangely sensitive lover in the sack. But he was not a thinker or strategic planner. Emotions rather than careful thought. And almost no education at all. In another life, if Trash hadn't grown up poor and in a nobody-gives-a-shit school district, he might have really been something. Now, she wasn't sure if he could grow past where he was at the moment. The End did that, she knew. It kind of froze people into who they were at the moment. Like they were playing roles in a movie and that's all they were allowed to do. Trash was tough-guy muscle. That was his role.

Trash, true to the script he lived, said, "Neeko's a pussy. He and Andy should have been able to fuck that old guy up and then we'd have had all that stuff. Now the cocksucker's been warned, he's going to be expecting something. If he's that tough, he could pop caps in some of our boys when we raid him. Mind you, if he does, I'm going to cut his balls off and make Neeko wear them as a necklace."

Dahlia wanted very much to roll her eyes like a teenager and say "*what-ev-errr.*" Would have been funny to do that. She didn't. Partly because Trash might actually do something that nasty, and partly because she might have to let him. Maintaining discipline in the Pack was accomplished partly through good leadership and partly through fear.

"Let's think it through, Trash," she said. "This guy could have killed our boys, but he didn't, so he earns a couple of points."

"You and your points," grumbled Trash. "Why is it always points?"

"Because that gives us perspective. You know what a meritocracy is?"

"Sure." He was lying, Dahlia knew, but that was okay. He always lied, and he was bad at it. Made thinks easy.

"It's a system where people are judged according to standards. Not looks or who your family is or how much money you have in the bank. Actions, words, whatever, that's what should matter. Before things fell apart, do you think *I* was the popular girl in school? Give me a break. No. Out here we have to go on what people do. So, I give points out and take points away so we can all get a good read on someone or something. It's how it works."

Saying "it's how it works" was one of those phrases that somehow made sense to Trash, Dahlia knew. He accepted it. Many of the Pack did. As if knowing it was a rule *made* it something they had to abide. Dahlia found it useful, but also a little sad. And a little scary. She tried to use it to help her people, to keep them from turning into a gang that just killed and took. While she was okay with theft, she had rules for that, too. Even killing had to have rules.

That, for her, was how it worked.

"Pick four fighters," she said firmly. "Maybe Nathan and Jumper, because they know how to move quiet. A couple others. Light kits, blades and handguns. One long gun. Soon as Neeko's done with the map, we're going to see about this tough old guy."

"We...?"

"Yeah," said Dahlia, "I think I need to see him for myself."

"And what if he's some kind of old retired soldier or cop or maybe a wiseguy from some old mob?"

"Then," she said, "I guess we'll have to kill him and take all his stuff."

Trash grinned, happy as a kid on Christmas morning. "Now you're talking."

– 6 –

THE WARRIOR WOMAN

"What we going to do with the kid?"

Jason adjusted the lacing on his bracer as he eyed Tommy with suspicion. He, Claudia, and Peter were hanging back, talking amongst themselves while Rachael and Alice tried to find out more about Happy Valley.

Pulling his shoulder-length dreads back into a thick rubber band, Jason added, "He don't look like he belongs out here, he's way too clean. Do you think that maybe there's a safe zone around?"

"Maybe," Claudia replied, watching Tommy curiously. She brushed a lock of dark, curly hair out of her face. "But I kinda think we would have heard about any actual surviving communities in the area before now. I mean, he's obviously well-fed and well-kept, so wherever he's from, they're well-stocked. His parents have to be missing him. Wouldn't be surprised if they're out looking for him."

"Maybe if we take him to his home, his people might let us stay for a while," Peter said hopefully. He settled down on a large rock, crossing his arms and stretching out long, boot-clad legs. "If they have supplies, they might have space, maybe even looking for more people."

"That's best-case scenario," Rachael said, rejoining them as Alice continued to talk quietly to the child. "In answer to your question—" She nodded at Jason. "—I want to take him back home, see if we can find his parents for him. It's got to be nearby, otherwise he'd be dirty and hungry." The others nodded in agreement. "But it might also be a trap. We just don't know what we're going to find there. Jason, you and Alice come with me. Peter, I want you to wait here for a few hours. If we don't come back, go back to Brett, tell him what happened."

No one argued.

"The Apple Man used to work for my daddy," Tommy said, hand tucked into Alice's. He'd grown more animated as the four made their way along the forest path. "And he was always nice to me. He always gave me apples right from the tree, even though he wasn't supposed to."

They rounded a large tree in the middle of the path and Rachael stopped in her tracks. A large, broad figure dressed in jeans and a dirty T-shirt faced away from them, short cropped hair dark against his neck, skin bronzed from the sun.

"Apple Man?" Tommy pulled his hand out of Rachael's and took a step forward. The figure turned slowly, one shoulder sloped lower than the other, head tilted to one side, mouth hanging open.

"Apple Man!"

"Tommy, no!" Rachael reached for the boy, fingers grazing his shirt and missing as he darted forward.

Cursing in Elvish, she bolted after him, pulling her dagger from her hip sheath. The orc was newly turned—Rachael couldn't see any decomposing flesh, but the closer she got, the worse it looked. Its jaw hung all crooked, like it had been smashed with something hard, its eyes clouded and yellow. Blood and sticky black gore stained the side of its face and shirt collar, a chunk of flesh missing from its neck.

Tommy didn't notice anything wrong. He ran toward the orc, who took slow, shambling steps forward, reaching for the boy.

"Tommy, stop," Rachael shouted as she dashed after him, pulling her sword from the scabbard attached to her backpack.

"He's a…he's a Bad Thing!"

Tommy faltered as he heard his own words echoed back, but he was already too close to the orc that was once his friend. It lunged at him, strong hands clenching around his arm. The sound of Tommy's horrified screams turned Rachael's stomach to lead and spurred her forward even faster.

Rachael raised her sword. It was an exact and functional replica of the Elven sword used by Arwen in the *Lord of the Rings* movies. The blade was made from exceptional steel and as Rachael aimed for the temple she prayed her aim was true. The blade glinted in the sunlight, sparks of light playing along the razor-sharp edge as Rachael brought it down, embedding it in the orc's forehead. The thing stumbled backward, pulling both Rachael and Tommy with it, its hungry moan filling the air as it opened its mouth and leaned down toward the boy. Tommy screamed again, struggling frantically to escape the orc's grasp. With the strength born of terror, he managed to pull free, running back to Alice.

With Tommy safely out of the way, Rachael stabbed up with her dagger into the back of the orc's skull. It resisted, hard bone fighting the sharp blade, but Rachael let go of the sword to grasp the dagger's hilt in both hands, pushing up with all her strength.

The orc crumpled to the ground.

Rachael closed her eyes, crouching down and taking deep breaths to steady her heartbeat and her adrenaline. She still wasn't sure she'd ever get used to this life. She had only ever lived her life being a hero in make-believe.

Being one in real life was much more stressful.

A crack of a branch to her left, the rustle of leaves to her right, and Rachael grabbed her dagger, pulling it from the back of the Apple Man's head with a hard tug. She retrieved her sword as a figure darted through the trees, faster than any orc she'd seen. Another shape followed, and she dropped into a fighting stance, ready to leap forward and strike.

"Don't move," a voice behind her threatened, and she froze, feeling the barrel of a gun press against her upper back.

-7-

THE SOLDIER AND THE DOG

Baskerville plowed the road, slamming into zombies with his massive armored body and then twisting to force the short, razor-sharp blades on his shoulders to slice through leg tendons. I drew my *katana* and followed, slashing at the falling bodies, taking off arms and heads.

Two of the three defenders were down, sprawled, screaming as the dead fell on them. I hacked the killers away and then hurried over to where the Arab was fighting. He wore the remnants of old National Guard battle dress trousers and jacket, but instead of military-issue boots he had a fairly new pair of Doc Martens. Hockey and kickboxing pads covered most of his body—as it did with the others—but he had a bad bite on the side of his elbow, where the pad was the thinnest. It doesn't take much of a bite. The *Lucifer 113* pathogen was designed to be an ultra-aggressive serum transfer bioweapon. It only takes a drop of blood or spit in an open wound.

I performed a vicious lateral cut with the katana and took off the arm and shoulder of the hand that had the guy by the throat. The zombie staggered, lost balance, and before it could recover, the soldier hit him with what I discovered was the lower third of a long-handled spade. The blade was bent from repeated impacts, but the soldier put some heart into it, catching the zombie just above and behind the ear. The dead body suddenly dropped, proof that the blow had damaged the brain stem.

I pivoted to put my back to his, and we met the rush of more of the dead. I'd counted nine, but now some of the soldier's friends were getting up and attacking. Baskerville snarled and growled like a timber wolf as he ran interference for us. I used my shoulder and hip to turn the soldier so that I took the brunt of the attack, and after a while we had a rhythm. Baskerville crippled them, they fell toward me and I cut heads. When I couldn't do better than taking off an arm, the soldier crouched and used his shovel—crushing skulls with the metal end or stabbing through the temple or eye-socket with the jagged end of the broken handle. It was brutal work. The screams of the other two soldiers faded and were gone, and then they got up and came at us, too. I heard the soldier sobbing as we killed his friends.

Maybe I did, too.

The fight seemed to go on and on, devouring the whole day, but when the last body fell I doubt more than two minutes had passed. I sent Baskerville out to run the perimeter and when he barked I ran and killed whatever he found. Five more zombies, three of them in uniform.

When it was over there was another of those haunted silences.

I relaxed, one rigid muscle at a time, and turned to the soldier. He had his last name embroidered on his jacket. *Al-Harti*. He was about twenty, with corporal stripes on his sleeves. A good-looking young guy who had laugh lines around his eyes.

I stuck out my hand. "Joe Ledger."

He stared at me, at my hand, and then licked his lips. Then he shook. "Abdul."

Then his knees buckled, and he fell.

I caught him under the arm and lowered him down, then helped him scoot back until he had his back to a sycamore. I snapped the blood from my sword with a sharp downward shake, then removed any lingering traces with a thick handful of green grass before resheathing it. Baskerville came and sat down, panting from his exertions. His body language told me that there were no more threats. I squatted down, removed my Wilson folding knife, snapped the blade into place and cut away the elbow pad and sleeve to expose Abdul's bite.

We looked at it, and he nodded. "I'm done."

"Yeah," I said. "Sorry, brother."

He smiled. "Me, too."

It was six months since the world ended. Everyone alive

knew the math. If he'd been resting, the pathogen would take all day to spread. But with elevated heart rate and respiration, and all the adrenaline in his bloodstream, it was already everywhere. Another design feature of the bioweapon—kill the soldiers who are pumped and engaged in resistance.

There is, I hope, a special place in hell for the kind of people who designed weapons like this. The reality was that he had hours before sickness took him and darkness blanked out his mind. After that it would simply be a matter of him dying and coming back. He wouldn't be himself anymore by midnight—maybe not even by full dark.

"You..." he began, and then lost the rest in a sob. I waited while he pulled himself together, my hand on his shoulder. Baskerville lay down with his head on his paws and whined softly. Abdul tried it again, "You should probably go, y'know, before..."

"Not a chance," I said. "I'm not double-parked."

"Why stay?"

I shrugged. "Why not? Wouldn't you stay with your buddies?"

He nodded. "But you don't know me."

"What do I have to know? Corporal Adbul Al-Harti, Maryland National Guard."

"Pennsylvania," he said. "My guys and I moved on with some refugees."

I tapped my chest. "Captain Joe Ledger, Rangers."

"Army?"

"Sure," I said. The truth was too complicated to waste time on; and once upon a time I had been a Ranger. "Retired, though. I was off the clock when this shit came down."

"Guess everyone who mattered was," said Abdul, hurting me without intending it. The two groups I'd run with, the Department of Military Sciences and then Rogue Team International were the cats who were supposed to *always* be on deck. We were the ones who were supposed to stop this from happening. The fact that we didn't was never going to stop twisting a knife in me.

I put a light dressing on his elbow, more to discourage flies than anything else. He sat with the arm held slightly out to the side as if trying to distance himself from the bite. Or disown the arm. I pretended not to notice and instead glanced around at the bodies.

"You guys kicked some ass," I observed. "Looks like it was a running fight."

"Long range patrol," he explained. "When the command structure fell apart a bunch of us kind of went out on our own, you know? Looking for survivors, helping them get out of tight spots. We've been sending them south."

"To Asheville?"

He brightened. "Yeah, you heard about that?"

"I've been doing pretty much the same thing." I explained about Dez Fox and Billy Trout, and Abdul began nodding.

"Sure, they were all over the news. Trout was doing those 'Live From the Apocalypse' news reports from inside a school in Stebbins. And Officer Fox was kicking ass and taking names trying to protect a bunch of kids. So, they got out?"

"Most of them," I said. He didn't ask what happened to the others or how many didn't make it. These days any bloody fool could write the script for those kinds of conversations.

Abdul nodded. "Glad the rest got out. Did they make it to Asheville?"

I shrugged. "God only knows. I haven't been there myself. Keep meaning to, but…"

He cut me a look. "But why not?"

We sat for a moment. The birds were singing in the trees now and sunlight slanted gently through the branches. It was as lovely as this kind of thing could be. It wasn't that tragic, shocked stillness but rather a quieter blanket of subtle noises. Bees and flies, birds, the rustle of squirrels chasing each other through the leaves.

"My family was waiting for me in Robinwood," I said. "I found ashes and bones, but…"

"Ah," he said, nodding.

We watched the bees. A doe stepped out of the woods forty yards away, moving with such delicacy that it made me want to cry. She looked around, saw us, watched for a long time, then moved farther into the sunlight. A pair of fawns followed on spindly legs. They couldn't have been more than a month old. Alive, despite all the hungry people and hungry things in the woods. I caught Abdul nodding at that, too. It was an affirmation of a kind. We were both going to die; him today, me sometime after...but the world was going to go on. It would be quiet and lush and beautiful when we were gone. Eventually even the hungry dead would starve and waste and turn to mulch. Life would continue, and after a few hundred years the forests would have reclaimed every inch of paved ground, turning cities into gardens. I knew that Abdul was thinking something along those lines, too. There was a strange peacefulness in his eyes. Acceptance, perhaps.

Abdul was already looking bad. His color had shifted from a healthy olive to a gray-green and greasy sweat ran down his cheeks. He shivered and sitting that close I could feel the heat of the fever that was igniting beneath his skin.

Damn.

After a while he began speaking quietly, telling me his story. And I think he did that because it matters that someone knows your story once you're gone. We all want to be remembered, as if being forgotten meant that our wandering souls might not be as immortal as we hope. Dez Fox told me that she spoke aloud the name of every zombie she killed, even if she had to pick their pockets afterward. A ritual of our shared humanity, as important—or perhaps more important—than anything I've ever heard said in church.

As I thought that, I heard the word "church" spoken aloud, and it snapped me out of my reverie.

I said, "Wait...what? What was it you just said?"

He paused, half-smiling. "I must be a riveting storyteller, Joe. You were miles away."

"I'm here now. What did you say about a church?"

"Huh? Oh…no, I was talking about the old guy. The one who was gathering up the survivors."

"Go back and tell me that part again," I insisted. "What old guy?"

"Just an old guy. Maybe ex-military or something, because people I know who met him said he was tough as nails. Like a general. Giving smart orders, seeing to details." Abdul wiped sweat from his eyes, looked at it and wiped it on his shirt. "I never met him, but I heard he was working through this whole area, looking for anyone left alive, giving them food and shelter, and teaching them how to *be* out here, you know?"

I nodded. "And…?"

"And for a while I thought it was one of those stories," said Abdul. "People grab at stuff like that because they want to know someone is out here who has his act together. Someone with a plan. Well, this guy, if he's real, is like that. That's one of the reasons my team came out here. We were hoping to hook up with him, see who he was, combine forces and like that."

"But you said his name…"

"Yeah, sure. They call him Old Man Church."

I felt my whole body tense and my heart wanted to jump out of my mouth. "What does he look like?"

"What's he *look* like?" Abdul thought that was a funny question. "I don't know. Old, I guess. I never saw him. All I know is that a couple of travelers who said they met him talked about his gloves. He wears black gloves. Not work gloves or bike gloves, but silk. At least that's what I was told."

I closed my eyes. "Jesus fucking Christ," I breathed.

"Why? What's wrong? Do you know this guy?"

I took a long time answering because I wanted everything he said to be real, and I was afraid of breaking the spell.

"I think maybe I used to work for him," I said.

"Old Man Church?"

"We called him Mister Church. Or sometimes the Deacon," I said. "If it's him…if it's really him…then I have to find him."

"Why—" began Abdul, but a sudden fit of coughing punched

its way out of his chest. Blood and something that looked like black oil spattered his hands and I instinctively moved away. Tiny threadlike white worms wriggled in the black stuff. The larvae of the parasite that was the base of *Lucifer 113*.

Abdul stared in horror at it, and any trace of peace that had been in his eyes vanished. He raised those eyes to me and they were filled with the total helpless pleading of the lost. Big tears rolled down his cheeks. Baskerville got up and backed away, growling low and deep.

"Down," I snapped, and the dog moved ten feet away and sat, eyes hooded and menacing.

"I...I..." Abdul began, then buried his face in his hands.

I got to my feet. "Tell me what you want me to do," I said as kindly as I could. When he looked up he saw that I had my pistol in my hand.

"Now or later?" I asked.

It took him a long time and cost him so much of what he had left to spend, but he got to his feet. Not his knees. His feet. That mattered. He lifted a trembling hand and pointed to the sword I wore.

"That's a samurai sword?"

"Yes. A katana."

"I...I saw you with it. You didn't just learn it...you know... *since?*" It came out as a question.

I holstered my pistol. "No. I've been studying and practicing my whole life. I stole this from a dojo in Hagerstown. It's a good sword. New, but top quality."

He licked his lips, winced at the taste, turned and spat. There were ghosts in his eyes. "Would it be fast?"

It was such a hard question to ask. And to answer. He was a soldier, though. A warrior. It was one warrior asking that question of another warrior.

"Yes."

"And you're good?"

"I'm better than that."

He didn't ask if it would hurt. He was already hurt. This was going to end hurt, and he knew it.

"Let me pray first, okay?"

"Sure."

He studied me. "Do you believe in God?"

I shook my head. "I really don't know."

Abdul nodded. He looked around to decide which direction was east, knelt, prayed. I moved away and cleaned my sword with water from my canteen. I did not pray, but I nodded to the sword as if *it* could understand.

Abdul finished. He used his own canteen to wash his hands. Thoroughly. And he dried them on the only clean part of his jacket. I came over and he held out his hand. He was infected but his hand wasn't cut, he wasn't bleeding. I shook his hand and we smiled at one another. Then he stepped back and began praying again in Arabic.

"*Inna lillahi wa inna ilayhi raji'un.*"

I'm good with languages. I knew the prayer. *We belong to Allah and to Him we shall return.*

There was a flash of silver fire in the sunlight and then the silence seemed to stretch on forever.

I cleaned my sword, put it away, sat down by the tree and did nothing at all until it was time to dig the grave.

− 8 −

DAHLIA AND THE PACK

Dahlia liked to be able to move like a ninja. It was much better than the way she used to move, which was more like a sick bear or a beached whale. A little unfair, she knew, but self-loathing was a hard habit to shake.

Nowadays, with all the practice of surviving out here, with actual things that want to kill you, every day was like a video game. Or VR. Or something. Seeing firsthand what happened to people who couldn't move quietly was a pretty good incentive program. She'd seen cops and soldiers get eaten because they made too much noise and drew too much attention.

So, for her it was ninja style.

She practiced it a lot with Trash and some of the other fighters, and also with Neeko and the scouts. It was kind of scary and kind of fun, and she could feel how it increased her confidence while also giving her some muscle tone. And if she thought about being a badass ninja while she ran those drills, well…no one else had to know.

Now it was critical for her to be truly as silent as one of those shadow warriors. Her gear was padded so nothing clanked or creaked. She and Trash took time moving through the forest, making sure not to step on twigs, watching for trip wires and booby traps as they got closer to where Neeko said the old fart was camped.

The forest was oddly lovely today. Sunlight slanted down through the treetops and painted big swaths of foliage with gold. There were all kinds of birds out here, and their combined songs filled the air with the kind of beauty that survivors often forgot about, or ignored. Dahlia did not ignore it. Without beauty, what was survival even worth?

Trash moved past her, angling down a slope toward the creek where Neeko got beaten up. For all his faults—and there were a lot of them—Trash knew how to move. His body was lean and muscular, and she loved to see him in action, even if it was just walking across a room. He looked pretty damn good naked, too, and that thought always gave her a flush. Trash was the first boy she'd ever slept with. She was moderately sure he didn't know she was a virgin that first time, but he was as gentle in the sack as he was brutal in a fight. And on missions like this one, he always reminded her of a panther or tiger. There was a phrase she read once in a novel: "moving with oiled grace." That was him. It was the kind of movement she aspired to, and seeing him glide past her and down the slope made her want him. Tonight was going to be one of the intense sessions, of that she had no doubt. He might have that oiled grace, but she had the stamina to wear him out.

The others, Nathan, Jumper, Serena, and Slow Dog, were spread out in a line a hundred yards wide. All four of them were tough, but each in different ways. Nathan was a bull in both looks and mentality; he was strong enough to smash through just about anything and liked to try. Jumper was all about Parkour and free-running. He was nimble, fast, and weird; and he did not relate to other people very well, so Dahlia figured he was some kind of sociopath. Serena thought she was Lara Croft, and had the body for it, but her mind was more like a snake—cold and ruthless. Slow Dog was probably the sanest of the Pack's fighters, but that was a pretty low bar. He was loyal to a fault and would do very bad things to anyone who messed with the Pack. He was a nice guy around camp but sometimes he totally lost it in a fight, going way over the top with the amount of damage he needed to inflict in order to win.

Right now, though, Dahlia felt comforted to have all of them at her back. And Trash. Psycho or not, he was an incredible fighter. The old bastard was never going to know what hit him.

Not that she wanted to hurt the guy necessarily, but she did want to take all of his stuff, and maybe let Trash give him a few dents because of what the man had done to the scouts.

That was the thought going through Dahlia's mind when every single thing went wrong.

She was looking for trip wires and saw one. She was even smiling as she lifted her foot and stepped over it. Dahlia had no idea what a pressure-sensitive field trap was until she heard the faint *click*. Then the tough, flexible pine bough that had been curved back, taught as a longbow, was released by the ground trigger hidden under dry leaves. The bough caught her in the stomach and folded her in half, lifting her completely off the ground, and swatting her backward into a tangle of berry bushes. The air was smashed from her lungs, but she managed a high, shrill, single-note wail of shock and pain. When she crashed down in the shrubs, Dahlia felt like she had been shot.

She briefly thought that's what had happened.

She lay there, punched deep into the shrubs, splayed like a starfish, gasping for air that seemed to have been sucked out of the whole world.

Nathan rushed over, pulling a heavy-bladed meat cleaver from a leather belt pouch, crying a warning to the others. Dahlia stared, confused, as the forest itself seemed to come alive and consume him. She saw leaves and branches move and fold around him, but there were sounds like knuckles on flesh, and then Nathan was falling, his eyes going high and white, his knees buckling, the cleaver gone from his big fist.

"There!" cried Jumper. "He's right there."

Dahlia forced her head to turn a half inch—an effort that seemed impossibly difficult—and saw Jumper leap toward a tree, step off the side of it, pivot in mid-air and drill a devasting punch toward a shadowy figure who moved away from Nathan. Dahlia knew what Jumper's leaping punches could do. They were bone breakers, neck-sprainers, teeth snappers. Except they needed to land in order to do damage. The figure— and she realized now it was someone wearing forest camo and foliage as a disguise—shifted away from the punch, allowing it to miss by an inch. Then a stiff forearm chopped laterally across Jumper's upper chest. The impact turned the arm into an axle and Jumper's body into the wheel; he rotated in midair and then fell hard on his face. The figure squatted and drove a two-knuckled punch into the base of Jumper's skull and the free-runner flattened out and did not move again.

Then Trash, Serena, and Slow Dog were there, crashing through the brush, each of them swinging weapons.

The moment seemed to slow down, almost to freeze, as Dahlia got a clear look at the face of the man in the camo. He was tall and blocky, with big shoulders and a barrel chest. He wore one of those full ski-masks on his head—a balaclava, Dahlia thought it was called—but she could see his eyes. They were dark and surrounded by crow's feet. For one fragment of a moment those eyes looked into hers and she couldn't read the emotions that should have been there. No anger, no fear, no hatred. Instead she saw disappointment and annoyance. As if her whole strike team was nothing more than an inconvenience.

Time speeded up all at once. The figure—the old man, she was sure of it—suddenly seemed to lose substance, to blur as he moved. Or maybe it was simply that he was so fast that she could not track him.

Serena tried to stab him and he punched her forearm, her bicep, her deltoid and the side of her jaw. Bam, bam, bam, bam. The knife fell; the arm itself seemed to die and flop down, and then the lights in Serena's eyes flickered and went out. She dropped in place.

Slow Dog wore brass knuckles on both of his huge fists and he swung a one-two combination that was as fast as it was brutal. The old man did not evade but instead stepped into the swings so that Slow Dog's huge arms wrapped around him and rebounded. Dahlia did not see what the old man actually did, but Slow Dog shrieked and staggered backward, blood spurting from his nose and mouth. He dropped to his knees and then fell over sideways.

Then Trash, faster than the others, grabbed the old man by the shoulder, spun him and drove a knife into his guts.

Except that's not what happened.

The knife was suddenly gone from Trash's hand and it struck the tree and buried itself in the bark, quivering with the impact. Trash himself seemed to leap into the air, twisting and turning. He hit the tree just inches below the knife, slamming shoulders and the back of his head into it.

The old man stepped back and let him fall.

Dahlia managed to pull her pistol out, even as her oxygen starved lungs clawed in a single breath. She raised the pistol and pointed it at him.

The man stopped. He looked at the gun. Then he reached up and removed his balaclava, revealing a weathered face and graying hair. His eyes were calm, without trace of fear or surprise. He did not look at the gun. Instead he looked directly into Dahlia's eyes.

"The day is going badly for you, little sister," he said. "You are not as good at this as you think. I'm going to give you a chance."

The gun trembled in Dahlia's hand.

"You can listen," said the old man. "You can run away. Or you can die."

"I...I have the gun," wheezed Dahlia. "I..."

He shook his head, the way a teacher would during a difficult lesson. Patient, but not infinitely so.

"Listen, run, or die," he repeated. "Those are the only three possible outcomes. Take a moment. Make a careful choice."

– 9 –

THE WARRIOR WOMAN

"Drop the knife or I'll shoot."

Rachael considered her options, hyper aware of the gun pressed against her back. She didn't think she'd be able to get the drop on him with her dagger or jump to the side fast enough before he pulled the trigger. She needed to put them off guard first, make them think she'd surrendered.

"Drop it."

Opening her hand slowly, she obeyed the command., the Elven dagger hitting the dirt path with a soft thump. Other than that, she stayed perfectly still, eyes trained on Alice and Jason, who both watched her intently, ready to go for their weapons on her signal.

She counted at least ten people. Didn't mean there weren't more out there. Most of them carried machetes or axes or hammers; only the guy behind her had a firearm.

Scratch that. A man carrying a shotgun stepped into her line of sight.

Overall, Rachael had never been great at math—her grades at school had only been average—but she *was* good at calculating combat situations, thanks to LARPing. Larger numbers of enemies didn't necessarily mean a disadvantage, but it did mean they needed to work smarter.

Disable the enemies with the guns first; ranged weapons would put them at a serious risk. Machetes and hammers next; they were one-handed weapons that could be swung fast, and cause more potential damage. Shovels and axes last; they usually required two hands to wield, had lousy balance and a slower hit rate. They would, however, do more damage if they did land a strike.

The other man with a gun had it pointed directly at Jason's chest. Her friend's gaze didn't leave hers, and she darted her eyes at the man holding the weapon. She hoped he got her meaning...and that their enemies didn't.

Jason give an infinitesimal nod and she looked over at Alice, who'd faded back into the trees, Tommy clung to her legs like a baby koala, his face buried against her stomach. "Stay back," she mouthed.

"Stand up, I don't want you getting any ideas about that knife of yours." The man behind her spoke again, accenting his words with another jab of the gun barrel. Rachael stood slowly, hands out in front, making sure not to make a move for her knife and sword—both within her reach.

She was going to have to do this on hard mode apparently. But that was their life now. Hard mode.

Without warning, she crouched and swung her leg around, hooking an ankle behind the man's knee and yanking hard before rolling to the side, dagger back in her hand. Unprepared, the man lost his balance, falling backward with a shout. He hit the ground hard, gun falling off to the side and into the brush. He lay there, the wind knocked out of him.

"Go!" she shouted to her team. Without waiting to see if they obeyed, she moved on to the next man, landing a strong kick to his chest as he swung his machete. He stumbled backward. Rachael pressed her advantage, slammed the pommel of her dagger against his wrist. He screamed and dropped the machete and she kicked him again, this time in the balls. He toppled over, hands folded over his groin.

She heard the sounds of combat behind her, punctuated by Tommy's screams. She turned and immediately ducked under the vicious swing of a shovel that would have taken her head off. Rachael grabbed the long handle and gave it a violent twist so that the attacker's wrist was bent at an extreme angle. The leverage snapped his thumb with a sound like a heel stepping on a green twig. The man shrieked and Rachael doubled him over with a kick to the groin as she tore the shovel from him. She whirled and swung the flat of the blade against the ankles of a woman rushing at her, sending the attacker flying forward into a bad fall. The woman hit the bent-over man and the two of them fell into a sloppy heap.

Another man rose up with a woodsman's axe and chopped down at her, but Rachael brought the shovel up in both hands, blocked the axe handle at an angle that sloughed off the brute force. Even so, the shock of it vibrated through her wrists like a thousand needles.

The axe man pulled back and tried a second and even more powerful blow, but Rachael was in motion, too. She darted sideways, reversed the shovel on her hands and rammed the blunt end of the handle into his solar plexus. He let out every molecule of air in his lungs and the axe chunked down into the dirt. Rachael spun the handle again and hit him in the back of the head with the flat of the shovel with such force that the man dove face-forward into the dirt.

A knife whipped past her head and *thunked* into a tree behind her, startling her so badly she dropped the shovel. Rachael turned, looking for whoever threw it, and her heart jumped painfully in her chest as another attacker burst from the woods with a knife in his hand identical to the one he'd just thrown. She backpedaled and tore the knife from the tree, did a pivot that was more like a choreographed pirouette and used the momentum to give her power for a throw of her own. It caught him four steps away and buried itself in the meat of his thigh. The leg buckled and the man screeched as he fell, dropping his own knife to try and stanch the sudden explosion of blood.

Rachael heard a cry and saw that Jason was fighting another attacker armed with another damn axe. Before she could take a step to help him, Alice rose up behind the killer and smashed him in the back of the head with the butt of her sword. The man's eyes rolled high and he dropped senseless to the dirt.

Rachael could see the first man she disarmed scrambling to find his gun. She snarled aloud as she ran toward him, snatched up his fallen machete and skidded to a stop with the blade pressed hard to the side of his throat. He froze, his fingers on the handle of the gun.

"You can be stupid or you can be alive," she said.

He stared at her.

"Right now none of your friends are dead," said Rachael, pressing the edge into his skin with such force that a bead of blood broke from his skin and rolled along the steel. "It's totally on you if you want to change that."

Behind her, she heard someone rack a shotgun. "On your six," said Jason.

The man on the ground drew his fingers away from the pistol.

"Good choice," said Rachael.

– 10 –

THE SOLDIER AND THE DOG

Baskerville and I went looking for Old Man Church.

Hope is such a fragile and dangerous thing, and I almost did not want to have it rekindled in my chest. I'd hoped to find Junie and Ethan at the farm. Top and Bunny had hoped to find their families, too. I don't know if they ever did, or if they ever made it to the base in Nevada. If so, they probably thought I was dead after all these months. They'd have given up hope on me.

Now there was the chance, however slim or unlikely, that Mr. Church was alive and somewhere near here. Alive and doing what he did, which was to impose order on chaos.

Once upon a time Church had been a field operator like me. Well, if any of the many tall tales about him were true, then not really like me. He was stranger, smarter, more dangerous—and more capable. He had been the adult in any room, the alpha of any gathering, even when he was among a few dozen SpecOps jocks. You couldn't really imagine him as a child any more than you could imagine him dead. He was more like a force of nature than a person.

Am I exaggerating? No, I really don't think so. The phrase "larger than life" kind of defines him. Christ knows how many times I'd wondered what he'd been doing when *Lucifer 113* got loose. If he hadn't been infected, then it was no surprise at all that he was still working to save the world. Or at least as much of it as he could. Who knows, maybe he's the one who decided that Asheville was the rally point. That wouldn't surprise me even a little bit.

The thing is, he actually *was* old. He was sixty-something when I met him, and I was in my early thirties at the time. Now he had to be pushing eighty. How much fight could there be left in him?

I had to find out.

So, with my dog running beside me, we followed trail after trail, mostly following the path Abdul's team had taken. It was clear enough because of the tread-marks from their shoes. Abdul's Doc Marten's, and a mix of combat soles and Timberlands worn by his guys. Easy.

By noon the next day I found a small pack of travelers walking down the center of a blacktop that was cracked and choked with weeds. Eleven of them, ranging from a woman of seventy down to a toddler in a stroller. They saw me coming and one of them pulled out a hunting bow and goddamn near killed me, but I stopped and put my hands up.

"Not looking for trouble," I called. "Captain Ledger, U.S. army. Looking for my unit." Again, a useful lie.

"Lose the hardware," called the old lady.

"Not a chance," I said, "but we can talk from here if you like." We were about seventy feet apart.

"What do you want?" she demanded. "We got no rations to share."

"Don't need any," I said, "but tell you what—how 'bout I go into those woods and come back with dinner? Then maybe we can we have a conversation that doesn't involve yelling or gratuitous violence?"

They cut looks at the surrounding woods. The old lady nodded. "Roger here is a darn fine shot. You try anything and he will put you and your dog down."

The guy with the bow stood rock steady and the arrow was aimed at my chest. I did not doubt what the old lady said. So, I walked backward a dozen paces, then turned my back to them and angled toward the woods. Baskerville lingered for a moment, maybe daring the archer to shoot. Have to admit I was sweating it a bit because getting an arrow in the back is a lot less fun than it sounds.

The area I'd come through was farmland and there were plenty of animals out there. I'd seen sheep grazing on wildflowers and clover about a mile to the east, and I went that way. These animals were born and bred on these farms and even though they were destined for somebody's plate before the dead rose, they weren't able to grasp the concept of freedom. Half the milk cows out here had already died because they'd been bred to be totally dependent on humans to feed and tend them. Sure, some of the bulls had taken down a fair number of zombies, but they'd fallen, too.

Not that sheep were smarter, but they didn't need to be milked. They simply grazed, pooped, fucked, slept, and did the same day after day. They weren't hard to find. I picked one that was about a hundred and fifty pounds and literally walked right up to it and killed the animal with my sword. It barely even noticed me. Made me wonder how they had not been eaten already by the dead, but maybe they—like Baskerville—could smell them and move away. Not sure; didn't care.

I popped my knife, bled it to reduce the weight, and then hoisted it across my shoulders and humped it back. That wasn't easy and I could feel every one of my years and every inch of scar tissue by the time I found the road. The small caravan had moved on, but I figured they would and picked a spot ahead of where they might be. Picked well, too, because I stepped out of the woods less than a quarter mile ahead of them on a straight patch of road.

They stopped and gaped at me. I grinned back, and Baskerville gave a snooty little *whuff*. No one shot me with an arrow.

– 11 –

DAHLIA AND THE PACK

Dahlia lowered her gun.

The old man gave a single nod of approval. He walked over to her and held out his hand, and Dahlia gave him the gun. He removed the magazine, ejected the shell, caught it, returned it to the mag, replaced the magazine itself, and put the pistol in his pocket. She watched with a strange fascination.

Around them, the strike team groaned their way back to awareness. The old man moved through the small clearing where the fight took place. He gathered up weapons, patted everyone down, placed the weapons out of sight behind a fallen log, and then did a second check on each. He helped them sit up, felt pulses and looked into eyes. He flicked a knife out of somewhere—Dahlia never saw where—and cut a strip from Slow Dog's sleeve, folded it into a compress, and showed the big young man how to hold it to stanch the bleeding. Then he went to Trash, who was blinking in stupid uncertainty as to what had happened, pulled him to his feet and probed the fighter's skull.

"It's not broken," said the old man, "but you'll be sick for a bit."

"I—" began Trash, then he whirled and vomited. The old man sighed and patted his back.

The others sat like naughty school kids on the ground, their backs to trees, while the old man went over and lowered himself onto the log. Dahlia heard the creak and pop of old tendons and joints.

"I thought I was past all of this nonsense," he said. He removed a cloth from a pocket and began sponging the greasepaint from his cheeks. He nodded to Dahlia. "You're the leader," he said, not making it a question. "What's your name?"

"Hey, fuck you," gasped Trash, but the man put a finger to his lips.

"Shhhh," he advised. "And sit down before you fall down."

Trash looked like he wanted to make a fight of it, to try and reclaim the moment and take back some shred of his personal power, but instead he lost his balance and thumped down on his ass.

"You blindsided us," he muttered.

"Of course I did," said the old man. "You came in force. What would you expect me to do?"

"You attacked two of our scouts."

"I *counter*-attacked. They made the first move."

Dahlia groaned as she tried to sit up. Her stomach felt like it was filled with hot splinters. She looked at the bough that had struck her. It was wrapped with thick pads of green leaves. When she glanced at the old man, he nodded.

"I could have just as easily sharpened the branches to spikes and positioned it at face height."

No one said a word.

"I could have dug pits lined with punji sticks and covered with infected blood," said the old man. "Or I could have positioned myself in an elevated shooting position and killed you all when you walked through the big clearing two klicks from here. Take a moment to consider that. Add to that math the fact that it would have been very easy to cut your throats while you were down here, or shoot you with this young lady's gun.

Ponder that. Ask yourself why I would do things the way I did rather than the way that would have been easier and less dangerous for me. Go ahead. Take a few minutes with that."

No one spoke.

The old man sighed.

"I made the young lady here an offer, and I'll share it with all of you. You can run away and not come back. I don't hold grudges, but I am not particularly tolerant when it comes to recidivism. Or you could do something stupid now and then I will bury all of you. Or," he said, "you can listen to what I have to say."

Serena and Slow Dog exchanged a look. Jumper was still in a semi-daze and Nathan merely looked scared and confused. Only Trash sat there with a face that was a mask of belligerence.

"What is it you want to say?" asked Dahlia.

The old man nodded approval, as if that was the right question. "If I was another kind of person I might be motivated to judge you solely on your actions. Based on that, I might regard you as below average in terms of intelligence gathering and mission planning. Your actual skill level, as measured by your attempt to execute your plan, leaves quite a lot to be desired. It's amateurish and naïve. Also, it speaks to a neo-militancy likely borne from fear and lack of any kind of long-term strategic thinking. Nod if you're following me."

After a moment Dahlia nodded. Slow Dog did, too. None of the others responded.

"Had you been better at this, you would likely be more seriously injured or possibly dead. Depending on how difficult you made it."

"Fuck you," grumbled Trash, but there was very little power in it.

"Shut up, Trash," said Dahlia quickly. Anger flared in his eyes, but he didn't say anything.

"What you should have done was try to parlay first," said the old man. "You could have come here under some kind of flag of truce, and even perhaps offered an apology—though for the record, I don't require them."

Dahlia licked her dry lips, tasted blood and dirt and dragged a forearm across her mouth.

"You could have had your fighters in reserve if the parlay went south on you. That's sensible. I could have admired that, and I would have responded to courtesy."

"How do we know we could trust you?" asked Serena.

"Because I did not kill the two scouts. It would have been easy. They were children. It's obvious you did not know I was here, so you wouldn't have known where to look if they simply failed to return. It would have been nothing to me to kill them and either make it look like a zombie attack, or make them vanish entirely."

The certainty with which he said it scared Dahlia. The look in his eyes told her that he wasn't bullshitting. Those eyes told her that he had done that sort of thing before. Maybe many times. He had to be some kind of ex-military. Maybe special ops. He'd taken on the whole strike team without so much as being touched. That was freaky scary.

"How many of you are there?" asked the old man. "In your camp. How many?" When no one answered, he smiled and nodded. "Sensible not to share your numbers. But, for the sake of discussion, let's say the number is sixty-seven."

That jolted everyone. Despite the pain in her stomach, Dahlia shot to her feet.

"How...how...?" It was all she could manage.

"Intelligence gathering is the most important component of any mission. Remember that."

"Who told you?" demanded Nathan.

The old man shook his head. "No one told me. I observed. I know that you sleep in the seventh tent from the edge of the woods." He pointed at Serena. "You have the blue bedroll. Should I go on? No. The point is made. As a group of survivors you are all managing things just above the subsistence level. Not bad, considering how many other groups, including better-armed groups, have fallen. You get points for that. However, you are acting like a gang, and you are not very good at it."

"We do all right," sneered Trash.

"You just got your clocks cleaned by a very old man who took you all on without weapons. You, on the other hand, had youth, numbers and were all heavily armed. Explain to me how that supports your claim that you're doing 'all right.'"

Trash's face colored and he looked away.

"You're spying on us?" asked Dahlia.

"Yes."

"Why? If you know all this about us, why not just leave before we came out here?"

"That," said the old man, "is a very intelligent question, and it deserves a straight answer. Pay attention." He leaned his forearms on his thighs. "Before the outbreak I spent quite a long time running teams of special operators. Sadly, the nature of the outbreak disrupted my lines of communication with any who may have survived."

"The EMPs," said Dahlia.

"Yes. An ill-advised voice of action, and one which most likely crippled any chance of an effective response." He laced his fingers together, and Dahlia saw that the dark gloves he wore were very thin. More like silk than canvas. "Since the collapse of the infrastructure I have been endeavoring to do what I could to help people get to places of shelter, and to organize so that they can survive in community form. We need to build our numbers because survival of the species requires a deep gene pool. Do you understand that?"

Dahlia nodded. A few others did, too.

"Being out here in the same woods as your group is not an accident. I became aware of you a few weeks ago and positioned myself where I was likely to be found. Your scouts work in a grid pattern, so I made sure that they would find me on a day when it was convenient for me. I made the same offer to the scouts that I have made to you. They chose to run. Fair enough. They aren't on the policy level. They reported back and you came to find me. It was unfortunate and disappointing, though not particularly surprising, that you came to attack me. That could have worked out very badly for you. None of the injuries I inflicted are serious. All of you will be able to defend yourself if attacked by the living dead. That fact should be suggestive."

Dahlia nodded again.

But Slow Dog asked, "Why? Why not just fuck us up and let us rot?"

"Or turn into walkers?" asked Serena.

"I'm not a fan of killing unless there is a tactical or strategic win involved. You are not formidable enough for that level of response from me."

"Ouch," said Nathan.

"And," continued the old man, "you are potentially more useful to me, and by extension the world, if you're alive."

"What do you mean?" asked Dahlia.

"You are not good at what you do, but you could be. You're all very young, very strong, and you have some experience with combat. I could bring you to a higher level of efficiency. I could train you to become a much more powerful and useful team."

"Why the hell would you want to do that?" asked Jumper, finally able to join the conversation.

"Because the war that we're fighting should only have two sides," said the old man. "Us—the living—versus *them*—the dead. The nature and severity of this crisis should have been an eloquent statement about the folly of warfare as we've always known it. *Lucifer 113*, after all, was created as a bioweapon. With the death of billions of people, do we really need more of a lesson?"

No one spoke.

"You are operating out here as if aggression and preying on each other is the only path to survival. It isn't. It is a self-tightening knot around your own necks. You will lose numbers through attrition and then you will be gone. Other, stronger gangs will overwhelm you. Or you will simply erode your own ability to want to live in a world that is defined by a constant struggle against extermination. You would, in a sense, be fighting on the side of living dead. And even if you managed to survive, your group is too small to survive in any generational way. You would pollute your DNA within a few generations and what is left to survive would be warped by genetical damage. Hardly a long game worth playing."

The old man stood up and walked over to Dahlia and stood looking down at her. She was tall, but he was taller and seemed to fill the whole clearing with his power.

"Or, you could let me train you to be better advocates for your own right to survive as well as soldiers in a very real fight to preserve humanity. There are probably hundreds of thousands of people left in North America. Maybe even millions. Globally, probably ten or twenty times that many. They will tear themselves apart if they follow the kind of mindset you clearly have embraced. And they have other dangers to face. The rise of diseases that were kept in check by the medical infrastructure and which will now return with a vengeance."

"Why us?"

"Because you're young," he said. "Because you have made mistakes but you haven't corrupted yourselves so thoroughly that you're beyond saving. Because you care for the people in your group, which means you still have compassion. Because I would rather take a risk on you than bury you."

Trash got to his feet. "Fuck this and fuck you, you old fuck. You can make all the bullshit threats you want, and maybe it'll work on some assholes, but not me. You're some kind of psycho motherfucker and we're out of here."

He looked around, clearly waiting for the others to join him. Nathan and Serena rose and moved to stand with him. Jumper and Slow Dog stayed where they were. So did Dahlia. She saw the surprise and hurt bloom on Trash's face.

"Dahlia...come on..."

"Trash," she said quickly, "maybe he's right."

"What? You're buying this shit? He's conning you, D. He's

conning all of us. He's running some kind of game."

She walked over to him. "Is he? He could have straight up killed us. All of us. If he was running a game, then explain to me why he didn't."

"I don't know why," yelled Trash. "He's fucked in the head. Who knows? All I know is I'm not going to start following some Obi-Wan Kenobi-acting motherfucker. If you do, then you're as crazy as he is."

They stood staring at each other and Dahlia could feel the air all around her crackling with tension. It hurt her heart. But at the same time the things the old man said sent a thrill through her, and a wattage she did not yet understand. And she wanted to understand.

She took a small step backward. "Then I guess I'm crazy."

The pain in Trash's eyes made them wet and glassy. "Dahlia...what about the Pack? What about us?"

"The Pack is mine," she said. "They'll do what I tell them to do."

"Fuck they will. I'm going to tell them to pack their shit and we are so out of here."

"No," she snapped, "don't you dare."

He got up in her face. "Just watch me. You think the Pack has *your* back more than mine? Let's see."

Dahlia suddenly shoved him with both hands. She had no idea she was even going to do it until it was done. Trash was too sharp, though. He swatted her hands to one side and raised his hand to slap her hard across the face. Suddenly Slow Dog was there, pushing himself between Trash and Dahlia, puffing out his chest, pushing it against Trash.

"You want to hit someone, bro, hit me."

A meaty hand dropped on Slow Dog's shoulder and Nathan stepped to him. "You better settle down, hoss. You don't want to—"

And Jumper shoved him sideways. Nathan nearly fell but Serena caught him. Trash pointed a finger at Dahlia. "This how you want it? You want to bust up your own family, D? All we been through and this is what you want?"

"I want us to survive," she yelled. "That's all I ever wanted."

Trash nodded. "Oh, I get it, you think because this old fuck has some moves that he's going to have a bigger dick and teach you to like it. Some kind of Lolita bullshit and—"

Dahlia slapped him across the face. It was a hard slap and it knocked his head to one side and tore a corner of his lip open, pulling thick beads of red from his skin. Slow Dog and Jumper flanked her, ready for what was coming, but Trash just shook his head. He touched his fingers to the cut, looking at the bright red, then reached out and wiped the finger on Dahlia's sleeve.

"You picked your side, D. You going to have to live with how this plays out." He pointed his fingers like a gun at the old man and dropped the hammer. "Next time I see you, motherfucker, you're going to need more than some kung-fu bullshit."

With that he turned and walked off. Serena and Nathan exchanged a long look, and Dahlia saw that they weren't sure about which side they were on. But Nathan tapped Serena's shoulder, nudging her in Trash's direction. They both glanced at their friends, but then turned and vanished into the forest. The others stood listening to the sound of their passage fade, fade, and then vanish.

Dahlia pawed tears from her eyes. Jumper put his arm around her shoulders but she shook her head and he let his arm fall. They turned toward the old man.

"Who *are* you?" asked Slow Dog.

He turned to him. "There isn't enough time left in the world to answer that question in any way you'd understand."

"I don't even know what that means," said Dahlia. "I mean… what's your name? Can you tell us that, at least?"

The old man studied her and although she saw lights flickering in his eyes she was unable to use them to decode anything about him.

The old man gave her a smile that made him look old and sad. "You can call me Mr. Church."

– 12 –

THE WARRIOR WOMAN

Rachael walked the path, gathering fallen weapons while Jason searched their would-be attackers for any more they might be concealing. Using the shotgun, he motioned for them to sit down one by one along the path, hands in plain sight. Alice sat off to the side with Tommy, holding him until his tears subsided.

The thumping of footsteps coming up the path made her tense and spin around, sword out. She lowered it when Peter and Claudia came into sight.

"We heard the screams," Peter gasped as they both leaned over to catch their breath, hands on knees. "Are you okay?"

"The Apple Man went orc and attacked Tommy, and then we had some unexpected visitors." Rachael nodded over her shoulder at the line of people. "We're all fine though. The kid's a bit shaken up, but no surprise there. Keep watch here, okay? I don't know if there's more of this crowd around, and I don't want to get surprised again."

Rachael picked up a Bowie knife and dropped it onto the now-sizeable pile of confiscated weapons, then strode over to the group of attackers. She looked at them one by one before crouching down in front of the man who'd held the gun on her.

"Look," she said evenly, "we don't want to hurt you, but I can't have you threatening me or my people, so tell me who you are and what you want. And if you're lucky I'll send you on your way. No harm, no foul." She tapped one palm absently against the hilt of the Elven dagger, once more sheathed at her hip. The man swallowed, his gaze never leaving her hand or the dagger.

She gave him time to work it through.

"I'm John, John Allens," he said at last. "We're from Happy Valley. We were on patrol, looking for one of our people. He went missing the other day, so we organized a search party. We saw you attack him." His tone turned harsh. "Attack and kill him."

Rachael winced. "I'm so sorry, but your friend was dead before I got to him. I don't know how he died either, but he was an—" She stopped herself from saying "orc" because they wouldn't understand. "He'd come back from the dead, just like most everyone else out there." She kept her voice calm, almost sad, wanting to show respect for their loss. "We mean you and your friends and home no harm, I can promise you that."

"M-Mr. Allens?" Tommy's voice was soft, almost scared as he peaked around Alice's leg.

"Tommy?" John Allens shot to his feet, apparently no longer concerned with Rachael or Jason's weapons. "What in the hell are you doing out here? Your family's got to be worried sick about you!"

Rachael stood as well, taking a step back as she looked from Tommy to John Allens. She kept her hand on her dagger hilt but made no move to draw it.

"Happy Valley? Happytown?" Jason muttered to her.

"Tommy, is Mr. Allens from Happytown?" she asked as the boy took a few hesitant steps forward.

The boy nodded sheepishly.

"We found Tommy wandering near the woods a little ways back," Rachael explained. "He was looking for someone called the Apple Man. I'm guessing that was your friend." She nodded toward the fallen orc. Allens looked over at the body and nodded. "We were trying to help Tommy find his way home when Pat attacked him. I had no choice but to quiet him."

"You okay, son?" Allens knelt by Tommy, checking him over for bites and scratches. The boy nodded, passively submitting to the inspection.

"What's Happy Valley?" Peter asked curiously. He was a thin, gangly young man with sandy hair and clear blue eyes. He looked like he should be playing sandlot baseball instead of being a part of this kind of violence. The self-aware hurt of that truth was evident in his eyes.

"We're a town about a mile down the path," Allens answered. "All survivors. Our community is gated, so nothing gets in, and we have been blessed with abundant land for farming and grazing, and lots of room for people. In general, we've been very lucky. Haven't had any attacks by gangs or walkers, and the homes are a good distance from the gates. It's a piece of heaven, even in these bad times."

Rachael glanced at their weapons in the pile.

"How do you defend it? Do you have a guard or any watch set up, or any reinforcements of your fences?"

Allens looked uncomfortable and scuffed his foot on the ground, not meeting her eyes.

"We've sort of relied on volunteers." One of the women in the group spoke up, her eye starting to swell from a close encounter with Jason's fist. "We have lots of people willing to volunteer, whether it's doing the farming or taking care of the animals or repairing the homes and fences or guard duty. A lot of folks willing to do the work, even though most of us don't have much experience."

"We had some firearms experience, but..." Allens paused for a moment before continuing. "Well, we ran out of bullets about a month in. Both of these guns are unloaded." Jason looked down at the shotgun in his hands and rolled his eyes. Allens noticed and gave a small chuckle. "Yeah, that shotgun usually gets people to back down before things escalate to the point where we'd have to call our own bluff."

The woman nodded. "Now we just have to rely on what we have, mostly garden tools, baseball bats, rackets, stuff we can find around. Nothing that's really good for defending against more than one monster at a time."

Rachael nodded, turning to glance at the rest of her group, eyebrows raised. Peter and Jason looked dubious, but Claudia and Alice both nodded.

"Do you want help learning how to defend yourself with the tools you have?" Rachael included everyone in the question.

The woman looked shocked. "Why would you help us when we tried to hurt you?"

"You were defending yourself, your homes, and your friend. I don't blame you for that. We're not the best or most technically trained fighters, but we've figured out how to use what we have to survive. There's different techniques for using different weapons, even shovels and axes. These techniques will help you use the weapons you have to effectively fight off the undead without needing bullets or more traditional weapons. Do you want to learn?"

A few of the men in the line nodded, while others looked skeptical. Allens and the woman spoke quietly for a moment. Then the woman stood, offering her hand to Rachael. "I'm Heather. Thank you."

Rachael shook Heather's hand with a warm smile. "Rachael. We all have to do what we can to help out our neighbors in these times. My friends and I need to gather our gear, and then we're ready to go with you."

She walked back to her friends, making sure to put enough distance between them and the Happy Valley folks to allow her to speak without fear of being overheard. "Tommy," she said, "how 'bout you go help your friends and we'll be right there, okay?"

He frowned.

"It's okay, sweetie," Alice said. "Go on, now."

Reluctantly letting go of Alice's hand, Tommy trotted down the path to Heather.

"Okay, gang. Thoughts?"

"It sounds great," said Claudia. Peter nodded.

Jason was less than trusting. "How do we know this isn't just a trap?" he said in a low voice. "How do we know they won't kill us once we drop our guard?"

"We need to be cautious," Rachael agreed. She thought for a moment, then said, "Alice, Peter…wait until we're far enough for you to follow at a distance. Stay out of sight. Once we find out where Happy Valley is located, go back to the school and tell Brett what's going on, and where we are."

Jason still didn't look happy, but he nodded in reluctant agreement.

"Sounds like we're going to be here for a few days, at least to help out," continued Rachael, "but maybe they'd be willing to let us *all* stay for a little while after we're done training them. Maybe we can share in some of their luck."

Walking back over to Heather and Allens, Rachael grabbed the shovel off the pile of weapons and handed it to the woman. As the Happy Valley folks collected the rest of their weapons, Rachael noticed that Jason didn't remove his hand from the knife at his belt.

She couldn't blame him. She wasn't sure how much she trusted these people either, but if they were telling the truth, she would be more than glad to help them protect themselves.

– 13 –

THE SOLDIER AND THE DOG

As it turned out, the old lady was a former middle school librarian named Abigail Smith. Thin as a rake handle but tough as steel. Shrewd-eyed and stern, but those were exactly the right qualities for this kind of survival. While the others cleaned and cooked the sheep, Abigail and I sat on roadside rocks and drank from a little bottle of bourbon she pulled out of a pocket.

I sniffed the whiskey, nodded, took a sip and was, for a moment, in a very happy place. Although Top and Bunny would likely label me a "beer guy," I could appreciate a fine whiskey. As I wiped my mouth after a second sip I caught Abigail studying me.

"You look like you have a story to tell," she observed, accepting the bottle back and taking a hellacious pull.

"Doesn't everyone?" I asked.

She shrugged. "Some more than others. You military? You have the look."

"Used to be."

Abigail shook her head again. "No. That's not you." She gave me such a calculating and intense stare that I wanted to check for dirt under my fingernails and pay any late-book fees she might ask. "Some people come home from duty, take off the uniform and go back to being who they were before. Most, maybe. Others always look like they're wearing that uniform."

"You're sharp. You ever serve?"

Another shrug. "I was one of those who went back to being who I was."

"No," I said, "I don't think that's entirely true."

We handed the bottle back and forth. I told her my story, even some of the stuff that was classified as above top secret because why not? Secrets didn't really matter. She listened, nodding, not interrupting. I like people who don't interrupt. When I wound down, she put the cap back on the bottle and gave me her tale.

She'd been one year shy of a late retirement, and was planning to fight it, preferring to grow old and die among her beloved books. When the dead rose, Abigail was among the people who gathered in an emergency shelter, but first the power went out, then the back-up batteries failed, and finally the food ran low. That's when she decided that waiting for help was likely to be a suicidal pursuit. So, she and a few others went out of the shelter to find a destroyed town filled with monsters.

There were younger men and women in the shelter, there were bigger and stronger people, but there was no one tougher. And by that, I mean tough of mind, tough of spirit. Over the next few weeks Abigail polled the survivors about their skills and put them all to work. Anyone who knew how to do basic household repairs or construction were assigned the task of reinforcing the shelter. Hunters were tapped to find weapons and ammunition, and to establish elevated shooting positions on the key routes leading up to, or away from, the shelter.

People who could cook from scratch were tapped to work with scavenging teams to locate bulk staples and oversee nutrition. Those with first aid training were required to teach that to everyone else.

That's how she did it. "Everyone has some useful skill," she said, "even if they don't know it yet. You get someone who played field hockey in school or was good at tennis or softball and you make them your front-line fighters. They may not know how to fight per se, but they're used to hitting things in ways that don't hurt their own backs and elbows and knees. The dead don't require finesse out of us, but fighting them requires efficiency."

I grinned and listened. The smell of roasting mutton filled the air and that was wonderful. Sentries with sharpened staves and bows patrolled the road.

"Then," continued Abigail, "you have to think about other skills. Not fighting or direct defense. Anyone who was a therapist or had been in therapy long enough to understand what it means to really listen. Anyone who could tell jokes, sing songs, tell stories, *read* stories, entertain in any way—they're important because once the walls are secure and everyone's fed we all have to get through those long nights, don't we? We have to have laughter and song because that reminds us of possibilities and it also reminds us that we're people. Civilized people. If we lose that, then it's a pretty short step downward into savagery and brutality."

"That's brilliant," I said.

She tried to wave it off, but there was a little bit of a blush on those lined cheeks. "It's practical, at any rate. I've always been like that, even as a little girl. Things should make sense, and if they don't, then we have to make them make sense."

"Preaching to the choir, sister," I said.

Someone grumbled about us making too much noise, so we drifted off to the verge beside the road. She spread out a big blanket and we lay down and looked up at the stars. Baskerville lay between us, dreaming doggie dreams.

"Staying alive has become quite a chore," said Abigail.

"A bit."

"You've lived a harder life than most. Tell me, does it ever get easier?"

"Easier? Sure. I suppose," I said. "You develop useful habits of survival. Routine helps with the fear and fills time so you don't always feel the loneliness. And there's always something new to learn, or a skill that you can focus on to improve. That lets you be more in your mind and less in your heart."

She nodded, accepting that. "Have you ever felt in danger of losing all connection to your heart?"

"Oh yes," I said. "And it would be much easier to be able to reach inside and pull the plug on all emotions. It would make the nights easier to get through."

"But you haven't done that…"

"No."

"I've met people who have," said Abigail. "Out there. Since the end. There are some people who seem genuinely dead inside. Bands of Rovers, I think they're called. Some loners, too. They seem to have forgotten what it's like to be human. To feel compassion. All they seem able to feel is greed and hate and lust."

"Those are emotions," I pointed out.

"Don't be pedantic. I'm talking about people who have lost both sympathy and empathy. Who are predators a lot more frightening than the living dead."

"I know," I said. "Met more than a few of those." I told her about the Nu Klux Klan.

"Exactly," she said. "The end of the world seems to have ended them."

I thought about that for a moment, then shook my head. "I don't think that's right. I think these people were always like that. Hatred, misogyny, racism, sexual abuse, and all the violence that goes with those things aren't a byproduct of *Lucifer 113*. No, I think what happened is that the comprehensive failure of the infrastructure took the cultural and legal shackles off of people who have always harbored those appetites. It's just now there's no one left to stop them or punish them."

She turned and gave me a long, appraising look. "There are people like you."

"Oh, hush now," I said.

The stars above us seemed to move as the world turned.

"It's a gift," said Abigail after a pause so long I thought she'd drifted off.

"What is?"

"The stars."

Above us the roof of the world was painted with ten trillion chips of diamond dust. Some were planets, some were stars, and some, I knew, were whole galaxies. We could see the sweep of the Milky Way, too.

She said, "Before the plague there were always lights and most people—most of us—never really knew how much those lights washed away most of the stars. Even in the small town where I lived, there were lights. Street lights, stop lights, car lights." She turned to me, her face edged with silver starlight. "Have you ever seen stars like this?"

"Before all this? Yes, but only in pretty remote places," I said. "On ships far out to sea, in Death Valley, couple of deep deserts. And Antarctica once. A few other places. It's humbling."

"It's everywhere now," said Abigail. "A new twist on the Dark Ages, I suppose. And maybe that's what this will be called. The New Dark Ages."

"And yet," I said, "look at how much light there is."

She said nothing. When I glanced over at her I saw she was crying.

Later—much later—we got up and began walking along the road. Baskerville ranged ahead, silent for all his bulk, to make sure that we were not walking into danger. The world was full of monsters, but they were not everywhere all the time.

"Why are you out here, Joe?" asked Abigail. "What are you looking for?"

"Would it be corny to say I'm looking for hope?"

"A little."

I grinned. "I'm looking for a man that I think is someone I used to know. Maybe you've run into him out here. Older man, very tough, exceptionally smart. Maybe wears black gloves…?"

"Oh!" she said, smiling. "Mr. Church."

I stopped dead in my tracks. "You've *met* him?"

She walked three paces more, then turned. "Yes. A lovely man."

"Wait, wait, stop," I said, touching her arm. "This is important to me. I need to know if we're really talking about the same person. Describe him to me."

"Why is it so important?" she asked, and I could almost see defensive shutters drop between us.

"Remember me telling you about the two special operations teams I used to run with? The Department of Military Sciences and—"

"Rogue Team International," she finished. "Yes. Why?"

"Church created both organizations. I worked for him and with him, and as far as I'm concerned, he is the strongest, smartest and most critically important person I've ever known. If anyone can help us beat this, it's him and—"

"'Beat this'?" she echoed. "Joe, much as I admire optimism, much as I like to think of the glass half full and a waiter coming with a fresh pitcher, there is no way to fix this. We lost the world. Millions of people are dead, possibly hundreds of millions or even billions. There is no infrastructure, many of the cities have been destroyed with nuclear weapons, the power grid is out, cell phones don't work, not even cars will drive. The soldiers I've met have all said that there is no one giving orders anymore. And all of those dead people are actively hunting a dwindling number of surviving living people. I'm not trying to kick you below the belt, Joe, but how can anyone *fix* that?"

"I…" But my words faltered. "*I* don't know, Abigail. That's the whole thing. He probably has a plan. When you talked to him, did he say anything about that? About how we're going to beat this plague?"

Instead of answering immediately, she began walking again and I fell into step beside her. We walked maybe a hundred yards before she spoke.

"Joe, I only spoke with him a few times. Maybe twice at any length. If he had any knowledge about how to stop the plague, or some way to reverse it, he never said so. Mostly we talked about how to manage things as they were. He had some very good ideas about scavenging, about locating and establishing a safe haven. That's why we're heading south now."

"Are you going to Asheville?" I asked.

"That's a long walk," she said. "We have a pregnant woman in our group and quite frankly I don't think she could make it. No, Mr. Church told me about a food distribution warehouse forty or so miles from here. It was overrun at first, but he said that the people who were there had not acted in practical ways. He found the place and cleared it out, then sealed it so that it would be accessible to travelers who knew how to get in. Even left an inventory of the supplies and refilled the tanks on the generator. He hid some weapons and told me where to find them. I had the impression that he was very particular about who he trusted with this information. He even told me a code phrase to use if someone else got there first, so they would know we were also sent by him. Does...that sound like the person you used to know?"

I smiled, and it was a genuine smile. Not forced. Not a wince. "Yes," I said, "it really does. May I ask what that code phrase is?"

She hesitated. "Look, Joe, I feel that you're a good man. You could have done us harm if you wanted to, but instead you brought us food."

"But...that's not enough for you to want to share certain details," I said. "No problem, I get it. Who knows, maybe I'd even be able to figure it out. Church would want to use a phrase that's easy to remember. Something simple but unique, and unexpected, given the circumstances."

She cut me a look. "I could give you a hint, if you like. Because if you *did* guess, then it would tell me something."

"Worth a try," I said. Baskerville was standing on the road watching something, but it proved to be an owl who moved from one tree to another. I let Abigail work out the risk/reward thing on her own.

"Okay," she said. "A hint. Something vague. Maybe too vague, because it's a literary reference."

"Hit me."

"Leonard Pine."

I actually burst out laughing. "I *knew* it!"

We stopped and she studied me as I laughed. A real laugh, even more real than my smile. It wasn't that it was all that funny, but it was proof. Real proof that we were talking about Mr. Church. No doubt at all.

I said, "Vanilla wafers. That's the code phrase, or something like it."

She gasped. "You *do* know him. And extra points for understanding the reference."

It was an old joke. I was always a huge fan of the novels of Joe Lansdale featuring a couple of down-on-their-luck private detectives, Hap Collins and Leonard Pine. Hap and Leonard never had a good day that couldn't go south on them, but no matter how weird things got, they always won out in the end. Hap was a white liberal, Leonard was a black conservative, but they were the best of friends and walked through hell together. One element in the books was that Leonard was absolutely addicted to vanilla wafers. It was a mania with him, worse than a junkie hooked on crack. And it was a love shared by Mr. Church, who always had a box of Nilla wafers close at hand. Even the first time I met him, when he interviewed me under deeply weird circumstances for inclusion in his black ops organization, the Department of Military Sciences, he had a plate of vanilla wafers. And Oreos for me. I can't stand fucking vanilla wafers.

But at that moment I'd have eaten a six-course dinner of nothing *but* vanilla wafers.

"Where is he?" I begged. "Please, I need to find him. I need to talk to him."

Her smile faltered. "I…I don't actually know. It's been weeks since I saw him last." She named a small town a hundred miles north and explained where Church had been camped, and how he was camped. A big travel trailer pulling a good-sized storage pod filled with supplies. "I doubt he'll still be there, though. He said he was looking for a place a few travelers had told him about. A gated community with a good wall that had never been overrun. I got the impression he wanted to see if it could be established as a town where he could send other refugee groups like mine. We couldn't wait, though, because of Sandra and her baby on the way."

"Where was this community?" I asked. "What do you know about it?"

"It had a name that seems so weird now, under the circumstances, I mean," she said. "Happy Valley."

"Yeah," I said, "that does seem a little weird."

Abigail looked into my eyes and then around at the dark forest. "The world has become weird, though. Weird and big and dark and scary."

"We're still alive, though. You and your people. Church and the people he's helping. Whoever's down in Asheville. We're not going to die out like some species on the edge of natural extinction. Somehow we'll win this world back from the dead."

In the cold starlight I saw a mix of emotions in her eyes. Some hope and some humor, some tolerance and some despair. Sadness, too, because any conversation about survival carries with it the memory of who has not survived. Seeing her pain, knowing it was tied to that kind of memory, made my own inner eye look at the empty places in my life. It twisted a knife with practiced, delicate precision.

We walked back to the camp, and she told me where she thought Happy Valley might be. Then we went to our bedrolls.

Baskerville spooned with me for warmth. The night passed. In the morning I went my way and they went theirs. I hugged Abigail and told her that I hoped we'd see each other again. She said that would be nice.

We both knew that we wouldn't. But lies are cheap and they sound good.

– 14 –

DAHLIA AND THE PACK

Life became strange for Dahlia. Surreal. That was the word, she decided. That said it all.

She had always loved that word. Before. It had been a vocabulary word in tenth grade, and she liked the description in one of the dictionaries she read. *Perception marked by the intense irrational reality of a dream.* That was fun, though she understood at the time that "irrational" did not necessarily mean "bad." It meant that it made no logical sense. That seemed to apply to a lot of things in her world. The whole concept of physical beauty—a lucky happenstance of genetics—being the yardstick by which people were judged made no sense at all. *That* was irrational. She was so much smarter than pretty much all of the "in crowd," the preps, the whatevers. Dahlia had been one of the smartest kids in her class, but because she'd always been fat the others discounted her intelligence. Waistlines mattered more than IQ or GPA. Which was nuts. That was surreal in a bad way. The fact that she knew that her brains would matter ten times more when they all graduated was another kind of surreal. Her ability to dive into literary worlds and become lost in them as if what lay between the pages was more real than anything in school...yeah, that was surreal. It was an escape hatch that kept her sane and made her smile when nothing else did.

Then the world came to an end and the rules changed. A lot

of the pretty kids got eaten. Those that still had enough meat on the bone to reanimate were now pretty fucking ugly. And their clothes looked like shit. How embarrassing to be wearing last year's fashions forever? That made Dahlia smile, even now. Even though it was petty and a little catty. It was also surreal, though. In a different way, and not entirely in a bad way. Not for her. While everyone she knew at school was dying, she'd come more fully alive. She'd become the leader of a roving band of survivors carving out their place in a post-apocalyptic world mostly populated by zombies. Actual zombies.

So freaking surreal.

And now...

Now this.

Dahlia stood in the center of a clearing, wearing a blindfold around her eyes, holding a Sharpie in each hand. Red in her left, blue in her right. Instead of knives. It was day seven of her training. And her life had now become some kind of action movie training montage. Weird exercises that were part wax-on, wax-off and part Jedi mind tricks. She'd tried calling the old man "Mr. Miyagi" or "Yoda," but instead of taking offense he'd merely told her to grow up. That stung. A lot more than she thought it would.

"Again," said Mr. Church.

She heard his voice but couldn't tell exactly where it came from. He was spooky like that. He made only exactly as much sound as he wanted to. He could vanish without her hearing him go, and could appear as if he'd teleported down from the *Enterprise*. Scary. Some Jedi mind tricks for sure.

In this exercise he circled her and would lightly touch her somewhere—shoulder, arm, calf—and based on that touch Dahlia had to react, determine the angle of his body to hers, and touch him with one of the markers. He wore a white boiler suit, like a Hazmat suit but without a mask. Any marks she made would reveal how accurate she was, how smart her choice of targets, how fast she moved.

So far she hadn't made a single mark on him. Not a dot.

She tried to stretch out with her senses. To hear and smell everything. To feel changes in the air around her. Had his voice come from her left side and a little behind? She thought so and shifted her weight to jump that way.

When it came, the touch was on her right hip. A fingertip against her hipbone. Dahlia whipped around and slashed right and left with the markers, crisscrossing the air in overlapping patterns.

There was no resistance.

"Again," said the voice out of nowhere.

Another touch. Another move, faster than before; really trying.

"Again."

"Again."

After ten more tries Dahlia stepped back, flung down the Sharpies, tore off the blindfold and spun around to find him. Church was directly behind her. His boiler suit was unmarked.

"This is bullshit," snarled Dahlia.

"No," he said, "it's not. You're getting better."

She glared around. Eighteen members of her Pack sat in cross-legged silence around the edges of the clearing. A few were smiling, but no one was openly jeering. Neeko even gave her an encouraging nod.

"I *can't* do this," snapped Dahlia. "No one can. It's stupid."

Church's face was hard to read, she'd learned that much over the last few days, but did she just see a flicker of something cross his mouth? A tightening, like a small wince? Was that disappointment or irritation? Or both?

Dahlia bent and scooped up the markers and held them out to the old man. "Okay, Yoda, you're big on asking us to do these dumb exercises and play your silly games, but why don't you show us how to do it...if it's even possible at all."

If she expected him to throw that back at her, she was wrong. Church nodded. "That is a reasonable request." Then he added, perhaps a little unkindly, "One you should have asked before now."

He waited while Dahlia pulled on a boiler suit, then allowed her to tie the blindfold around his head.

"Satisfy yourself that I can't see," suggested Church. "Otherwise this has no value."

She tied it tight and peered at it until she was sure. The gathered members of her Pack exchanged some looks. More of them were smiling now, though she couldn't tell if they were happy that the old man was going to get schooled, or because they thought Dahlia was setting herself up. Maybe a little of both.

The old man rolled the markers between his fingers and then shifted his grip so that they were more like scalpels in a surgeon's hands than combat knives.

"Whenever you're comfortable," he said.

Dahlia began moving around him, creeping with utmost stealth. The boiler suit made soft noises, but she turned to Neeko and mimed clapping her hands. He grinned and began clapping with a rhythmic beat. The others joined in slowly, but soon everyone was smacking their hands together and the clearing was filled with so much noise that any rustle of the boiler suit was completely buried.

Dahlia leaned far over and tapped Church on the right rear shoulder blade.

She never saw the move he made. It was a blur and when he stepped back there was a blue mark on her stomach.

The clapping paused for a moment as everyone gaped.

"Don't stop," she roared at them, and the clapping was renewed with increased fervor. She moved and touched. He moved and marked her.

Over and over again.

It very quickly rose from exercise to frenzy, and her taps became hits. Or attempted hits. She struck and struck, and no matter how, or from what angle, or how fast, he reacted. Her rage and frustration rose together, throwing fuel on the fire in her chest. Finally, Dahlia screamed and swung a kick at him, trying to hit him in the groin.

He stepped into it and let the force of the powerful kick

expend itself on his thigh. Then he put the flat of his palm on her sternum and gave her a small push. There was no trace of emotion in it, and not even a lot of force, but the angle was good for him and bad for her and Dahlia fell. A sob broke from her as she landed hard on the ground. The noise from the Pack died immediately and there was silence everywhere.

Mr. Church reached up and removed the blindfold, blinking momentarily in the bright sunlight that slanted down through the trees. He fished his tinted glasses from a pocket and put them on.

"You cheated," she growled, but he waved that away as if it was nothing more important than a gnat. That made her madder, but then she saw that Neeko was staring at her. Not eye-to-eye, but at her stomach. She looked down at the red and blue marks on her boiler suit. They were not random marks. They were words. She twisted the material and cocked her head to read them and saw that they were not in English. It was a short phrase written in Latin. The son of a bitch hadn't just marked her, he'd actually written on her. She was so absurdly stunned that she could not move except to mouth the words. "*Dum spiro spero.*"

Dahlia could read it. Latin was one of her languages at school. Had she mentioned that in one of her conversations with the old man? Yes. Probably.

She spoke the English translation in a tight whisper.

"'While I breathe, I hope.'"

She remembered the lesson in school. The words combined ideas from two different philosophers, Cicero and Theocritus, and was thought to be paraphrased by St. Anthony.

Mr. Church came and squatted down in front of her. "Listen to me," he said gently, but with a voice pitched loud enough for the others to hear. "Listen. You've survived this long on a useful combination of wits and natural talent. That's good, but it's not enough. There are tougher and scarier things out here than you. I'm one of them. The dead are a threat, but there are people out here—living people—who are far more powerful, more frightening, and much more dangerous. If you ran into any of them, you'd be dead. You all would." He paused and gave her a tiny smile. "Lessons like this are frustrating and they're hard. They're supposed to be. I won't make them easier. You need to rise, become craftier, refine your senses, get stronger and faster, become wiser. If I didn't think you had that potential, we would not be here in this moment. If I thought you were just a thug, like your friend Trash, then you'd either be recovering from wounds received or be dead."

He rose and looked around at them.

"Understand this," he said. "I am not a nice man. I am not particularly patient and in no way forgiving. Not before the outbreak and less so now. I am not interested in whether you think these exercises are fair or fun. They are neither. I am not interested in complaints of any kind. If you have assessments, useful opinions, insights or ideas, then that door is always open."

He turned back to Dahlia.

"You make a lot of jokes about *Star Wars* and *Harry Potter* and *The Karate Kid*. I get them. Maybe if the world hadn't turned into a horror movie then they might be funny. They're not. They are both inappropriate and a waste of our time. Either discard them or find something useful in their themes to draw on. Stories often contain wisdom." When she began to speak he held up a finger. "We will do this exercise again, right now. You will do better this time. You'll endeavor to take your ego out of gear and stop pretending to be tough...and simply *become* tougher. Do I make myself clear?"

Dahlia got slowly, heavily, to her feet. The others sat in silence, none of them daring to speak a word or make a sound. She wanted to grab a knife and stab the old man. She wanted to tie him down and let the dead have him for lunch.

Instead, she unzipped the boiler suit and tossed it to him, then bent to pick up the blindfold so she could put it on again.

That night, they all crouched around a set of maps that Church spread out on the ground. Everyone had eaten and was full, and the firelight painted them all in soft tones of orange and yellow. The woods around them were pitch black, but there were trip wires everywhere, and noise-maker alarms to signal if the dead were coming.

The maps were marked with pieces of color-coded Post-it notes to indicate where pockets of resistance were or were rumored to be. He asked Dahlia a series of questions about how their Pack might approach each group, and why. The conversation went on deep into the night.

They did not see or hear the figure crouched high in a tree, his body covered with a black canvas tarp. The flickering firelight did not reach far enough to glimmer on the lenses of the high-powered binoculars. Trash watched the camp with cold eyes. Inside his chest was a heart grown colder still.

– 15 –

THE WARRIOR WOMAN

Rachael, Jason, and Claudia walked quietly behind the Happy Valley group as they led them toward their home. The man with the knife wound to the thigh was supported by the others, and Rachael stirred around in her emotions for some sympathy. Found a little; not a lot. Maybe once she saw how things were in their town she might carve off a thicker slice of compassion.

Beside her, Jason was visibly tense, prepared for a trap that never sprang, his eyes darting around as they traveled, hand practically glued to his knife hilt.

Rachael wanted to believe that these people were good people. That she and her friends had finally gotten lucky and this wasn't a trap. She wanted to create a community like the one John and Heather described, one where people could find a permanent home. Where they didn't have to constantly be on the run and fear for their lives. Where normality could resume.

She missed the mundane activities of her former life. She missed attending classes and going to work. Missed seeing her friends and having dinner with her parents. She knew she was never going to get that life back, but God damn it, she would make sure someone else got to have that life, even if she had to fight every orc on the east coast to do it.

Before long, the woods ended, opening out onto what had once been a beautiful area. It looked almost like a park, with large old-growth trees and hilly, grassy fields spotted with wildflowers. Closer inspection showed that the flowers were interspersed with tall weeds and bramble-bushes that made the going difficult.

"There's a road up ahead," John explained. "It leads into the community. You can't really walk through the field—we let it grow wild to discourage people and keep the monsters away."

Rachael nodded, following silently as they made their way down across the edge of field to the road. Beyond the wall of green forest was a wide space of cleared land and the walls of the town of Happy Valley. Ten feet high and the color of a sunwashed peach, those walls looked solid and reliable, as if to say that, yes, there is safety here. She could see a few guards walking along the top of the wall and standing on either side of a big double-gate that had once been decorative wrought iron but which was now backed by lashed timbers on the inside.

The open space was empty of orcs, which surprised her. No wanderers, no throng of them trying to claw their way in. Either the town was so remote that the dead simply had no reason to come here, or the residents were diligent about clearing them out. In either case, the residents of Happy Valley had managed to create the perfect siege castle, even if by fluke of nature. Rachael took mental notes. If they were going to build their community, they could learn from this.

The sun was low in the sky by the time they arrived, approaching a wide, tall wall covered in peach stucco bisected by a heavy metal gate. Rachael dropped back to have a few quiet words with Alice and Peter.

"We'll see if they have enough beds for all of us, and tomorrow you two can head back to Brett."

They nodded, and Rachael jogged ahead to catch up with John, who walked in the lead. "So tell me a little more about Happy Valley." She kept her tone light, going for casual curiosity.

John smiled at her. "Well, we have a great community, a lot of wonderful residents, and volunteers who make sure that everything runs smoothly. A lot of good people. We all look out for each other, make sure that we can continue the quality of life we once had, even if the world out here has gone to shit. Pardon my language."

"Do you know how many?"

John shrugged. "No clue. I don't think we've done a count lately, and even if we did, I don't have the numbers. Not my wheelhouse. Some people find us by accident, some on purpose. Some choose to stay, others leave."

Rachael nodded, looking up at the gate as they stopped. John called out to someone out of sight, and the gate rolled slowly open.

Heart pounding in her ears, she stepped inside after him, stopping to make sure that all of her team followed, nodding at each of them and smiling at Tommy, who still clung to Alice's hand like a lifeline. When the last of them entered, the gate rolled shut with a loud, somehow ominous clang.

Heather turned to the newcomers and smiled. "The council won't be meeting tonight," she said, "but we can get you some beds and a place to shower, and tomorrow we can show you around, introduce you. In the meantime, let's get you folks settled."

As the sun set, solar lights set in the ground glowed to life, giving the town a warm ambient glow and a feeling of home that Rachael hadn't felt in quite some time. Many of the residents of Happy Valley were out and about; families on porches, sitting at picnic tables or just strolling. Men, women, and children, clean and well-dressed, looking at the newcomers curiously, whispering among themselves.

Rachael suddenly realized just how out of place they appeared, with their tattered superhero garb and armor and swords, covered in dirt and blood and sweat. She shifted the bag on her shoulders uncomfortably, taking care to smile at everyone who looked her way, but she hadn't felt so self-conscious about how she looked since New York Comic Con, right before the shit hit the fan.

"Mommy! Daddy!" Tommy let go of Alice's hand and ran past Rachael to a young couple out in front of one of the homes. The worried frowns that had marred their foreheads smoothed out when they saw their son. The couple scooped him up, hugging him close and kissing his head over and over with frantic joy.

Rachael's heart hurt, watching that. As happy as she was for Tommy and his family, she would never have that reunion with her own parents. Tears pricked at her eyes, and she swallowed hard, looking down at the ground as she tried to compose herself.

A hand on her shoulder snapped her out of her unwelcome thoughts. Alice gestured toward Heather, who had stopped in front of a beautiful two-story house. A veranda wrapped around the front and the lawn was well-tended, with purple flowers creating a splash of color against the cream-colored outer walls.

"You can stay here tonight," said Heather. "There are enough beds for all of you."

Rachael looked up at the house, her eyes wide.

It was beautiful and perfect. Too beautiful. Too perfect.

It was the sort of home you aspired to move into one day with your family, back in the world before; not the sort of home people could have in the world now.

It felt…wrong.

There were three bathrooms in the house, all bigger than her college dorm room. Rachael finally chose one, stripped off her armor and clothes, piling them to the side, and turned on the shower.

It had been months since she had a real shower, and she would have settled for a cold one. So when hot water streamed out of the showerhead, Rachael nearly dissolved in bliss. She scrubbed herself down with lilac scented soap, watching months of dirt swirl down the drain.

Drying herself off, she felt like a new person. Giving her clothes the same treatment—at least as best as she could with hand soap—she wrapped herself up in an oversized towel the same cream color as the house, and picked out a bedroom, hanging her wet clothes over a chair.

Absently detangling her hair with her fingers, she leaned against the window, looking down at the street and the houses below.

This was what she wanted, a community like this that could thrive and survive. This is what they needed to build back home.

She was running. Running. She didn't know what she was running from, but she was running for her life. There was something chasing her, something fast, and she didn't know what it was, didn't want to wait and find out. It wasn't an orc, not if it moved that fast, but she knew that if she stopped she would die. She could hear Brett in the back of her mind, telling her to run, telling her not to stop. Suddenly the ground beneath her feet ended, and she was falling, falling, and it was dark, and she didn't know when she would hit the bottom.

Rachael sat up in bed with a start, dagger clenched in her hand, sweat beading along her forehead and dripping between her breasts, heart racing. It took her a moment to remember where she was. Sun streamed through her window—how could it be morning already?—and she lay in what was probably the softest bed she had been in since…well, maybe ever.

Breathing a sigh of relief, she put the dagger down, letting herself collapse back against the pillows.

A knock at her door forced her to leave the soft warmth of the bed, but she did so with a grumble, her bare feet padding across the plush carpet. Running her fingers through her hair to smooth the morning tangles, she opened the door a crack, remembering almost too late she was only in her underwear. Luckily it was Alice. Heavenly smells wafted through the inch opening.

"The council brought us breakfast," she reported. "They want us to arrive, without any weapons, in an hour."

"Arrive where?"

"Open the door," demanded Alice. "This is heavy!"

Rachael did so, stopping short when Alice offered her a large plate of food. Pancakes dripping with maple syrup and a bowl of fresh fruit. Rachael stared at the plate as though she'd never seen food before.

"Right?" Alice exclaimed. "They have eggs too, and toast with butter. I haven't had bread or butter in…well, it feels like forever."

After nearly inhaling the food, Rachael pulled on her still damp jeans and T-shirt, grimacing at the feeling of cold, soggy fabric against her skin but reveling in the smell of jasmine soap. Oh, to have clean clothes…Like much else in Happy Valley, it seemed too good to be true.

Heather waited for them downstairs, impeccably dressed in a floral spring dress that made Rachael feel like a hobo in her Batgirl T-shirt and worn jeans. Heather led them on a pleasantly meandering trip through the community to a sprawling building that screamed "country club," with beautiful orchards and gardens surrounding it.

"This is our community center and town hall," said Heather. "We have our own government now that everything else has failed. We have a mayor, Margaret Van Sloane, and a town council. It's all very proper…we had an election and everything. It really works wonderfully."

As they walked through the entrance of the main building, she looked through sparkling glass windows that overlooked the gardens and orchards where a good dozen or so people were at work trimming leaves, picking fruit, pruning flowers, and weeding.

The council was set up in a spacious room, a long table with eight chairs on either side running the length of it. The chairs were all occupied by men in slacks and dress shirts, and women in dresses similar to Heather's. A single chair sat at the head of the table, occupied by a painfully skinny woman; the kind of skinny that was once considered chic amongst the wealthy. Rachael stood at the foot of the table, Jason and Claudia standing beside her.

"Welcome to Happy Valley." The woman at the head of the table stood, offering them a tight smile that made Rachael think of Botox. "I'm Margaret Van Sloane, the mayor of this community. What brings you here?"

Rachael cleared her throat.

"Good morning. I'm Rachael, this is Jason and Claudia. We were looking for supplies for our group when we found Tommy. He'd gotten lost so we decided to help him find his way home. We came across some of your people looking for one of your men, Pat. Long story short, we talked, Heather and John said the residents didn't have much experience defending themselves, so we offered to come and spend a few days here to teach your people the basics."

"I thought John said there were five of you."

Rachael felt rather than saw Jason tense up beside her. "There were," she replied readily. "But they wanted to rejoin our group rather than come here so we parted ways back in the woods."

Van Sloane gave a small, satisfied nod.

"Well then, we will be glad for your help. Heather and John both maintain that you're very competent fighters."

"We just get a lot of practice," Rachael deflected the compliment awkwardly. "I'd rather be as lucky as you all, and not need it."

The mayor gave the same tight little smile she'd offered upon their arrival. "Regardless, you're welcome to stay as long as you'd like. And your friends as well, of course." She nodded toward

Jason and Claudia without really looking at them.

"You're welcome to use the house you stayed in last night for the time being. In time, if you choose to stay with us, we'll assign more appropriate quarters."

More appropriate how? Rachael thought. What she said, however, was, "Thank you. Please let me know when you'd like us to begin training your people."

"We can arrange some time tomorrow for you to start, see if anyone would be interested in learning what you have to teach. We have plenty of space where you can hold lessons." Margaret Van Sloane nodded to one of the other council members, an older man with a full head of silver hair. "Tony, make sure it's arranged. But, we won't keep you longer. Heather will be happy to give you a tour." With that, Van Sloane turned back to her council, clearly finished with the conversation.

Guess we've been dismissed, Rachael thought

Heather smiled, but it seemed a little forced. "Well, let me show you around." Once again Rachael and her friends trailed after her like ducklings, back out through the building and surrounding gardens and out into the development, where they were given a cursory tour of the town and amenities the community had to offer.

Rachael took quiet note, however, that armed guards were always around. They hung back and tried to look nonchalant, but she wasn't fooled.

She could understand it, though. Several citizens of this town had been injured by strangers dressed in—she had to admit—pretty bizarre costumes. Caution seemed entirely reasonable. Even so, she didn't like it and made sure to keep track of every guard she passed.

"Does anyone else see what I see?" Jason murmured to Rachael and Claudia as they entered another subdivision.

Rachael looked around, wondering what she was supposed to be looking for.

"I noticed it," Claudia whispered back, crossing her arms almost protectively over her chest. "I thought maybe it was just a fluke at first, but now I definitely see it."

Rachael scanned the area for any possible threats, finding none.

"What are you two talking..." Her voice trailed off as she finally understood what Jason and Claudia meant. "Oh."

They were on yet another beautifully maintained street where people sat relaxing on their porches drinking sodas, children played happily on well-manicured lawns. In stark contrast, a handful of workers were trimming some of the bushes along the sidewalk. As Rachael looked—really saw what was in front of her—she felt sick and stupid for not noticing it before.

While the happily playing children and lounging residents all wore clean, expensive looking clothes and looked like they'd just come from a hair salon, the workers were all clad in what looked like hand-me-downs, mainly jeans and plain T-shirts. None of their clothing was ragged, but the contrast between workers and residents was easy to see if one paid attention.

Everyone on the council, everyone relaxing and enjoying the day...they were all white. All the people working in the gardens or cutting the trees or cleaning the City Hall was a person of color. Black, Asian, Hispanic, Middle Eastern. All those lovely shades of brown skin doing the labor while the extremely white residents of town sipped their iced tea and flexed their toes in the green grass of well-manicured lawns.

Oh, this is bad. Rachael thought to herself, stomach roiling. *Oh, this is very,* very *bad.*

– 16 –

THE SOLDIER AND THE DOG

We spent more than two weeks trying to find Happy Valley. I scavenged a bunch of maps, but it wasn't on any of them in the area Abigail said to look. Which told me there wasn't actually a place called that, but was likely a development or gated community of that name. Likely a new build shortly before the dead rose. None of that helped. Would have been a snap with Google maps, but that ship sailed, caught fire, hit an iceberg and sank.

So I roved. Going where the road took me. Sometimes following instincts; sometimes following whim.

I found it by pure luck. I stopped for a night in what had once been a real estate office. Those are the kinds of businesses no one ever thinks to raid. No obvious stores of food, weapons, medical supplies or other things. No sign anyone had even slept there before me, except for animals. I killed some time sweeping out the manager's office and beat the cushions of a leather couch to make sure I wasn't going to lie down with bedbugs or lice. Then I made a fire in a metal trashcan and put a brace of fat rabbits over it to slow roast. While that filled the offices with a mouth-watering aroma, Baskerville and I prowled the rest of the suite of offices.

I found a file cabinet near the reception desk, bottom drawer crammed with boxes of power bars, two bags of Twizzlers, and several big bags of wrapped mints. I took all of that. Then I hit pure gold in a small breakroom. There were eight five-gallon bottles of spring water for the lobby cooler, and all the makings for coffee, including four pounds of bulk coffee already ground, and maybe six or seven hundred packs of Starbucks instant coffee, along with sealed bags of sugar packets and powdered creamer. I nearly wept.

So, I used another metal can to build a fire to boil some water and brewed some actual coffee. Nothing has ever tasted better in my whole life. I drank five cups. After a while my eyes were twitching and I was able to smell colors and taste sounds. Who cares?

I split the rabbits with Baskerville and after dinner I prowled the office again, hoping for more hidden goodies. There was no more food, but in the executive office, I found a handgun and a nearly full box of shells. It was a Springfield XDs 45 ACP. A small-frame gun, the kind useful for concealed carry. Decent stopping power but it's for up close and personal defense, and it has a single stack magazine that holds only six rounds. I didn't need another gun, but I took it anyway, because what I needed at that moment and what I might need later were vastly different things.

While I wandered the office, I thought about the cache of supplies I'd gotten here. If I could find a good-sized cart, like one of those big laundry hampers, all that spring water, the coffee and the gun might make a nice gift to bring to Happy Valley when I got there. Church would appreciate the gesture.

And that's when the universe decided to get weird on me. Not nasty weird, which is the route it usually takes, but downright coincidental to the point of being weird.

I looked up from the gun I'd taken from the head honcho's desk and there, on the desk, was a lease agreement for a two-bedroom, two-bathroom townhouse in Happy Valley.

I shit you not.

I set down the pistol and snatched up the lease, then went searching for a map. There were several and I matched the mailing address to the map and there it was. Maybe fifteen miles from where I stood. My heart pounded in my ears and I wanted to run for the door but did not. It was late, and there had been dead ones wandering around this little town. Morning was safer.

We left at first light.

There were only two of the dead in sight, both of them looking more confused and sad than scary. A teenage boy in sweatpants and Nike sneakers, and a bald older man wearing a hospital gown. Both of them had visible bites and were missing important pieces of meat. The fact that they were mostly intact was likely due to having been attacked by only one of the living dead. It takes a while to chew your way through healthy flesh. And for some reason I don't understand, the zombies stop eating shortly after a person dies, and won't take so much as a small nibble of their own kind. Maybe it has something to do with the way *Lucifer 113* was bioengineered. The parasites needed sustenance, but the imperative of the design was to attack healthy hosts and spread the disease. Before Dr. Volker changed it, the base bioweapon had been designed to have an enemy population infect itself in as short a time as possible, leaving the physical assets of buildings and resources intact.

When I think about that I wonder if we actually deserve to survive, and that somewhere Charles Darwin is spinning in his grave. The flip side of survival of the fittest is extinction of those who maybe should go into history's dust bin.

Cheery thought. Call me Mr. Sunshine.

The zombies weren't a threat to me, but I killed them anyway because they might be a threat to someone else. There was a lot of good stuff in this area, and survivors should have a chance to use it. I found my cart, though. A big landscaper's plastic bin that rolled on four low-pressure rubber tires. Good for hauling small trees with their root balls. Now it had as much bottled water as I could carry, and all of the damn coffee. And three paperback novels I found in the break room. One by James Moore, one by Christopher Golden, and one by Mary Sangiovanni. Horror novels, but hey...it was in keeping with the world around me.

We made a stop in a PetSmart and I loaded up with maybe a hundred pounds of canned dog food. I opened two of them for Baskerville and he was in doggy heaven. All of the bags of kibble had been torn open and devoured by rats and raccoons, but vermin still haven't figured out how to work a pull-tab. Also found a six-pack of light beer, but...fuck it...the world may have ended but I still wasn't *that* desperate. I left it in case a hipster had survived.

We headed west, going out of the small town and through farmland. According to the map, Happy Valley was not actually in a valley, which was one of the reasons it had been hard for me to locate. It was on a hill that backed up against a pretty steep mountain. There was a small river that came down from the mountain bringing snow melt, and the gated community was surrounded by a very dense and very deep section of protected land. No public roads passed it, and the only ways into it were two small private roads. One was a service road that wound around to the back corner and might as well have had "tradesman's entrance" painted on it. The other was a crushed shell road that was probably quite lovely once upon a time. Pink shells, lined with decorative stones. But it was not easy to find because someone had gone to great lengths to plant a bunch of fast-growing weeds and shrubs in front of the entrance, and over the last six months it had all grown wild. The decorative rocks had all been pushed aside and the shell gravel raked away. I found traces of it, enough to know what it had been.

"Someone's being very careful," I said aloud. A squirrel dropped an acorn on me. Not sure how to interpret that.

Baskerville sniffed around and seemed content that all was kosher, but then a breeze rolled our way from deep within the trees. The dog lifted his big head and sniffed it and immediately went into his aggressive fighting stance—wide-legged, head lowered, ears pivoting to hear everything, nose sniffing out the complexities of odor. I smelled it, too. A sickly-sweet stink I knew too well. Rotting flesh. But there was something else mixed in, an underlying strangeness or something.

The dead rot for a bit, but they don't completely decay. The genetically-altered parasites prevent that, keeping the infected in a state near death but not actually dead. You see, that's the thing. There are the living, the actual dead, and the living dead. It's a third state of existence. The body is in a semi-hibernative state, with all nonessential organs and tissues shut down so that the essential systems can stay online. There is actually some respiration and blood flow, though it is almost impossible to detect. Otherwise the zombies would have rotted to piles of goo within a week or two after the outbreak.

The upshot of this is that the stench of decay for them is different than that of an ordinary human body left to rot. It isn't as sweet because the parasites need the energy of those sugars.

The smell riding the forest breeze was very sweet. Which meant that it was not infected flesh. It could be an animal, although most animals have their own aromatic signature if you have the experience to discern one from the other. This smelled like human flesh.

I touched Baskerville's shoulder and bent low to whisper to him. "Find. No hit."

He was off like a shot. In the months we'd traveled together, I'd spent hundreds of hours teaching the mutt a lot of tricks. Verbal commands, finger snaps, and silent hand signals. He didn't yet have the vocabulary that my first combat dog, Ghost, used to have, but Baskerville was learning. He was a damn smart dog, and we were a pack now. As he vanished into the woods I took a moment to look around and let my own—admittedly less acute—human senses do their jobs. There were a lot of birds singing in the trees, including two noisy crows. There were no moans that I could hear; no voices or cries for help, either.

I left the cart where it was, loosened my sword in its sheath, and followed Baskerville.

The smell was too strong to have traveled far, and within a couple of minutes I came upon the big dog standing just inside the shadowy woods on the edge of a clearing. His ears twitched as I came up behind, but his eyes were set and fixed on what was inside the clearing. The smell was much stronger here, and now I could tell that there was more than one kind of rot troubling the air. The sweetness of human rot and the stranger, muskier stink of zombies undergoing their ultra-slow process of decay. The closer I got the more of that I smelled.

As I crept up behind Baskerville, I could hear sounds, too. Moans, but oddly muffled, and some creaking, rasping sounds. And the buzz of flies. Hundreds of them. Thousands.

Baskerville and I peered through a break in the leaves and stared into the mouth of hell itself.

– 17 –

DAHLIA AND THE PACK

Dahlia stood at the edge of the big clearing. Neeko stood facing her across the open space, and several of the others were there as well. A skinny black girl named Bailey; Pepe, a squat, broad-shouldered Chicano; and one of the last kids from Dahlia's old school, Skye. The interior space of the clearing was filled with all kinds of devices rigged by Mr. Church. Pieces of logs balanced by ropes, camouflaged pits, trip wires, and dozens of small targets made from paper plates dripping with fresh white paint. Control wires snaked out in all directions, each of them held by other members of the Pack. Scattered throughout the clearing were bundles wrapped in cloth or old newspaper. Weapons or other tools.

The exercise was a bitch. Dahlia and the others had taken a real beating during it several times over the last few weeks. She could still feel the bruises. And it was never the same way twice. So far none of them had gotten all the way through. There were no set rules except Church's expectation that everyone did it and anyone participating in the exercise try to get all the way through. No quitting.

Church did not give his combat or survival exercises names, but Neeko always did. He called the drill with blindfolds and Sharpies "Ghosting." This was the Arena.

"On deck," called Church. He stood just inside the wall of shadowy trees.

Dahlia eased forward into a crouch, exactly the way she'd been taught—knees bent, weight shifted to the balls of her feet and equally balanced, hands loose and ready, eyes focused on the whole clearing instead on any one object. A phrase hung in her consciousness. *Mushin no shin.* A Japanese word for "mind of no mind." It was a concept Church had been teaching them all. To be ready for anything while being without expectations or preconceptions. A pure, reactive state that allowed a warrior to fight the actual fight rather than what he or she expected. It was Zen, not Jedi, but it amounted to much the same to Dahlia. A mind trick.

She waited for the moment to tell her what was happening so that the long weeks of training could allow her reflexes and muscle memory to dictate how to move. It was even harder than it sounded.

"Go," said Church. He did not shout it. He said it quietly, almost conversationally.

Neeko and Dahlia moved into the clearing first, breaking right and left as they entered. The goal was to find a small bundle, the contents of which were different every time, and then escape the Arena with it intact.

There was a sound—a faint whisper of something—and Dahlia shifted, turned, ducked, then flattened completely as a branch was released from a tether and snapped through the air where her stomach had been. The painted plate missed her back by half an inch, and she immediately rolled sideways and came up fast, following the branch, grabbing it above and below the plate and giving it a savage wrench. The green wood cracked, and she spun off it to see Neeko twist himself nearly in half avoiding a bunch of small stones that fell from a net bag released by one of the Pack. One stone struck his forearm and he cried out but kept moving. The stones weren't soaked in paint, and therefore indicated injury but not an infected bite.

Pepe, Skye, and Bailey moved in now, treading carefully, looking for traps.

Skye made it three steps before stepping on something hidden under leaves. A pint of paint dropped from the "ceiling" onto her head with a heavy *splat*.

"Shit," she cried. Immediately the three Pack members closest to her side of the clearing began counting out loud. Infection was quick, and quicker still when someone was moving fast and pumping blood. Increased heartrate spread the parasites throughout the body too fast for amputation or any other preventative method. Church allowed them fifteen seconds in the drill, after which they would have to play zombie and try to attack the others. Before the world ended that would be a fun, if weird, game of tag; now it usually resulted in heavy bruising and the occasional broken bone.

Pepe grabbed her and shoved her toward a pair of paint-soaked plates hung on wires. Skye set her jaw, leaped at them and tore them down, bearing both to the ground so Pepe could run past her and get clear.

Dying are either a burden or an ally to the living. One of Church's many combat sayings. If a soldier was injured during a really intense firefight, then helping him would draw resources from the battle. A medic and stretcher bearers. Two to three soldiers. If the team was badly outnumbered and the injured person could somehow fight, then Church said they were obliged by honor to do so. The concept was horrific and made Dahlia sick to her stomach, but she knew that Church was right. Anyone bitten would become a zombie, sooner or later. There was no cure and no hope, so what was actually the most humane choice? To endanger others or save them?

She recited another of the sayings in her head as she moved deeper into the circle. *The war is the war.*

Awful, but true. And this was war.

Two branches suddenly broke free of their tethers and slashed at her, but Dahlia stepped into them, bashing one down with her left forearm so that the paint spattered the ground; and catching the other with her right hand and shoving it backward. She twisted it and broke the branch. Broke its neck. It sagged down and she moved. She had paint droplets on her, but not an impact splash. Not a bite.

"On your six," yelled Church, and Dahlia whirled to see three Pack members in white boiler suits come rushing out of the woods. This was new. They reached for her with hands that dripped with fresh paint. The attackers looked weird, too big, and she realized that they were wearing padding under their clothes.

Dahlia darted to the right so that she was on the outside of the line rather than letting them all come at her like a wave. She slap-parried a reaching arm and then stepped in and shoved the outside attacker with all of her considerable weight. Although she wasn't as heavy as she used to be, Dahlia carried a lot of mass, and beneath the fat there were newly trained and very tough muscles. The outside "zombie" crashed into the others and they all went down. As they fell she spotted a wrapped bundle on the ground. Not the prize, but a tool. She dove for it, rolled with a measure of grace, ignored the thump of her shoulder on the ground, and came up with the prize, whipping off the rags as she did so. Inside there was a plastic water pistol but it was nearly empty. How many squirts? Two? Three?

She brought it up and almost fired it, but stopped. Three squirts meant three bullets. Not a lot of ammunition but a lot of noise. With a growl she thrust the water pistol into her pocket, snatched up a piece of broken branch and ran over to where the three *faux* zombies were trying to untangle themselves. She jabbed the closest one twice on the back of the skull.

"Dead," she cried, and the zombie collapsed down.

Dahlia knelt on him and reached over his bulk to repeat the action with the second.

"Dead."

The third was thrashing and she hit him four times before she got good placement on the temple.

"Dead," she cried.

"Miss!" called Church. "The temple is lethal to humans, not to the dead."

She cursed. Church was always a stickler for accuracy. It wasn't just any part of the brain that killed the zombies; only a few specific areas would work. So she climbed over the two "dead" ones, ignoring the grunts and cries of the Pack-members inside the padding, pushed the third zombie's head down and stabbed really hard on the brain stem.

"Ow!" cried the zombie.

"Dead," yelled Dahlia.

"Don't wait for applause," said Church. "Move!"

She moved.

Everything in the Arena seemed to be in motion and she tried not to focus on any one part. *Mushin no shin.*

"Thirty," yelled someone, and suddenly Skye wheeled on Pepe and grabbed him. She bent forward to try and bite his neck, making it look way too real. Pepe howled in pain and surprise as he shoved her away, and then the Pack members began a new count. For him.

Then Bailey was there, and she had a ten-inch length of plastic garbage hose that was taped at one end. A training knife. She stepped up behind Skye, grabbed her paint-smeared hair, pushed her head forward and stabbed her four times in the back of the neck.

"Dead!"

Pepe was still standing there, a hand pressed to his neck. Red leaked between his fingers. Skye had actually bitten him. From the ground, Skye cried out, "God, I'm sorry."

Then another branch was released, smacking Bailey and Pepe both with gobs of paint. The Pack members howled and began counting in total confusion. Dahlia started in that direction, then spotted a large bundle on the ground.

Fuck, she thought, torn for a split second with indecision.

The War is the War.

She dove for the bundle as another branch whipped a paper plate at her. It painted a skunk-tail of white along her back, but there was no straight impact. Still no bite. She dropped to her knees by the bundle and snatched it up, surprised at how heavy and awkward it was. When she tore off the wrapping her heart nearly froze. Inside the bundle was a waterproof canvas bag filled with water balloons, and tied to the front of it was the plastic face of a doll. A baby. The water in the balloons was warm, and Dahlia immediate understood. This was a child. Alive.

God.

In that moment the bundle in her arms *was* alive. The part of

Dahlia that was the ironic and caustic chubby girl in high school wanted to scoff at the feelings that rose up in her. The aspect that was Dahlia, who created the Pack and survived the apocalypse, wanted to dismiss the bundle as a burden, as a liability.

But the version of Dahlia who was here now? The part that had chosen to step away from Trash and stand with Mr. Church had a completely different take. It wasn't any maternal gene kicking in. No, that wasn't her, and she knew it. Instead, she was feeling an urge that was both older and newer at the same time. It was the core survival instinct of the Pack needing to protect its own, particularly the young, because without babies the Pack died. Any pack, which is why everything from whales to wolves raised and cared for their babies. That was part of it.

The other part was the world was being emptied like a broken hourglass. If all the sands ran out there was nothing left to fill it. Time, at least for humanity, would end. Babies were proof of the potential to rebuild, regrow, reclaim.

And all at once Dahlia understood that this was the core of the lesson. Maybe of all of Old Man Church's lessons. Protect the Pack but also make sure it grew.

This chain of logic and analysis flashed through her mind in a microsecond.

Then Dahlia was moving, the baby tucked against her side as she angled toward the closest edge of the clearing.

"Neeko," she roared, and the little scout whirled away from a trap he'd just evaded. He saw her, saw the bundle, and as if a burst of telepathic communication shot like lightning between them, he nodded and ran to help her. Two more of the zombies in boiler suits rushed out of the woods, and as Dahlia turned to avoid them, Neeko—smaller and weaker than her—darted in, using his lack of size to evade grabs, and his thin limbs to whip out with his makeshift weapons. He had never moved this fast before. She had never run as fast. The tricks and traps of the Arena tried to kill them both. More zombies chased them. It seemed as if the whole world wanted to catch them, kill them, kill the child.

Dahlia felt herself shifting, transforming. She wasn't a kid anymore. She wasn't who she was before meeting the old man. She was pretty sure she wasn't who she'd been seconds ago. Somehow, she was becoming who she was going to be. If she lived. If they all lived.

She was fifteen feet outside of the circle, with a panting Neeko crouched beside her, before she even realized was safe. The moment froze.

She looked around and there was Church standing a few feet away. The man almost never smiled. But he was smiling now.

– 18 –

THE WARRIOR WOMAN

When Rachael cut their tour short, saying she needed a drink of water and some food, Heather seemed almost relieved to be done playing native guide. She pointed them toward, unbelievably, a coffee shop. "Just tell them you're new here and that the mayor will arrange for payment."

The three watched her walk off and out of sight before turning to look at each other.

"So I'm not the only one totally creeped out by this place, right?" Jason asked.

"Hell, no," replied Claudia. "There is something seriously fucked up going on here."

Rachael nodded her agreement. "Okay, this is what we're gonna do. I want to find out what I can about this place and what's going on here. I totally understand if you two want to hole back up in the house while I play detective. I don't want to put you in any situation here where you don't feel safe or welcome."

"I'd rather have them have to look at my face." Claudia's voice was cold as she watched a Hispanic teenager on his knees weeding while a white couple and their dog walked by as if he didn't exist. That was strange, because dogs were rare out in the woods. Orcs had eaten most of them and the rest were smart enough to stay away from anything that walked on two legs. This one, though, seemed like an ordinary pet. Strange.

"Okay then. I'm gonna check out the coffee shop. Do you want to split up?" she offered. They nodded, Jason and Claudia continuing up the street while Rachael went in the other direction, heading out of the subdivision toward the wall and the outer perimeter of the community.

The first person she ran into was John. *Jackpot*, she thought. Greeting him with polite—and fake—enthusiasm, Rachael thanked him for bringing her group to Happy Valley.

"I do want to ask though," she continued, pretending to be much less intelligent than she actually was. "What's the story with all the workers? I mean, you told us a little bit about how things work around here yesterday, but I'm still not sure I understand."

"Why, sure thing." John gave her a broad smile, seemingly forgetting she'd beaten the shit out of him the day before. "Most of the families living here were part of the original homeowners when Happy Valley was first built. The community wasn't completely full, but a good portion of the homes had residents. When things in the world fell apart, and it was no longer safe outside, it was decided to bring in as many people as we could support. Thing is, even when resources were stretched thin, we didn't want to turn people away who needed help. So, we offered to let newcomers work for us for an agreed upon period of time, to earn their place here or supplies, if they want to move on. If that's the case, we help them find a safe place to go." He smiled knowingly.

"How long do they have to work?" she asked with *faux* wide-eyed interest, the words "indentured servitude" running through her mind.

"There's not really a set time," John replied, "maybe a few weeks or a month or so. It really depends on the type of work, whether they want to go or stay. And if they want to join us permanently, we want to see how much they're willing to do to prove they're dedicated to the community. Now, if you will excuse me, I'm meeting my wife for lunch." He gave her a wink, and she smiled back.

As soon as he turned his back, her smile instantly faded and she slipped back into one of the subdivisions. She wanted to talk to one of the workers and see what they had to say.

It took a little while for her to find some workers who weren't under the watchful eyes of residents or the occasional security patrol, but she turned up and down a few streets until she found a small group of three men and two women taking a break from painting the exterior of one of the spacious homes.

"Hi there," said Rachael in friendly tones. All of them startled and jumped to their feet, talking over one another to apologize for taking a break.

Holding up her hands, she quickly said, "It's alright, I'm not a resident. I'm new here. I just wanted to talk to you for a few minutes, if that's okay."

Most of them looked uncomfortable, unwilling to meet her gaze, but one of them finally stepped forward, a young black woman. She had her hair pulled back into a bun, splashes of pale blue house paint across her cheek, a stark contrast against her dark beautiful skin.

"Can I help you, ma'am?" she asked in hushed tones, her nervousness palpable. Her gaze flickered left and right, as if scanning the area for possible observers.

"I just wanted to find out your story, how you got here, if you want to share." Rachael did her best to sound reassuring. "My friends and I are trying to decide if we're gonna stay here. I'm Rachael, by the way." She held out a hand.

After a brief hesitation, the woman took the proffered hand, gave it a quick shake and dropped it. She did not, however, offer her name. The woman shrugged. "I've been here since the cars died and everything went to shit."

"What happened when you got here?"

"They took all my stuff, my supplies, said that it was the price I needed to pay to enter, and that they'd let me live here for a while, stay here, and I would be able to work off the food they gave me and the supplies and clothes and shelter." The words poured out of the woman in a rush, like a stopper had been pulled out. "That it would probably only take a few months, that everyone who came in did it. And that once I worked it off, they would help me and my family find a safe place to go to where we could set up homes for ourselves, build a community."

"And that was six months ago?" Rachael asked.

"Yes, ma'am." She paused, shooting a dark look off into the distance. "They lied, I haven't seen anyone work off whatever debt these people claim we have. If anything, they keep saying us workers are using more than we're earning. That we need to earn more. Work harder."

"That's happening to all of you?"

The woman nodded.

"Why don't you just leave?"

"Where would we go?" She gave a harsh laugh. "And even if there was somewhere—"

"Paloma!" One of the other workers, a man who looked like he could be the woman's brother, shook his head and drew a finger across his neck. She caught herself and turned to go back to her work. Then she stopped and looked at Rachael once more.

"Better just to keep your head down, keep your nose to yourself. For us, and for you and your friends. You don't want them knowing you're poking around. You'll get us in trouble, you'll get yourself in trouble. And you don't want that, ma'am."

Rachael watched the workers all turn away, pretending she didn't exist, and her heart sank. This wasn't the world she wanted. Not at all.

– 19 –

THE SOLDIER AND THE DOG

There was movement in the clearing, but there was no threat.

Well, not an immediate one. So much was implied, though. I kept my palm resting on the handle of my sword, but this was less of a combat situation than it was a crime scene. I was a cop before I was a soldier, but really anyone could tell that bad things had been done here.

This wasn't a slaughter scene of the kind I'd seen a thousand times since the dead rose. It wasn't zombies versus human survivors. It wasn't gangs of roaming asshole humans doing harm, either. Seen enough of that, too.

No, this was something else. Something wrong in an entirely different way. Maybe something evil.

With Baskerville beside me I walked into the clearing and stood there, turning in a slow circle, trying not to vomit.

There were bodies there. Maybe forty of them. They were not sprawled on the ground as they might have been after a battle. There was no sign of a fight here at all. And yet there was violence and death everywhere I looked.

The bodies stood around me. They looked at me. They reached for me with withered arms and grasping hands. Their eyes stared with that grotesque blend of vacuity and hunger.

They were all zombies.

They were all tied to trees.

But it was worse than that.

None of them could open their mouths. Not to scream, not to moan, not to bite. You see, someone had made that impossible. There were ropes or belts or strips of leather tied around their heads, the loops under the chins and neat bows or shiny buckles on the crowns of each head.

Ropes lashed them each to a separate tree, with coils of it around waists and chests, leaving the legs free to kicks and stamp, and the arms free to...

To do what?

I stopped by one of them—a woman of about thirty, with long black hair and Mexican features. I studied every detail and the more I looked the more bizarre the evidence became, painting a picture that was as strange as it was hideous.

There was blood caked on her hands; dried now but clearly having run red and thick from the smashed fingers and metacarpals. Edges of bone stuck out through the skin and blood had crusted thick around them, dried now to a chocolate brown. There were bloody scrapes all over her face, and more blood on the ropes that held her to the tree and on the heavy leather belt cinched tight to keep her jaw shut. Her dead eyes were filmed over with a blue-white mist, but I swore I could see the last fading echoes of the panic and terror she'd felt as she died.

There was not a single bite on her that I could see. Not one.

The zombie thrashed and flopped and struggled but she was powerless to do anything. Not a goddamn thing. And instead of feeling scared by it, I felt a trapdoor of sadness open up in the bottom of my soul. Her smashed hands reached for me but there was so much damage to nerves and tendons that even if I was closer she couldn't have grabbed me. She couldn't do anything.

"I'm sorry," I told her. There were mad lights in her eyes. Most people say that once a person turns there is nothing at all left of them inside. I don't believe that. I think it's far, far worse than merely having died of an infection and then having your body reanimated and hijacked by genetically engineered parasites. That kind of thing should, by any measure of reason, be worst case scenario. It wasn't, though. Lingering self-awareness was so much worse, and I thought it's what I saw; but there was no way to test the theory. There was no way to reach from where I was to where she was. No way on earth.

I turned away. Call it grief or cowardice or the impotence of being unable to help. I moved from one to another to another of them and saw the same thing in each case. The hands were mangled. Smashed. Fingers broken and twisted. Wrists cracked. None of them had bites. All of them were injured, though. I could see evidence of broken noses, cracked and broken teeth, bruises that were faded now to black smudges beneath leathery skin, broken bones, facial trauma.

But no bites.

The math was scaring me. It was making me sick, too. I counted them. I was wrong about there being about forty. There were fifty-three of them. They were thin, wasted, but their clothes were the wrong size for people who had been skinny. These people had been starved.

No. That's imprecise. These people had been starved to death. They had been left to die out here from starvation and exposure.

But it went deeper than that. It was worse than that.

Those broken fingers that reached for me but were unable to grab. Those broken hands. I could feel my mouth go dry. There was no other possible answer than the very bad one that was banging around in my head. Whoever had brought these people out here had crippled their hands and then tied them to these trees. They left their arms free even though there was no way these people could untie themselves or even remove the bindings on their heads to allow them to scream. It wasn't just murder, it wasn't just physical torture; these people had been left here to suffer. This was about torment.

All of these people had died in hunger and pain, in terror, surrounded by proof that no one else was coming, that no one else had escaped. The enormity of it was staggering. It was one of the most awful things I had ever seen, and I have seen humanity at its worst.

I wanted to throw up, but I forced it back down.

One of the dead was dressed differently than the others. He wore a heavy leather jacket with silver studs, and had leather pads on his knees and elbows. A biker, I judged. He had an enormous black beard and a crooked nose and looked like someone who, in life, was probably extremely dangerous. Now he was wasted and covered in bites and there was a lingering expression of desperation and fear on his features. I felt bad for him. I felt sick for all of them.

Baskerville must have caught my mood because he stood next to me, growling softly. He wasn't directing it toward the thrashing corpses. He kept looking into the woods, and I realized that he was studying a narrow path of beaten grass that wandered between trees and vanished into shadow. In the direction of Happy Valley.

"Well, well," I said, but my voice sounded wrong. A little too calm. A bit too ordinary. That was never a good sign. I took a couple of determined steps in that direction, but then I stopped as something occurred to me. I turned and stood looking at the dead faces.

The unlife that is the effect of *Lucifer 113* tends to make the skin pale and leathery, creating a kind of homogenized sameness to skin tone. But it's not really the same. The gray pallor is more often a product of dying skin cells and accumulated dust. Beneath it are the remnants of actual color. White and yellow, brown and black.

Except when I looked around me, I didn't see any zombie who looked like they might have been white. I saw two Asian faces and a whole lot of shades of brown. Latino and African American.

None of them were white.

Which meant what?

Could those Nu Klux Klan sons of bitches have a chapter out here? Or was it something else?

One thing I knew for sure was that if Mr. Church was anywhere around here, he would not have let something like this stand. No sir. Which meant that either he wasn't at Happy Valley or he wasn't able to stop this kind of savagery. Either way, I had to find out.

I clicked my tongue for Baskerville and we faded into the woods. Hunting for more than answers.

– 20 –

DAHLIA AND THE PACK

Days became weeks. And Dahlia became something else.

She knew it. She could feel it happen.

After that one afternoon in the Arena, something inside Dahlia shifted. Maybe inside a lot of the others of the Pack, too. Outwardly she looked the same—big boned, carrying a lot of weight and a lot of curves, lots of black hair. But the eyes that looked back at her from the mirror each morning were different. Older, maybe, though not in years. Or, maybe it was that she looked wiser. If that was something that could show in the eyes. There was less outward fear, fewer flickers of uncertainty, and more visible confidence. All of that.

Some sadness, too. Dahlia missed Trash so much. She missed what he could have become if he'd stayed and learned from Old Man Church. Trash's own father had been a brute, and that's the lesson about manhood he'd learned. Church was so different. So much stronger, but he didn't reek of testosterone and anger. Dahlia liked who she was becoming, but it was hard to go there alone. At night, alone in her bed, she ached for Trash. For the surprising gentleness of which he was capable when no one else was looking. Of his kisses and the way he touched her—with strength but with respect, his big hands gliding over her skin rather than grasping or grabbing.

Where was he? Was he even still alive? There hadn't been a single sign of him, or of the others who went with him. Serena and Nathan, and a handful of others from the Pack. The rest had stayed, waiting for Dahlia, and then joining Old Man Church's little army.

Now, the Pack really *was* an army. Fit and fast, coordinated and efficient. Neeko, freed from his fear of the older and bigger Pack members, had proven himself to be a good fighter and a natural leader. Church taught him a lot of useful skills about tracking, spying, gathering intelligence. Neeko's group—which now ran under the nickname of Bravo Team—had found more than a dozen groups of survivors. Some of them were part of Church's army, while most had been sent on—provisioned and with reliable maps—toward Asheville. With every life saved, Neeko seemed to swell, to become physically larger and more self-assured. Dahlia asked Church about that one morning while the two of them were out on a patrol in the deep woods.

"It's validation," said Church.

Dahlia frowned. "Of what?"

"Of himself," he said as they began climbing a steep hill. He moved well for his age, but she could see that he moved with care. "Neeko hasn't received a lot of support in his life; he was never properly nurtured. Abusive homes are like that. He was told that he was worthless so often by the authority figures in his life that he came to accept that as an inarguable truth." Church took hold of a sturdy maple sapling and used it to pull himself up onto flat ground. "You started that process, Dahlia. You trusted him as a scout and praised him for the things he did right."

She scrambled up after him, only slightly winded from the climb. Beneath her extra pounds was a lot of useful muscle. The weapons and tools she wore were all in padded holsters or sheaths, and Church had taught her how to move through the woods without making noise or leaving sign of her passage. She felt a little like a girl version of the ranger, Strider, from *The Fellowship of the Ring*.

"I was hard on Neeko when he screwed up, though," she said.

Church shook his head. "From what he said, you corrected him pretty sternly, but there's nothing wrong with that. You needed him to be safe and you wanted his intel to be accurate. That's discipline, not abuse."

She started to argue, but let it go. She never won those kinds of arguments with the old man. They moved deeper into the woods. Old oaks and sycamores rose high above them and the air was filled with bees and butterflies. Clouds hid the sun and cast the forest in a softness of gray-brown shadows.

"Neeko will continue to mature and grow stronger," Church said after a moment. "I have high hopes for him."

"He deserves to survive," she said, and was surprised at her own words.

Church turned to her. "Most people deserve to survive," he said. "More importantly, most people deserve some measure of enduring happiness. Even now. Even after all of this."

Dahlia studied him for a long while. "You don't look happy."

Church turned away. "I said that most people deserve happiness. Not everyone."

She asked him what that meant, but he didn't answer. Instead they walked for nearly an hour though the forest. Finally, he checked the angle of the sun and told her to continue the patrol while he went back to camp to give another lesson to the some of the newer recruits.

When she was alone, Dahlia felt strangely vulnerable and had to work to shake that off. It was easy to lean on Church, or lean close to his power, and she did not want that. Nor, she suspected, did the old man. He wanted her to be strong and self-reliant. Sometimes that was like pushing a rock uphill. Easy at first, but every time she paused for a breath it got heavy and wanted to roll down.

Like her ego. Like her feeling of personal power.

She spent a little time mentally telling herself to grow the fuck up and get a fucking clue.

Then she began moving through the woods again.

Beyond a stand of trees ahead of her there was a patch of brighter light. Not sunlight, but less of a canopy of leaves to block the glare from the cloudy sky. Dahlia removed her compact binoculars and adjusted the focus, seeing a patch of dusty black. A road. When she shifted the binoculars again she saw that there were three figures on that road. People...though it was impossible to tell more than that.

Dahlia nearly cried out when she saw them, and if the sound had escaped it would have been a scream. She bit down on it, clamped it in.

213

Trash was there.

He was *right fucking there.*

Talking with two other people. She wanted to keep staring at Trash, but she forced herself to follow her training. *Learn everything about a situation that you can,* Church had told her. *Don't be distracted by any one thing.*

So she forced herself to study the other men with her former lover, and Dahlia immediately felt a sudden coldness grip her. The men were older, in their thirties, dressed in camouflage clothing that had a military or paramilitary feel to them. Lots of gun belts with bulging ammunition pouches; lots of knives. Lots of guns. Each wore at least one holstered handgun and held automatic rifles. One had a combat shotgun slung over his shoulder. They looked hard and *hardened,* as if the end of the world had driven them away from all traces of ordinary humanity. Their eyes were cold, their mouths smiling but without humor. One of them, a big man with enormous shoulders and what looked like shrapnel scars on his face, wore a necklace of some kind around his bull neck. It took Dahlia a long time to understand what was wrong with the necklace. It was big and chunky, set with oversized and unusual stones.

Except they weren't stones at all.

She tightened the focus on the binoculars and stared in horror.

The necklace was strung with human ears.

Forty-one of them.

The man to his right wore a similar necklace, though his was made up of thumbs. Some of them looked fresh. Dahlia's heart hammered in her chest. She stared through the lenses at the grisly objects. If the world was still kind, if the world had not torn free of the hinges of sanity, then those trophies would have all been caked with blood that was as black as night. With the blood of the dead.

But the world was offering no mercy that day. It offered no kindness and the very air seemed to babble with madness. The blood—dried now to a chocolatey brown—was not from the infected. It was human blood.

Then the day, already spiraling down toward darkness, got so much worse. Trash said something to the men, then turned and pointed into the woods.

Pointing to where Old Man Church's camp was.

Pointing to where Dahlia lived.

– 21 –

THE WARRIOR WOMAN

Rachael thought they'd found a model for heaven in the World After, but instead she found hell.

Catching back up with Claudia and Jason, Rachael had filled them in on what she'd found out and they'd shared their own grim stories. They'd managed to talk to more than one of the non-residents; evidently their own skin colors made it easier for the workers to trust them. With each new story things got worse. Rachael felt sick. Finally she walked with her friends back to their temporary home, but after grabbing her dagger and tucking it into her belt under her shirt, she told them she was going out again.

"I want to see if I can talk to Tommy's parents."

It took a little wandering to locate their home again, but she found Tommy outside drawing on their walkway with colored chalk. He gave a friendly wave when he saw her. Ruffling his hair, she asked, "How are you doing, kiddo?"

"I had a bad dream about the Apple Man," he said sadly, but then shrugged, going back to his chalk drawing, the trauma of the previous day easily forgotten.

His father answered the door, a handsome Caucasian man in his early forties. There were some soft lines at the corner of his blue eyes and hints of gray beginning to shade his temples. He looked untouched by any of the horrors outside the walls of Happy Valley.

He frowned when he saw her. "Can I help you?"

"I'm Rachael. My friends and I brought Tommy home yesterday."

At that, he smiled and shook her hand emphatically. "You're the girl who saved him! I'm Will Manners. Please, come in. My wife will want to thank you."

He gestured with one arm, waving her inside. She stepped across the threshold gingerly, feeling out of place as soon as she entered. A beautiful grandfather clock, expensive pieces of art, and artfully arranged flowers decorated the interior, and that was just the entrance hall.

Brushing her wavy brown hair out of her face, Rachael looked around with a smile, putting on a pleasant mask to disguise her feelings.

She followed Will through an extravagantly decorated living room to a large kitchen, all black granite and stainless steel; marveling at how neat and clean everything was. Too clean, especially for a family with a child living in a world at war with the dead.

A petite blonde woman, hair in a perfectly trimmed bob, was at the sink, arranging flowers in an Oriental vase. She turned as Will and Rachael entered, face registering polite surprise at the presence of a stranger in her kitchen.

"Will?" she asked, confused.

"This is Rachael, Abigail. She's the girl who saved Thomas."

Abigail Manners nearly knocked Rachael over with the force of her hug. Tears welled up in her large blue eyes as she squeezed Rachael tightly. "Oh, thank you. Thank you! You saved our boy…you saved my Tommy. How can we ever repay you for what you did?"

Rachael patted her back awkwardly, not sure how else to handle the crying woman. When Tommy's mother finally released her from the hug, Rachael said, "I have a few questions about Happy Valley and was hoping you could answer them for me."

"Oh, of course! Please, sit down." Abigail gestured to the dinette on the side of the kitchen, carefully set with more flowers.

Rachael nodded graciously and took a seat, smiling her thanks as Will set a bottle of soda down in front of her, popping the cap off it, and one of his own before sitting across from her. Abigail sat down next to him, grabbing for his hand and holding it tightly as if she was afraid to lose him too.

Both of them looked as stereotypically upper-class suburban as Rachael could imagine. Will in his striped polo and pressed khaki slacks, Abigail in a soft pink cardigan over a white blouse. These were people accustomed to comfort, to a certain standard of living. She doubted they'd last a day outside the walls of Happy Valley, though one thing that Rachael had learned over the last six months was that people could and would surprise you.

She thought about what Paloma had told her.

People could and would surprise you, for good or for bad.

"So what can we do you for?" Will asked in a hearty voice that grated against Rachael's ears.

"I'd really just like to know how you like living here. Are you some of the original residents?"

"We are indeed," Will said proudly. "Happy Valley has been around for nearly a decade. It was built as a community for residents who were looking for a safer way to live, away from the hustle and bustle of cities, but without being strictly rural. It was a nice, safe place to live. It wasn't always as self-sufficient as it is now. Most things were brought in via delivery. Most of the shops we have now, for instance, are old homes or community buildings that we repurposed. But it's always been a little piece of heaven, especially for those of us who were trying to find a way to leave the city life behind us."

"Will used to work in New York City," Abigail offered, "but we moved here when he got the opportunity to switch careers. I never wanted to raise children in the city, and Happy Valley seemed so perfect. So many good people, and so safe, especially compared to the high crime rates and bad schools in the city."

Rachael nodded. "And after everything happened, I'm sure it seemed like it was meant to be."

"God, yes," Abigail exclaimed, "it was like it was destiny. The world presented us with a problem, and Happy Valley was the answer. We could stay in our homes, safe, and surrounded by good people we trust. We had a variety of people with different skill sets, and they figured out how to set up gardens and generators and water purifiers. It's such a lovely, safe community, filled with good people."

"What about the workers?" Rachael prompted.

"Sometimes people make their way here, either because they've heard about us in passing or find us by providence," Abigail replied, scratching at the back of her neck absently. "We don't have a lot of space or extra supplies, but we do what we can in exchange for an honest day's work."

"That's right," said Will. "We offer them jobs, temporary assignments, so that they can earn a wage, pay for supplies, and sometimes in exchange for safe passage to another community we have a few miles away. It takes a lot of energy and manpower to get them safely there, but we're willing to do it, provided that they put in the work to earn it."

"But you don't make the residents work?" Rachael asked, staring at the Mannerses unblinkingly.

"Why would we?" Will seemed genuinely surprised. "They're all good people who worked hard to be here. This is their home, and we're the reason it's safe to live in Happy Valley. The residents are the reason we've all been able to survive. These people are given food, shelter, and safety. We just ask that they earn it."

"With hard labor," Rachael said quietly.

"They're allowed to work for us. I mean, it's the least they can do in payment for us saving them from what's outside."

"What if they bring supplies with them? Wouldn't that mean they don't need to work as hard since they're contributing to the community?"

"When they come in, we ask that they turn over the supplies that they have, which is the basis of their debt, if you will, with the community. As they work, more value is added to that tab based on the jobs they do; the amount of time they spend working. If they cause any destruction of property or disturb any residents, then a penalty is taken out. It is all part of an agreed upon contract. It's all made very clear from the start." Abigail's voice grew strained, agitated under Rachael's steady gaze. "We just don't have the space for just anyone to come here and be a resident. The person would need to show their true value to the community, prove that they are a good person who can contribute to Happy Valley."

Rachael sipped her soda, thinking of the seemingly empty homes she'd noticed during their tour and subsequent explorations.

"For example," Abigail continued, "for everything that you did for us, for saving Tommy...Will and I would speak to the council, and you could live here without needing to work off anything. Happy Valley could be your home, just like it's ours."

Rachael pretended to think for a moment.

"And my friends? Could they live here too?"

Will and Abigail looked at each other.

"They would need to work for a place here, just like everyone else." Will finally said, shifting uncomfortably in his chair under Rachael's gaze. "They would need to prove they're good people, prove that they're a good fit for our community."

Rachael could hear the meaning behind his words loud and clear.

She could stay because she was white. Because she was useful and fit their image of what they wanted for their "perfect" home. Her friends, who were as capable as her, but with darker skin tones, were not welcome to become residents. Only indentured servants like the rest.

– 22 –

THE SOLDIER AND THE DOG

We moved as quickly as safety allowed, and both of us were good at that sort of thing. I have hunted a lot over the years, and mostly my prey has been other people. As it was now.

Baskerville went wide and ran parallel but a little ahead, sniffing out our trail, following the scent of the last person—or persons—to have visited the clearing where all those people were left to die. I followed, checking the landscape for trips and traps. Finding none even as we got closer to Happy Valley. That troubled me, because any community of people surviving in a world of the walking dead should have set traps. Tin cans filled with stones strung on wires would be enough; a simple sound alarm that the dead would be too stupid to avoid. There were also spots that were natural observation points—sturdy trees where a deer-stand could be erected, knolls where a fortified sentry post could command a view of the surrounding woods. Like that. I saw none of it.

What I did see as I reached the edge of the densest part of the woods, was a walled town. A big, sprawling, gated community with a ten-foot-high wall, probably cinderblock, covered in peach-colored stucco. There was razor wire along the top and I could see sunlight sparkle on a thousand tiny points, which I took for broken glass set into the cement. When I pulled my binoculars to take a closer look I was amused to see that the glass was all in decorative colors. Clearly a design feature of the original build rather than something added later. Besides, broken glass wouldn't deter the dead. The razor wire wouldn't do much, either.

I knelt in shadows between lush trees and scanned everything I could see. There were heavy gates fifty yards to my left. And when I zoomed in on them I could see a very expensive security box. Digital and thumbprint scanner, I thought. Inoperative now, but suggestive of high-income residents. The place was remote, though a highway was moderately close, and—according to the map I'd found—so was a heliport, a small private airfield, and a regional rail line. Over the top of the wall I could see a lot of trees, though some of them looked prematurely withered, and the upper floors of two and three-story McMansions. The architecture looked modern. Maybe two or three years before the outbreak. Not older. The wall, too. This place had been built as a retreat for the very wealthy. That much was obvious.

Had it protected them? Time would tell.

I wondered how they were surviving, though. Where did they get the resources to sustain a community? It was impossible to tell from where I knelt just how big the community was, though it looked sizable on the map. Did that mean there was arable farmland inside? Were these wealthy residents really tilling their own fields? It seemed unlikely, though before the End Junie and I visited an intentional community in Central California made up of upscale organic farmers and artists. Was this like that? A place that had been built as a sustainable village before the need for such a thing became absolute?

A lot of questions.

"Come on, fuzzball," I said softly to Baskerville as I started to rise, but then I saw him staring intently off to my right, and I settled back down. "What are you seeing, boy?"

His answer was a low, soft growl.

I trained my glasses on the vista, scanning the walls of the town, the open space between that and the woods, and then the tree-line itself.

That's when I saw them.

Four men knelt in shadows very much as I was. They were rough-looking characters dressed in leather and denim, with lots of knives and guns at their hips or slung across their backs. Two of them had binoculars and were intently studying Happy Valley.

I made a small hand sign to Baskerville, telling him to scout quietly. He was off in a flash, but for all his bulk and armor, he knew how to move like a ghost when he wanted to. I put my binoculars away, loosened my sword in its sheath, checked the magazine in my sidearm, and followed.

The watchers were pretty intent on studying the town, but it didn't mean they were oblivious to everything else. Caution has kept me alive all these years. Knowledge of how to move through the woods the right way has always been key. There's a way to do it right. You listen to the woods. They're never actually silent, and quiet is relative.

Once you open up your senses to the life of a forest, you begin a conversation. You listen in order to learn and form opinion, but you have to be careful not to allow assumption or judgment. Truth is absolute in the natural world. However, you need to interpret the truth and understand it. There is no guile in the way tall grass or leaves move in a breeze; there's no lie to the way mud dries around a footprint or how crickets react to the presence of things that frighten them. If you are experienced and passive, you can hear sounds that don't belong and see things that are out of place.

The reverse of that is to move in ways that are in harmony with the natural world. If you don't want to be seen, move in the way the forest moves. Walk no faster than the breeze and when it stops, you stop. Find places to step that won't easily take a footprint. Look for things on the ground that will crack under your weight. Consider how well your clothing and face and equipment will blend into the existing landscape.

I knew how to do this. It's kept me alive, allowed me to hunt, kept the dead ones from spotting me, and brought grief to people I don't like.

The four men watching Happy Valley did not hear me. They didn't see me. I stood beside a tree ten feet from them and they had no idea. Baskerville lay in the tall weeds eighteen feet behind me, and they had no idea. The wind was blowing the wrong way for them to hear us approach or smell us.

I watched them. Learning them.

Two of them were twenty-somethings with lots of colorful

tattoos. Naked women, monsters, cartoon characters. One guy was in his thirties and was obviously a hardass biker type. Less expensive tattoos, including some amateur shit. Symbolic more than decorative. Scars and hard hands. But it was the fourth guy who interested me most. He was late forties and had a body that looked like it was made from bundles of piano cable and roughly smoothed rock. His face was like an eroded wall. Some Native American blood, I think. Or Russian. Mongol eyes in either case. A long beard that was prematurely white. Prison tats everywhere, and tear drops on his cheek. I could only see him in profile when he turned to talk to the others. That was enough to let me know a few things. He was the leader of this crew and he was the most dangerous. If it came to a fight, I'd kill him first, and kill him quick, because guys like that are dangerous as long as they can still draw breath.

Not that the others were sissies. Even the younger guys looked like they knew how to dance.

What troubled me most was what they were wearing. Not the clothes, which were somewhere between *de rigueur* biker gear and retro Mad Max stuff. That was fine. When so many things want to bite you, leather was a smart choice. No, what drew my eye were the necklaces they wore. The younger guys each wore human fingers strung on leather. The thirty-something had noses on his. And the older guy had scalps on his. Yeah. Actual scalps. Maybe fifteen or twenty of them. Strung with beads and a few feathers.

Holy shit.

They spoke together in low tones. The younger guys whispered, which is stupid. Whispers carry because of the sibilant "ess" sounds. The older guy was smarter and spoke quietly.

"Four per shift," he said. "Three shifts a day."

"They're keeping watch," said one of the younger guys.

"They're being stupid," said the older guy. "They got all those people and they have the guards working full eight-hour shifts. Use your damn brain, Chickie. They don't know we're coming, so they're probably bored as fuck by now. Two, three hours into each shift and they're getting distracted. Five or six hours in and they're either not paying attention at all or out on their feet. That's when we move."

"Why not wait until, like, seven hours in?" asked Chickie. "Won't they be more tired?"

I expected the older guy to give a harsh answer, but he fooled me. It was obvious he was schooling the younger guys. "Nah," he said, "seven hours in and they're starting to count down to end of shift. And they wouldn't want to risk dozing off then because they'd get in the shit with whoever their boss is."

The others nodded. I had to agree. That was a reasonable assessment.

What I couldn't see yet was where these guards were that they were discussing. Then I saw it when one of them moved. High on the corner of a wall was a small shed-like guard tower mostly hidden behind the leaves of a big sycamore. The tree blocked the tower from sight until one of the men inside opened a kind of hatch and poured a bucket of water over the edge. Probably from a chemical toilet. The grass below the tower was all withered and dead.

With the hatch open I could just about make out other figures in the shed. Three of them. Two men and a woman, sitting on folding chairs. Pretty sure they were playing cards.

"Fucking clown college," said the older man. "Their line of sight's for shit and they got Dumb and Dumber standing guard."

"You got that right, Snail," said the thirty-something. "They might as well just hang out a welcome sign for us."

"Pretty much what they're doing," said the older man, Snail. He looked up at the sun. "Getting late. Let's boogie."

They backed into the shadows before they stood up. I stayed right where I was and they passed within five feet of me. I could have taken them right there. Hit them hard from one side and let Baskerville close the trap from the other side. And maybe I should have. The nature of gathering intelligence is that you have to understand the larger picture and I didn't want to fall into the assumption trap. Sure, they were hardcases and their necklaces were not the post-apocalyptic version of Boy Scout merit badges. That said, it didn't mean they were actually evil. Maybe the trophies came from zombies they'd killed. I couldn't tell without a closer examination. For all I knew, they could be rough-edged good guys working to protect a group of travelers. Hell, from any distance I looked like rough trade myself.

Add to that math the bodies in the clearing. I couldn't easily concoct a scenario where these guys were responsible for that. Some of those people had been there for a long time, and if these men were just now assessing the sentry patterns, then it seemed likely they were newcomers. Which meant that the people on the other side of that wall could be bad guys.

Maybe, maybe not. They could have put those poor bastards in the clearing as a warning. Each of those zombies could have been a scavenger or some other kind of bad guy, and the clearing could be a place of public execution. Harsh, sure, but these were End Times. Harsh seemed kind of ordinary.

In either case, I didn't know enough to warrant action. I won't take a life based on an assumption. So, I let them pass.

When they were gone I walked over to where they'd been and stood for a while in the cool shadows. Baskerville came over and sat nearby, watching the path the men had taken. He didn't like them worth a damn, that was obvious.

One thing occurred to me. Something that the librarian, Abigail, said. I couldn't recall the exact words, but she'd mentioned gangs of rovers. That clicked with a bit of information from way back before the End, when I was a cop in Baltimore. There was a biker gang known as *the* Rovers. They were a real bad bunch, too. Well known for violence and brutality on a scale that made other gangs steer clear. There was even a case once where seven members of the Warriors, another biker gang, had been murdered in a drug deal gone bad. The right hand of each of the murdered bikers was missing and never found. The detectives working that case concluded the hands were taken as trophies.

Trophies. Like ears, noses, and scalps?

Could Abigail have been referring to a specific group rather than making a general comment? If so, were these boys part of that old gang? Too many things lined up all at once for me to dismiss the possibility, and that included my own gut instinct.

Which meant they were probably bad guys after all.

Even so, they hadn't killed those people in the clearing. So... what in the wide blue fuck was going on out here? I glanced at the peach-stuccoed walls, with the incompetent security and the strange goings on in the nearby clearing. I did not believe for one second that Mr. Church was in Happy Valley.

All sorts of emotions warred inside my head and heart.

I clicked my tongue for Baskerville and together we faded into the woods. We'd found people. Now we wanted answers. And maybe we both wanted some blood, too. Seemed about the right time for that.

– 23 –

DAHLIA AND THE PACK

Dahlia found Church cleaning up the equipment after a training session. Neeko and some of the others were limping off to recover from a grueling combat drill. Church turned before she could call his name and stood waiting, frowning as she came close.

"What's wrong?" he asked.

Dahlia was winded and had to take a moment to catch her breath. The extra weight she carried helped her in fighting, but it was not her friend in a flat run through the woods. Sweat streamed down her face and throat, and her clothes were pasted to her.

"Tra—Trash," she gasped.

Church glanced around to make sure no one else was close, then guided her to a pair of camp chairs. She thumped down in hers and gratefully accepted a canteen. After three gulps her throat felt less raw.

"Tell me," said Church, and she did. The frown he wore deepened as she described the men Trash was with. When she was done he had her go through it again, slowing down, describing everything in minute detail. By now she was used to this. Church was all about the details. What he called "deep intelligence."

When she was done he sat back in his chair and was quiet for a moment, then he nodded slowly. "I expected them to come this way soon, but I thought we'd have at least another month."

"Wait…you know those guys?"

"Not specifically," said Church, "but I know *of* them. They called themselves the Rovers. The core group used to be a biker gang."

"Sure," she said, "I heard about them. On the news, I mean… before. They were always in trouble for something. Drugs, I think."

"Drugs were a big part of their activities," agreed Church. "They also trafficked in arms. Gun, explosives. Civilian and military grade. Selling to other gangs, to organized crime outfits, and to militia groups from Pennsylvania to Mississippi."

"They sound like a bunch of assholes."

"What they are," said Church, "are extremely dangerous. They are organized, ruthless, and efficient. The fact that they don't have working motorcycles anymore does not decrease the threat they pose. If anything, it increases it because it makes them more localized. And it has turned them into scavengers as well as predators. Call it a locust mentality. They have been attacking settlements, camps, and refugee centers. I've seen what they leave behind." He paused and looked into the forest as if he could see the Rovers. "They are the reason I've been training the Pack so aggressively. Fighting the dead is bad, but doing so requires a smaller skill set and it is, as you often put it, 'rinse and repeat.' The dead don't learn from experience. The Rovers do. And they are both merciless and unforgiving."

And Trash is with them…" breathed Dahlia. "Oh, god…"

"You said that he pointed in the direction of this camp?"

She nodded. Tears stung her eyes, but she tried not to let them fall. She didn't want to cry. Not for Trash. Not if he had joined a group like that. And yet...maybe he didn't know who they were. Or how bad they were. Maybe they tricked him somehow.

"Dahlia," said Church, and she looked at him. His eyes, even mostly hidden behind the tinted lenses, were intense. "Listen to me," he said in a voice that was kind but not soft. "I know you love Trash. You've never said as much, but trust me when I say that I know the look of heartbreak. You've been very brave because you're the leader of your Pack, but I know that you're hurting. And I know that you're holding hope inside. You want Trash and the others to come back to the Pack. To come back to you."

She brushed at her eyes but did not trust herself to actually reply. He nodded anyway.

"Trash made his choice. He could have stayed with you and with the Pack. He could have joined what we're building here, but he chose not to do that. If he has thrown in with the Rovers, then you have to accept the possibility that he is lost."

"No..."

Church took both of her hands in his. The silk gloves he wore were cool and the fingers beneath them as hard as iron. "A war is coming. I've been preparing for it since I first learned about the Rovers. I've fought a lot of wars in my life. I will fight this one and I intend to win. I am going to tear the Rovers down. I intend to end them. Do you understand what that means? It means I'm going to war under a black flag. With people like them there is no chance of a reconciliation."

"Doesn't that make you just as bad as them?"

Church's mouth hardened. "Does it? By what logic? No, I want an actual answer. How does killing a monster make you a monster?"

"There was that old saying, from...Nietzsche, I think. Something about 'If you fight monsters you become one.'"

Church sniffed. "Nietzsche is often misquoted and nearly always misunderstood. What he said was: '*Beware that, when fighting monsters, you yourself do not become a monster...for when you gaze long into the abyss, the abyss gazes also into you.*' His words were a caution, but he wasn't speaking in absolutes. The logic many people infer from that quote is that if you do monstrous things you will inevitably become a monster, but that isn't so. Are you so close-minded that you think every soldier who has ever killed for his or her country immediately and irrevocably became a monster? That the act of killing makes everyone irredeemable?"

"No...that's not what I..."

"You're a very smart young woman, Dahlia, but even smart people can be lazy in thinking. You are speaking from a place of hurt and fear, not from a distance that allows for insight and understanding. Consider...when this war happens, Neeko will likely have to fight and he may have to kill. Will that condemn him to a changed nature where he will be defined only by what he had to do? Shouldn't he be viewed through the lens of context? If he kills to prevent the Rovers from raping, brutalizing, and killing many others, does that truly make him as bad as them?"

Now she was crying. Slow tears fell crookedly down her cheeks as she shook her head.

"Wars are fought by *people*," said Church. "Some of those people become monsters. A few. Not all. Not most. The rest...? If they're lucky, they go home to be with the people they fought for. They find a way to lay down their weapons and most of them manage it. And although they carry some scars, in flesh and soul, they are allowed to stop being soldiers." He paused and tilted his head to appraise her. "Tell me...do you *want* to go to war with the Rovers?"

"God, no!"

"Will you if they attack this camp?"

"Sure, but—"

"Would you step in to fight them if you saw them raiding

one of those caravans we sent to Asheville? The one last week, for example. There were sixteen children under ten, and eight people over seventy. If the Rovers were trying to murder them and the only thing you could to do stop them was to kill them all…would you?"

"That's not fair."

"Of course it's not. Answer the question, though."

"Yes," she snapped. "Yes, I'd kill them. To save all those little kids, of course I would, but that's my point. It makes me a killer."

"Ah," he said, smiling sadly, "that is where you're wrong, Dahlia. The killers are the ones who choose to do that. If you chose to stand between the helpless and people who wanted to harm them, even if you were forced to kill, it doesn't define you as a killer."

"Yeah? Then what the fuck does it make me?"

"It makes you a warrior."

She stared at him, and the word seemed to burn in the air.

"Warrior…?"

"Oh yes. A soldier follows orders, right or wrong. A warrior, a true warrior, steps into harm's way to save the lives of those who cannot defend themselves." He released her hands. "I'm teaching you how to fight, how to kill, but I have no intentions at all of turning you into a killer. Even if you kill a hundred of the enemy. I want you to *live*, Dahlia. When I'm gone you will need to lead your Pack, and you will need to transform it into a community. Maybe into a nation. But before we can rebuild the world we have to preserve it."

He stood.

"The Rovers are coming for us," said Mr. Church. "The difference between them and you is that they *want* a war. They *want* to kill."

Dahlia got to her feet. The tears were hot on her cheeks but she didn't wipe them away. "What…what do you want me to do?"

Her voice was shaky, her heart was breaking, but she stood firm.

"Gather the pack," said Church. "Call in the scouts. We need to find out how many are coming."

"And then?"

"And then we pick where *we* want to fight. They have numbers and there is an arrogance that goes with that. You are a woman, most of the Pack are kids. I'm an old man. If Trash has told them about everything, then that is what they will expect to find. It is not," he said, "what they *will* find."

"No," she said.

"What is it they'll find?" he asked.

"Warriors," said Dahlia.

Mr. Church pulled her close nd hugged her.

"Welcome to the war."

– 24 –

THE WARRIOR WOMAN

"We are getting out of here." Rachael's voice was low as she handed her extra knives over to Claudia. "I don't want the town to decide that we've outstayed our welcome as guests and decide we need to participate in their fucked-up work program."

It was past midnight as Rachael, Claudia, and Jason loaded up their weapons and bags onto their backs, strapping down anything that might make noise so they could move as stealthily as possible. The town was dimly lit at this hour, something Rachael hoped would work to their advantage. The solar lights along the edges of the sidewalks glowed softly, providing just enough light to navigate by.

She'd spent most of the afternoon and early evening unobtrusively spying to see how regular the guard shifts were, where they patrolled, and if there were any weak points they could use in their favor. There were. For instance, the town seemed to rely primarily on sheer dumb luck. There were only two guards monitoring the main gate at any given time. These were apparently the only jobs they didn't trust to their non-resident workers, instead relying on a steady stream of volunteers from their community residents.

The walls of the community were high, at least ten feet, higher than any of them could climb without aid, but Rachael had paid attention to where the ladders the workers used were stored, and she had an idea.

She just hoped that some of the town's dumb luck would be on their side tonight. They were going to need it.

The three of them left the house, well-worn boots falling softly on the grass and pavement. They kept to the deep shadows between houses, ducking into the darkness at any signs of movement. The streets were pretty much deserted; most of the town was already asleep, preparing for a new day.

The storage building was adjacent to the country club turned city hall. A risk, but a calculated one, and one that Rachael hoped would pay off. She sent Claudia and Jason to the east wall where they'd wait for her, and she would meet them by the side gate. It was further out of their way, but the further away from the front gate, the less chance of them being spotted.

She wound between the buildings, keeping to the darkness, eyes darting for any signs of movement, of life, of danger. The town was silent, eerily so, but no one seemed to be awake in this section.

Good.

The storage building bordered the road that led to the city hall. It was small and unassuming except for the large padlock on the front. Rachael crouched down and studied it. She'd learned how to pick locks years ago for her LARP character, but she was out of practice and didn't have the right tools with her. She was going to need to rely more on brute strength.

Pulling one of her throwing knives from her belt, she jammed the tip into the lock, rocking it back and forth, lodging it in, before twisting sharply, trying to jam the lock.

"Fuck. Work!" she grunted under her breath, forcing all of her strength into the knife.

Rachael froze, heart pounding as a sound carried to her ears. Was there someone there? The hairs on the back of her neck stood on end, along with the certainty she was being watched.

She looked around, eyes darting to all the darkened windows and long shadows. She couldn't see anyone, but that didn't mean anything. She needed to work faster.

She tried again, but the knife gave, bending against the force and snapping the tip of the blade off in the lock. Cursing softly, she threw the knife into the grass and grabbed her big Elven dagger. Lodging it between the lock and the door, she braced herself and pushed.

The clank of the metal latch snapping sounded like cannon fire to her ears, and Rachael froze, holding her breath, heart racing wildly. Surely someone had to have heard.

But ten seconds passed, then twenty, and no one appeared, so Rachael pushed open the door and grabbed the largest ladder she could find and a bundle of rope. Gripping the ladder tightly under one arm, she bolted for the wall as quickly and quietly as she could.

She found Jason and Claudia, crouched and tense, in the shadows by the east wall. Rachael could almost feel the fear and tension ripple in the air around them.

"Ladder," murmured Rachael. Jason raised it and placed it quietly against the wall, extending it as high as she could. There was still a good seven-foot gap between the top of the ladder and the top of the wall, and her heart sank as she thought about the drop on the other side.

Jason seemed to read her mind. "Parkour?" he asked with a strained smile. Rachael nodded, tying the rope to a sturdy sapling and handing it to him, hoping it was long enough to help them slide down to safety.

Jason climbed the ladder first while Rachael held the bottom steady, hoping their luck would hold. She hadn't heard any sounds, but the voice in the back of her mind that had saved her many times in LARP was sounding warning alarms now. Something was wrong.

Rachael watched nervously as Jason reached the top of the ladder. He was tall, a little over six feet, with wiry lean muscles that allowed him to pull himself to the top of the wall easily. He dropped his bag and the rope over the other side as Claudia began to climb.

Claudia was six rungs from the top when Rachael heard the incoming footsteps behind her, the sudden flicker of a flashlight throwing long shadows across the wall.

"What the fuck do you think you're doing?" The shout came from a few feet away.

"GO!" she screamed as Claudia reached the top, arms outstretched to Jason. He grabbed her hands, pulling her from the ladder rung to help her scramble to the top of the wall, handing her the rope to climb down the other side.

Rachael turned before they dropped out of sight, her Elven sword already in hand, threatening. She had to squint into the glare of a flashlight. "Back off right the hell now," she snarled. "Just let us leave and no one gets—"

She barely caught the blur of movement as someone swung a heavy rake at her. Rachael brought her blade up to try and parry it away, but the edge bit deep into the wood and she nearly lost the weapon. The attacker tried to use the opportunity to pull her knife from her hand, but even half-blinded, Rachael pivoted and kicked out. The flat of her heel hit something solid and the attacker sagged back, losing his grip on the rake. Rachael freed her weapon with a deft snap of her wrist.

Then she spun and dropped into a fighting crouch, legs spread, weight shifted onto the balls of her feet, ready for anything. Three more flashlights flared to life and she was completely blind now.

She never saw what it was that knocked her legs out from under her. Maybe a shovel, maybe an axe handle. Whatever it was whipped her feet into the air and then she was down, landing flat on her back. Too hard, too fast, no chance at all to break her fall. The air was knocked out of her lungs and she made a scream like a dying rabbit as she tried to suck some oxygen.

"This is for you, you fucking bitch," growled a man's voice and she had the briefest image of a thick boot moving toward her face. The kick knocked all the lights out of the world and Rachael plummeted into a bottomless pit of darkness.

– 25 –

THE SOLDIER AND THE DOG

I didn't catch up with Snail and his crew of spies, though I found a spot on the dirt shoulder of a feeder road that showed clear signs of bicycle tires. Still biking, though not in the same thunderous style. Whatever. Bicycles were practical, they didn't need gas, and they were quiet. I gave Snail some grudging points for that.

Baskerville and I scouted along the road in the opposite direction, following where the road arced around to the far west corner of Happy Valley, and there we got lucky.

Three bikes were set against trees just off the road and loosely covered with leafy branches. Enough cover to keep away nosy humans, and totally indifferent to the dead. Not that there were a lot of zombies in the area. No real reason there would be. I hadn't seen many homes or farms within miles, which meant that population was pretty thin on the ground to begin with. Maybe any stray walkers had been cleared out by either the Rovers or the residents of Happy Valley. There were some bones in the weeds, including skulls that displayed clear head trauma.

The bikes were in good shape and the branches had been only recently cut. I let Baskerville sniff the seats and handle-grips of each bike and then told him to find. I gave him the verbal command to find only. Not "find and own," which would have left me no one alive to chat with.

Baskerville crept off, sniffing the ground, picking up speed as he locked onto a scent. I followed at a light jog-trot, conserving my wind in case there was a fight.

It took my dog twenty-four minutes to find the Rovers. They were crouched down behind a Lexus that had burned to a shell. Like the other crew, they wore too much leather and had grisly trophies around their necks—ring fingers, big toes, and ears.

It's hard to develop warm fuzzy bunny feelings about guys like that.

The sun was rolling toward the west and the shadows were getting long. I didn't want to waste what was left of daylight watching these three sit and scratch at flea bites. I was about to do something when they rose and turned and began walking back through the woods. I ghosted them. As they began pulling the foliage away from their rides, I came up behind them, drew my gun and stood with it in a very comfortable and steady two-hand grip. Close enough for easy kills, too far for them to make any sensible moves.

"Yo," I said, "assholes."

They whirled, reaching for their guns, but then froze. I was really close and I had them dead to rights. Anyone could see it.

"Do something stupid and I will kill you," I said.

They looked scared and confused. Only one of them looked dumb enough to try something.

"Lose the hardware," I said. "Do it slowly and do it now."

"Who the fuck are—"

"I'm the guy with the gun," I said, cutting him off. Then I clicked my tongue and Baskerville trotted out of the woods and came up to them. He is a really big fucking dog. The armor and spikes and all make him look like a gargoyle, and not a happy one at that. He seemed to sense which of them was twitchiest and looked him right in the eye. Sure, they all had weapons but they also had no chance at all.

"Take your pick. Bullet in the brainpan or have your nuts torn off." I smiled. "Third choice is taking your weapons out with two fingers and dropping them on the ground."

They hesitated for one moment longer, but then one of them—the leader, I later learned—said, "Do it."

His men disarmed, and they made quite a pile of goodies. Guns, hatchets, skinning knives, combat knives, a couple pairs of wire cutters—probably for taking souvenirs—and one old pineapple-style World War II hand grenade.

"Listen to me carefully," I said. "If even one of you is jerking me off and trying to hide something, I'll kill all three of you. Take a moment and then make the right decision."

The asshole who looked like he was going to try something flushed and removed a knife from a concealed sheath in his boot.

"Nice," I said, and shot him through the face. The bullet exited through a big and messy hole and struck a tree across the road. The shot was loud but hollow, as gunfire outside usually is. The echo bounced off the trees and vanished into the sky. Even if someone heard it, there was little chance they'd be able to accurately determine where it came from.

The other two men cried out and started to move, tried to catch him, almost ran, and all of it at once, meaning they accomplished nothing.

"Why...why...why...?" stammered one of the others. "The fuck you shoot him for? Donny did what you said."

"Not the first time I asked," I said. "Let's all take that as a teachable moment."

They stood rock still and gaped at me, caught between the gun and the dog, with all of their options leaking out of Donny's head.

"Now, here's what is going to happen next, kids," I said. "You're going to take your belts off and let your pants drop around your ankles. No, don't look at me like that. This isn't that kind of weird. Belts off. Good. Pants down. Now, take your belts and wrap them around your pants, knot them up tight and cinch the buckles. Make a good job of it or I'll have Baskerville bite something off you don't want to lose."

The dog gave a deep-chested *whuff*.

I watched as they followed my orders, creating a useful version of leg irons. Sure, they could get out of it, but not quickly.

The younger of the two wore stained blue boxers; the other guy had the nastiest, clingiest pair of tighty-whities I'd ever had the misfortune to see.

"Guess we're all happy neither of you decided to go commando today," I said. They looked down at the ground, too scared and embarrassed—and confused—to say shit. I crossed my legs and sat down ten feet from them. Baskerville sat so close to the older guy that hot slobber fell on the man's thigh. I told them to sit, and they did. "Let's play truth or dare. Rules are simple. I ask questions and you give me absolutely true answers. Full and complete answers. And don't you *dare* fuck with me." Flies were beginning to buzz around Donny's head, which added eloquent emphasis. They both nodded.

"First," I said. "Names."

"Barry," said the younger guy. "Barry Niles. People call me Diver."

"Why? You skydive or skin-dive?"

He colored. "It's, um…"

"He's a muff diver," said the older guy. "Can't get enough of it. Always smells like pussy."

"Fair enough," I said. "What's your name?"

"Loki."

"Real name?"

"Left it behind a long time ago," said the older guy. He was about forty, with red hair and green eyes and a knife scar that bisected his left eyebrow.

"Okay," I said. "Loki was the god of mischief. You planning on trying something clever?"

"No," he said, then in case he thought I wasn't going to believe him, added, "No, sir."

"Good. Next question. What's the name of your outfit?"

Loki paused for a heartbeat and then said, "Rovers. Pittsburgh chapter, and some others."

"Thought so. Who's running the Rovers these days."

"Dude," said Diver, "he'll cut our nuts off if we—"

Loki turned to him. "Shut the fuck up, dumbass. Grown folks are talking here." To me he said, "Same cat who was riding first bike before the biters ate everyone. Big Elroy."

"Never heard of him."

"You will," said Diver. "You shot Donny and—"

Loki turned and punched Diver in the side of the head. Really hard. The lights in the younger man's eyes dimmed for a moment. Baskerville shot to his feet and was about to take a bite out of the older man, but I snapped my fingers.

"Enough," I said sharply. Diver clutched his head and moaned. "Loki, keep your hands to yourself. And Diver…? Next time you open your mouth it better be to answer a question or it won't be your friend here who clobbers you. I'll blow your kneecaps off. Both of them. Want me to do that? No? Then mind your fucking manners."

I gave them a minute to get their shit together. Then I gave Loki and Diver a nice, big smile. The big hunting cats smile like that. Or so people have told me.

"Now, fellas," I said, "what's your interest in Happy Valley?"

− 26 −
DAHLIA AND THE PACK

Dahlia and Neeko moved through the woods together. A small two-person scout team.

Old Man Church had sent them out to gather intel while the rest of their friends packed everything they could and began the process of moving the camp. A lot of things would have to be left behind, but there was nothing that could be done about that. The presence of the Rovers, and the betrayal of Trash, made haste more crucial even than the bulk of supplies.

Before they left, Dahlia said to Church, "Maybe the Rovers will see all the stuff we're leaving and just be happy with that."

"Is that what you think?" asked Church, "or what you hope?"

When she didn't answer, Church gave her shoulder a reassuring squeeze and sent Dahlia on her way. That had been three hours ago and the brief conversation was still sticking pins in her. She *wanted* to be right. Was there something wrong with wishful thinking? Was it wrong to hope for an outcome that didn't involve fear and fighting and horror?

Neeko, sensitive to her mood, kept cutting her looks but didn't actually say much. They kept walking. Dahlia tried to keep her head in the game, but that's the problem with emotions like heartbreak; it's an easy set up for distraction and for failure.

"Well now," said a voice from off to their left, "will you look at this shit right here."

Dahlia and Neeko jolted to a stop and turned toward the voice.

They were there. Five of them. Three men and one woman in their thirties and one woman in her late forties. All in leather. All of them smiling in ugly ways.

Rovers.

"She's cute," said one of the women. She had a muscular body and a face made of sharp lines and no softness. A leather cord was strung loosely around her neck and from it hung more than a dozen human ears. "Dibs."

"Fuck that," said a tall, lean man with filthy dreadlocks and a necklace of little fingers. Three of them looked like they were cut from the hands of children. "I saw her first."

"Yeah, but I called it first, asshole."

The others laughed, and the man relented. "Okay. But leave something for me."

They all thought that was funny, too.

"Wh-hat d-d-d-do you want?" asked Neeko, but he tripped over nearly every syllable.

"Wuh-we whah-want duh-do wuh-we whah-want?" mocked a short, blocky guy with Asian eyes and bleached blond hair. "Tuh-take a guh-guess."

Dahlia held up her hands, palms out. "Look, we don't need to do this. Just let us go and we'll be out of here. You'll never see us again."

That was apparently hilarious to the Rovers.

"Hey," said Dahlia, "we're leaving some supplies behind. A lot of them. I'll tell you where they are, okay? That's fair, right?"

The second woman, who was in her late forties and wore a pair of eyeglasses that had been repaired several times with tape, shook her head. "Sorry, honey, but that's not how it works. I mean, sure, you *will* tell us where the stuff is, but it's not going to buy you a Get Out of Jail Free card. You do know that, right? I mean, you're not actually stupid." She paused. "Are you, Dahlia?"

Dahlia stiffened at the use of her name, and it tore a small cry from Neeko.

"How...?" she began but didn't finish. There was only one way they could know her name, and it was as obvious as it was awful. "Trash," she breathed.

"Trashy-boy is our friend," agreed the woman with the glasses.

"He told you about me?"

"Hell yeah, he did. Told us all about all ya'll. That little shit is either Mince or Neeko. Probably Neeko. He's a scout and you think you're Queen Shit, am I right?" The woman seemed very happy and she beamed a great smile. "Dahlia the Pack Leader. Dahlia, the fat girl with a knife who thinks she's the baddest bitch in the apocalypse."

Dahlia's heart was tearing loose from its moorings and sinking in her chest. She wanted to throw up. She wanted to kill Trash. She wanted to crawl into a hole and die.

Instead she drew her knife.

It wasn't the one she'd used to fight her way out of high school a million years ago. This was a heavy-bladed *kukri* knife, the signature weapon of the Ghurkas of Nepal, one of the fiercest fighting forces in history. Mr. Church had taught her how to use it, showing her how the weight of the blade could be used to generate a lot of whipping speed, and how it could be used to cleave through bone. Dahlia always liked knives, and that one seemed to want to be in her hand. It came alive when she drew it and maybe she did, too. What had the woman called her? *Fat girl with a knife. Had those really been Trash's words?*

Dahlia was heartsick and terrified. Once the handle of the knife was seated into her fist, the blade curving outward with its graceful and deadly elegance, the fear seemed to recede.

"Get behind me," she said to Neeko, and Dahlia barely even recognized her own voice.

Neeko didn't move.

The five Rovers laughed. At her. At the fat girl with the weird knife.

And then she was among them.

– 27 –

THE WARRIOR WOMAN

The first thing Rachael was aware of was the wrongness.

She was in darkness and yet moving. She was not walking but her feet were moving. She was in pain.

A lot of pain.

Her head felt like it was broken. Cracked. Shattered. There was warmth on her cheeks and in her hair. Blood. She blinked, trying to clear her eyes, but there was so much blood there, too, that for a time she was blinded.

"She's coming out of it," said a voice. Her traumatized brain tried to tie the voice to a name, a face, but there was something wrong with her memory. Pieces of it seemed to have been hammered into meaningless shapes or broken off entirely. She wasn't entirely sure she could recall her own name. However, two other names floated through the churning waters of her thoughts.

Jason.

Claudia.

Who were they?

She wished the world would stop moving so she could pull the cracked pieces of herself together. If they would stop dragging her along she could figure it all out and...

Dragging.

Yes. She was being dragged. There were hands under her armpits. Strong hands. She understood now that two men were half carrying her and that the toes of her shoes were scraping along over dirt and grass.

Jason. Claudia.

Suddenly the question was no longer who they were, but *how* they were. And where. With that Rachael felt herself coming back. All at once she knew who she was.

She also knew how much trouble she was in. Happy Valley. The slave labor. The escape attempt. The kick to the head. All of it. Her eyes were still caked with blood, but from the sounds and the grunting effort of the men as they hauled her over rough terrain, she reckoned she was outside.

Why, though? What was going to happen out here? Were they going to kill her? Rape her? It had to be something serious, otherwise they'd have simply tossed her outside the walls, slammed the gate and be done with it. This wasn't expulsion, it was...

What?

Abruptly she was released and falling. She landed hard and badly, and the impact with the ground tore a cry from her. One of the men laughed.

"Yeah," he said, "she's awake. Good."

Rachael felt sick and weak and knew that was from the kick to the head. In the old movies the heroine could get knocked out and then wake up ready for the next big action scene. Not in the real world. Trauma severe enough to knock her out did damage. The muscles and tendons in her neck hurt abominably, and there was a persistent ringing in her ears. She lay where she'd been dropped and brought weak hands up to paw the muck from her eyes. The world emerged. Daylight. Blindingly bright; she winced and hissed as if scalded, turning her head to the side to avoid the glare.

That's when she saw the dead people.

So many dead people.

Orcs and…others. Some of them simply dead. But it wasn't actually simple, was it? No, she told herself. This was wrong in a lot of very bad ways.

The corpses were tied to posts, straight poles with crossbars that stood all of the dead up like a grove of scarecrows. The corpses were in horrible shape. Emaciated, starved; their faces marked by their screams and suffering. She turned to see them, to see all of those faces. Every one of them had died hard out here. Many had been fed upon, with parts of arms and faces and bodies eaten away. Others slumped down in final, total defeat; unmarked by bites but clearly dead. On some of those, Rachael could see single post-mortem wounds from where someone had quieted them. A small mercy. A very cold comfort.

Then she saw two figures lashed to crossbars who were still alive.

God, she hoped they were still alive.

Jason.

Claudia.

Covered with blood. Strung up like scarecrows. Like sacrifices in some bizarre and perverse ritual. Other people—townsfolk—were finishing the process of tying their arms and legs.

"They look pretty," said a voice behind her. "Don't they?"

Rachael turned her head, which was enormously painful to undertake. The two men who'd carried her stood there. One was coiling a length of rope. The other was lighting a cigarette. He grinned at her through the smoke.

"What the fuck are you doing?" growled Rachael, but it came out hoarse and weak.

"Maintaining order," said the man. He took a deep drag and exhaled blue smoke into the air. "You and your friends could have had it all. Clean beds, food, shelter. Instead you had to go and piss in the punchbowl. You're too stupid to even know when you're on top."

The man with the rope smirked. "I'd like to be on top of her," he said.

The other man took the cigarette out of his mouth and

pointed to the other four townsfolk. "You do that shit again, Kyle, and they'll dime you out to the mayor. Miss Van Sloane doesn't like it when we get grabby and you damn well know it. Or do you want to spend another week shoveling shit alongside the helpers?"

"Might be worth it," said the second man, eyeing Rachael. "Look at the cans on her. Bet she be—"

Rachael kicked him in the balls.

She kicked him as hard as she could, and he doubled over, eyes bugging, a thin whistling wordless howl bursting from his mouth. She wanted to kick him again, harder, but a wave of dizziness and nausea slammed her back onto the dirt. The other four townies turned and came hurrying over, demanding to know what happened. The man who'd been kicked was entirely unable to manage a single articulate word.

The guy with the cigarette waved the others off. "It's nothing. Kyle was making a joke and this little slut tried to get cute. Come on, help me get her up."

They left Kyle on the ground and the five others crowded around Rachael, swatting aside her attempts to punch and kick, howling and cursing when she slipped one in. They slapped and punched her and finally dragged her by sheer force to her feet and as a group hauled her over to an empty post. She screamed and tried to bite them, but there were five of them and one of her, and they won.

Rachael never stopped fighting, though. Not for a moment.

– 28 –

THE SOLDIER AND THE DOG

In stories about heroes the good guy is often hamstrung by a moral dilemma. He knows he *should* kill the bad guys when he has a chance, but he has this code. Like Batman and the Joker. Batman's supposed to be a champion of moral behavior, his being a violent vigilante notwithstanding. He won't kill the Joker even when that psychopath tells him he should. Instead, he locks him up in Gotham's prison or in Arkham Asylum, both of which are notorious for the frequency of super villains escaping. And the result? Batman feels smug about making the good moral choice, and then gets to wallow in self-absorbed angst when the Joker breaks out and slaughters a shit-ton of people. I bet some comic book scholar actually took the time to tally up how many people died because Batman didn't use the razor edge of a batarang to end the reign of terror. Numbers are likely in the five digits. And don't get me started on Superman.

Me...?

I'm not Batman or Superman.

Once I had all the information the Rovers were likely to give me, I killed them. I did it quick and efficiently. No torture. Just a flip of life's fragile little switch. They begged, of course, but aside from not being a superhero, I'm not a judge or jury. They were making a plea to the hangman.

Any twinges of regret? Sure. I'm not inhuman. But I did the math and decided that, thin as the human population was right now, we didn't need them in the gene pool. Call it preventative surgery. Call it whatever. I had regrets because I'm still moral; but there was no hesitation because I'm practical and this was a war where the good guys were badly outnumbered.

I used the cut branches to hide them, and completed the extra step necessary to make sure they wouldn't reanimate. The bikes were potentially useful, so I hid two on the other side of the road behind some dense bushes. The third one had to be sacrificed, though, because I figured I might need a grappling hook if I was going to sneak into the town. I busted it apart and used part of the frame to make a sturdy hook, tying it securely with rope from my pack. Be Prepared, that's my motto.

Then I headed to Happy Valley.

The intel I'd gathered was interesting. And disturbing.

Happy Valley had been built as an upscale incorporated town with an exclusive population. Lawyers and money had to be involved in setting it up. Only invited persons could move there. There were just under three hundred residents, and an unknown number of "workers."

When I asked what that meant, the Rovers told me that there was a special arrangement for anyone who wanted to live there. They had to agree to do manual labor—cleaning, farming, basic repairs, trash collection, and so on—in exchange for being able to live inside the walls. These workers also had to turn over their own supplies and needed to earn them back before they were allowed to leave. Or they could leave with no supplies at all and maybe some consequences.

"Those fuckers in there are all about consequences," said Diver.

"What kind of consequences?" I asked.

Loki said, "You been to the grove?" He nodded in the general direction of the clearing where I'd found the corpses tied to posts.

"You're saying the people of Happy Valley did that?"

"You see one guy with a big black beard? That was Buckeye. He was one of us. He was sent in as a, you know...spy and shit. We wanted the lowdown on the place 'cause we heard some shady stories. He went in and for a couple of days was able to get word out to us. Wrapped notes around rocks and used a sling shot to send them over the walls. And then, poof—nothing. Messages stopped. We didn't hear a peep for over two weeks. Then Snail and his crew found him dead in the grove. They'd tied him up and left him to starve to death. That's fucked up."

"And you didn't take him down and bury him?" I asked.

He looked at me like I was from Mars. "Why? He was dead as shit."

Nice guys. They said Buckeye managed to get a rough guess as to the amount of stores and supplies. There was a lot, but not enough for all those people. Maybe three months' worth at half rations. And the workers were being fed quarter rations with a promise of thirds if they worked extra hours to earn it. Also, the residents were raising livestock in there. Rats, which were the principle source of protein for the workers, and dogs to feed the residents. There was a big kennel attached to a slaughterhouse and kitchen.

Not exactly sure which part of the story punched the worst buttons in my head—slave labor or dogs as cuisine. It was at least neck and neck. Maybe a little more the dog thing for me.

"What was your game plan once you raided the place?"

"Fuck...what else?" said Loki. "Food, supplies, walls, and a prime location. That's going to be our kingdom, man. Rover-ville or some shit." Then he smiled. "Besides, Buckeye said there's some quality tail in there. Rich bitches who probably never had nothing more than pencil dicks. Most of them white and clean and, like, *ready for it*." The son of a bitch actually winked at me. "You're a tough motherfucker. Big Elroy would welcome you like a brother. Shit, you could have first crack at all that trim—"

Loki wanted to say more, but then he was dead. Diver, who had been nodding at what his friend was saying, never spoke another word.

Baskerville pissed on their corpses. Eloquent and appropriate.

As I walked away it amazed and disappointed me that a shared crisis did not encourage everyone to drop all their old bad habits and rise to stand together. It would be nice to believe that would be the defining characteristic cited in history books written years from now. Not that I believed it, but it would be nice. If there was a future. I really believe humanity could outlive and outlast the plague of the dead. It was groups like the Rovers who made me doubt if the human race had the collective right to survive. Fighting the urge to give in to a cold and unforgiving cynicism was a real bitch, and it felt like every day I lost a little ground. Days like today made me feel like I was sliding down a hill smeared with slippery human sewage.

It was twilight now and when I reached the tree line I could see lights coming from beyond the walls. Pale and flickering for the most part, which suggested firelight; but there were some of the colder and steady blue-white lights consistent with camp-ing lanterns. The illumination wasn't very evident and probably leaked out from under canopies. It barely reached the upper branches of the surrounding trees, and there were no clouds to reflect it. So, basically not a "come eat me" sign. That was about the first smart thing the residents had done.

Well, semi-smart. There was enough light for me to walk the entire perimeter of the place, staying inside the forest shadows, and get a really good idea of where and how to scale the walls.

Bottom line was this—they probably thought they'd all stayed safe because of the walls and their own brutal treatment of anyone who came knocking at the gate. I doubted anyone was ever allowed to leave. The walls kept out the dead, and the guard towers allowed for just enough vigilance to reinforce the distorted feelings of safety, and as the months went by, complacency set in. That brings with it a certain skewed and naïve logic: if it's worked this long it must mean it'll keep working. It falls somewhere between arrogance and optimism.

I retreated into the woods to eat, feed Baskerville, and think it through. The dog, free of his armor, shook himself all over and promptly found something disgusting to roll in. Not that I cared. We both stank. There'd been some cans of Vienna sausages and creamed corn in the Rovers' backpacks. I opened them and split the goodies between us.

While we chowed down I looked at the big dog. "You don't think Mr. Church is in there at all, do you?"

Being a dog, Baskerville just looked at me. His tail thumped twice.

"Me neither," I said.

An owl began to hoot softly in the gathering dark, and a million crickets and cicadas sang their love songs. A deep sadness wrapped itself around me and I felt more alone than I had in months. I thought about Junie and the baby and my brother's family. I thought about Top and Bunny and wondered if they were alive. If not, would they have been alive had I been there? Sure, that's arrogance talking, but my inner parasites are neither kind nor helpful.

At one point I thought I saw Junie's pale, lovely face watching me from the shadows, but when I went over it was just the owl sitting on a low branch. My movement chased it off and I shambled back to the desultory little fire I'd started for warmth.

The stars came out and looked coldly down at me. Baskerville came over and pushed himself against me until I wrapped my arms around him and buried my face in his fur. If I wept for a while, he did not seem to care.

In the morning I kicked dirt over the last coals of my campfire, strapped Baskerville's armor on, checked that my gun was loaded, and went back to Happy Valley. I was not in the best of moods. So I figured, God help anyone who decided today was the day to fuck with me.

– 29 –

DAHLIA AND THE PACK

Dahlia fought for more than her life. More even than Neeko. She fought for the whole Pack. She fought with anger and heartbreak and passion.

She fought with coldness, too. And that was strange for her. Even as she moved she was aware that the heat of rage was not there, or...not real, at least. Instead the furnace of her heart seemed to be stoked with shovelfuls of ice. When she attacked, it was no blind rush, but instead an attack designed to disrupt the group of Rovers and sow the seeds of confusion. It was strategic rather than impassioned.

It was how Mr. Church had trained her.

The Rovers were positioned in two knots: three in front, and two behind. She went straight at the knot of three and as they shifted to meet her charge, she suddenly jagged right and struck the Rover at the edge of that group. Not with the knife, but with her hand, parrying his reach with her forearm and then bouncing off of that impact and using the resulting force to power a blow with the open Y of her hand formed by thumb and index finger, so that the big knuckle of the index finger struck the man's Adam's apple. He gagged and sagged back.

Most people are right-handed, Church had said, *and most right-handed fighters are awkward when fighting a left-hander.* Although Dahlia was right-handed she had been relentlessly trained to fight ambidextrously. Church had insisted on it. He'd been inflexible, almost cruel about it. As the Rover canted backward and crashed into the smaller of the two women, Dahlia understood why.

Don't stand and admire your work. When you create an advantage, press it.

She followed the Rover's fall, reaching now with the heavy *kukri* knife and striking with a loose, deft flick of her wrist. The blade caught the dreadlocked man across the bridge of the nose. He screamed and reeled back so sharply, grabbing at his face, that his elbow struck a tree trunk. He screamed and fell, landing on top of the man she'd hit in the throat.

When in a pincer attack, don't turn to see what danger is behind you. Keep moving and turning. If you're in the center, then you are trapped.

Dahlia jumped sideways, turning in midair and slashing with the *kukri* as she did so. The blade encountered a stab from the leader of the gang. The muscular woman had a military bayonet and had lunged forward with a powerful blow that was intended to end the fight there and then. The blades rang off one another, striking sparks but drawing no blood. The fifth Rover grabbed Neeko and wrapped a tattooed arm around the little scout's throat.

"I'll fucking kill him," roared the Rover, but then he grunted in pain and surprise as Neeko struck backward to hit the man in the crotch with the side of his fist. Immediately the scout turned inside the choke, pushing his chin into the crook of the arm to create a narrow margin for breath, and twisted his whole body toward the muscular arm. A turn-away would have tightened the choke, but turning toward the shoulder of the choking arm created exactly the opposite effect. For a split second the arm was a cage and inside that cage was Neeko and everything on the Rover's body he wanted to hit.

When you create an opportunity for counter-attack you must waste no time and show no mercy. Overwhelm the attacker with as many strikes, kicks, head-butts and bites as you can manage. Do not let up because if you give him even a moment to catch his breath he will come back harder. Take that option away completely.

Neeko did exactly that. In the space of a single fractured moment he head-butted the Rover in the nose, kneed him in the crotch, stamped on his instep and ground the man's foot-bones, bit the side of his neck, boxed his ears and punched him in the throat. All of the blows were sloppy with fear, and no single strike was crippling, but the cumulative effect was akin to being dropped into a threshing machine. The man staggered and Neeko pivoted to kick him on the kneecap with a flat-footed attack that filled the air with a huge dry-stick *crack*.

Dahlia saw all of this out of the corner of her eye, but all of her other awareness was drawn to the leader of the Rovers, who drove at her with a furious attack. The bayonet slashed and chopped and stabbed. The woman was shorter but very solid, with ropey muscles and catlike speed. Her attacks drove Dahlia back step by step.

Never allow the enemy to fight his fight. The rules are yours to change.

Dahlia suddenly threw herself sideways into a tight shoulder roll and came up with a handful of dirt and small stones. She rose and hurled them at the woman, forcing her to shield her eyes and turn away. The woman tripped over a root and fell heavily, losing her knife.

That's when Dahlia made her first mistake.

Mr. Church taught her to press an advantage, to never leave an enemy able to regroup. One part of her knew that and understood the logic of it, but another part—an older, less confident and perhaps more moral part—shouted that to press the advantage meant killing these people. All of them. She was not sure she could commit five murders. Not in cold or hot blood.

Killing the living dead was one thing; this was something entirely different.

And so she ran to Neeko, grabbed him by the shoulder and propelled him into the woods with all of her strength.

"*Run!*" she yelled.

He gaped at her and looked past Dahlia to where the Rovers were all climbing back to their feet. Then he gave a small cry and vanished into the woods. Dahlia knew that in a flat race no one was going to catch the little scout. He was as fast as a weasel and slippery as an eel, and terror put wings on his feet.

Dahlia tried to run, too, but she was neither as fast nor as nimble. She tore into the woods, but with howls of fury the Rovers gave chase. The air was abruptly split by the sound of whistles—like the gym teacher in high school used—and after a moment there were answering whistles from deeper in the woods.

That's when Dahlia realized the full scope of her mistake. If she'd done as she was taught, then maybe there would have been a way out. Now she was caught in a trap with who knew how many of the killers.

She ran.

Other bits of Old Man Church's training came to her, guiding her. She cut left and right, avoided collision with bushes whose branches might be damaged by her passing and thereby be proof of her direction. She stepped on flat rocks and leaped over obstacles, then changed direction two or three times after landing. She cut back across her own trail to confuse pursuit. All the time the whistles screeched, signaling one to the other as the Rovers tried to catch her. Some blasts were long and steady; others short and staccato. There was some kind of pattern to it, but there was no time to suss out what it was. The Rovers were likely using the whistles to talk to each other.

She heard one whistle directly ahead and dropped low, becoming absolutely still as a Rover broke from the woods, a hunting hatchet in his hand. He looked left and right but did not see her, and then ran to follow the call of another shrill whistle blast. As soon as he was gone, Dahlia rose and moved into a dense stand of pine trees.

And there was a Rover directly in front of her. Tall. Powerful. Familiar.

She jerked to a stop and stared with horrified eyes.

"Trash…?" she whispered.

Time seemed to freeze into a bitter nothing as they stood there, six feet apart. He was dressed in leather now. Like them. She looked for a necklace of grim trophies, but he wore none. Dahlia wasn't sure if that was a relief. Maybe it only meant he needed to start his collection. Which part of her would he cut off to buy his way into their trust?

Whistles in various patterns cut the air. Trash lifted his head to listen, then his eyes dropped back to meet hers.

"Dahlia," he said.

"Please," she begged.

He raised his whistle and put it between his lips. Those lips. The ones she had kissed too many times. The lips that had whispered such sweet things to her in the nights. The lips that had kissed her when she woke from nightmares.

"Please…" she whispered and raised her knife.

He blew his whistle. Three short blasts.

"Go," he said fiercely. "Go south. Now!"

She lingered a moment longer, seeing the terrible pain in his eyes. Then he gave a single small, sad smile.

She bolted and ran, heading into the woods, angling south. Behind her she heard voices. The muscular woman and Trash.

"You saw her?" demanded the woman.

"Yeah," said Trash. "Caught just a glimpse of her going north, maybe northeast. C'mon, I'll show you. She can't be too far ahead."

There were more whistles and the sounds of shouting.

Going northeast.

Going away.

Tears fell down her cheeks.

"Trash…" she said so softly that it was little more than a breath. She turned.

And Mr. Church was there. Right there. Four feet behind her. She hadn't heard him at all. He had a pistol in his hands, the barrel pointing where Trash had stood. His eyes searched hers. She nodded, and after a moment he responded in kind. He lowered his weapon very slowly.

Then, without a word, he holstered the weapon, turned and led the way through the woods to where Neeko and the rest of the Pack waited.

After a long, long time, Dahlia ran to catch up to Old Man Church.

– 30 –

THE WARRIOR WOMAN

Rachael fought.

But there was one of her and six of them. Kyle, the one she'd kicked, joined the others, his face bloated and flushed, naked hatred in his eyes. He muscled his way between the others and punched Rachael in the stomach. It was an ugly, brutal blow that drove the air from her lungs and would have dropped her to the ground had the ropes not already been wound around her waist. She screamed and then gagged, trying to suck in air, but there didn't seem to be any left in the whole world.

Kyle grabbed her face, pinching her chin between his thumb and fingers and leaned close to spit in her face. Then he gave her a grin that was beyond malicious, crossing over into true malevolence.

"I hope the walkers don't find you for weeks, you little whore," he said. "I hope you starve out here."

Her legs were bound, as was her right arm; Rachael tried to tear her left free so she could stick a thumb in his eye or punch him in the throat, but the others held her.

"That's enough," growled the man with the cigarette. "She's done. Let it go."

"She's done when I say she's done," growled Kyle. He reached for the frayed collar of her Batgirl T-shirt, clearly intending to rip it open. But then the moment, the day, and maybe the world changed as a voice spoke from the shadows of the woods.

"Now ain't this interesting as all shit?"

They all whipped their heads around as a woman stepped from between two big pines. She was muscular, with a sharply-etched face and a necklace of human ears.

"Who the hell are you?" asked Kyle. He shook Rachael by his handhold on her blouse, tearing the collar. "More of your pussy friends?"

"Well," said the woman, "I don't know this little cutie but I'd like to. Mind if we join the party?"

Before Kyle could ask what she meant by "we," he found out as three other strangers came out of the woods. They were all dressed in leather; they all had grisly necklaces. They all had knives or axes or hatchets in their hands.

Rachael stared at them and felt her heart sink. For one tiny second she thought that the universe was going to cut her a sliver of luck. That hope faded as she looked into the faces of the newcomers. They were hard, brutal, amused. The townsfolk spread out, drawing their own weapons. Only one of them had a gun, but it was a shotgun and not even a pump-action. The strangers were spread far apart and none of them looked particularly frightened of the weapon.

The woman took a couple of steps into the clearing. "Which one of you pencil dicks is running this cluster-fuck?"

"I am," said the cigarette guy, who tossed the smoldering butt away. "Who the hell are you?"

"Me?" said the woman, contriving to look surprised at the question. Then an oily smile broke on her thin-lipped mouth. "My name's Glory and I'm the goddamn angel of death."

The man with the shotgun tucked it into his shoulder and pointed the barrel at her.

"Yeah? Well I've got a load of buck shot that says you ain't shit."

Glory turned to him—not her whole body, just an insectoid pivot of her head. She raised her hand, kissed her fingers and blew him a kiss. "Buh-bye," she said sweetly.

Rachael saw a fragment of the forest shadows shift and break off and she began to cry out in warning, but the sound caught in her throat. Who would she warn? And why? She had no friends at all in this place, of that she was absolutely certain.

The shadow moved with blinding speed and suddenly the man with the shotgun grunted, stiffened, seemed to rise to his toes. His eyes bugged wide and his mouth opened to let loose a scream, but all that came from his throat was about a pint of dark red blood. Then the shadow rose up behind him and became something else. A man. Young and tall, with a handsome face twisted into a brutal mask. The shotgun sagged down and with a spasmodic jerk of dying fingers blasted the buckshot impotently into the dirt. The dying man fell to his knees and then the killer braced a knee against his back and tugged, jerking free a thick-bladed butcher knife. The shotgun man fell limply onto his face, twitched twice, and then lay still.

The townsfolk all cried out in shock and then flinched backward as a fifth leather-clad stranger stepped out of the woods, a big nickel-plated revolver in his massive fist.

"Jesus *Christ*," gasped Kyle.

The cry woke Jason, who opened his eyes and looked around in sudden panic. He was bound, bloody, bruised, and tied to a cross in a grove filled with dead people and armed killers. Claudia still hung limp. Maybe dead.

"Ra—Rachael...?" he murmured weakly.

Glory was still smiling at the townies. "You assholes are all from Happy Valley, aren't you? Yeah, no need to answer. You're the elitist jerkoffs hiding behind the wall thinking you're better than everyone. Thinking that you have it all solved, that you own this fucking world. That your shit don't stink. Well, newsflash, kids...as wake up calls go, this one's going to be a real bitch. Trust me."

– 31 –

THE SOLDIER AND THE DOG

In the morning I patrolled the perimeter of the town again and found two more sets of Rover scouts in concealed observation posts. Three Rovers in each. Baskerville wanted to start the day with some red fun, but I told him no. I was still in the intelligence-gathering mode. I had a pretty good read on what the Mad Max crowd had in mind, but I thought it might be useful to verify what Loki and Diver had told me about the residents of Happy Valley.

If the people inside the walls were forcing travelers into slave labor, then I wanted to do something about it. Only problem was that the Rovers I'd interrogated didn't know if there were any forced workers still inside. Their man, Buckeye, hadn't filed his last report. If there were no slaves in there, then fuck it. I'd let the Rovers and the elitist pricks inside kill each other and write the whole place off my list.

If.

But I had to find out, and I didn't want to risk alerting their wall sentries if taking out the Rover teams got loud. Instead, I circled the town until I found a place where I could scale the wall with little or no chance of being seen by Rovers or sentries. I took the grappling hook I'd made from the bike frame, gave Baskerville some commands to stay free and alert and not engage unless attacked. Dogs are smart and if you train them they can understand complex orders. Ask sheep farmers and the show-dog crowd. Ask soldiers and K9 cops. I mean…you could have asked them if they were still alive.

Fuck. Sigh. The world really blows.

Point is…my dog would be safe. He couldn't climb the walls anyway.

My line of approach was by crawling through a drainage ditch that took rain runoff to a creek. The thin weeds were tall and blew constantly in any breeze. When it came to security, the residents of this town had their collective heads way up their own asses.

I made it to a pair of crooked slash pines and was up into the branches before you could say kiss my hairy white butt. I crouched among the bristles, dislodging and annoying a squirrel who fled to a higher branch and threw pieces of pine cone at me. Little asshole.

The wall was ten feet away and there were metal struts standing upright every six yards to anchor the razor wire. I was just starting to wind up to throw the grappling hook when I saw movement down on the ground, forty yards from me. There was a small side gate in the wall and a group of people stepped out into the morning sunlight. Six of them. Five men, one woman. Each pair of them was carrying a third person, so there were nine in all. The three being carried—well, dragged, really—looked to be either dead or unconscious. A tall guy, a waifish girl, and a very solid-looking woman.

I used my binoculars but could only see the strong-looking woman from my angle. She wore dark wash jeans, a faded grey T-shirt with batgirl logo in yellow, dirty knee-high black combat boots, leather bracers on her forearms and an old-fashioned pauldron on one shoulder. The armor pieces were probably looted from a museum or handmade by someone who spent a lot of time in Renaissance fairs before the dead rose.

Two men carried her along so that the toes of her boots dragged through the grass. I couldn't see her face very well because her forehead and cheeks were covered in blood, and more of it matted thickly in her long dark hair.

They lugged her across the apron of open ground and vanished into the woods. The other pairs likewise hauled their burdens, moving quickly and cursing frequently. From the direction they took I had a good guess where they were going.

The clearing.

"Son of a bitch," I said under my breath.

Three minutes later I was back in the ditch, worming my way

back to the woods. Baskerville either saw me or smelled me, because he was waiting inside the forest shadows, looking like he wanted very much to bite something.

"Let's go hunting," I said.

– 32 –

DAHLIA AND THE PACK

"He could have turned me in," said Dahlia.

Church said nothing.

"He didn't have to lie for me."

Nothing.

"That says a lot, doesn't it?" she asked. "It means that he's not really *with* them. That he's not as bad as them."

Church kept walking and said nothing at all.

Finally Dahlia couldn't bear it and she ran around and stood in his way, forcing him to stop. The rest of the Pack stopped, too. All of them looking nervously at the two of them. Church took a breath and let it out slowly.

"What would you like me to say, Dahlia? Trash saved your life. Yes, that's good. Yes, it shows that he has some redeeming quality. But he also betrayed the entire Pack and told them where our camp was. If you hadn't seen him do that then we might have been raided and slaughtered. We don't know how many of them there are. You got lucky today. That's the bottom line."

"He *saved* me," she insisted.

"Which is why I didn't kill him," Church said coldly. "That's his reward. Trust does not come with it." He stepped closer and lowered his voice. "Understand this, Dahlia, if it comes down to Trash's life and a single member of our family, then I will end him."

"I won't let you."

His eyes were like flecks of black ice behind his tinted lenses.

"What is more important to you? Saving Trash or saving the entire Pack?"

"Both," she said immediately.

"And if both is not an option?"

Before she could answer he walked around her and continued leading the Pack through the woods toward Happy Valley.

Dahlia stood where she was, fists balled, heart beating in all the wrong ways in her chest. Hating Church. Hating herself and everyone. Wanting them all to die. Wanting herself to die. Being a damn zombie would be so much easier than this.

As the Pack moved past her she gave them brutal death stares, daring anyone to show pity or say a fucking word. No one did. Not even Neeko, who lingered for a moment, looking hurt and confused.

When they were all gone, Dahlia stood alone in the slanting sunlight. She almost wished there was a zombie or four to fight. Or some random thug who just tried to give her shit. Someone she could happily stomp to death.

But the woods remained calm, with bees and butterflies and songbirds.

Dahlia wanted to light a match and burn it all down.

"God damn it, Trash," she snarled. When she uncurled her clenched fingers and looked at her palms, there were crescent-shaped nicks in the skin. Two of them welled with blood.

She bent and snatched up a fallen branch, whirled and smashed it against the trunk of a tree, sending splinters of wood flying in all directions. The sound was startlingly loud and it froze her. She looked up as if she could see the echoes bounce off the trees and flee across the forest.

"Shit..." she breathed.

The birds were silent now and she could feel them watching her. Ice formed around her heart as she wondered who else had heard that sound.

"Shit, shit, shit."

She ran to catch up with the Pack.

Neeko was waiting for her a few hundred yards along the

trail, chewing on a stem of sweet grass and pretending it was just any ordinary day.

"Hey," he said.

"Hey," she said. They fell into step together.

After nearly two miles, he said, "So…think it might rain?"

"Oh, shut up," she said, but she laughed as she said it.

Then one of the younger kids came running back to find her. "The Old Man wants you," she gasped. "We're there."

Dahlia and Neeko broke into a run and followed the girl back to where Church and several older Pack members crouched in the shadows beneath a massive weeping willow. Sunlight shone brightly on a broad space of cleared land, and beyond that was a large, wide wall covered in peach stucco.

"Happy Valley," said Neeko.

"It looks intact," said Dahlia. "No zombies. No signs that it's been overrun."

Church, hearing her comment, came over and knelt beside her. "The other scouts have reported in," he said. "There are packs of Rovers all through these woods. Estimate one hundred minimum, and likely more if there are groups in other parts of the woods. They're moving in the direction of the town. Some of them are carrying ladders, likely looted from building sites or stores. Others are pulling wagons of premade Molotov cocktails. Dixie said she saw several Rovers with grappling hooks."

Dahlia felt the blood drain from her face. "They're going to attack the town, aren't they? I mean…like right now."

"Yes," said Church. "There's no other target of substance in the area. The scouts estimate that we have one hour before they're here."

"Well…shit!" She instantly began to surge forward, but Church caught her arm and gently pulled her back.

He held up a finger. "Never rush into things without considering all of the pertinent data."

"Like what? The Rovers will slaughter a bunch of innocent people."

Church said, "How sure are you that the people of that town

are innocent? You've heard some of the rumors the refugees have told us."

"What, about Happy Valley being like a slave plantation? Come on, do you expect me to believe that crap?"

"I expect you to consider it and prepare for that eventuality, just as you prepare for other things. Strategic planning is best done from a distance and with a cool head."

They studied the landscape for a bit as she chewed on that.

"So, Dahlia," he said after a time, "what do you think we should do?"

"Me? I thought you were Obi Wan and we were all Padawan learners."

"This is real life," he reminded her. "Besides, it's *your* Pack, Dahlia. It's never been mine, and it won't be mine when this is over. It's up to you to make a decision, and to plan for various likely contingencies. For example, you could head southeast, skirt the perimeter and move out of the area. There's still time for that. And there are half a dozen other possible options."

"Like…?"

He shook his head. "You tell me."

Dahlia turned and looked back at the members of her Pack, all of whom were crouched down in the weeds and behind bushes. She knew and loved them all. She'd done so much to protect them and keep them out of harm's way. On the other hand, she'd also talked them into joining with Old Man Church. That hadn't been for fun and games. He made no secret about the fact that he was waging a war out here. Against the dead and against the predatory living.

Against people like the Rovers.

She took a breath and told him what she thought they could do. Church listened and then nodded.

"You see?" he said. "You are a leader."

They spent a few minutes discussing the plan and some variations. Church offered a few suggestions, but mostly let her shape things. The more they talked, the more Dahlia felt that there was a logic to her idea. Even a strength. But then darkness drifted over her heart. She lowered her voice so that only Church could hear her. "If we do this," she said, "some of them could get hurt."

"Some *will* be hurt. That's unavoidable."

"Some of them could die."

He nodded. "Yes." Church adjusted his black gloves and stared into the distance. "This is the shape of the world, Dahlia. We can't wish an idyllic paradise into being. Maybe other people can do that, but I doubt it. Sometimes peace comes at a price. The question is, are you, as leader of the Pack, willing to pay that price?"

– 33 –

THE WARRIOR WOMAN

Kyle drew the hatchet from his belt and brandished it at Glory.

"I'm going to cut me a big chunk of ugly off your ass," he announced, and ran at her. Glory sidestepped to avoid his swing, and although she still smiled Rachael could see that the woman was surprised at the speed of the attack. Kyle was a jackass, but he was quick. The two of them began jabbing and slashing at each other, missing by hair's breadths each time.

For a moment, everyone else on both sides seemed to be caught in a moment of stupid spectatorship. Maybe the townies were unprepared for this and not as aggressive as Kyle; maybe the gang members had expected the townies to cave more easily. In either case, the moment held, stretched, and then finally snapped. The man who'd smoked the cigarette flung himself at the young man who'd stabbed the shotgun guy. The leap was powerful, but the killer either saw him coming or had good reflexes because he began to turn as the rush hit him, so instead of being smashed down, both men fell and rolled over and over.

Then everyone was fighting. They went from shocked immobility to a madhouse melee in a fragment of a second. Rachael wasted no time. Her left hand was still free and she immediately began tearing at the knots that held her right to the crossbar. Jason was shaking his head, trying to shake off the battering he'd received; and even Claudia was beginning to twitch, roused by the shouts and screams.

Everywhere she looked Rachael saw terrible violence. It wasn't just a fight, it was like watching rabid dogs tearing at each other. The townsfolk fought with terror, which gave them incredible speed and a desperate ferocity. The gang members fought with a vicious cruelty that was more natural brutality than skill. They were evenly armed and both groups knew they were fighting for their lives. There were no fancy moves, no tactics or strategies. This was mayhem and murder.

Rachael got her right hand free and began working on the lashing around her waist. Her T-shirt collar was torn, but not badly, and the townies hadn't even bothered to remove her few pieces of armor. Her weapons were gone, though. Damn.

"Rachael...?" called Claudia weakly. "What's...what's happening?"

As the last knot came free, Kyle came staggering toward her, his eyes wide and both hands clamped to his throat. Blood, red as madness, spurted from between his fingers. Glory, her face bruised and lacerated, caught up to him and began hacking at him, stabbing him in the shoulders and head and back, all the while uttering a long, continuous inarticulate scream of pure rage. Kyle, dying, collapsed forward, releasing his throat and grabbing hold of Rachael as if with some insane desire to drag her down into death with him.

Even then Glory kept chopping at him. Rachael couldn't tell if this was a reaction to Kyle injuring her or the way this wild woman always fought. Either way, it was terrifying.

Then, as if a switch had been thrown, Glory stopped, locked for a moment in place, her knife and knife-hand dripping with blood as Kyle sank lifelessly to the ground. Glory's eyes stared at him and then slowly rose to stare Rachael in the eyes. The mask of mindless fury transformed all at once. The mad lights in her eyes were replaced by a sudden look of hunger. A naked and terrible look of gluttony.

"Mine," said the woman softly as carnage raged all around her. "First you, and then your whole damn town. *Mine.*"

Rachael tried to tell her that Happy Valley wasn't her town. That she was no part of any of this. That this was all wrong.

But there was no time left for any of that.

– 34 –

DAHLIA AND THE PACK

Dahlia got up and walked out of the forest.

After a moment, and in ones, twos, and threes, the rest of the Pack joined her. Church followed last. Jumper and Slow Dog were right behind her. They all walked quickly across the cleared space, heading for the main gate. Dahlia was aware that the Rover teams they'd spotted hiding in the woods were able to see all of this happen. She thought she could hear whistles blowing deep inside the forest. Or maybe it was just the wind. Hard to say, and too late now anyway.

She walked straight up to the front gate, stopping far enough back so that the guards on the wall could get a good look at her. At all of them. The Pack had grown since she'd joined Old Man Church. Strays, refugees, and small parties swelled the ranks so that there were now about a hundred of them.

"Everyone stay cool," she'd ordered. "Weapons slung. No one says anything. No one acts like a dick, okay?"

Her people nodded. Even those who were a good deal older than Dahlia. To all of them, she was the leader of the Pack, and she was answerable only to the strange old man with the tinted glasses and black gloves.

Church came and stood near her, but slightly back and to one side. Allowing her to own the moment. Dahlia felt a little bit like a kid in a school play with her father watching, but that was okay.

"Hey," she called. "Hello in there."

Above her a figure appeared. A woman of about sixty with iron gray hair, dark eyes, and severely angled cheekbones. Two men flanked her and laid the barrels of hunting rifles on the wall, the barrels pointing down.

"Who are you and what do you want?" asked the older woman in a voice that was very clear and very sharp. "And who are all these...*people*...with you?"

Dahlia did not like the woman's voice or attitude. It was an instant decision, but it came from her gut. Even so, she put on her best debate team voice and plowed ahead.

"My name's Dahlia. These are my friends. We heard about Happy Valley and came to see if it was still standing."

"It is, as you can see," said the woman. "What of it?"

"Well, not to be blunt, but it's not going to be standing much longer, ma'am."

The woman gave her a cold smile. "Oh really? And is that supposed to be a threat of some kind?"

"A threat?" Dahlia was actually surprised. "No. It's a warning, I suppose. We heard about some people—a big gang of bikers and such—heading this way. They call themselves the Rovers."

One of the men on the wall leaned close and whispered something to the woman and they spoke together for several seconds. Then the woman nodded and turned back to Dahlia.

"How do we know you're not Rovers yourself?"

Dahlia glanced at Neeko and a few of the other younger ones, then back up. "Seriously?"

"Yes, I'm very serious."

"Um, because the Rovers are a motorcycle gang. At least they were before the EMPs killed their bikes. They go around wearing leather and studs, and they wear necklaces of body parts they've cut off of people. Most of us are teenagers, or close enough. I don't think we're actually rocking a killer biker army vibe. I mean...do you?"

The woman gave her a cold appraisal for a long ten count. "Why come and tell us?"

"Common decency?" said Dahlia, inflecting it as a question.

"And what would you expect in return? We don't have food to share."

"We have plenty of food," said Dahlia. "We don't actually need anything from you. Look...can we come in so we don't have to stand out here shouting?"

The woman's eyes seemed to focus on Church for the first time. "And who is that? Your father?"

Without hesitation, Dahlia said, "He's my uncle. He used to be a—"

Church cut in and Dahlia was shocked to hear him speak with a New England drawl that was thicker than his own accent. "My name's John Deacon," he said, "of the Hampton Deacons. Steel exports. What my niece here is trying to say is that we've been out here for some time and we're doing fine. Have a good place with all the comforts of home. Even make a good martini, as long as the olives last. But these Rovers have been raiding a lot of settlements and causing all kind of trouble. Some of these young folks are scouts—we have a barter system of field work of all kinds in exchange for room and board. Works out very well, if you follow me. Well, we sent some teams out to keep an eye on the Rovers and they overheard mention of Happy Valley. So, I came out here, gathered up the scout teams. Wasn't sure if you were all safe here or if you needed some warm bodies to sort those thugs out. Not looking for anything because, quite frankly, I can't think of a thing you have that we need. But what pains me is to see..." and here he paused to pour acid on his words, "...*those people* come and take away what rightfully belongs to decent Americans."

The speech shocked Dahlia but she kept it off her face. She saw Neeko and Jumper exchange deeply surprised expressions; though Slow Dog was nodding in appreciation. Church sounded like a completely convincing rich asshole, from the imperious tilt of his head to the word choice. It bothered her that he could play this role so well.

The woman on the wall cleared her throat. "The Hampton Deacons, you say?"

"Yes. We helped build half of New York, or at least the bones of most of the buildings. Shame what happened to it." A beat. "I mean *before* this whole outbreak thing. Used to be a decent place, once upon a time. People you met on the street could speak English, if you know what I mean."

"Yes," said the woman. Church smiled up at her, and damn if she didn't smile back.

"What are you doing?" asked Dahlia in a tiny whisper.

"Roll with it," he said, hardly moving his lips. In a much louder voice he said, "My niece wasn't exaggerating about the Rovers. They're quite a savage bunch. Unwashed, unintelligent, uncouth, but there are a lot of them and they *are* coming."

The woman was still unconvinced. Dahlia saw her eyes roving over the rest of the Pack. There were people of all colors in her group, and they looked pretty raw and wild, too.

Before the woman on the walls could answer, there was a sudden shrill blast of whistles from the woods. Not one, but many.

Church pointed to the forest. "That's them. They're coming. Either let us in and we can fight them together, or we'll get out of here before they show up. I certainly don't like the idea of fighting all of them in an open field."

The whistles were still distant, but it was clear they were drawing closer. Dahlia wondered if it was intended to spook the people behind the walls, or to gather the various gangs of Rovers together. Or both.

The woman on the wall pursed her lips, giving her face a pinched, shrewish cast. The same man who'd whispered to her earlier now produced a pair of binoculars and handed them to her, pointing to a section of the forest three hundred yards to the west. The woman looked for a moment through the glasses and then jerked them away from her eyes, her shrewish expression instantly replaced by one of naked fear.

Before she could speak, Church turned away and said, very loudly and clearly, "Okay, kids, we need to move. Everyone head to the east woods. We don't want to be here for this and—"

"No!" cried the woman. "No, please, come inside."

The gates began to swing outward.

Church gave Dahlia a wink, but he sustained his drama for a bit. He stopped, glanced up at her with a troubled, doubtful face; then cut looks at the woods and at the Pack.

"Maybe we'll do better on our own," he said slowly.

"Please," cried the woman, "they're coming. I can see them."

Dahlia had to fight to keep a smile off her face. She understood how Church was playing this. Instead of begging, he made *her* ask. Made her, in fact, beg.

With a show of great reluctance, Church sighed, nodded, and then walked toward the open gates, curtly waving for the Pack to follow. Dahlia hurried to fall into step beside him.

"You played the entitled white asshole card pretty well," she said quietly.

"I've met more than my share of them," said Church. Then he added, "Stay sharp and play your role, too. I don't like this set up at all. Keep your eyes open and your emotions in check."

"Yes, Obi Wan."

"Hush now."

The Pack entered the town of Happy Valley. Dahlia turned to see the doors being swung shut and a heavy crossbar being fitted into place. It spoke of security, but it also scared her.

Outside the whistles rose in volume and one of the guards on the wall cried: "They're coming."

– 35 –

THE WARRIOR WOMAN

Rachael screamed and backed away, but her back slammed into the crossbar, and before she could twist away Glory clamped one iron hand around her throat. The bloody knife rose and then plunged downward.

Rachael twisted and slammed her leather bracers at the madwoman's wrist, deflecting the knife and causing the point to drive two inches into the crossbar. Then Rachael kneed the woman in the crotch and tried to head-butt her, but Glory twisted her waist and took the knee against her own thigh, changed angle and slammed her own forehead into Rachael's face. The savage blow missed her nose and instead mashed an eyebrow, which split and spurted blood.

Then Glory seemed to jerk backward and Rachael saw that Jason had somehow managed to free an arm and caught the killer's sleeve. Glory staggered and went down to one knee, but was up in an instant, slashing with her weapon. Bright rubies filled the air and Jason screamed and sagged back, his inner arm, shoulder, and throat opening with a terrible wound.

"No!" screamed Rachael and launched herself at the woman. Glory snarled and spun back to Rachael just in time to parry a kick. Her blade whipped out and drew a burning line across Rachael's abdomen. The T-shirt parted like a gaping mouth and blood welled as Rachael backpedaled, not knowing how seriously she was injured. Jason sagged down against the restraints as Claudia began screaming and thrashing.

Then a hand clamped around Rachael's ankle and she looked down in horror to see that Kyle—*dead Kyle*—had grabbed her. The newly awakened creature struggled to rise as he snapped his teeth in her direction. Glory backed up a step, uncertain of her next move, though she was still smiling.

She's enjoying this, thought Rachael. *She's worse than the orcs.*

Rachael kicked at Kyle, but he caught her foot with his other hand and she fell hard on her butt, her head snapping back against the upright post. Claudia kept screaming and everywhere there was blood and death.

Then, like a grenade being tossed into the middle of it all, a voice boomed out with such strident force that everyone— gang members, townies, Claudia and Rachael, and even the undead Kyle—paused in their acts of murder and turned toward a figure standing at the edge of the clearing. He was tall, muscular, heavily armed, and there was some kind of armored creature with him. Maybe a dog. Maybe a *warg*, for all Rachael knew. The world was crazy enough. The man's words echoed like thunder.

"*What in the wide blue fuck is going on around here?*"

Rachael's heart leapt in her chest. She knew that voice.

She knew the man.

She even knew the monster dog.

"Joe!" she screamed.

– 36 –

HAPPY VALLEY

The woman came down from the wall to meet them. She was tall and as slender as a rake handle and stood in that peculiar attitude Dahlia had seen used by some of the mothers of the richest and prettiest girls in school. A sort of slouch of the shoulders while keeping her head up at a disapproving angle; one hand on her hip and her pelvis cocked forward. It looked uncomfortable and Dahlia had no idea what it was supposed to convey.

"Mr. Deacon," she said, "it's a pleasure to meet you. I'm Margaret Van Sloane of the—"

"Of the Hewlett Bay Van Sloanes," Church said, cutting in smoothly. "I thought so. A pleasure, Margaret. I knew Bryce Van Sloane quite well."

"Bryce? Oh, how lovely. He was my uncle. Did you do business with him?"

"Our paths crossed a few times," said Church smoothly. "He was very sharp. A killer in business." He offered his hand and took Van Sloane's birdlike hand in his, giving it a delicate shake.

Dahlia had to resist rolling her eyes. She thought he was laying it on a bit thick. On the other hand, the skinny hag seemed to be eating it up.

The whistles were blowing in odd patterns now, some closer and others farther away. Margert Van Sloane flinched at the sound.

"How many of these…*Rovers*…are coming?" she asked.

"A hundred at least," said Church, "and possibly many more." Church quickly explained about the Rovers—that they started out as a biker gang and grew into a horde in the months since the dead rose. He laid this part on thick, too, telling Van Sloane about the trophies and the brutality of the gang. Dahlia watched what his words did to the woman. Without being explicit, Church made it clear that they were, to all intents and purposes, the Visigoths and Happy Valley was Rome on its last day.

The Pack clustered together near the gates, and several of the guards seemed to be watching them more closely than what was happening on the other side of the wall.

While Church spoke, Dahlia looked around. Happy Valley looked like something out of a brochure for an upscale real estate brokerage. There were streets lined with lush trees, and houses that, though cookie-cutter, were individually beautiful. Two and three stories, with lots of gables and stained-glass dormers and fancy brickwork.

It was weirdly orderly to her, because everywhere she'd been since the catastrophe had been changed in one way or another. Whole cities, towns, and villages had been the scenes of slaughter and conflict where bullet holes pocked all the walls and doors, where cars stood in awkward positions in the roads or smashed into one another, or were left where they'd died when the EMPs fired. Bloodstains were everywhere, and you could barely walk without stepping in a patch of dried gore or on spent shell casings. Some towns were wholly given over to the living dead, with the gray people randomly wandering the streets or standing like grotesquely vigilant tombstones near the places where they died. Other towns belonged only to ghosts and to the animals that had come searching for food. A few had become armed forts where desperate groups of survivors struggled day-to-day for enough to eat and a safe piece of ground on which to sleep. There was nowhere in the world of living people that remained unchanged because the world itself had irrevocably changed. How could anything not reflect that?

Except here, in Happy Valley, there was no sign of that catastrophe.

The lawns were green and trimmed, the hedges sculpted to geometric perfection, the trees shady and lovely, the streets clean, the pavement swept. None of the houses were burned shells; there was no sign of violence of any kind. The residents were even well-dressed and well-groomed, with clean nails and expensive haircuts and fine jewelry.

That's what Dahlia saw first. It was so compelling an image that she felt momentarily displaced, disconnected from her own understanding of reality. How could *this* be here? Even with the walls and the protective geography, how could the end of the world not have touched Happy Valley?

She heard Church and Van Sloane talking. Heard them discuss the defenses, the threat, the coming fight, and it seemed unreal. Like that belonged in a much different story than this.

And then...

As if the universe was tired of its joke and wanted to hurt with a cruel punch line, she looked *past* the obvious and saw a bit deeper. A young man stood on the lawn of one of the closest houses. Not in the center of the lawn, not like he owned the place, but to one side, standing partly obscured by a hedge. By, in fact, the hedge he had been working on, a pair of clippers in his hands. He was a black man, much thinner than the other residents, dressed in grass-stained jeans and a plain T-shirt.

Why he caught her eye, and what was different about him, was not immediately obvious. Then Dahlia saw two other people, both Latinas, carrying bags of trash out to a wheeled cart. They grunted as they swung the heavy bags up. One paused to drag a forearm across her brow to wipe away sweat. They also wore jeans and plain T-shirts. Their hair was not expensively coifed, and they wore no jewelry of any kind. They wore sandals and gave furtive looks, meeting no one's eyes.

Then Dahlia saw the guards. A pair of young white men with sunglasses were pacing along the street. At first Dahlia thought they were coming to reinforce the walls, but that wasn't it at all. Instead they looked left and right as they walked, glancing at the black man trimming the hedges and the brown women hauling trash. And at others. A skinny white kid in ragged jeans with long unkempt hair and lots of tattoos who was pushing a broom along the street. A heavyset black woman with two white children in a stroller. An Arab with a wheelbarrow full of freshly picked vegetables. The guards looked at them and maintained their stares until each worker, in turn, paused and nodded.

The nods were small, but definite, and they troubled Dahlia. They looked like bows. Like statements of obedience. None of the people who bowed were smiling. The Arab man had a bandage across the bridge of his nose. The heavyset black woman had pink scars on her arms. The tattooed white man had the raccoon eyes you get with a broken nose.

And that's when she understood. That's when she knew how Happy Valley had survived. That's when she understood why Old Man Church had adopted the persona he had—white, entitled, condescending. That's when the whistles that still filled the air seemed less of a comprehensive threat and became instead one half of a pair of jaws.

She looked around, trying not to let anything show on her face, and saw that although the men on the wall were looking out, rifles and other weapons ready, there were plenty of other people—men and women—clustered around Van Sloane, and standing in a large circle around the Pack. All of them were armed, many had handguns, and if their barrels were not directly pointed at Dahlia's friends, there was more than a suggestion of that.

Which is when Dahlia tuned back into the conversation between Church and Van Sloane.

"...your weapons, of course," Van Sloane was saying.

Dahlia turned, fighting to recapture all of what the woman said. "Wait," she said, "you want us to give up our weapons?"

"Fuck that," said Slow Dog, placing a hand on the hilt of a

big machete that hung from his belt.

"No, no, not give *up*," assured Van Sloane. "We want to inventory everything and then we can decide who gets what based on our assessment of the real threat."

"Are you out of your mind?" demanded Dahlia. "The Rovers are coming *right now*."

"And we will respond appropriately. See...we already have people on the walls." In the last few minutes the sentries manning the wall had quadrupled. Now they crowded together, all of them heavily armed.

"Why take our weapons, though?" asked Jumper, looking nervously around.

"As I said..."

"No," insisted Dahlia, "why take them even for two minutes?" She turned to Church. "I guess you were right after all."

"Right about what?" asked Van Sloane. Dahlia did not answer the question. Instead Mr. Church walked toward the mayor.

"How many fighters do you have?" he asked casually.

"Enough."

"Really?" interjected Dahlia. "'Cause it looks to me like half of them are standing guard over the people you have *working* for you." She painted that word with acid. "Are you going to give the workers weapons, too?"

Van Sloane said nothing.

"What happens to the workers when this shit all goes down? Do you let the Rovers have them or—?"

"Our helpers are very well cared for," said Van Sloane.

"'Helpers'? That's a convenient word. If they're helping you, why do you have guards watching them? How come all of them look like they've had their asses kicked? What the fuck is going on around here?"

Van Sloane bridled. "Watch your language, young lady. This is *my* town. I'm the mayor here and we have survived very nicely while everything else fell apart. There's a reason for that. We have a system. Everyone does their part and everyone is taken care of. You are here out of courtesy. While we appreciate you coming to give us a warning, don't pretend that your actions are anything but self-interest. *We* are protecting *you*. Just as we protect our helpers. From the dangers outside and from themselves. We keep them fed and provide shelter and clothing—"

"And brush their coats and give them dog yummies. Yeah, I get it. I've actually read history books," sneered Dahlia. "Anyone with two eyes can see how you're running Happy Valley, Miss Mayor. I'll bet you were happy as fuck that the world ended and the government collapsed, taking the Constitution with it. All those pesky amendments. Like the one about slavery."

"Oh, please," said Van Sloane with a laugh. "There are no slaves here. Everyone here in Happy Valley wants to be here. Everyone came here willingly. No one was dragged in."

"Maybe, but how many of them are allowed to just up and leave?"

Van Sloane shook her head. "They stay because it's safer here. It's better here. There is food and shelter and walls and—"

"And beatings and what else?"

Mayor Van Sloane exhaled a long, weary breath. "Enough. Mr. Deacon, I can see that you cannot control your niece. It makes me question your motives in coming here. You could have a half dozen of your people in the forest blowing whistles and pretending that there is a threat. So, let's cut the nonsense and get right to it." She snapped her fingers and every single one of the armed men and women circling the Pack raised their weapons. "I want your people to drop their weapons. Do it carefully and slowly and be smart about it. Put all of your supplies in a pile. Everything."

Dahlia sighed. "You were right about everything," she said to Church.

Again, he spoke to Van Sloane. "The Rovers are coming whether you believe it or not. Given that, it would be encouraging to know if your guards and sentries are any good at their jobs."

Van Sloane took a step closer to him, smiling like the Florida alligators Dahlia had seen when her family was on vacation. A lot of teeth and no trace of warmth or mercy.

"Oh, my people are good," she said. "It would have been better for you and your niece if you hadn't pushed this."

"Yes," said Church, "everything could have been easier."

The whistles blew closer and louder. Church sighed and raised his hand. Van Sloane looked at it. The guards looked at it. He snapped his fingers.

The arrow was a gray blur that struck hard into the dirt in the narrow space between Church and the mayor. It hit so hard that it quivered and thrummed.

Suddenly there were people everywhere, coming out from between houses and rising up from behind hedges. Dahlia grinned as the Pack raised their weapons—guns and crossbows and compound bows and slingshots. For all his size, Slow Dog moved like greased lighting and tore a rifle out of a guard's hands, reversed it in his grip and shoved the barrel up under the man's chin, lifting him to his toes. Jumper took away a handgun and a hatchet with a balletic spin that was so smooth it looked choreographed. He pointed the gun at Van Sloane. Neeko and another scout seemed to come out of nowhere, taking the guns deftly away from the guards who'd been checking on the "helpers." All at once the people surrounding the Pack were themselves surrounded. The sound of hammers being cocked back and shotguns being racked crackled through the air. Dahlia's *kukri* knife flashed silver and the blade came to a sudden stop a millimeter from Margaret Van Sloane's throat.

Church, who had not made a single move, shook his head. "We could kill you all right now. It would be easy. It shouldn't be easy, but you've made it easy. And you've made it tempting." He pointed to the walls, where more of the Pack now held guns while others took weapons from the sentries. "Those whistles are real, Margaret. So are the Rovers. They're coming, and there are more of them than there are of us. They are a more professional army. Dahlia and I took your town with a group composed mostly of kids. Imagine what the Rovers will do."

His smile was somehow much colder and less human than Van Sloane's alligator leer.

– 37 –

THE SOLDIER AND THE DOG

So, there's this young woman, Rachael Elle. Smart, feisty, tough as hell, and a little weird. Dresses up like superheroes and calls the walking dead "orcs," like out of Tolkien.

Now, there is nothing wrong with being crazy. A good argument can be made that going nuts is an entirely appropriate way of dealing with the end of the world and the rise of the living dead. Sanity is certainly no buffer against that.

A similar argument can be made, and successfully litigated, that I, myself, am—in purely clinical psychological terms—as crazy as a bag of hamsters. This is not a news flash to anyone who's known me since I was a teenager.

However, sometimes things are so downright loony-tunes that even I wonder if my insanity dial has been turned to eleven.

Mind you, as a rule I am too old to be shocked by much anymore. I have both been there and done that and seen a lot of this world's weirdest shit. Trust me on this. Sometimes, though, the universe just up and tries to fuck with you.

Case in point.

The random woman being carried into the woods was Rachael. Don't ask me how the hell she got from where I last saw her to here. Don't begin to ask me to calculate the odds or explain the probabilities of chance necessary to put the two of us together again like this. Stephen Hawking couldn't have worked out those numbers. It not only proves there's a god, but He's also out of his fucking mind.

I stood at the edge of the clearing, with Baskerville at my side. Everyone else was frozen into a tableau of felony murder and aggravated assault. And Rachael Elle—the tough-looking woman I saw being dragged out here—was sitting on her ass with a dead guy holding her ankle and a crazy lady with a knife poised to stab her. Everyone else seemed to be a mix of Rovers and the Happy Valley residents who dragged Rachael and her two friends out here. At the moment, one of those two friends looked dead, or as near as makes no never mind. The other, a girl, looked like she'd gone all the way over the edge into total freaksville.

The moment was not a happy one for anyone.

I, however, thought it might be entertaining as fuck. Baskerville did, too. He sniffed the air in the direction of Rachael and gave a big, happy *whuff*.

The sound he made seemed to pop the balloon of frozen silence that held everyone immobile. And just that fast everyone was trying to kill everyone else again.

Way I saw it, the people in Happy Valley were murderous dicks. And the Rovers were a step down from sewer rats. The only civilians in this mix were Rachael and her friends.

I pointed to the three of them and told Baskerville they were friends. Then I told him to play. Actually, what I said was: "*Baskerville—hit! Hit! Hit!*"

He hit like a goddamn missile.

And I did a little damage my ownself. Can't let the damn dog have all the fun.

As we rushed in, I heard a sound from the woods closer to the town. Whistles. Dozens of them blowing in patterns, like drills sergeants ordering around their troops. I knew that couldn't be good.

One thing at a time, though. Rachael and her friends needed help right damn now.

– 38 –

THE SIEGE OF HAPPY VALLEY

Neeko hurried over to Dahlia, grinning while also casting uneasy looks at Van Sloane.

"You were right," he said, "they only had like one guy on the back wall. I mean, there were five originally, but after the

Rovers started blowing their whistles, they left just the one. He didn't even know I was there until I was up the tree, over the wall, and standing behind him. Me and Brenda and Tonk."

She kissed his cheek. "You're like a little ninja. You're so adorable I could eat you up."

He flushed to the color of a ripe tomato and squirmed away from a hug. "It wasn't anything special. Anyone could have—"

"Hush," she told him. Then she glanced at Van Sloane. "Neeko's sixteen. Brenda and Tonk are fifteen. They scaled a tree, jumped over the wall and captured the *only fucking guard* you left to defend the rear wall of this town. Seriously? Did you think that bad guys only break in one door at a time? No, don't answer. Clearly you're just not that smart."

"Watch your mouth," snapped Van Sloane, but although she bridled with indignation it was clear to everyone that her outrage had no power behind it. And nowhere to go.

"We could have taken over the whole damn town and killed you all in your sleep if we wanted to," continued Dahlia. "Hell, a couple of halfwit hamsters could have—"

Church touched her arm. "Stop showing off," he said mildly. "It's unseemly and inefficient. Clock is ticking."

The whistles were getting louder, emphasizing his point. People were coming from all over the town—many of them— and as they approached, the members of the Pack moved among them in pairs, one pointing a weapon, and the other taking any weapons held by the townies. It was a process that should not have been easy, and Dahlia had expected violent resistance, but the clockwork efficiency of the Pack, the confusion, and the obvious lack of training on the part of the townsfolk made the process a rinse-and-repeat. There were only a few instances of townies resisting, but the Pack members won every tussle. There were a few bruises and one smashed nose among Van Sloane's people, but that was all. It was very nearly a bloodless takeover.

That was not a comfort to Dahlia, though. The Rovers were coming and she had no idea how many of them there were. Or how well-armed they were.

Dahlia nodded and addressed Van Sloane in a calmer voice. "Listen, *Mayor* Van Sloane, those whistles are the Rovers. That's not a joke. I think the reason they're making so much noise, and the reason they aren't already climbing over the walls, is that they're playing a game. They're drawing your attention here. It worked, too, because you pulled most of your guards away from the rest of the walls. It's a magic trick. They make a big show of letting you see how empty their hands are, but they already have a bunch of stuff hidden in little pockets. Bunnies and scarves and stuff. Point is, you fell for it. They're going to hit you hard right here at the main gate and as soon as they're sure they have your complete attention, they'll hit you from behind."

"You can't know that," said Van Sloane, but there was no confidence in her tone.

"Sure we can," said Dahlia. "Nothing else makes sense. The Rovers want this place. They don't want to destroy it to take it, so distraction and infiltration makes perfect sense."

"I..." began Van Sloane, and then she faltered.

More whistles now. Louder and louder.

"Here's the way this is going to work," said Dahlia, raising her voice so everyone could hear. "Anyone in this crowd who came here looking for shelter and has had to work for it, step forward. Anyone who is a 'helper.' Anyone forced to work. Anyone who's had their stuff taken away. All of you step forward."

Out of a crowd of nearly three hundred people, more than a hundred people moved through the crowd toward Dahlia. They looked at her, and then at each other, and it was clear to her that they were surprised at how many there were. Van Sloane had probably kept them in small groups so they wouldn't have exactly this kind of realization.

The people were a mix of races—several kinds of Asian, and every shade of brown skin, from one couple who looked more African than African-American to Latinos and Middle Eastern faces. There were some white people, too, but they might as well have had "fringe crowd" tattooed on them. They were skaters, squatters, street kids, and others. No one who would easily fit into the world of manicured lawns, upscale socials, or summers in the Hamptons. They were dressed in a kind of uniform—as much as available clothing supplies allowed, she reckoned—jeans and T-shirts. All soiled by hard work, except for the ones who probably worked indoors or with kids.

As Dahlia climbed up onto a low brick decorative wall, she felt a whole speech rising to her lips, but she had to bite it down. Anything she said would be obvious to everyone, and they would all know that this wasn't an aberration. This was an extension of how it so often was—of an affected few using force, or laws, or trickery, or money to subjugate anyone who did not have the same skin color, the same politics, or belong to the same exclusive bloodlines. It made her want to stab Van Sloane in the face. A lot. It made her want to take all of the assholes who ran Happy Valley and toss them over the walls so the Rovers could do whatever they wanted to them. It made her hate being who she was—a child of privilege herself, a white girl. Fuck, it made her loathe being a carbon-based lifeform in this twisted world.

What she said aloud was different, and it took a great deal of willpower to say what she needed to say rather than what she wanted to say.

"This is all going to happen fast, so here's the deal," she shouted. "The helpers are free. No debts, no obligations, no bullshit. Anyone from Happy Valley who doesn't like it—too bad. But here's the thing. A gang called the Rovers are about to attack the town. Those whistles you hear are them coming. There are a lot of them. They won't give a crap if you're a resident here or a slave. They're coming to take this place away from all of us, and they aren't going to be nice about it. We don't have time for a debate and this isn't a democracy. I'm in charge."

"Says who?" growled one of the men from town. One of the helpers, a tall black man wearing work gloves and with grass stains on the knees of his pants, got up in his face.

"How about you shut the fuck up while you can still make

that choice on your own? Right about now she's the first person to say something I want to hear in a long damn time."

"You watch your mouth, nig—"

And that was as far as he got before the helper hooked a hard right fist into his gut and then brought his knee up as the man folded.

Then everyone was fighting.

– 39 –

THE WARRIOR WOMAN, THE SOLDIER, AND THE DOG

There were about a dozen of them, give or take. Everyone looked pretty well battered from the brawl they'd been engaged in. That didn't seem to matter, though, because by now they were all pumping adrenaline by the gallon.

Baskerville went crashing through them to Rachael, and his bulk—with all of the leather and spikes—slammed into the zombie holding her ankle. Baskerville is trained not to bite the dead, but he has no issues at all generally and enthusiastically fucking them up. I saw parts fly and then Rachael shimmied backward with the hand still clutched around her ankle, but no arms attached to it. She kicked it off and got immediately to her feet without wasting time on shock and surprise. Smart.

The Rovers and the townies were caught in a moment of indecision as to whether to fight me or each other. That was stupid. They should have fought me.

Ah well.

I didn't bother with my gun. Too noisy and bullets are hard to find. I had a katana and forty-plus years of practical experience with it. So I laid in with a will.

The blade is so perfectly made. The layered steel hammered and honed to a thing of art by a master sword maker. It's not a chopping weapon; it's surgical, and in the hands of an expert it seems to melt its way through flesh and bone with long, sweeping movements. I am an expert.

So, long story short…they all died.

Rachael killed a few. Baskerville took some. I killed everyone else. The forest was ringing with whistles and war was coming, so there was no time for anything but the killing. There was no time for mercy or giving quarter or anything else.

Does that make me a monster?

No. It makes me alive.

– 40 –

THE SIEGE OF HAPPY VALLEY

It all nearly fell apart right there. Right then. The crowd seemed to come alive in the wrong way and surge toward each other like a raging surf and a fragile levee. People were going to die right in front of her, and then no one would be left to fight the Rovers.

Suddenly a shot rang out and everyone froze. Mr. Church had climbed up next to Dahlia and he held an automatic pistol in one gloved hand. The gunshot and the gun itself were nothing compared to the actual palpable presence of the old man. He *owned* the moment and every single person there knew it. Felt it.

"Dahlia was speaking," he said into the uneasy silence. "She was telling you how you can all survive this. Be smart and listen."

He lowered the pistol but did not put it away. It lifted Dahlia's heart to have him there, but in the brief fight she had seen her Pack members move to break up the battle rather than descend into mindless violence. That lifted her even more. Even Slow Dog seemed to want to calm things down rather than bust heads.

"You people from town, you have to make a choice right now," said Dahlia. "Either you fight with us, or you go into those pens where you kept your helpers."

None of them spoke. She saw hard faces and resentment and anger. She wanted to see remorse. She wanted to see light-bulbs of understanding flash on, but this wasn't one of those old Hallmark movies. This wasn't a Disney ending.

She turned to Slow Dog. "Do it."

Immediately the bigger members of the Pack began herding the townies toward the pens. The few members of the Pack who had guns—their own or those taken from the townies—had to use the threat of them for emphasis. No shots were fired, though. No one died. There were angry, ugly words, and some people still had to be pushed, but it got done. Mayor Van Sloane turned coldly and walked, with a show of great dignity, after them.

That left the helpers—a word she hated but had no immediate replacement for—and her own Pack. An army of two hundred. She immediately had everyone share out arms and count ammunition. Forty-nine guns but not enough ammunition for a war. Plenty of bows and arrows, though.

"Okay," she said, "here's what we're going to do…"

– 41 –

THE WARRIOR WOMAN, THE SOLDIER, AND THE DOG

When it was done I hurried over to Rachael, who was flushed and weeping. She stood by the guy who had been tied next to her, and as I approached I saw that she wept for more than what had happened to him. She wept for what she had to do. Her friend's eyes were open, but they were empty of everything except that bottomless hunger. The other intended victim, the girl, was crying hysterically, banging her head against the pole to which she was bound.

"I'll do it," I said, reaching for the weapon Rachael had removed from the dead fingers of the woman she'd been fighting. But Rachael shook her head.

"Jason is my friend," she said. Using "is," not "was." That hurt to hear. I waited until she'd quieted the young man before I cut her friend loose. The girl wrapped her arms around Rachael, clung to her.

I cut Jason down and laid him on the dirt. The two women knelt with me. The younger one, I learned, was Claudia. She bent forward and buried her face against Jason's chest and wept with deep but silent tears.

Rachael grabbed my wrist. "Joe…how are you even *here?* I feel like I'm in a weird dream."

"There's no time for campfire tales, kiddo," I said. "Those whistles are trouble coming." I gave her the rundown on the Rovers and she told me about Happy Valley.

"Is it me," she said, "or has a disproportionate number of total fucking assholes survived the apocalypse?"

"Sadly, it's not you." The whistles were constant, but they weren't that close to where we were. That wasn't all that much of a comfort.

"They're heading to Happy Valley," said Rachael, reading the sounds correctly.

"Yes. Do you still have friends there?"

"No, but there are a lot of people who need our help."

"Pardon me for saying this, but fuck the residents."

She shook her head. "Not them."

Rachael told me about the "helpers." "I can't just leave them there. Even if the townies stop the Rovers…"

"Yeah," I said and sighed. "Guess this is going to be a long day."

She started to say something, then stopped and smiled, shaking her head.

"What?" I asked.

"No…it's just that I almost said that it isn't your fight, but that's dumb. The Nu Klux Klan wasn't your fight, either. Neither was helping me and Dez Fox and those kids."

I got to my feet, then glanced down at Claudia. When Rachael caught me looking, she nodded and moved to put her arm around her friend. They spoke together very quietly for a few minutes, then Rachael kissed her cheek and came over to me.

"Claudia's had too much lately, you know," she said very quietly. "She's going to see to Jason. Bury him if she can. And she wants to cut down all of the other people the townies brought out here. Don't worry, she's pretty smart and sharp and if the Rovers come out this way, she knows how to hide."

I didn't ask if Rachael was sure about all this. It was her call to make. I clicked my tongue for Baskerville, who bounded over like an overgrown puppy, despite the blood splashed on his armor.

Without another word we set off into the woods.

As we ran, I had no real idea how this was going to work. The odds were looking really damn long. We were a young woman barely out of her teens, an overgrown dog, and a crazy middle-aged guy. Against an army of Rovers and a town full of assholes.

Shit.

– 42 –

HAPPY VALLEY

Dahlia positioned her army on the walls, doing a lightning fast survey of skills. Anyone who had skills with weapons or who could swing a stick or bat became fighters. Anyone with first-aid knowledge was ordered to set up triage centers. Those who weren't able to do either task were assigned to protect the children. The guns were put into the hands of the Pack members who could shoot or helpers who'd either served in the military or hunted.

She had runners collect wheelbarrows full of rocks and river stones used in decorative gardens, and these were hauled up to the walls for those fighters who said they could throw. One older Latino man used to be a pitching coach for AAA ball and swore that he could hit whatever he aimed at.

The whistles were louder than ever and just as Dahlia turned to look up at the wall, Neeko twisted around and yelled down at her. "They're coming!"

Dahlia hurried up to see. At first there was nothing but the sound of those damn whistles. And then a figure broke from the woods. If it was a Rover, though, then he was dressed differently. Instead of wearing leather, this one wore a set of mechanic's coveralls and what looked like a kind of screen-covered head net. The sound of the whistle came from beneath the head covering. And there was something strange about the coveralls. They were wet. They glistened, as if covered with oil.

"God almighty," she heard someone breath and Dahlia turned to see the black man who'd fought with the loudmouth. John, she thought his name was.

"What is it?" asked Jumper. "What am I seeing?"

John pointed. "It's black blood," he said, and when Neeko didn't seem to get it, the man explained. "His clothes are covered with zombie blood."

A second person came out of the woods, and this one wore painter's coveralls, similarly smeared with infected blood, and a similar head covering. He too was blowing a whistle.

"Oh...shit," said Dahlia. She and John exchanged a frightened, knowing glance. They knew what was coming. Five more of the Rovers came out of the woods, each of them dressed similarly. Then ten more. More and more. They were spaced out in a wide line at least two hundred yards wide. All of them blowing whistles. Some of them walking backward and waving their arms.

"What are they...?" asked someone, but the words trailed off as the whole front of the forest suddenly trembled and the dead came stumbling, walking, shambling, lumbering into the sunlight. Following the whistles.

Dahlia's mouth went dry.

This was not an army.

This was an *ocean* of the hungry dead.

She wanted to scream. She wanted to turn and run through the town, climb the rear wall and run away.

Instead she looked up and down the length of the wall. Everyone stood staring in shock. In terror. In helplessness.

Smaller groups of Rovers, similarly dressed, came out of the woods along a game trail. They were pushing big green carts on fat, low-pressure tires. Dahlia recognized the carts as the kind used at a chain of big home and garden centers. She squinted through the sun glare and tried to make out what the carts were filled with. Bottles…? No, it was worse than that. Each bottle had a piece of cloth stuffed into its mouth, with the edges bouncing as the carts rolled over the uneven ground. Dahlia fished for the word for this, but John supplied it.

"Holy god," said the man. "Molotov cocktails. They're going to burn us out."

The Rovers pushed the carts forward, running between masses of the dead. A few zombies took weak swipes at them, but the black gore on their clothes kept the Rovers safe from any real attack.

More and more of the dead poured out of the forest. There had to be a couple thousand of them. This was no random attack. That was obvious. The Rovers must have been planning this for a long time. Gathering supplies, working out details, and meticulously planning the siege. She could hear the people on the walls begin to buzz with nervous chatter.

"Hold fast," she bellowed. "The dead can't climb the walls. We got this. We…"

Her words faltered as another group of Rovers walked out of the surging mass of the dead. There were five of them in protective clothes smeared with infected blood. Untouched. Unmolested by the monsters because they, too, smelled dead. They ran in a knot, outpacing the zombies and the Rovers pushing the carts as they dashed toward the walls. Two of them carried rifles, but Dahlia didn't care about that. It was the other three that really scared her. They carried larger weapons, running with them in both hands. Like oversized rifles but with a big bulbous thing sticking out of the barrel. Dahlia knew what they were. She'd seen movies. She'd watched news footage of the wars in Iraq and Syria and Afghanistan.

She knew what a rocket propelled grenade was.

Just as she knew that the walls of Happy Valley were not built to withstand that kind of attack.

Not one chance in hell.

– 43 –

THE WARRIOR WOMAN, THE SOLDIER, AND THE DOG

I didn't think a straight run to town was the smart move. Turns out I was right, but not for the reasons I thought.

The obvious danger was packs of Rovers. That would have been bad enough, but when there were brief pauses in the sounds of whistles we heard something else. Actually, Baskerville smelled it first and went rigid with tension. We stopped, crouching on either side of him, listening.

There it was.

The moans. It was like a wave of sound that seemed to come from everywhere. Birds fled from the trees and escaped into the western skies. A pair of deer bolted from within a nest of fallen branches and ran like mad past us. Squirrels chittered as they ran from tree to tree. Everything that lived in these woods and had enough intelligence to be frightened was fleeing. The moans, and the dark intent implied by that sound, seemed to chase them.

"God," breathed Rachael. "*Orcs.*"

"A whole goddamn lot of them," I agreed.

Suddenly the woods transformed from being a cloud of relative safety inside which we could hide and move, to a cloth of sickness into which we were sewn as fragile threads. I checked my ammunition. Two full magazines and a third with seven rounds. Rachael had a shotgun from one of the townies, but it was a single shot version and there were four rounds plus one in the breech. Not enough for a war, and too loud to risk using.

I tapped her shoulder and we moved off. Every now and then we caught glimpses of the horde—that's the only word that really fit—and it chilled us.

"How can there be this many of them?" asked Rachael as we ran. "And why are they all heading toward the town?" Then she raised her head as a fresh burst of whistles filled the air. "Oh," she said, then amended it. "Oh god."

Happy Valley was in deep shit. We'd started out thinking we were going to be able to help. Now it seemed as if all we'd be able to do was maybe bury the dead.

– 44 –

HAPPY VALLEY

"Down!" screamed Dahlia as she dove for cover. John and Neeko and the others scrambled away, tripping and falling. People flung themselves from the walls, landing hard on the ground ten feet below.

There was a sharp, rising sound like steam escaping from a boiling kettle and then the whole top part of the wall seemed to lift itself from the structure of reality and fly through the air. A massive red flower of superheated gas bloomed, spreading burning petals arching into the town. Trees caught fire and people screamed as fiery debris landed on them, igniting clothes and hair.

For Dahlia the world went red and then black as she lost

herself for a moment. Seconds? Longer? When she opened her eyes, she was still on the wall, but she was alone. Her ears rang with a sound like an electronic wail and her hair was burning. She panicked, swatting at it, slapping her scalp, her face.

"Ne—Neeko...?" she croaked, but if there was an answer she could not hear it. The noise in her ears was too loud. It took her a thousand years to climb to her feet. Hot smoke scorched her lungs and every breath rubbed her throat raw. "Neeko," she screamed.

A figure moved in the smoke. Blackened and unreal. Staggering as it moved toward her. Shambling. It was Neeko sized and Neeko shaped, and it moved with artless clumsiness like one of the dead things. It reached for her with gray hands.

Dahlia backed away. Of all the horrors in her world, she could not bear this. Not Neeko. Not him.

She saw his lips move but there were no words.

"No..." she begged.

Dahlia drew her *kukri* knife and tried to brace against a kind of pain that could not be endured. Neeko stumbled toward her.

She raised the knife.

A voice rang out. Harsh, and loud enough to punch through the incessant ringing in her ears.

"*No!*" roared Mr. Church.

Dahlia turned to see him come striding toward her, a pistol in one hand, his tinted glasses gone, dark eyes filled with pain and concern. Neeko turned toward him and reached for him instead.

And Old Man Church wrapped his free arm around the little scout's shoulders and pulled him close.

"You're okay, son," said the old man. "You're okay."

Neeko clung to him, and Dahlia saw that he was alive. She had not been able to hear him speak because of the ringing. His skin was gray because he was covered with dust. She staggered over and nearly tore him away from Church and kissed him and then crushed the boy to her chest. Then she looked around. Others were not so lucky.

Down on the street level, a Latina who had been one of the helpers manning the wall was struggling to rise, but it was clear the fall had killed her. A huge piece of jagged masonry stood out from between her breasts and her eyes were empty of everything. The black man, John, was backing away from her, shaking his head. Unwilling in the moment to accept it.

Church raised his pistol and shot the woman through the forehead. She puddled down into true death. And John stood there, still shaking his head, tears glistening in his eyes.

Dahlia turned away. The damage to the wall was significant. The RPG had struck a few feet from the top and it was as if a giant had bitten a half-moon shaped chunk out of the peach stucco and cinderblock. The gap was eight feet wide and a yard deep, which meant the bottom edge of it was only seven feet from the ground. An easy climb for a man. If all those dead crammed the walls, the ones in front would be crushed and the others would simply crawl or climb over them to get in. Plus there was a pile of debris at the foot of the wall. In effect, there was no real defense.

"God, look," said one of the remaining guards on the wall. She did. The Rovers were aiming a second rocket-propelled grenade.

"Down," she cried, and they all leapt from the wall as the missile tore through the air and detonated. It struck fifteen feet to the right and struck in the middle of the wall, blowing a hole clean through. The gap was only three feet high, but there were cracks all around it.

"Get everyone back to their jobs," Church said to Dahlia. "Keep them busy. Stick to the plan."

"We didn't plan for rocket launchers," she gasped. "How—?"

"Stick to the plan," he said again, leaning into it. "We need people on every wall. We need to find every possible weapon. You thought it through, Dahlia, now *see* it through."

"But...what are you going to do?"

"Buy you some time," Church said. "We can't take too many more hits." He looked around and spotted an armed helper running for the wall. "You! Your gun. *Now.*"

The man skidded to a stop and looked doubtfully at the white-haired old man. "You even know how to use this?"

Church took it from him without answering. It was a sturdy Weatherby Vanguard RC bolt-action hunting rifle with a twenty-four-inch barrel. He checked the loads and found that he had only three .300 Winchester Magnum bullets.

"Is there more ammunition?"

"Took it from one of the townies," said the man. "He didn't have any extra rounds on him."

"Find more or find me another rifle," ordered Church as he climbed to a spot between the two breeches. Out on the field the Rovers in protective clothing were still blowing their whistles while the forest continued to vomit forth the dead in an unending stream. They were all coming from the sections of the forest where the Rovers themselves had emerged, suggestive of them having followed the whistles like the children of Hamelin following the Pied Piper. He frowned because there was something about that process that seemed wrong to him.

First things first.

He crouched behind an unbroken section of wall, propped his elbow on the top and leaned into the stock as he sighted his target. One of the Rovers was crabbing sideways to get a better angle on the wall twenty feet to the left of where the first grenade had hit. His frown deepened because it a was poor choice of targets. Whether the Rovers themselves wanted to invade the town or if they intended the dead to be a forlorn hope, it was a bad choice of target when you wanted to break down a wall.

If, in fact, that was their plan at all.

Time to sort it out later. Church sighted through the deerhunter's scope and drew his bead. Then he fired, leaning in to take the shot, keeping the weapon steady. He exhaled and squeezed the trigger just as the Rover was pulling his. The heavy bullet struck the launcher's metal tube and ricocheted along the weapon, exploding the fingers of the man holding it and then glancing off to punch a red hole through his lower lip and out through his cheek. The Rover screamed and his finger jerked the trigger, but the launcher spun and twisted as he fell and the grenade went skittering and hissing across the grass toward the oncoming tide of bodies. It struck the ankle of one of the Rovers in bloody coveralls and exploded, flinging red rags across the faces of the dead.

The zombies went mad with the smell and taste of fresh meat and suddenly the driving herd was a disordered mess. The Rovers with the bloody clothes and whistles had to back sharply away from clutching hands. Two Rovers were splashed with blood from their dead companion and they vanished beneath a wave of the dead.

Closer to the wall, several of the zombies turned to rush at the man Church had shot. The bullet had done terrible damage, but he was alive. However, he was splashed with his own blood, as were the others in the RPG team. A dozen zombies swarmed over them, driven wild by the smell and sight of fresh human blood. It trumped the nullifying effect of the zombie blood on their clothes. Church watched this with a cold eye, noting the effect and nodding to himself.

He worked the bolt and shifted the rifle to another target—a pair of Rovers leading a huge mass of zombies—and fired a single shot. He aimed for a stomach shot and hit the Rover just off center. With only muscle and organs to punch through, the bullet went all the way through the first Rover and into the groin of the second. Lots of blood.

The effect was immediate and appalling. The zombies following the Rovers went from a shambling mass drawn only by the whistles and became a pack of predators sparked to frenzy by blood. They fell on the wounded Rovers and even from that distance Church could hear the screams.

He shifted and used his last round to get a similar gory effect on the left flank of the assault.

Dahlia stood watching from the wall and was amazed at the effect of three carefully chosen shots. It was surgical, calculated, and horrible. But it was perfect, too, because now the attack was in total confusion.

What disturbed her, though, was the complete lack of emotion on the old man's face. He was not only an excellent shot, but ice cold, too. No flicker of human emotion showed at all as he caused people to die in awful ways. She wondered if that was something she should aspire to, or something she should fear.

– 45 –

THE WARRIOR WOMAN, THE SOLDIER, AND THE DOG

We could see daylight through the trees and I signaled Rachael to stay low and be very quiet. She moved well, and we crept to the edge of the forest. Up ahead were three people dressed in what looked like white hazmat suits covered with black muck. There were no obvious rents or tears in their clothing and they moved with the coordination of living men, not the awkwardness of the dead. Baskerville sniffed and looked uncertainly from them to me and back.

I waved Rachael to a spot behind a tree and held a finger to my lips. She nodded and crouched, still but ready. I gave a hand signal to Baskerville to circle and take up a flanking position. While he was doing that I crept forward for a better look.

The three people in the white suits were struggling with a big plastic cart. The left rear wheel had come off and they were trying to fix it without the use of any tools. There was a lot of cursing. Dead people don't curse. Their language was very colorful and included descriptions of improbable sexual acts that would have been both gymnastic, humiliating, and painful. I caught one comment, though, that told me who they were.

"Big Elroy's going to have your balls," said one of them.

"Yeah, well fuck your mama with a donkey dick," was the reply. "Are you going to help me with this thing or not?"

Ah. Rovers. Nice people. Bet they're great at family picnics with Grandma and all the kids.

The fact that Rovers were here, dressed like this, and splashed with zombie blood made a lot of things make sense. The whistles and moans had a clear logic to them now. It was a smart plan, and there was a damn good chance it would work, especially considering how goddamn stupid the people manning the walls of the town were last time I checked.

I shifted around so I could see past them, and my heart sank. Out in the field between the forest and the town was a fucking war. Other Rovers, dressed just like these three, were leading masses of zombies toward the town. The walls of the town were smoking and there were two big holes. How had the Rovers accomplished that level of damage?

The answer came with the sound of a gunshot. A heavy-caliber rifle. I took out my binoculars and saw zombies swarming over a badly-injured man. Other men stood with him and they carried shoulder-mounted RPGs. Well, hell. That wasn't good. From the carnage around them, though, it was clear someone from the town had returned fire and the fresh blood had trumped the protective clothing. Either a lucky accident or a smart plan.

There was a second shot, and a third. In each case the victim was wounded rather than killed. In both cases there was a lot of damn blood, and that's not a happy thing for them when you're surrounded by an army of flesh-eating ghouls. I watched with some amusement as the living dead tore into the wounded Rovers, and anyone else splashed with their blood. I waited for more shots from the walls, but there were none.

Even so, whoever had fired those shots was a cold and clever bastard. Shame he or she was a resident of Happy Valley. It's hard to admire talent in someone who is otherwise a total rat bastard.

The three Rovers near me were watching all this, too.

"Shit," said one of them. "Those dead cocksuckers are going batshit."

"No," said another, pointing. "The handlers are working them. See?"

And it was true. The flurry of murder did not last long, and from what I could tell it accounted for only about eight or ten of the Rovers. There were many others, and they ran along the ragged lines of the dead, blowing their whistles and shoving them toward the town. I saw several more carts like the one near me, and some of the Rovers were reaching into them and removing bottles. One person at each cart lit something—a torch of some kind—and the other Rovers leaned toward the flames, lighting cloth streamers stuffed into the necks. Molotov cocktails without a doubt. Then they ran and hurled the bottles, smashing them onto the ground. The oil or alcohol in each splashed out and the flames leaped up.

At first there didn't seem to be a use for this, because they weren't even trying to reach the walls. For a moment I thought they were afraid of more gunfire, but then as more and more of the Molotov cocktails exploded, the sense of it became obvious. The Rovers had lured the dead out of the forest with whistles, and now they were creating lines of fire on the field to drive the dead along corridors of flame that narrowed down to where the walls had been breached. Zombies shy away from flames—not sure if they're afraid of it or because there's nothing about the burning heat that smells of life or food. In any case, they shifted away and moved toward the smell of life beyond the walls.

It was another sign the Rovers had thought this through.

I glanced back at the three Rovers and the cart near me. By standing on my tippy-toes I could see the necks of dozens of bottles with rags stuck in the mouths. More cocktails for the garden party.

I grinned. Sometimes I love being who I am and thinking the way I think.

I drew my pistol and walked around behind them. They were really focused on what was happening on the field. I took up a solid shooter's stance, raised the gun in a two-hand grip and said, "Hey, fellas."

They whirled.

They saw the gun. Then they saw Baskerville come loping out of the brush. Their weapons—an axe, a scythe and assorted knives—stuck up from a corner of the cart.

"Who the fuck are you?" demanded one of them.

I pointed the barrel at his face and said, "Shhhhhh."

They shushed.

"You cats have one chance here," I told them. "Strip off those hazmat suits. Do it right now. No...no talk, no questions. That's it, good boys."

They removed the garments and stood in their leather and spikes, with their necklaces of ugly parts. And, as it turned out, it was two men and a woman.

"You," I said to the guy who'd asked who I was, "pick up the clothes and put them over there next to my dog. Be real careful about it, too. Baskerville hasn't eaten yet this morning and although you probably have too small a dick to fill his belly, that *is* where he'd take his first bite. Feel me?"

He apparently did, and moved with all the delicate care of someone walking blindfolded through a minefield. He dropped the mucky white garments a few feet from Baskerville.

While he did that, Rachael came quietly out of the woods and stood on the far side of the cart. They glanced at her in surprise. Not unreasonable, considering Rachael wore parts of old-fashioned armor, had blood matted in her hair, and a big tear in the front of her Batgirl T-shirt. She was also giving them a look that would have frightened a crocodile.

"Who the hell's she supposed to be?"

"I thought that was pretty obvious," I said. "She's Batgirl."

I said it in a Christian Bale raspy voice, but they looked blank. Wrong crowd, or maybe the movie was too old for them. Whatever.

"Okay, assholes," I said, "what's the plan for Happy Valley? I mean, the whole plan. I want details and I want them now."

The first guy snorted. "You're out of your fucking mind if you think—"

I shot him in the face. He fell backward and down and I took a step forward and pointed the gun at the woman, who'd stood closest to him and whose face was now painted with blood and brains. Rachael shifted toward the second man, and Baskerville moved quickly to stand within easy kill range of both Rovers.

The Rovers jumped and cried out when I fired my shot, but then turned to statues. Their eyes were wide, mouths open, and it was clear that any power that they perceived in themselves had crumbled away.

"I only need one of you to answer my questions," I said, moving the barrel from one to the other. "That one gets to walk out of here."

As it happened, they both decided that it was a good time for a conversation. Once they got in gear, I could hardly shut them up.

– 46 –

HAPPY VALLEY

Dahlia recoiled from the flames that sprang up in long lines across the field. The living dead stumbled forward in their hundreds. A few staggered too close to the fires, and flames leapt onto dried flesh and rags of clothing, turning them into torches. Here and there some of these walking bonfires collided with other zombies, but the Rovers were there with long poles to knock them away before they could start a conflagration.

The mass moved on, getting closer to the wall. Soon they would be climbing toward the breech.

"Archers," yelled Dahlia, and those members of the Pack who had real skill with bows drew arrows and began firing. The first volley hit home, with every arrow finding undead flesh, but only two zombies fell. "Aim for the head!"

They tried and the second volley was almost entirely wasted. Arrows struck eyes but the archers were shooting down and the barbs drove at the wrong angle. Most of the arrows passed over their heads and hit the chests of the creatures behind them.

The zombies surged forward through the alley of flames.

"Wait," yelled Dahlia. "Legs. Shoot their legs."

The archers stared at her for a moment, then one by one they understood and reached for new arrows. They took careful aim and fired. Of the nineteen arrows fired, seven struck the big muscles of the thighs in the front rank of zombies. There was minimal blood and no trace of pain on the faces of those who were struck, but five of that seven fell as the damage from broad-bladed arrows caused muscles and tendons to tear themselves apart. Even the dead need muscular integrity to stand and walk.

The five that fell were like a tripwire to the dozen behind them. Suddenly the ruse was a collision, with ungainly bodies tripping over them and the mass behind continuing to press forward.

"Rocks," bellowed Dahlia and a wave of helpers snatched up pieces of broken cinderblock and handfuls of river stones and hurled them down at the zombies. Trying to smash heads, and sometimes managing it. Other rocks broke arms or legs.

The archers kept firing and the helpers kept throwing rocks with frenzied energy, and Dahlia's army built a bulwark of corpses fifteen feet from the breech.

Down on the ground level, Old Man Church had handed off the empty rifle and hurried over to the pen where the townsfolk were kept under guard. He ignored the stares of resentment, fear, and hatred.

"Open it," he told Slow Dog, who was standing guard. Slow Dog obeyed at once and then took up a position with a double-barreled shotgun just outside. Church walked past him into the cage.

"You're going to regret this," began Margaret Van Sloane, but Church walked past her as if she was nothing. Less than a gnat. He stopped in the center of the pen with enough people surrounding him that if they wanted to kill him, everyone there knew they could. He had no weapon in his gloved hands, and he was an old man.

"Listen to me," he said. "The Rovers are here. You can hear it. You heard the explosions. The front wall is badly damaged and Dahlia, her Pack, and the people you enslaved here are fighting against a coordinated attack that can, and very likely will, be too much for us to stop. The Rovers will get in here. So will several hundred of the living dead. Happy Valley is going to fall." He looked around at a sea of faces. Even the most hardened of them looked scared. "If the enemy breaks in, we will all die. That is certain."

The sounds of the battle—screams, explosions, whistles, moans—filled the air.

"You people know this town. Maybe you have resources here Dahlia doesn't know about. Extra weapons and ammunition. Materials that can be used as explosives. Body armor. Cans of hairspray that can be used as blow torches. Anything that can give us a better chance."

The people said nothing. Some people could not, or would not, meet his eyes.

"We need those resources," said Church, "and we need fighters. We need any of you who are willing to fight *with* us rather than against us."

Van Sloane gave a loud, derisive snort. "You have to be out of your mind if you think any of us would lift a finger to help you and—"

"I'll do it," said a young woman of about twenty. She was slim and fit, with blonde hair and bright blue eyes.

"Be quiet, Bree," snapped Van Sloane. "Nobody asked you."

"Me, too," said a tall teenager. Maybe seventeen, with broad shoulders and a receding chin.

"Yeah," said another young man, and then two twenty-something women nodded and stepped forward. Several of the older townies cried out in protest, and one caught the wrist of Bree, the first girl who'd spoken up.

"What are you *doing*?" demanded the woman.

Bree looked at her and then jerked her wrist away. "I guess I'm doing what you won't, Mom."

Others stepped forward, and it was clear that the ones who volunteered were all young, from twelve up to maybe twenty-four or -five. None older.

"We have some guns in the basement," said the broad-shouldered teen.

"Thomas," said an older man, "*no*."

Thomas turned to the man, who was clearly his father. "I've been meaning to ask you this for a long time, Dad," he said. "So...tell me, what the fuck is wrong with you?" He looked around at Van Sloane and the other adults. "What the fuck is wrong with all of you?"

Bree shook her head. "What's wrong with *us*?"

Church held up a hand. "Much as I would love to moderate an existential debate, we have a war to fight. Anyone who wants to help save the whole town, come with me."

All the young people moved forward and a few of the adults made to follow. Church stepped into their path.

"Be very careful with what you decide," he said. "If anyone comes out of this cage with anything but a desire to help *every-one*, I will kill them. Look into my eyes and ask yourself if I'm joking."

Two of the men glanced at each other and then stepped back. They cut looks at Van Sloane, but she said nothing. The other adults nodded to Church and followed the younger residents out. Church went last and lingered for a moment in the doorway.

"You're choosing to remain in a cage rather than fight along-side your own children. You're staying here rather than fight for your own lives." He shook his head. "I've seen a lot of flavors of human cowardice and aggressive stupidity, but quite frankly, you amaze me. And you disappoint me."

With that he turned and left, and the cage was locked behind him.

The battle at the wall was going better than Dahlia thought. The combination of precise archery and then the hurling of stones was creating an actual wall of writhing bodies that, so far, was keeping the main army of the zombies away.

But it was working a little too well.

As she walked along the wall, directing the fight, Dahlia tried to apply all of the lessons Church had given her about tactics and strategy. From a certain distance, the Rovers' plan was solid: herding the dead onto the field, using the RPGs to weaken the wall, and then creating walls of flame to funnel the dead toward the breaches. All sound.

Except that it wasn't.

She chewed her lip and peered over the walls at the enemy outside the gates. There were so many of the dead, and there were some wild spots where random walkers burned. Rovers used their poles to keep the burning wanderers from setting the whole mass of the dead alight. The teams with the Molotov cocktails made sure the fires didn't go out.

So…what was wrong?

She stopped and stared.

There had to be at least thirty Rovers on the field, each doing different jobs.

Thirty.

Thirty?

"Oh…*shit*," she said, and then she turned and leaped down from the wall. Although she hated to run, she ran now as new and sudden terror exploded inside her heart.

They were going to lose this fight, and now she understood why.

– 47 –

THE WARRIOR WOMAN, THE SOLDIER, AND THE DOG

Rachael, Baskerville, and I ran as fast as we could. My arms and the dog's saddlebags clinked and clanked with bottles and we stank of gasoline.

Better than the stink of the living dead blood on the white hazmat suits Rachael and I wore. And the body odor stench of the guy who'd worn it before me.

Oh, and for the record, I lied. To the two Rovers who I'd interrogated. I promised that they could walk if they told us everything they knew. No. They weren't walking anywhere, not even as the walking dead.

If I expected Rachael to give me a hard time about it, I underestimated her. Maybe the death of her friend Jason was too fresh in her mind. Or maybe surviving out here in this broken world has changed her. She watched me kill the Rovers and did not so much as blink.

It made me a little sad, actually. For her.

We skirted the edge of the field, catching glimpses of the fight. From what I could see, the Rovers had told us the truth. The massive frontal assault was still under way, but it was obvious the Rovers weren't really trying to take the town.

Not from the front anyway.

No, the Rovers were being very smart and very devious.

And so we ran, hoping there was still some time left on the clock.

– 48 –

THE SIEGE OF HAPPY VALLEY

The Pack member left in charge of the rear was named Tammy-Ducks. She was nineteen, short and fit and smart. Until two months ago she'd been with a group of college kids who'd had to fend for themselves after the outbreak spilled over into a small sports venue where a gymnastics competition was underway. Tammy-Ducks was a gymnast, specializing in floor routines and the balance beam. She also had a little bit of judo from a two-credit course she took during her freshman year, and a lot of rough-and-tumble fighting tricks from growing up with four older brothers. The last seven members of her team were absorbed into the Pack after Dahlia and Slow Dog saved them from a large swarm of zombies.

Tammy-Ducks had loved the training provided by Old Man Church—who she privately thought was sexy as hell, despite being really, really old and really, really scary. Like the other girls on the team, Tammy-Ducks was coordinated, fast, and knew how to learn.

Now she and her teammates were in charge of keeping the rear wall safe.

However, Tammy-Ducks was pretty sure they were all going to die.

There was a sloping hill behind the wall that rose pretty sharply upward, and not a lot of open ground. Scrub pines littered the narrow gully between wall and hill, though, and obscured good lines of sight. There were people moving behind those trees, but she couldn't tell how many. All she was sure of was that they were not dead people. They moved quickly and furtively, and every now and then she caught a quick flash of something. Possibly the reflection of sunlight off of binocular lenses. It made her deeply uneasy, because someone out there could see her more easily than she could see them.

"Yuki," she called to one of the other girls, "get me some binoculars, okay?"

After a minute Yuki came along the narrow walkway inside the top of the wall and handed a pair to her. They were not very good glasses, but then again the distance wasn't very long. Tammy-Ducks took them and peered through, adjusting the focus.

"You see anything?" asked Yuki, squinting from beneath a shading hand.

"Yeah, hold on…"

There was definitely movement in the trees. She saw several Rovers in leather moving quickly from right to left. They ran with unusual orderliness and then she realized why. They were running in pairs, each set carrying a ladder. Big aluminum extension ladders. The Rovers followed the uneven terrain away from the rear gate, though.

"Crap," she said.

"What?" asked Yuki.

"Wait, I see something else," said Tammy-Ducks, draawn by another of the bright flashes. She rested her forearms on the wall to steady her sight and studied the shadows between two pines that grew very close together. Something was glinting there.

Yes. There it was. Not binoculars at all. Only a single lens of a—

She never heard the shot. The sniper's bullet punched through the right lens of her binoculars and blew out the back of her head. Tammy-Ducks fell backward off the wall without making a sound.

Old Man Church ran with the young residents as they went from one home to another to retrieve hidden weapons. A pair of fine Winchester rifles, four .9mm handguns with multiple magazines, and a pump shotgun with two full boxes of buckshot. He handed out the weapons to the Pack members and a few helpers who'd come with them. One of the helpers, a good-looking Jamaican-American named Zack, accepted a Glock but then fumbled with an attempt to load it. The young man named Thomas held out his hand.

"Let me," he said. After only a moment's pause, Zack handed him the gun. Thomas ejected the magazine, checked that it was loaded, and slapped it back in with a great show of competence. Then he reversed the weapon and offered it butt-first. "Like that."

Zack took it and for a moment they eyed each other with some level of communication that had nothing to do with their individual ethnicity or their place in the former structure of the Happy Valley community. When Zack took the weapon, his fingers brushed Thomas's and there was a flicker in the air between them. Thomas smiled and turned away.

"Get a room," muttered Slow Dog, but the two men ignored him.

The group moved on.

Members of the Pack were running wildly to and fro carrying bags or laundry baskets or pushing wheelbarrows filled with bags of fertilizer, cans of hairspray, boxes of matches, bags of nails and screws to use as shrapnel, red cans of gasoline, containers of soap powder. All of the things Dahlia would need to construct fragmentation bombs and incendiary devices. Church approved and led his own team on, kicking in doors to find what they needed, taking direction from the young residents. Once everyone was armed with something—firearm, bladed farm tool, or baseball bat—Church led them to the western wall.

"Start here," he said. "Up on the catwalks. Walk the walls in pairs. Scout the woods."

"Shouldn't we be back at the gate where the fight is?" asked Bree.

"No," said Church. "We should not."

Dahlia reached the rear wall in time to see Yuki pitched backward as the sharp crack of a heavy rifle bounced off the walls. Tammy-Ducks lay in a heap along with two others. Tammy-Ducks would never rise, but the other two were already beginning to twitch as the parasites in their blood reanimated them.

"I got this," yelled Jumper and he quickly quieted each with dagger thrusts to the backs of their necks. It was horrible, and she could see how this cost the young man.

Dahlia looked up at the wall and took a breath.

"You can't go up there," said one of the gymnasts, who'd leapt down and was forcing words out through terrible sobs. "He'll kill you, too."

Dahlia went up anyway, though she kept low and only took tiny, brief looks over the wall. On the third try a shot chipped out a piece of masonry four inches from her head. A single shot.

She closed her eyes and tried to replay what she'd seen in those brief glances. Trees, a slope. People running. Heading to the western side of town. That's where Church was. Dahlia came down and sent a runner to warn him.

"Aren't we going, too?" asked Jumper.

"No," she said. "It won't be here."

"What won't?"

"The real attack. This isn't where they're going to come over the wall. There's not enough room for them. The hill's too close. And I don't think it's going to be the west wall either."

"Why not?"

"Because they're letting us see them carrying ladders that way."

Without another word, she wheeled around and ran along the wall, heading east.

I stopped Rachael and Baskerville at the edge of the woods on the east side of the town, and it's a damn good thing I did. The forest beyond where we stood ran up and over a rocky ridge. There were several Rovers on our side of the ridge and no one out in the field, but there was a weird vibe to the air. Call it a sense of expectant dread. Whatever. Or maybe it was a case of the willies.

"What is it?" asked Rachael as we hunkered down behind a boulder.

"Listen," I said, pulling off the white hood.

She glanced at me for a moment, then did the same. She cocked her head toward the west. At first she frowned and shook her head, then she went still and I saw it on her face. She heard it, too.

"People," she said, lowering her voice to a whisper. "A lot of them."

"Yeah."

Rachael looked over her shoulder the way we'd come. "No orcs over here."

"Nope."

I studied the open space and saw something else. I touched her arm and pointed.

"What...?"

I handed her my binoculars. "See the grass there? Right there, at the base of the wall? Tell me if it looks right to you."

She used the glasses to study where I'd indicated. Another frown. "The grass looks torn up. Kind of clumped."

"Uh huh. Want to take a guess what's under those clumps?"

She thought about it, glancing back to the ridge a few times.

"If that's where most of the Rovers are," she said slowly, "and if all that stuff going on out front is a big distraction, then..."

"Keep going," I said, "you're doing good."

"Then how are they going to get over the wall here?"

"How indeed?"

She lowered the glasses. "You think they have ladders hidden under the grass?"

"I'd actually be kind of disappointed if they didn't. All things considered it's a pretty snazzy plan. Good chance it's going to work, too."

"Can we do anything? I mean...there's a lot of them, right? What can we possibly do now?"

I grinned and pulled the hood over my face. "Not sure about you, kiddo, but I intend to misbehave."

"'*Aim* to misbehave,'" she said.

"What?"

"It's a quote from *Serenity*," she said. "The old movie. The spinoff of *Firefly*...?"

I patted her shoulder. "You may very well be the toughest absolute nerd girl left on Earth."

"Thanks," she said. And meant it.

We got up and, yes, we misbehaved.

Dahlia found Church and told him what she thought.

"Go back to the main gate," he said. "It may be a dodge, and I rather think it is, but it's still a major threat. We need to change the dynamic there. Your original plan is still a good one, but the mission has changed. Adapt to that. We need to shift the swarm. Do you understand?"

"Got it," she said.

"I'll leave Jumper and some people here and take the rest to the east wall."

"What about the sniper out back?"

"Let him stay in place for now," said Church. "We can deal with him later. We have a war to fight."

Dahlia returned to the front wall and when she climbed up again she looked out on a scene from hell itself. There were no longer hundreds of the living dead out there.

Now there were *thousands* of them. Seething masses of the dead, boiling out of the woods like cockroaches from a collapsing building. The Rovers in their white garments beat and shoved them into the corridor of flame that led to the front gate. The archers were nearly out of arrows and some had taken to simply throwing river stones at the zombies. The mountain of corpses was now higher than the broken wall and Dahlia saw it tremble as more of the dead slammed against it from behind or writhed, still in their parody of life, within it. It was going to fall soon. There was no doubt of that. Once it did, there would be a highway of rotting bodies high enough to allow the living dead to enter Happy Valley.

If they got into the town, then it would be carnage. Maybe—just maybe—the Pack and the helpers and the few allied residents could fight the zombies. But not the dead *and* the Rovers. Happy Valley was too spread out inside and too poorly prepared for attack outside.

Dahlia wished that the plan had been to lure the Rovers in and then let them have the damn place while her Pack and the other survivors snuck out and faded into the woods. She'd even proposed that to Church early on. But now she understood why Church had turned it down. She'd seen proof of why. The Rovers were attacking on all sides. Even though the groups to the rear and west were smaller distraction forces, they were there. They were armed. They could possibly stall the Pack long enough to draw the whole Rover force in for the kill.

No. The only real way to win this was to use the town itself as a weapon.

And so she rallied her people. The supplies brought from the houses were there and she climbed down and began distributing them. There was no good plan. Only plans marginally less suicidal than others.

She recalled a snatch of conversation she'd had with Church about this as they drew near to Happy Valley.

"Some of the members of the Pack want to know why we're bothering," she said to him. "Those aren't our people in there. We don't even know how many slaves are inside the walls. Or how many Rovers are out here."

"That is the kind of question soldiers often ask on the eve of battle," he had answered. "In World War II, in Iraq, in other wars, soldiers were often asked to go fight and possibly die for people they didn't know, people they would not otherwise have met. We are not a conquering army, Dahlia. We are not the ones who start a war. We don't get to choose whether war happens. What's left to us is to decide is whether the people caught in the path of a war deserve our commitment to try and save them. Or free them. Or even avenge them. No one fights alongside us because of coercion. You don't."

"No," she'd admitted.

"No one is forced to go with us to free the slaves in Happy Valley. Not one member of this Pack is required to do that."

"No."

"So, tell me," he asked gently, "why are we going to fight this war?"

She thought about it for miles of that walk.

"Because no one else will," she said, then paused and amended that statement. "Because no one else will bother."

He nodded. "Give me more."

"Because...if we walk away, if we let what they're doing to people in there stand, then we are allowing it. We're...what's the word? Complicit."

Church took her hand and raised it to his lips and kissed it. There was nothing remotely romantic or sexual about it. He held it for a moment and then let it go. He said no more to her about it. Now, maybe there would be no time to ever finish that discussion.

All there was left, was the war.

− 49 −

THE WAR

Big Elroy had ridden with the Rovers for years before the dead rose, but not his whole life. Before he was a biker he'd been a soldier. A sergeant in the army who'd served with distinction in Iraq and Afghanistan, and then was brought up on charges of rape. The victim, a thirteen-year-old girl, ignored threats against her own life and those of her family to testify. The army believed her and Big Elroy was stripped of rank, given a dishonorable discharge, and barely avoided jail time. If the girl had been white, he knew he'd have served time.

He wasn't out of work long before receiving a job offer from Blue Diamond, a security firm that provided, among other things, military contractors. No one called them mercenaries anymore.

Big Elroy spent eight wonderful years on gigs in the Middle East, Africa, and Central America. He did not much care who cut the checks to Blue Diamond. What mattered was that he was having fun and getting paid well. Blue Diamond respected his skill set and his understanding of tactics and strategy. By his eighth year, Big Elroy was running his own team and designing complex mission plans.

Then he got shot. For a soldier it would have been called a million-dollar wound; the kind of injury that insures you'll never have to see the hell of combat again. For a contractor like him, it was like being pissed on. He had a limp he'd never shake and some nerve damage in his left hand. He lost more than seventy percent of the sight in his right eye. They gave him a severance package and a swift kick in the ass. Within six months he was riding with the Rovers.

Now he *was* the Rovers. He'd been on the rise within the club before things went to shit, and when the dead rose and the top tier management of the Rovers club began eating each other, Big Elroy stepped in to fill a critical vacancy.

Now he had two hundred and twenty soldiers in this region and another two hundred out in scavenging teams throughout Pennsylvania, Maryland, and Virginia. By tomorrow, he'd even have his own kingdom.

Happy fucking Valley.

Maybe he'd call it Rovertown. Maybe he'd call it Elroytown. Either way, it was his. All he had to do was take it.

He stood like a general from some old Napoleonic war painting, sitting astride a horse on a hill that commanded a wide view of the valley. There were fires burning out front. There were fake-out teams and snipers on the east and in back.

And the main force of his army was ready to rock and roll.

Waiting for his word. He wished he had one of those cavalry sabers so he could hold it high and slash it down to signal the charge. Fuck, he should have thought of that. Ah well, a fire axe would work. He raised his. The lines of Rovers on the far side of the ridge tensed. The east was as pure and untouched as that girl in Iraq had been. Ready for the big meat.

He raised his axe and then paused with it over his head. There was something weird down there on the field. Two of the Rovers in white hazmat suits were walking along the base of the wall, doing something he couldn't quite see. The distance was too great.

"Jesus Christ," he roared, and turned to one of his lieutenants, "what the fuck are those two jerkoffs doing down there? They're going to be *seen*."

"I…" began the lieutenant. "It, um, looks like they're checking on the ladders."

It did look like that. The pair of Rovers were moving from one concealed ladder to the next and bending over them for a moment each.

"Get them the hell out of there, for Christ's sake. They're going to screw up the charge."

"Wait," said the lieutenant, "they're moving off. Maybe they were just checking to make sure the stuff was good."

"Why in the hell would they do something like that?"

"I..."

"Never mind. Find out who they are," said Big Elroy with a snarl. "I'm going to hang them by their balls."

"Yeah, you got it," said the lieutenant. "It looks clear."

"Okay," said Big Elroy. "Signal the teams. Light it all up."

The lieutenant ran back to the edge of the woods where a runner was waiting. He waved his arms and them gave a fist-pump signal. Within seconds whistles began blowing in the woods. Not the same patterns as before, but a strident and sustained three-note signal.

The herding team outside of the front gate heard the whistle signal and everything went into high gear. They relayed the signals around the whole perimeter.

In the back, the sniper kept up continuous fire.

To the west, a team of Rovers rushed the wall with ladders while others fired guns and lobbed Molotov cocktails to give them cover. The attack had to look real, and so Big Elroy had picked forty Rovers who were too stupid to understand the concept of "cannon fodder." They were given promises about first picks among any women captured inside, and other incentives; and they were amped up with amphetamines and cocaine, so they were wired to the gills. Like Viking berserkers, they bellowed and roared as they rushed the walls, throwing their ladders against the peach stucco and scrambling up.

Slow Dog was in charge of the west wall defense. He smiled

as the berserkers rushed the wall. Five ladders with eight men per.

He raised the first bucket of gasoline and waited until the topmost man was almost up, then he poured it over him and let the rest splash down over the other seven. Then he scraped a kitchen match on the top of the wall and let it drop.

The others manning the wall did exactly the same.

The screams were terrible.

Mr. Church and his team knelt out of sight on the catwalk at the top of the east wall. He had sixty fighters and hoped that would be enough.

"Look," said Bree, "what's that?"

Church looked over the edge and saw two Rovers in white hazmat suits go running from a place of cover and bend over a piece of torn lawn. One of the Rovers was tall, the other shorter and clearly female.

"What are they doing?" whispered Thomas.

That was a good question. The Rovers had bottles tucked under their arms and seemed to be pouring the contents over sections of grass. Church studied the lawn out there and after a moment grunted.

Zack had his gun out. "I can take them both. From this distance it would be easy."

But Church shook his head. "No. Pass the word. Leave them be."

"Why?"

"Call it a hunch."

As he said it he saw a movement in the woods nearby. An animal. When he shaded his eyes, he saw that it was a very large dog dressed in armor that was set with spikes.

"Now isn't that interesting," he murmured.

Dahlia worked furiously, mixing chemical fertilizer and soap flakes and gasoline in the exact amounts Mr. Church had taught her. ANFO, it was called, short for ammonium nitrate/fuel oil.

A simple but powerful explosive. As she completed one batch she handed it to Neeko, who filled metal gasoline cans with it and then poured in handfuls of nails and screws. Another Pack member sealed each can and attached a fuse. They had seven of the little bombs and enough cans to make six more. Other Pack members filled glass containers with any kind of flammable material they could find. The younger ones sealed them and carried them in batches to helpers on the wall.

Dahlia was sweating heavily, heavily, her brain swirling with a cocktail of adrenaline, fear, and fatigue.

"Let them come," she said to herself as she worked. "Let them come."

They came.

With a howl that shook the sky, the Rovers and their legion of the undead assaulted the front gate. The intention was clearly to create a ramp of the dead all the way to the breech and then let as many zombies inside the walls as could manage the climb. It did not matter to Big Elroy if the living dead got into the town. He had enough people to clear it all out, and the zombies would do a lot of the killing for them. *Shock* troops in the truest sense of the word.

The handlers in the field blew their whistles and used their poles and lit their fires exactly as they'd drilled a hundred times. It worked perfectly. The dead, drawn from all over this part of the county, followed the noise and avoided the flames and went for the living people they could see and smell on the walls.

The defenders on the wall had no arrows left and were throwing rocks. *Rocks*, for god's sake. That's all they had to fight with. The Rover handlers, emboldened, walked right up to within thirty feet of the wall. Outside of the effective range of a heavy stone. Fearless in their sure knowledge that the people inside were all going to die.

Gutter, the head of the field team, stood closer than anyone. He was laughing as the mound of dead finally fell forward, filling the trench and bridging the gap between them and the shattered wall. The dead surged forward. A huge cheer went up from the Rovers all across the field, and they ran in close to be ready to follow the zombies into the doomed town.

"Now," yelled Dahlia as she grabbed a red gasoline can by the handle, lit the fuse with a Zippo lighter, shot to her feet and hurled it over the wall. She'd risked a short fuse because she didn't want to give it time to land.

Then she flattened down a split second before the ANFO bomb exploded.

Gutter saw the red can and laughed at that, too. He thought that it was a last-ditch attempt to do damage. Throwing any old shit they could pick up. What was next, he thought, a porta-potty?

That was the thought in his mind when the ANFO bomb detonated with such force that it stripped the hazmat suit from his body and most of the flesh from his face. The spinning shrapnel of nails and screws and pins scythed through him as if he was made of paper. All around him Rovers and zombies were caught in the blast.

Only the zombies survived. In pieces, but they survived.

The next bombs came arcing over the wall toward other groups of Rovers.

Then thin-walled plastic bottles filled with alcohol and trailing blazing strips of cloth smashed down amid the zombies. The fragile plastic burst apart or was stepped on, and the fires leapt up to bite into torn clothing and withered skin.

The flames shot hot into the sky. They were visible for miles. And certainly visible from around the corner, on the east side of the wall.

Big Elroy grinned. Gutter and his boys had done it. They were breaching the walls. He could see the flames licking at the sky and it made him feel like Napoleon. Like Genghis Khan.

He raised his axe, paused for a moment, and then swept it down.

The forest seemed to burst apart as hundreds of Rovers ran out in a weird, ghastly silence. No cheers, no battle cries. This was the real attack. Cold and precise and silent. While all eyes and ears were drawn to the sniper, the ladder teams on the west and the big assault at the front door, the army of the Rovers raced across the open lawn to where their ladders were hidden beneath blankets of loose sod. It was clockwork. Three men flipped aside the sod; four men grabbed the ladders and rushed the walls; teams of shooters knelt and trained weapons on the wall in case anyone was up there. They needed only thirty seconds to do this and then the wall would be theirs. Once they were inside, they had the numbers and the training, and the town would fall.

This, Big Elroy knew, was how battles were won—training, nerve, imagination, and discipline.

The ladders rose. One, two, three, four…all the way up to twelve. Big men took up positions to brace them as other Rovers swarmed up, weapons slung, ready to take and own the wall.

If any of them noticed the stink of alcohol or gasoline on the rungs of the ladders, there was no time to stop and check it out. There was no time to comment on it. They had to move fast, fast, fast.

Only a few of them saw the two handlers in white Hazmat suits stand up from behind a hillock. Those few saw the Molotov cocktails and did not understand. Was that part of the assault? If so, when was that added to the plan? And why?

And why were the handlers throwing the flaming bottles toward the base of the ladders instead of trying to lob them over the wall?

From his hill, Big Elroy saw this with a clearer perspective.

He felt the blood drain from his face.

"No," he said. But he said it to himself, and he said it too late.

The bottles broke and splashed flames everywhere. On the lawn, where the Rovers clustered, waiting for their turn to ascend. On the ladders themselves, which were doused with accelerant. On the men crowding every rung of each of a dozen ladders. Everywhere.

The whole eastern wall became a sheet of flame.

In the space of five seconds, seventy-nine of the Rovers were burning. In the space of five more, the spilled gasoline on the turf chased down many more.

Big Elroy watched a third of his army burn.

And then above the flames, all along the walls, there were people. Men and women. Even from that distance, Big Elroy could hear the crackle of gunfire.

The Rovers tried to run. And died.

They tried to fight back. And died.

A few swatted at the fires that consumed their friends. And died.

Some dropped to their knees and begged for mercy. They died, too.

Several of the Rovers abandoned the fight and ran for the closest section of woods. There, in the shadows beneath the trees, were two figures. A woman and a man, dressed in hazmat suits but without the hoods.

No one who went into those woods came out again.

The sniper in the back heard the screams and saw flames coming from the east, which made no sense. That wasn't part of the plan. He signaled to his spotters and the three of them ran along the slope, hidden by the pines, hurrying to offer support to Big Elroy. They wanted to be part of the big push anyway.

They got about halfway there when they saw something coming down the slope toward them. Something that ran on four feet, but was an impossible shape. Like a dog but with spikes.

The sniper turned and raised his rifle, but he was one full second too late.

The army of the dead was burning.

Burning.

Dahlia stood on the wall. Her face was covered with soot, her eyes stung. Her mind was numb and she was half deaf from all the explosions. Out in the field, the whole mass of the living dead was burning.

Thousands of them.

Burning.

There was no sign at all of the Rovers. Not living ones, anyway. The bombs had done terrible work. The ANFO and the Molotov cocktails. The zombies had done the rest, killing even while they burned.

Dahlia wiped something away from her cheek. She thought it was going to be a drop of someone's blood. It wasn't.

She stood there for a long, long time looking at the wetness of her tears on her fingertips.

Mr. Church stood on the wall. The Pack and the helpers were still firing. The Rovers, those few that remained, were falling. Dying. Ending.

Far across the field, on a knoll, Church saw a big man on a horse. Another man was running toward him, wearing a hoodless hazmat suit with something strapped across his back. A sword of some kind, though the distance was too great to tell. It was almost certainly the man who'd thrown the fire bombs at the ladders. The one who'd boobytrapped the ladders. He was going after the mounted Rover with the axe. From what Church had learned over the last few weeks, he judged that the horseman was Big Elroy, leader of the Rovers. He had a couple of men with him, and they rushed to intercept the stranger. One of them had an automatic rifle; the other had a pair of long-bladed knives.

The running man drew a pistol and fired while running. A difficult shot, even for an expert. The rifleman suddenly sat down and then fell sideways, the gun sliding from his hands. Then the running man tossed his gun away—empty, apparently—and reached over his head for the handle of the sword, drawing it with a flash of silver fire. A katana, thought Church. The Rover with the knives tried to intercept him, to keep the swordsman from Big Elroy, but the sword swept him away, cutting the man's head, shoulder, and right arm off with a savage diagonal cut. Blood geysered up.

Big Elroy charged down the hill, raising his axe for a murderous blow.

The swordsman feinted toward the right, almost into the path of axe and horse, then pivoted left, turning into a full circle so that he came up on the horseman's left. The blade flashed again and Big Elroy was falling, his foot still in the stirrup but the leg cut through below the knee. The Rover fell hard, and Church watched as the swordsman walked over to him, paused for only a moment, and then made a single, final cut.

There was something about the man's posture as he stood there looking down at the dead Rover. Something about the set of his shoulders, the way he turned to look back at the town.

Church straightened slowly and wiped his eyes with his black gloves, hoping to clear his vision.

"No," he said softly.

EPILOGUE

-1-

The day wore on. Long and sad and bloody.

A few Rovers, not yet knowing they'd already lost, tried to

climb the walls. Others—a scant few—fled into the woods and were never seen again. Or, if they were, they did not wear necklaces of grisly souvenirs or claim to know anything at all about any gang by that name.

The fires burned. Three houses in Happy Valley caught fire from drifting embers.

Dahlia counted her own dead. Of the Pack members who'd followed her to Happy Valley, there was nineteen dead. Jumper was one of them, though no one had seen him fall. The town girl, Bree, was dead, killed by a shot fired from the field. Eleven helpers were dead, too.

And more than two hundred Rovers.

The living dead in the front field were left to burn. Some of the forest burned, too. It was later discovered that the clearing where helpers had been left to starve had burned. Claudia escaped, though, and found her way back to town.

Joe Ledger, Rachael, and Baskerville came up to the back gate and knocked to be let it. It was Mr. Church who opened the door.

The two men stood looking at each other for a long, silent time. The people around them—Rachael, Dahlia, Neeko, Slow Dog, and many others—waited them out. None of them understood.

It was finally Joe Ledger who stepped forward and offered his hand. Church looked at it.

"I...um...never figured you for the hugging type, boss," said Ledger, his voice thick with emotion.

"Times change, Captain," said Church and he pulled Ledger into a fierce embrace. They stood there, hugging each other while Baskerville barked and wagged his tail.

When Ledger finally stepped back, he said, "How?"

But Church shook his head. "Stories for another time." He paused. "But...Junie...?"

Ledger shook his head. Dahlia swore that Church aged ten years in that moment, and for the first time he really did look old.

-2-

The Pack stayed in Happy Valley. So did most of the helpers. A few left, needing to look for friends or family from which they'd become separated because of the forced servitude. Church sent them on their way with supplies and bodyguards.

Rachael and Claudia lingered for a week, healing, grieving for Jason, and taking counsel from Ledger and Church. When the warrior woman finally left, there were tears in her eyes. She kissed Joe on both cheeks and hugged him for a long time. Then she left.

The adult residents of Happy Valley were not released from captivity quickly because Dahlia was afraid they would be murdered. And, in fact, two of the helpers were caught trying to steal automatic weapons to exact justice for the horrible crimes.

Dahlia asked Church what to do and he told her that she should make the decision. After days of deliberating, she decided to have a public hearing. The younger residents spoke for their families, but they did not make apologies. Some of the adults confessed and submitted themselves for any punishment offered.

Dahlia used a blind lottery to create a jury of twelve. The trial took days, and everyone who wanted to have a say was allowed to do so. Everyone. When it was over, the jury went into one of the houses to deliberate. It took them three days to come to a decision.

While Neeko counted out the votes, everyone sat in tense silence. Some people were crying. Helpers and residents. The verdict was given to Dahlia in a sealed envelope. People cried while they waited for her to read it. Residents, helpers, and even some members of the Pack. Dahlia held the sealed envelope and closed her eyes for a moment. Ledger stood beside her, his sword over his shoulder, a gun at his hip, and the big dog beside him. No one else was armed.

The trial was held in a small town hall used for concerts and plays. Dahlia stood looking at everyone.

"Okay," she said and held up the envelope. "I have the verdict, but I want to say something first. I guess I need to make something clear, okay?"

No one spoke.

"I'm the judge. Mr. Church suggested it and you all voted on it. I'm the judge."

No one spoke.

"That means that I get to decide on the punishment. The sentence. Whatever. I get to decide and you all have to accept it."

In the front row of the seats reserved for the defendants, Margaret Van Sloane sat straight as a ramrod, but her eyes were haunted. She was deeply afraid. No one seemed willing to offer her comfort. A lot of people gave her looks of unfiltered hate.

Dahlia continued. "If the verdict is guilty, I can decide on what's appropriate for punishment. I could have everyone on trial here locked away forever. I could have you shot. I could even take you out to the woods and tie you up like you did to all those people. I could do that, and I have enough people here to make sure that whatever I decide gets done."

No one spoke.

"Same goes if the verdict is not guilty. I can impose all sorts of restrictions on you and make sure you work in the fields for the rest of your life. Even if the verdict says not guilty. I'm the judge and that means I guess I get to make the rules."

Ledger cut a look at Church, who gave a small shake of his head.

Dahlia took a breath, then tore open the envelope. She read it, nodding to herself. When she looked up at the crowd, they were all staring at her, intent and tense.

"Guilty," she said. "I mean…of course they're guilty."

There was a sob from one of the defendants. There were sobs from some of the helpers, too.

Mr. Church cleared his throat. "And what is the sentence?" he asked.

Dahlia nodded again and let the paper fall to the floor.

"The world ended," she said. "Maybe as much as seven billion people died. We're pretty close to being extinct and yet you parasites dragged old thinking into this world. Hatred, intolerance, all of that. You had the chance to leave all of that behind and yet you didn't. You tried to make it part of this world. You're no better than the Rovers. You do know that, right?" She walked over to stand looking down at Margaret Van Sloane. "We killed the Rovers. Every last one of them we could find. And why? Because they were predators and monsters a lot worse than the living dead. All they wanted was to take, to own, to have. They weren't going to give anything back to the world. So...tell me, Mayor Van Sloane, what should we do to *you?*"

Van Sloane tried to meet her eyes, tried to stare Dahlia down, but she could not. Not one of the defendants could do that.

"I should have you all killed," Dahlia said to them. "I should. Hell, I know that's what you would do."

She hooked a finger under the mayor's chin and forced her head up.

"*Look at me,*" she snarled.

Van Sloane raised her eyes, though it clearly cost her the last of her dignity to do it.

"I want to live in a better world than that," said Dahlia. "I want to live in a world where people like you don't get to make the rules. I want to live in a world where people like me do. And my friends. And the helpers. And, fuck, your own kids."

The room was absolutely silent.

Dahlia released the woman's chin.

"My ruling is this. No one dies. No one goes to jail. No one gets staked out in the woods." There were gasps and some small cries. Ledger rested his hand on the butt of his pistol and Baskerville got to his feet. To the defendants, Dahlia said, "And no one forgets, either."

She stepped back and licked her lips, which had gone paste dry.

"The defendants have a choice. Something they didn't give to the people who came here asking for help, for shelter. You can stay, but if you do, you have to leave all your old world shit behind. Racism, sexism, and all of that. Gone. Done. It dies right here and right now. I don't care how you manage it. Pray, or do yoga or whatever. I don't care. You take a scalpel and cut it out of who you are. If you can do that, then you can stay. I'm a sucker for a good redemption story. But," she said, and the word was like a punch, "it better come from the heart, because we'll be watching. This is *our* town now. The Pack and the helpers and anyone else who wants to make this a place worth living."

She bent over Van Sloane one last time.

"If you *can't* do that, then you're gone. We won't hurt you. We'll even give you weapons and supplies and help you get clear of these woods. But you can't ever come back here, 'cause if you do then I swear to God I'll kill you myself."

Dahlia looked at everyone.

"I'm going to give the defendants one day to decide. One day. If any of them leave, and you're related to them, you can choose to go or stay. If you stay, you know my rules."

The silence that filled the room was massive and heavy, and she did not see acceptance on every face. She didn't expect to. When she glanced at Mr. Church, though, she saw approval and something else. A smile. Small, but there.

Thomas was the first person to start applauding. It wasn't some cliché slow hand clap. He leaped to his feet with a cheer and began beating his hands together. So, too, did Zack. Despite all he had been through, so did Zack.

After that it was thunder.

Only a few of the defendants did not clap. Most did. Not all.

— 3 —

Joe Ledger stayed in town for a month.

He spent many long hours talking with Mr. Church. He spent most of his days overseeing the repairs to the wall, including a massive and ambitious upgrade to the overall security. He trained scouts and fighters.

Church was the unofficial mayor of the town, but after a few weeks he announced that Dahlia was a better candidate. There were a lot of arguments, but he won every single one of them.

Ledger came to see him one evening and they sat in the backyard watching the stars. Most of that evening had been passed in silence. They'd told each other their tales.

"You're leaving, aren't you?" asked Ledger.

"Eventually. I want to help Dahlia for a while. She's a remarkable young woman."

"She treats you like a father."

"There are worse things in the world to be," said Church.

"Look, why don't you come with me? I'm going to see if I can find Top or Bunny. Hopefully both. Then maybe push west, see what's happening on the west coast."

Church thought about it. "Maybe. But you go first. I have some things to do and then, if I can, I'll find you out there."

Ledger looked at him. "Seriously."

"Yes," said Church, "but I make no promises. Finding you here was a stroke of odd luck. Maybe I'll get lucky and find some other people."

Ledger knew who he was talking about. Church had been in love with a strange and dangerous woman named Lilith. She'd been on a mission in the Middle East when things fell apart, and he'd had no word of her since. Ledger was pretty sure he was going to try and find her.

They sat in silence for a long time as the stars turned overhead.

"The world is still alive," said Church. "That's something."

"Yeah," Ledger said. "That really is."

Behind them, from one of the other houses, there was the music of a Spanish guitar and the sounds of people laughing.

Mr. Church leaned back in his chair and smiled up at the sky, his eyes closed. Joe Ledger laced his fingers behind his head, leaned back, and listened to the laughter. How rare and beautiful a thing it was. Around him, the world did not appear to be broken at all.

THE END

THE ZOMBIE APOCALYPSE CHRONOLOGY

The Joe Ledger series is first, beginning with PATIENT ZERO. Not all of the books deal with zombies. A character named Sam Imura (older brother of Tom Imura) is introduced in book #4 as the sniper on Echo Team, Joe's special ops squad. The Joe Ledger series (so far) includes:

JOE LEDGER/DEPARTMENT OF MILITARY SCIENCES

1. Patient Zero (2009; St. Martin's Griffin)
2. The Dragon Factory (2010; St. Martin's Griffin)
3. King of Plagues (2011; St. Martin's Griffin)
4. Assassin's Code (2012; St. Martin's Griffin)
5. Extinction Machine (2013; St. Martin's Griffin)
6. Code Zero (2014; St. Martin's Griffin)
7. Predator One (2015; St. Martin's Griffin)
8. Kill Switch (2016; St. Martin's Griffin)
9. Dogs of War (2017; St. Martin's Griffin)
10. Deep Silence (2018; St. Martin's Griffin)

JOE LEDGER - ROGUE TEAM INTERNATIONAL

1.   Rage (2019; St. Martin's Griffin)

JOE LEDGER SHORT STORY COLLECTIONS

1.   Joe Ledger: Special Ops
   (2014; JournalStone; short story collection)
2.   Joe Ledger: The Missing Files
   (2012; Blackstone audio collection)
3.   Joe Ledger: Unstoppable
   (2017; St. Martin's Griffin; anthology, various authors)

DEAD OF NIGHT and FALL OF NIGHT are set fifteen years after the Ledger series. They are also the official story of how "First Night" (the zombie apocalypse from Rot & Ruin) happens. The books in this series include:

THE DEAD OF NIGHT SERIES

1.   Dead of Night (2012; St. Martin's Griffin)
2.   Fall of Night (2014; St. Martin's Griffin)
3.   Dark of Night (2016; novella; JournalStone; with Rachael Lavin)
4.   Still of Night (2018; JournalStone; novella and short stories; with Rachael Lavin)

NIGHT OF THE LIVING DEAD

The movie, written by George A. Romero and John Russo, takes places approximately two days after the events in Dead of Night.

SHORT STORIES AND NOVELLAS

There are various short stories and novellas that bridge the gap between FALL OF NIGHT and ROT & RUIN. They are included in various anthologies and in my short story collections.

The titles are:

Concurrent or directly after FALL OF NIGHT:

- Hot Time in the Old Town Tonight
- Chokepoint
- Fat Girl with a Knife
- Jack and Jill
- Sunset Hollow
- A Christmas Feast
- Valley of Shadows
- First Night Memories
- Lone Gunman (included in the anthology, NIGHTS OF THE LIVING DEAD, which I co-edited with George Romero—writer/director of Night of the Living Dead. George was a huge fan of DEAD OF NIGHT and asked me to write a story that officially connected my series to his movie.
- Saint John (origin of the villain from books #3 and #4 of the ROT & RUIN series)

Two to five years after FALL OF NIGHT

- The Wind through the Fence
- Jingo and the Hammerman
- Overdue Books
- Back in Black (with Bryan Thomas Schmidt) (a Joe Ledger/Tom Imura crossover)
- Dead & Gone
- In the Land of the Dead
- Rags & Bones
- Hero Town
- Tooth & Nail

Then there's the ROT & RUIN series, which takes place fourteen years after the events of First Night. Then a new series spins off from that one, BROKEN LANDS.

THE ROT & RUIN SERIES

1. Rot & Ruin (2010; Simon & Schuster Books for Young Readers)
2. Dust & Decay (2011; Simon & Schuster Books for Young Readers)
3. Warrior Smart (2015; graphic novel; IDW publishing)
4. Flesh & Bone (2012; Simon & Schuster Books for Young Readers)
5. Fire & Ash (2013; Simon & Schuster Books for Young Readers)
6. Bits & Pieces (2015; Simon & Schuster Books for Young Readers)
7. Broken Lands (December 2018; Simon & Schuster Books for Young Readers)
8. Lost Roads (December 2019; Simon & Schuster Books for Young Readers)

JONATHAN MABERRY is a New York Times bestselling author, 5-time Bram Stoker Award-winner, and comic book writer. His vampire apocalypse book series, V-WARS, is in production as a Netflix original series, starring Ian Somerhalder (LOST, VAMPIRE DIARIES) and will debut in 2019. He writes in multiple genres including suspense, thriller, horror, science fiction, fantasy, and action; and he writes for adults, teens and middle grade. His works include the Joe Ledger thrillers, *Glimpse*, the *Rot & Ruin* series, the *Dead of Night* series, *The Wolfman, X-Files Origins: Devil's Advocate, Mars One*, and many others. Several of his works are in development for film and TV. He is the editor of high-profile anthologies including *The X-Files, Aliens: Bug Hunt, Out of Tune, New Scary Stories to Tell in the Dark, Baker Street Irregulars, Nights of the Living Dead*, and others. His comics include *Black Panther: DoomWar, The Punisher: Naked Kills* and *Bad Blood*. He lives in Del Mar, California. Find him online at www.jonathanmaberry.com

Rachael Lavin is a LARPer, cosplayer, part time forest witch, full time nerd. Call Center representative by day, she rejects this reality and replaces it with her own. When she's not writing, she can be found hunched over her sewing machine, taking pictures, or running around the woods with foam swords. When she's not living in a fantasy, she resides in Hamilton, NJ with her boyfriend and a large number of fish.

CPSIA information can be obtained
at www.ICGtesting.com
Printed in the USA
LVHW051119261119
638403LV00003B/108/P